ANGHELLIC

Feathers and Fire Book 8

SHAYNE SILVERS

ARGENTO
PUBLISHING

CONTENTS

Shayne Silvers

Anghellic

Feathers and Fire Book 8

A TempleVerse Series

ISBN 13: 978-1-947709-49-2

© 2020, Shayne Silvers / Argento Publishing, LLC

info@shaynesilvers.com

BLASPHEMY IS A VICTIMLESS CRIME...

Callie Penrose has taken over Castle Dracula all for herself, finally feeling like she has time to take a breath and relax.

But the forces of Heaven and Hell have other plans. Callie quickly learns that removing her mother's protection of binding Excalibur to her soul had very serious consequences.

Namely, that it unleashed the Seven Deadly Sins on Kansas City. But they aren't in town for mayhem—not directly.

They came for a wedding. And a very dark prophecy that could bring the age-old Angel War to the streets of the City of Fountains.

But it's hard to focus on fighting when Hell is trying to fit her with a wedding dress...

But that is only the least of her concerns, because her mother kept secrets that could rock the Pillars of Heaven and rattle the Foundations of Hell.

The only problem is that her mother was so scared to share it, she didn't write it down anywhere.

And that might just signal the end for Callie Penrose...

<u>DON'T FORGET!</u>

FOLLOW AND LIKE:

Shayne's FACEBOOK PAGE:

www.shaynesilvers.com/l/38602

I try my best to respond to all messages, so don't hesitate to drop me a line. Not interacting with readers is the biggest travesty that most authors can make. Let me fix that.

The ice cream parlor was a secret gateway to Hell. It was the only logical explanation.

"It's fucking December," I muttered as I stared down the dark street. It was the only place still open at this time of night; the rest of the buildings in the area consisted of office space. I quickly tugged up my hood as a mother herded a troop of giggling eight or nine-year-old Girl Scouts out of the ice cream shop. They began walking straight towards me, whispering to each other conspiratorially. I narrowed my eyes suspiciously, glaring at them from beneath my hood as I relaxed my hands, preparing for an attack. Which one of them was the demon? I swiveled one boot on my heel in an arc so that my toes swept over all of them. My boots tingled when they pointed at demons.

I relaxed, realizing the Girl Scouts were not demonic.

That's when I heard the distinctive sound of a pistol cocking. The Girl Scouts bolted behind a nearby minivan parked on the street, moving in perfect formation—like a military unit. I slowly raised my hands in clear view as I looked up to see the mother now pointing a pistol at me; her face was as calm as a winter pond. A quick once over showed me she was in her early thirties, wore a blue Royals baseball cap, an open jean jacket, and a t-shirt underneath that said *I love vegans. Especially when they're cooked medium rare.* I bit my lip so as to not burst out laughing, because she looked like the kinda gal who had been waiting her whole life to justifiably pump a dangerous criminal full of lead.

"Keep your eyes to yourself, freak," she said, keeping the pistol trained on me as she unlocked the van. "Get in, girls. Now. On the double!"

Jesus. They really were trained soldiers. "Misunderstanding," I assured her. "A young girl stole my niece's backpack and ran this way," I lied, letting a little emotion into my voice. "It had her brand-new laptop inside, and…I don't have the money to get her a new one."

The momster's outrage faltered…slightly. "Well, I haven't seen any girls run by here. We were eating ice cream," she said, barely shifting her chin to indicate the nearby shop. Her eyes never left me, and her pistol remained steady. She saw me eyeing the weapon and lowered it from my face, still keeping it trained on my lower body as a precaution. Definitely trained. "Strange times," she explained. "You should get going."

I nodded, slowly, keeping my hands up as I side-stepped away from her. She turned with me, keeping the pistol between us until I was a safe distance away. Then she climbed into her minivan and was driving away in less than five seconds—at a reasonable speed rather than peeling out in fear.

I let out a nervous sigh. "Christ. Almost got myself killed by a Regular," I muttered. I walked to the ice cream shop, opened the door, and slipped inside, discreetly sweeping the space with my eyes and boots. I felt no tingle and saw nothing suspicious, although the place was packed. This only made me more concerned. Where had the demon gone?

Most of the place consisted of exhausted parents allowing their sugared-up kids to scream, laugh, and liberally pour ice cream on every part of their face, except for their mouth—using their fingers instead of the plastic spoons. One group of college kids sat at a table near the register, and I rolled my eyes to see that it was less of a group and more of a harem. One handsome guy wore sunglasses, a hipster man-bun, and he was grinning as three overly bubbly girls took turns fawning over him.

"Ice cream is great, but they don't hold a candle to Frappuccinos," he told them. "Especially with the whipped cream and chocolate drizzle," he added in a suggestive tone. "Everything is better with whips and chocolate."

They laughed or shrieked in feigned outrage, and one of them even tried to debate his point by shoving a spoon of her ice cream into his mouth. Of course, she had to lean forward rather far, showing off her cleavage so he could get the full experience of the mint chocolate chip. I checked the group with my boots and felt nothing demonic. I sighed, stepping up to the counter and doing my best to tune out their existence. Their shameless lack of pride was appalling.

Needing to fit in until I officially cleared the building of demonic presence, I approached the beefy kid behind the register—who was obviously only working there to pick up girls. He was handsome, didn't much like the suave hipster behind me, and looked like he worked out at the gym more often than he worked for a paycheck.

He lifted his gaze from the counter, taking me in from the waist up in slow motion, a grin stretching across his face as he finally met my eyes.

And he blanched in apparent recognition, jolting so hard that he knocked over his workout shaker bottle. "White Rose," he said in a muffled hiss.

I tensed, glancing left and right to make sure no one had heard him. Then I settled my glare on him. "Shh!" I warned in a firm whisper. "How do you know that name?"

He nodded, shakily, carefully setting his palms on the counter where I could see them. "Everyone knows your name." He indicated for me to look down at them, moving only his eyes. Then he subtly checked that his two coworkers couldn't see. For a brief second, fur grew out of his knuckles. Then it evaporated and he let out a nervous breath. "Werewolf," he whispered. "You're not here to kill me, are you?"

My eyes widened. "No! Just give me a scoop of chocolate!"

He nodded in relief, snatching up an ice cream scooper. "Of course," he stammered, dropping the spoon in his haste to obey my request. "Please don't kill me," he murmured like a mantra. He scooped up a liberal dollop of vanilla into a cup and then frowned at it. He added a scoop of lime sherbet, still looking confused by my complicated order, and then dropped the scooper onto the ground. He slid the cup of ice cream towards me and plastered on a fake smile. "Have a nice day!" he practically yelled into my face, dry washing his hands.

"Have you seen anyone suspicious enter in the last fifteen minutes?" I asked, quietly.

He shook his head anxiously. "No. I p-promise," he stammered.

I held out a ten-dollar bill and he stepped back as if it was poison, lifting his hands. "No charge for the White Rose," he whispered.

I stared at him, thankful that the table behind me hadn't taken note of the bizarre exchange. I shoved the money into a tip jar and smiled reassuringly at him. "Thank you. I've never had chocolate like this," I said with a teasing smile.

His eyes widened in horror. "I'm so sorry! Here, let me—"

"No. It's fine. Really. Thank you." I grabbed a plastic spoon from the counter and I turned around before he decided to set off the fire alarm or something. I bumped right into the hipster who had been backing away from his table, fending off three force-feedings now. I stepped back quickly, relieved that I hadn't spilled the ice cream.

He turned around and flashed me a dazzling smile. "I'm so sorry," he said.

"Don't worry about it," I said.

He took off his glasses and cocked his head. His blue eyes were deep and dreamy, and I suddenly had more sympathy for the desperate girls behind him. He truly was handsome. "Did it hurt?" he asked, sounding concerned. He gave off no magical aura, and he didn't appear to recognize me like the werewolf ice cream server had.

"What?" I asked, confused. He'd barely bumped me. The girls behind him practically hissed at me, arching their backs, and skipping sideways like yowling alley cats.

"When you fell from Heaven," he explained, somehow managing to keep a straight face. "Did it hurt?"

I blinked at him and then I burst out laughing at the terrible pick-up line. "Wow. Okay. Enjoy your night, Rico Suave," I said, rolling my eyes. I turned and made my way to the door, giving up on demon hunting for the night. I'd attracted far too much attention, unfortunately. I'd been so surprised to randomly pick up a demon's trail—which had practically been on top of me—after weeks of nothing, that I had pounced on it. And then lost him thanks to Sergeant Mom and the terrified werewolf.

"It was worth a shot!" the blue-eyed hipster called out, chuckling. "You miss one hundred percent of the shots you don't take."

He made a good point. "Keep shooting," I said from over my shoulder, and then I stepped back out onto the street. Kansas City was quiet tonight, but I spotted a couple walking their dog on my side of the street and a car driving past. I took a bite of my vanilla-lime concoction and grunted. "That's not half bad," I admitted.

The hair on the back of my neck suddenly rose and I looked up to see that the car had stopped moving about fifteen feet farther down the road, looking as if it had been frozen in time. I glanced over at the couple walking their dog to find their faces locked into smiles and each with one foot in the air, frozen in mid-stride.

I dropped my cup of ice cream, scanning the street warily. Nothing moved. I stepped away from the door to the ice cream shop, risking a glance inside. Everyone within was also frozen—ironically—and the blue-eyed hipster was laughing as he fended off the three groupies and their spoons of sans-dignity flavored ice cream.

I heard a steady metallic tapping sound and spun to see an old man walking down the sidewalk across the street, tapping a cane on the pavement with each step. He wore an old-fashioned suit and a bowler hat with a black feather in the top. He paused when he was directly across the street, and then turned to face me with a genuine, grandfatherly smile. His bushy, curled, white mustache twitched at the motion.

"Hullo," he said, waving jovially. "Finished with your ice cream? I thought I would be forced to stand out in the cold all night! I'm accustomed to warmer climates, I'm afraid. Blame it on old age," he said, shuffling across the street at the speed of an old man strolling through the park.

Despite his non-threatening demeanor, the hair on my arms rose up on end as I stared at the amicable gentleman, fearing for my life. Because as my eyes flicked over the bright yellow cufflinks peeking out from under his coat sleeves, I caught the smell of sulfur, and my boots were suddenly tingling like mad.

Which only meant one thing.

"Demon," I hissed. Rather than me finding him, he had found me.

2

He tipped his hat with a bubbly chuckle. "Right you are!" he said. "Now, let's get down to business, shall we?" he asked, his immortal eyes twinkling mischievously. And then he began humming *The Devil Went Down to Georgia*, even dancing a faint jig on his way to a bench affixed to the wall outside the ice cream shop. He set his briefcase down and took a seat, crossing his legs as he waited for me to...

Well, I didn't have a clue what he wanted. Was he here to kill me? In those loafers? As I assessed his threat level, I grew confident that I could kill him without breaking a sweat. He was nowhere near as strong as Samael.

Which only made me more suspicious and concerned. He'd been waiting outside for me earlier, and none of us had been the wiser. In fact, it seemed pretty obvious that he had lured me here.

"Who are you and what do you want?" I asked, carefully, angling one of my boots towards the dog-walkers to see if they were part of the ambush, or if he had any friends waiting to join our party.

"Oh, we know all about your fancy boots," the demon said, chuckling. "Darling and Dear are the best, after all," he said, indicating his own fancy loafers. "First stop I made after busting out of the slammer." My eyes widened a fraction of an inch to hear he sported magical shoes as well.

What powers did his old man loafers have?

And how had he just broken out of Hell? Was that a new trend?

Something about his comment made me feel like a spider crawling down my spine.

"How long ago did you break out of Hell?" I asked, masking my concern in what I hoped passed for nothing more than a lazy delaying tactic.

But the demon's amused grin was all too knowledgeable. "Oh, I'd say about three weeks ago. About six hundred and sixty-six seconds after you removed your protection," he said, chuckling.

Shit. That was right around the time I had repaired Excalibur and given it to the new King Arthur—a man named Alex Arete. Who was a friend of Nate Temple's, of course.

Because I had carried around a piece of Excalibur my entire life, unbeknownst to me, and it had hidden me from both the forces of Heaven and Hell. Giving it up had removed that ward of protection, and it had apparently encouraged this demon to break out of Hell.

My heart began racing in my chest.

I snapped out of my thoughts to see he was thumbing open the clasps on his briefcase, humming to himself and bouncing his foot—his legs still crossed—to the beat. Despite his compromising position making it more difficult for any physical attack, he could have had a grenade or a gun in his briefcase, for all I knew.

"You'd look really funny with a loafer shoved down your throat, demon," I warned, pointing at his briefcase. "Hands where I can see them."

He slowly lifted his hands, obedient but unafraid. "Just grabbing some paperwork, my dear. If I wanted you dead, I wouldn't have made my presence known," he said, amicably. "See for yourself."

I nodded for him to proceed as I stepped laterally so that I could get a look inside the briefcase the moment it opened. I held a shield at the tip of my mind, ready to snap it into place if he tried anything stupid.

He slowly opened the briefcase to reveal a rolled parchment and a circular beer coaster. It had swirling, cursive handwriting on it—in gold ink.

He used two fingers to carefully pluck up the coaster and then handed it to me. "Congratulations," he said.

I licked my lips warily, but I couldn't sense anything dangerous emanating from it. Rather than touching it, though, I read it from afar, quickly realizing it was not a beer coaster—it was an invitation.

I leaned back, frowning at the demon. "You're kidding me," I said, deadpan.

"Afraid not."

I folded my arms. "My own wedding invitation. At the Garden of Eden."

He pulled a pair of spectacles from his coat pocket—why wouldn't he—and read the wedding invitation. Then he glanced back at me from over his reader spectacles with a nod and a polite smile. "That is correct."

"I missed the name of the groom," I said, dryly, "because it's not on the card."

He pinched one end of his curled mustache, smiling jovially. "My client was quite specific about wanting his identity to remain a surprise. Love is a mystery, is it not?" He sounded entirely genuine and harmless rather than threatening. But if this man was a demon, there was zero doubt that his client was of the same ilk. What the hell was this—literally? The old man reached for the seemingly ancient parchment and began unrolling it. "Now, if you could please sign here, here, and here, I will be on my way." He tapped the requisite spots on the ridiculously long, ridiculously archaic, legal document. It looked to have been handwritten a thousand years ago in meticulously artful, cursive script.

I laughed incredulously. "You're kidding. A pre-nup?" I hooted. "Why would you even waste your time giving me this? You already know my obvious answer."

He frowned, glancing over at me. "But you haven't read my client's agreement yet," he said, sounding puzzled.

"It's not the fucking pre-nup!" I snapped. "I'm not marrying someone I don't know, and I'm *definitely* not marrying a *demon*. We haven't even gotten to that," I said, pointing at the legal protection document—protections for the mysterious demon. Couldn't let a vengeful wife divorce you and take half of your Hellish assets.

"If you do not sign, Kansas City shall burn," he said, squinting his eyes as he read a part of the partially unrolled document. Then he tapped it to show me, extending it my way. "It says so right here, if you wish to read it, first."

I scoffed, not bothering to fact-check him. I checked our surroundings, pretending that it wasn't strange for everything to still be frozen. What was his angle? "You're going to need a lot more back-up, pal."

He frowned over at me, pinching the end of his mustache again. "Now, that is just rude. We've been perfect gentledemons."

I narrowed my eyes, wondering why he'd said the plural when he was obviously alone. "Who are you, and what is this, really?"

"We are Legion, Miss Penrose."

I stiffened, taking an involuntary step back as my stomach squirmed unpleasantly. Legion. That was the demon who was more than one demon if memory served. Denzel Washington had made a movie about it. Which meant the kindly old gentledemons, as he called himself, had *plenty* of backup.

He noticed my anxiety and nodded. "We mean you no harm, Miss Penrose. You are the beautiful bride, after all."

I stared at the parchment. "You're a crossroads demon. That's a contract for selling my soul."

"Oh, don't be ridiculous. This is about much more than your soul, my dear."

This was no longer a joke. This—whatever it was—was deadly serious. I couldn't afford to piss him off and be taken away by a bajillion demons with one hive mind. I was good, but not that good. At least, I didn't want to test that tonight.

"And what do I get out of this arrangement?"

He smiled approvingly. "Negotiation. Very good. Let me see," he murmured, reading the tiny words on the long contract as he ran his finger down an insane number of lines. "Ah. Here it is. Kansas City shall not be immolated."

I suppressed the almost blinding surge of fury encouraging me to rip out Legion's heart with my bare hands. For now, I needed to gather as much information as possible. I didn't want to offend the demon until I'd had a chance to come up with a game plan and considered all of the consequences.

"And what does my husband get?" I asked in a flat tone.

He continued reading. "Kansas City, and you, of course." He picked up a quill from within his briefcase. The tip was red, and I knew beyond a shadow of a doubt that the ink was blood.

Likely from the last person who had used it to prick his finger and sign away his soul. Legion squinted at it and then took out a silk handkerchief to clean off the razor-sharp tip. Then he held it out to me. "There. All clean. Now, if you could please sign—"

"I'm going to need to think on it, Legion."

He turned to look at me and I prepared myself for an all-out brawl. A slow smile crept over his face and he nodded, setting the quill back inside his briefcase. "Good for you, girl. You'll want to have your lawyer read over it, first, no doubt. I commend you for that. Too many idiots running around, signing things all willy-nilly," he grumbled, rolling the parchment back up and setting it down on the bench—along with the wedding invitation. He closed his briefcase and gently locked the clasps.

Then he climbed to his feet, not taking offense at how rapidly I shuffled backwards a few steps. "Right. My lawyer. He's...very busy. So busy."

Legion smiled warmly, causing his mustache to wiggle. Then he doffed his hat in a polite bow. "I shall check back in one week, Miss Penrose. Act swiftly. If more money is needed to get your lawyer's attention, I have the authority to add his fee to the contract. One of my men will personally pay him a visit for you," he said, his eyes twinkling dangerously. "Your fiancé is quite determined to stick to the schedule. He's already made the invitations, after all," he said, pointing at the card with a faint chuckle.

I nodded, hesitantly. "That won't be necessary. I didn't see a date for the ceremony," I said, my mouth suddenly dry. "And I always expected a more traditional proposal," I added, trying to stretch out the deadline.

He beamed. "My client seems fairly set on Christmas Day. Stick it to the Man, as the kids say these days."

"Jesus' birthday," I said, forcing my voice to remain steady.

"And I will inform him of your demand for a traditional proposal. It is an excellent idea." I opened my mouth to assure him that it wasn't necessary because I already had my answer, but he spoke right over me. "Oh, and you may have six in your bridal party." Of course it was six. "Well, I'm sure you have much to think about this evening. Let me be the first to say, welcome to the family, my dear."

Then he bowed again, and shuffled down the sidewalk, tapping his cane as he began to whistle a song that had probably been popular a hundred years ago.

My knees wobbled, but I forced myself to remain standing, staring at the departing demon—even after he'd rounded the corner and my surroundings suddenly returned to normal speed. The dogwalkers hurried past me with an annoyed look since I was standing in the middle of the sidewalk.

I made my way over to the bench and snatched up Legion's parchment and invitation with a snarl. I almost hoped they did poison me on the spot.

Tonight had gone to shit. Officially.

I hadn't even gotten a proper proposal. Unless Legion had a talk with my husband-to-be. Why had I said anything? Now, I had to worry about being jumped in the street by a demon wanting to express his undying love—probably with a display of gratuitous violence to however many people happened to be standing around me at the time.

"Gentledemon," I muttered, as I considered where I wanted to go. I definitely didn't want to talk to anyone about my feelings or explain why I had a wedding invitation with only my name on it.

I tore open a Gateway and stepped through to Solomon's Temple.

It was fair to say that I already had cold feet.

3

I didn't want my friends terrorizing Kansas City in search of me, so I pulled out my phone and sent Claire a brief text.

I'm fine. Went to clear my head.

I had snuck away from Castle Dracula without telling anyone, needing to get away from the constant hubbub of being the new Dracula—a figure everyone feared and obeyed. I'd wanted to walk the streets of a city where I could feel invisible again. A place where no one was afraid of me.

Except...the terrified, ice-cream serving werewolf had reminded me that, in Kansas City, many were afraid of me. There, I was the White Rose—a notorious vigilante who killed any monsters who did so much as jaywalk. And now I had this Legion bullshit to deal with. His mysterious demon client wanted to marry me, or he was going to burn Kansas City to the ground.

I pocketed my phone and leaned my elbows on the railing, staring out over the vibrant green gardens and fields stretching into the distance like a patchwork quilt. Everything was lush and nurturing, except for one specific spot. Where I had moved Castle Dracula was a black stain on the land, because the walled domain was enshrouded in the darkness of eternal night. From my higher elevation at Solomon's Temple, I could make out a few of the most notable landmarks like the Clocktower, the Castle Keep—where my friends were probably pacing with worry—and what I thought might be the Observatory.

One of the first official decrees I had made was to announce that Castle Dracula now operated on central time since I was from Kansas City. Depending on the time of year, and whether daylight saving time was in effect on Earth, *Callie Standard Time* and *Callie Dracula Time* covered all the acronyms. No one at Castle Dracula had cared since it was always dark, but I had considered it a win.

The grounds were enclosed within a daunting fifty-foot tall stone wall with bricks the size of small cars. Despite how impossible it seemed, I saw a pale, glowing orb within the sky over that stygian darkness—Castle Dracula had its own moon, independent of the sun and moon at Solomon's Temple. From here, it was oddly chilling, like I was staring into an evil snow globe.

Seeing the sunny fields and glowing white structure of Solomon's Temple from within the perimeter of Castle Dracula was equally unsettling. You were standing in eternal night yet could clearly see a sun in the distance. It was like looking through a murky window.

My evil snow globe was filled with murderous monsters who were still coming to terms with their new non-vampire boss. A small faction had even rebelled and occasionally caused some murder and mayhem before retreating back to their unknown hideout. So, Ryuu, my ninja bodyguard, and Xylo, formerly known as Abel, were constantly waiting for danger. Xylo walked with a pep to his step, these days—his time with Cain had given him a newfound confidence in himself. He still suffered bouts of pessimism, but they were lessening; Cain's exuberant optimism was taking firm root in his long-lost brother, much like a lifeline thrown to a drowning man at sea.

Which was a great way to say *sorry for murdering you, bro.*

I let out a frustrated sigh, not wanting to think about the rebels or Castle Dracula's politics right now. I didn't want to think of my friends. I didn't even want to think of Nate Temple—who had been brought to the forefront of my mind thanks to Legion's visit.

Kansas City will not be immolated, he had said. As long as I married a demon. Presumably, someone high up on the food chain if the guy had Legion running his errands.

But the biggest concern was that Legion—and whomever else—had escaped Hell the moment I removed Excalibur from my soul. Was that why my parents had wanted to hide me? Had they known that a demon wanted to marry me? Even as a baby in the womb?

That was beyond unnerving, let alone disgusting.

But my parents hadn't just been hiding me from Hell. They had also wanted to hide me from Heaven. Should I be expecting a marriage proposal from an angel soon? I grimaced at the thought. They were trying to force me into choosing a groom from either Heaven or Hell. Either choice would result in a war.

With Kansas City in the middle.

"This is batshit insane," I growled, turning away from the balcony, and walking into the temple. I knew Sanguina was sleeping in my mother's laboratory. Maybe she would have some insight; although, the powerful Beast didn't strike me as the type of friend for weddings and boy talk. Power and destruction, sure.

Thankfully, neither Solomon nor Richard—who went by Last Breath when in his bipedal white lion form—were awake. Or at least they weren't walking around the place to find me lurking, unannounced. Solomon had a very unhealthy desire to study Sanguina, so it was safer for everyone if my visit—and her presence in the laboratory—remained unknown.

My morning had started off eventful. Knowing how loyal and unquestionably brave Phix, the Sphinx, had been in keeping my city safe in my absence over the last year, I'd finally asked her if she wanted the job of being my figurative horse in my role as Horseman of Despair. She'd spent a few minutes dancing around excitedly and purring like a locomotive before adamantly accepting. And about two minutes later, the Horseman of Death had made an unannounced visit, declaring that Phix was required to join him for a training camp on the job particulars.

I had not invited him or told him about my decision to choose Phix as my mount.

But a quick call had confirmed that Nate Temple's unicorn, Grimm, and an unnamed third horse would be joining Phix for the training, so I had reluctantly agreed. With three mounts picked, it meant only one member of our new squad needed to find one. Either Gunnar, the Horseman of Justice and alpha werewolf of St. Louis, or Alucard, the Horseman of Absolution and Daywalker Master Vampire of St. Louis, were without a ride.

Phix would let me know the details when I saw her next—which I hoped would be soon. I could use her comforting presence and razor-sharp claws on my hunt for rebels in Castle Dracula or demons in Kansas City. Especially now that I was marriage material.

As I quietly made my way to the lab, I found myself absently fondling the silver butterfly charm in my hand—my Horseman's Mask. I'd based the concealment design on a romantic gift Nate Temple had given me when we'd first kissed. Tonight's visit from Legion had stirred up feelings I had suppressed for entirely too long, and for good reason. My romantic feelings for Nate were a mixed bag these days.

Scratch that. The part of my heart that held him close was currently barren and storming.

We'd played the longest courtship game in modern history, teasing each other with a single kiss and a whole lot of sexual angst over *years*. I missed a step, pausing in the middle of the dim hallway. "Am I really *that* horny?" Solomon's Temple provided no answer, leaving my voice to echo into nothingness.

Typical.

I analyzed the part of me that longed for the day Nate and I could finally focus on us. We'd always pushed it down the line, promising each other we would do so *later*, when monsters and gods were not actively trying to wipe their asses with the very fabric of reality and flush humanity down the drain.

My frustration had all seemingly come to a head during our last encounter several days ago, when I'd caught him trying to steal a book from me. In an act of pettiness, I'd allowed Ryuu to secretly hold a sword to Nate's back, wanting to teach him a lesson for trying to rob me. Except it had backfired when Nate sensed the ninja, trapped him, threatened to kill him, and then called me out for risking my ninja's life by not stopping it sooner.

It had been the perfect storm, bringing up emotions I hadn't known I'd been carrying around. He'd made a mistake in trying to steal from me—even though it had only been a book I'd been holding onto for him, and he'd only stolen it so as to give me plausible deniability with the Norse gods. Nate's good intentions in trying to keep me out of the blast radius of whatever Norse pipe bomb he had been fiddling with had been both endearing and infuriating. In his aims to keep me safe, he had inadvertently succeeded in blowing up a bridge between us—or at least damaging some of the key supporting arches.

My mistake had been reacting emotionally—understandably so, after being robbed—by using Ryuu to teach Nate some humility. I hadn't spoken to Nate since.

Upon later reflection, I realized that the tension had been building up between the two of us for quite some time. I'd unknowingly been harboring anger at him for not making our relationship a priority during the recent, relatively peaceful, month. He hadn't called, asked me on a date, sent me flowers, or even invited me over for a movie. The only other encounter I'd recently had with Nate had been a few weeks ago.

Pandora had called to tell me that Nate urgently needed my help to fight Mordred, and that it was finally time for me to return Excalibur's sheath to the new King Arthur, a young man named Alex Arete, who was friends with Nate.

The legendary sword had been broken up into numerous pieces and hidden away over the past couple decades. One of those pieces—the Name —had been hidden inside me, of all places, when I was a baby. It was how my loving parents had come up with my name—ex-*Callie-bur*.

That decision—made by my parents collaborating with Nate's parents, because of course they had been friends without informing us somehow— had actually protected me from the forces of Heaven and Hell hunting me down as a result of my parents' long list of crimes. It had served as a protective ward. But it had been time to give it back—to re-forge the infamous sword, Excalibur.

Alucard and Gunnar had also gotten calls from Pandora to help Nate in Fae.

And that was when Nate gave them the other two Horsemen Masks— Absolution and Justice, respectively—and finally completed our posse. The act of handing out the last two Masks had served to heal Nate's own damaged Horseman Mask, because the new Four Horsemen were a brotherhood, and functioned best when working in harmony.

Since Nate had delayed handing out the other two Masks for so long, his own Mask had fractured—hence, Pandora's call. So, I'd arrived in Fae, and given Alex the sheath and power of my Name to fully repair the mythical blade. We'd all put on our Masks, and then...

Well, a whole lot of nothing had transpired on our ends. Because that had pretty much been all Nate needed from his new Horsemen. Alex had stepped in and helped Nate destroy Mordred.

While the three other Horsemen sat on our thumbs. Then we'd all gone home. That had been my only other encounter with Nate. I'd given Excal-ibur—part of my soul—away at the expense of my protection from Heaven and Hell. If that wasn't sacrifice, I didn't know what was.

Long story short, we had squandered our month of reprieve, crossing paths only the one other time, when he'd tried robbing me. And the results had been predictably disastrous—one or both of the men could have been killed.

Thankfully, the two had parted as respected, hesitant allies, and Ryuu had kept the offending katana that Nate had melted as a reminder of his near death experience. Because he was a man, and men did stupid things like that all the time.

Then again, women did plenty of stupid things like that all the time, too.

Like, for example, secretly wanting to test Nate's strength and ability to lead the Horsemen by sending a highly trained, and extremely lethal, ninja against him. To see just how good Nate really was, and if his abilities lived up to his rapidly growing reputations.

But that was just a hypothetical example...right?

Either way, the experiment had been concluded with clear and concise results, leaving behind a warped katana like a bold exclamation mark.

4

Afterwards, Nate had been forced to talk to me on a professional level—Horseman to Horseman. Captain to soldier, because he led our squad of Horsemen, and me allowing Ryuu to hold a sword to the lead Horseman's back was clearly a grievous error in judgment. Nate had not allowed me to hide from the consequences of my decision. If he had let it slide, I probably would have—subconsciously, at least—lost a lot of respect for him for being too soft. As Horsemen, we rose and fell together, and we were only as strong as our weakest link.

Some pains were necessary. They strengthened us. God knew Roland had embarrassed me dozens upon dozens of times, in equally disparaging ways, over the course of my ten years of training with him. The school of hard knocks was not forgiving. A slap on the wrist was for children.

I couldn't tell the world I was a Horseman and then cry about punishment when I had blatantly jeopardized my boss' life. And to top it off, I'd done it in front of Alucard, another Horseman, among others.

I'd also put Ryuu's life at risk, and he depended on me to always have his best interests at heart, not to treat him like a lowly pawn to toss to the meat grinder any time I felt like throwing a temper tantrum.

Although Nate did all sorts of wildly stupid things when angry—who didn't?—I knew he never would have let one of his allies or guards hold a sword to my back. Not in a million years.

It was no secret that Nate's most prized virtues were earned loyalty and trust. He gave it and demanded it in equal measure—holding himself to the same standard he expected from others. Family—not by blood, but by actions—was his bedrock. Period.

And no one fucked with the bedrock. No one. Friend or foe.

If I took out the romantic aspect of our relationship, his very direct reprimand had made perfect sense. I would've done the same in his shoes.

Except there *had* been a romantic aspect to our relationship. And reprimands did not nourish romance.

As Nate Temple, my friend and potential lover, he hadn't wanted to do it. As the Horseman of Hope, my boss, he'd had to do it. Hell, even as an allied city, from one leader to another, he had been right to do what he'd done.

But doing the right thing was sometimes different from doing the *right* thing. And now, the amalgamation of events had permanently changed the dynamic of our relationship, no matter what either of us wanted. Sometimes, lightning struck. It didn't ask your permission.

Don't get me wrong. I wasn't trying to beat myself up over my mistake. I was trying to understand the situation so that I didn't make the same mistake twice.

Which was why I'd spent the time since our blowout undergoing anger management therapy, searching for more productive things to do than sitting around and blaming Nate or myself for our non-existent romance.

Because I'd quickly realized that every single thing I had been blaming Nate for not doing...

I had been equally as guilty.

I hadn't reached out to him to suggest a date. I hadn't sent him any gifts or showed up unannounced for dinner. I hadn't even called him to chat, other than to talk business. Instead, I'd chosen to spend my time training with Ryuu, learning the Omegabet with Sanguina, exploring Castle Dracula, spending time with Xylo and Cain, and getting to know my Greater Demon godparents, Samael and Lily.

Relationships took two people working together, not one expecting the other to do all the work to keep it functioning.

There were two types of people in this world. Those who saw a problem and immediately searched for someone or something to blame were characteristically bitter and unhappy. Self-proclaimed victims, and claiming it was virtue.

And then there were those who saw a problem and immediately searched for a solution. They were usually excited and anxious to overcome problems, treating each one as a test to become a better, stronger version of themselves.

If you weren't part of the solution, you were part of the problem.

Assessing blame did not solve the problem. Blame was a preventative tactic—to make sure the problem didn't happen again...in the *future*. It did nothing for the *now*.

Sitting on the side of the road with a blown-out tire sucked.

Spending thirty minutes raging about how the government hadn't fixed the potholes, or the company who made the tire had obviously used shoddy material, or the mechanic who had put on the tire hadn't done it properly... only resulted in an angrier person sitting on the side of the road with a blown-out tire.

The tire didn't magically fix itself when you picked the winning number on the blame lottery.

The only way to do that was to roll up your sleeves and fix the flat tire.

Solutions came first. Assessing blame came after the problem was solved.

Which was why the event had so suddenly put things into perspective for me.

It had revealed something that I hadn't wanted to think about, let alone admit to myself. On some level, I was not willing to put in the time for my relationship with Nate. I'd been assessing and accepting blame, waiting for it to fix itself.

And that had shaken me to my core.

I reached my mother's lab and found Sanguina sleeping on a chair. A lone lamp burned on a stone table, illuminating the room in a romantic, calming glow. I set the parchment and wedding invitation down beside the lamp and let out an overly loud sigh to wake up the lazy Beast.

In place of eyes, she had empty eye sockets. My mother had taken them out and put them into me—via some unknown process that probably had an exponentially high ick factor. Then again, she'd been pregnant with me when she took Sanguina's eyes, so it could have been as simple as that. They should put it on those pregnancy brochures—*don't lift anything over fifteen pounds, and don't do battle with interstellar monsters made of raw magic*. Now, Sanguina's hollow eye sockets were crusted with molten silver, as if they had been burned out. She opened those haunting peepers and let out a cute little foxy yawn. Sanguina was the answer to the age-old question of how to make nuclear level magic more terrifying—

Put it in a cuddly, furry mammal.

It's why I'd given her a standing order not to use her powers unless specifically requested. She could annihilate someone over the most innocent of infractions, so I was her conscience.

My relationship with Sanguina was not just master to minion, but also a shared essence. I...

I was part Beast, technically speaking. A conduit of sorts between the mysterious, elusive, cataclysmic beings from...wherever she and her ilk had lived. She powered Castle Dracula much like Falco powered Nate Temple's mansion into a sentient being.

So being in Castle Dracula had felt strange for me, at times. Because it was almost like being inside myself. If Sanguina powered Castle Dracula, part of me did as well. We both had the Beast in us. Did Nate feel the same way inside his ancestral home? I shook off the thought.

"Anything new?" I asked her.

No, she answered, speaking directly into my mind. She'd learned how to stop shouting at my brain, diminishing the number of headaches I'd suffered in the beginning of our relationship. She could even speak out loud if she wanted to. She often preferred not to, so as not to frighten my friends with her words.

Lucky me.

"Well, a demon proposed to me a little while ago," I growled, trying to restrain my fury.

She tensed, sitting up warily. *Explain.* So, I did. Quickly and focusing only on the facts. She didn't offer comment, but she did look troubled, her tail swishing back and forth in a restless gesture.

I left her to her thoughts and began walking through the laboratory.

Qinglong—the decades-long bouncer and only other person who could enter without my express permission—wasn't here, so I had free reign to explore my mother's old workshop. Of course, the Azure Dragon was one of the mythical Divine Creatures, and he could Shadow Walk so fluidly that he could appear behind me without a sound and slice my throat before I even registered his presence.

It might say something about me—and my crappy night—that this thought barely registered as a concern as I continued about the room. I trailed my fingers against items laid out on the desks, stacks of books, and random collectibles, imagining my mother touching them on her own troubled nights. It was pleasant to think that mother and daughter, although separated by death, could still touch each other through her most cherished collection of magical artifacts.

I paused beside the two tubs of black and white marbles that held my mother's memories, pursing my lips thoughtfully. All I had to do was place one on my tongue to hear her voice and see through her eyes.

I hadn't come here much in recent weeks, fearing that focusing on the past would wind up consuming me. And that wasn't even considering the marbles.

I wasn't confident that I was strong enough to handle them yet, so I settled for touching her old possessions. It was safer.

But now that I was here, I began to wonder...

Had she left anything else out for me to find? Things I had overlooked during my first visit? Maybe the solution to some upcoming conflict I would face—like the identity of the asshole demon who thought he could claim my hand in marriage with an engagement ring of extortion? My gaze drifted back to the marbles for a brief moment. Surely, any instructions from her would be there. In fact, three marbles had been singled out from the tubs and set on their own velvet pillow, as if important.

But as much as I wanted to taste them, I was also very bitter about the whole thing. About what she had done to me. How she had used me. Even knowing it had been for my own good. She'd protected me from a demonic marriage proposal—theoretically. That protection was now gone.

I sat down in a nearby chair, pursing my lips. "I need information," I said, seriously considering heading back to my suite at Castle Dracula for some sleep.

Sanguina remained silent.

"No. I need answers. Solutions. To problems I cannot comprehend because seeking out information on the problems will only put me into debt with the wrong people. A demon wants to marry me, and he brought his lawyer and possibly his extended family into town for the big night. He was only able to escape Hell after I sacrificed my link to Excalibur," I mused.

"Which was bonded to me to protect me from Heaven and Hell." Excalibur's sheath had been lying on my mother's desk my entire life, undisturbed.

"Let me know when you have a question," Sanguina murmured.

I grunted, noticing a metal box tucked under a stack of books on the table beside me. I removed them to get a better look at it. A phoenix was etched into the lid.

I studied the fiery creature warily, thinking of the Vermilion Bird, one of the four Divine Creatures like Xuanwu, the Black Tortoise, and Qinglong, the Azure Dragon. Qinglong and Xuanwu had both worked with my mother and Samael—their own private club. But no one knew where the other two were—the Vermillion Bird and the White Tiger.

I sensed no power from the box and admitted that I was letting my imagination run wild. Perhaps I was reading too much into things. Not everything was a conspiracy.

I opened the box with one finger, already funneling my power into a shield in case I unleashed a djinn or something worse. Nothing remotely magical or deadly happened, and I let out a sigh of disappointment. Then I silently admitted that I was a psychopath for secretly hoping for such a reaction. Sanguina sniffed primly, reading my thoughts.

I peered inside the box to see a fiery flower. I hissed instinctively, wondering why the box hadn't been hot to the touch before I even thought to consider how the thing was still on fire. I stared at it for a few seconds, wondering if it would make the *Super Mario Bros* sound when I touched it.

The petals seemed to be ever-smoldering, not actually flaming. And...it was beautiful, resembling a lotus blossom.

I held my fingers over it, surprised to feel no heat. Rather than risk touching it, I inspected the rest of the box. I saw three sets of matching metal rings—nothing fancy, just simple bands. As I focused on them, I sensed traces of power, but only when I stared at them, which was strange. Careful not to touch the fire lotus, I scooped a pair of the rings up, clinking them together thoughtfully. There was a faint magnetic attraction between them, but it wasn't strong enough to defeat the inevitable force of gravity. *Like my love life*, I thought with a sullen frown. The pair was still trying, though, giving off a kindred spirit vibe. I sensed nothing malevolent about them, so I decided to keep them for myself. Maybe they would make me lucky in love. Later. I shoved them into my pocket and peered back into the box to find a note that somehow hadn't caught fire from the flower.

I flicked it with a fingernail to discern that it was a white metal placard the size of a credit card, not paper. My breath caught, wondering if it was the equivalent to the figurines I owned for Xuanwu and Qinglong—totems with the ability to summon them. Although theirs were actually animal figures.

Still, white metal was one of the White Tiger's aspects.

Except nothing happened. I had felt more magic from my Target credit card than I did from the metal.

But the Target card truly was magical, of course. Fight me if you diagree.

I frowned as I noticed that something had been etched into the card's surface. I picked it up, tilting it in the dim light to make out a spear broken into equal thirds. My breath caught. The Spear of Destiny had been broken exactly like the image.

Except it had been healed, and it currently resided inside my freaking *soul*. I called it up—something I had been working on a lot in the past few weeks—and it winked into existence in my hands. I studied the fracture lines—which were still visible, but no longer fragile. Instead, the Spear was stronger than ever. And it looked *identical* to the one on the card.

Archangel Michael had once wanted this Spear very, very badly. Under-standably, since it was the one that had pierced Jesus' side on the Cross.

I lifted the card closer and studied it, searching for additional clues. The broken spear appeared to be supported on either end by two triangles, making it look like a bridge between two mountain peaks.

And over the top of each mountain was an X. I angled the card, noticing a fainter marking—more like a hologram—of a sword stabbing down through the center section of the broken spear. It was barely even visible, and I wondered if I was simply imagining it.

The way the sword bisected that center section of the spear made it look like a Crucifix. I touched the Spear of Destiny to the card and held my breath for the world to end. Nothing happened, and I let out a disappointed huff.

"What do you expect of me, Mother?" I whispered to myself, setting the metal card back inside the box with the rings and fire lotus before carefully closing it. I let the Spear of Destiny wink out of existence—back into my body—and leaned back in the chair, interlacing my fingers, and setting them over my stomach.

Sanguina glanced up at the sound of my voice and regarded me without comment. She had taught me how to shield my thoughts from her—so she could *remember what peace and quiet felt like*, she'd said. I applied her teachings now, regarding her back just as snootily.

Sanguina spoke very rarely, and when she did it usually gave me chills. Like a toddler with the power of the universe, and as temperamental as a hurricane. She wasn't evil.

She also wasn't benevolent.

She was an emotional child, abandoned here long, long ago. Bonding to Dracula had saved her life, in a way. At the expense of his soul. He hadn't been strong enough to sustain her, turning him into a vampire so that she could siphon off the power in the blood of his victims. It wasn't ideal—for either of them—but it had sufficed.

Now, with me, she had found a source of power capable of keeping her in line—and we were biologically bonded as well as magically bonded. I hadn't been turned into a vampire as a result of that connection, and I frequently found myself wondering whether that was a favorable or terrifying factor.

I was sympathetic to her situation, though. She didn't want to destroy everything. Much like a child didn't *want* to throw a temper tantrum in the middle of the grocery store.

But damn it, she would sure as hell throw one if she didn't get her candy bar right friggin' *now*.

So, we were both learning.

For her part, she seemed relieved to finally have a parental figure capable of keeping her in line. I think. It wasn't as easy for me to read her thoughts as it was for her to read mine.

"Do you know anything about the Divine Creatures?" I asked Sanguina absently.

Surprisingly, she spoke out loud this time. "I cared only for blood and affection. Not daemons of metal and fire or water and wood," she said, referencing the elemental aspects to each Divine. We'd talked about them before —since Qinglong occasionally made appearances here in her favorite spot, and I hadn't wanted the two of them killing each other by accident. I'd never heard her use the word daemons before, though. "Those are dangerous toys for children to play with." Her tone let me know she was taking a shot at me. She must have sensed my thoughts from a few moments ago.

I cringed guiltily, wanting to clarify my earlier thoughts. "I care for you Sanguina, and it pains me to learn how you were treated. How you were left behind to fend for yourself. It wasn't meant to be an accusation or a judgment, it was intended as pity and sorrow. Sympathy for someone I care about."

She regarded me pensively, and I could tell she was blocking me from reading her thoughts.

Maybe she didn't want my pity. I totally understood that. So, I continued. "However, like the troubled, abandoned child, your experience has transformed you into something remarkable. You are stronger as a result," I said, smiling. "I was also abandoned as a baby. I empathize with you because my experience is similar, and it made me stronger. You have done more than any Beast I've heard about, and you did it all on your own, without help. That is beyond impressive, Sanguina," I told her, meaning every word. "So, when I compare you to a troubled child, it is only an acknowledgement of my respect. I am awed by how much you accomplished despite your tribulations. It is inspiring. *You* are inspiring."

I waited for her response, hoping I hadn't made her angrier.

She studied me for a long moment. Then she finally nodded, begrudgingly.

I made sure to lock down my thoughts for the night. We'd just had a moment, and I didn't want to ruin it.

I finally turned away from her unblinking stare and found myself staring at my mother's journal on the nearby desk. It was filled with pages and pages of the Omegabet—the language of the end. Sanguina had been teaching me a little of that, sharpening my ability to decipher strange drawings and read prophetic madness that—more often than not—resembled the drunken results of a fridge magnet sentence. The one where you get a few hundred random words that you could arrange into bizarre, often humorous, messages for your fridge.

Studying the strange amalgamation of symbols, runes, and characters scribbled on those pages made the hair on the back of my arms stand on end.

Because, subconsciously, I seemed able to read it or comprehend it. I couldn't sit there and go word-for-word, or anything, but staring at it for more than a few moments caused my mind to wander with dark, terrifying thoughts. I would snap out of it some time later—perhaps hours—realizing I had learned quite a bit. Often, things I had not wanted to learn or visualize.

Like walking in on your parents having sex, except less of the carnal sense and more of the apocalyptic.

I shuddered at that visual and shrugged off thoughts of the Omegabet.

The vampires of the Sanguine Council were a safer problem. The Sanguine Council had been recruited by the Masters—a secret, clandestine group of monsters and gods who wanted to set up their own new world order. They'd blackmailed the Harkers—my predecessors—into building them an army at Castle Dracula. One that they could use during the upcoming Omega War, as I'd heard it indirectly called a few times by Nate Temple. Others called it the All War, or the End War.

All alluded to the same thing. A doozie.

Because now that I had defeated Dracula—one of those secretive Masters—I had earned my own place in their little club. There was a meeting with them in about six weeks, and the new Master Dracula had been cordially invited. Probably so they could reassure they still had their army and that I understood the past obligations of my predecessors.

I'd met with the members of the Sanguine Council and commanded them to join me at Castle Dracula for an executive retreat. They assumed it was to curtail their feeding habits—which was true, but they didn't know that I also intended to come up with a better solution than handing them over to the Masters. I'd postponed that meeting since I hadn't yet pinned down the particulars of how to achieve my goals.

In addition to the vampires not knowing what to do with their new vege-tarian boss, some of the residents of Castle Dracula didn't quite know what to make of me either. They were also unhappy to learn that their old boss had been a fraud. Johnathan and Mina Harker had killed the real Dracula long ago, taking his place with none the wiser. That secret was now out, and it only added to the bubbling cauldron of angry monsters.

Not all were in favor of their new ruler. Enter the rebels, stage left.

I was hoping the Sanguine Council could help me with that. That the residents of Castle Dracula could see me coordinating the world's most powerful vampires into a new, cohesive unit. Likewise, that the Sanguine Council could see me ruling over Castle Dracula without issue. That the two problems would solve each other as long as I could keep everything stable for a little while longer.

If that didn't work...I wasn't sure what I would do.

I reached into my pocket and withdrew a thick card. I opened it, reading the words for the hundredth time. It was an invitation to Dracula for the upcoming Master's Ball—which was still more than a month away. It was addressed to *Dracula*, not Jonathan or even Mina Harker. Technically, that now applied to me.

They'd cleverly combined the word Master with masquerade—Masterade —because they were *oh, so evil*. Attending a party with the Masters could be suicide. It could also be helpful.

I tapped the card against the table, considering my options.

The protection my mother had given me from Heaven and Hell was now gone. A demon wanted to marry me on Christmas Day, three weeks from now. I had political drama to deal with regarding Castle Dracula and the Sanguine Council. The only party I hadn't bumped into yet was Heaven. With Legion making his move tonight, I was betting Heaven wasn't far behind.

My parents had put me in this position—as a chew toy between Heaven and Hell—working closely with Nate's parents to keep me safe until now. Quinn MacKenna was even the byproduct of our three families scheming together. The three of us were integral to the fight against the Masters. Our parents had set us up so that we would have the requisite strength to defeat them when the time came. Nate would play a significant role in the upcoming war as the Catalyst—whatever that actually meant.

I didn't know Quinn's part, nor my own. I wasn't a Catalyst, so what was my role? I'd be damned if I'd been put here to play sidekick to Nate Temple or to marry a demon. Nate had enough yes men on the payroll. I was no lickspittle. And I was in Kansas City. If I were meant to be his tool, I would have wound up there. Nate's parents had set me up here in Kansas City at Abundant Angel Catholic Church as a baby orphan.

Maybe it was time for me to stop reacting and to get ahead of the curve. To find out what I could do on my own that would help our cause. I was part nephilim. I was the descendant of King Solomon—able to trap angels and demons in my ring. I was part Beast. And I was the first one of our trio to make it into the Masters Club as a VIP.

I hadn't inherited anything in my life like Nate had. I'd fought and clawed for everything—even my Solomon inheritance. Everything had had a price. Solomon's Temple had forced me to survive the Doors.

Rather than waiting for Heaven to approach me, I decided to expedite it.

I scooped up the items Legion had left me and shoved the Masterade invitation back into my pocket. Then I motioned for Sanguina to follow me. "It's time to go pick a fight with an angel."

She hopped down off the couch. "Now?" she asked in a calm tone, speaking out loud.

I frowned. "No. Sleep, first. We'll do the angel thing after breakfast or something."

"Why didn't you just say, *it's time to go to sleep?*" she asked, sounding amused.

I scowled down at her. "Because that would have been lame."

She glanced up at me. "Then let's go be lame."

"You know, I really thought we were having a moment earlier," I said, condescendingly.

"We were not."

Well. "Then let's go be lame." I sighed, ripping open a Gateway to the Master Suite at Castle Dracula—my nefarious, spacious penthouse away from Kansas City. The bed there was to die for.

6

A click and a squeal snapped me awake like a gunshot. I sat up, panting heavily and immediately realizing that I had sweated through my sheets. I wore a long pajama tee and it was drenched.

For some startling reason, Ryuu stood beside my bed with his black katana drawn, bleary-eyed and hair disheveled. The only reason I didn't kill him on reflex was because he was facing the door in a menacing pose. Samael and Lily practically drop-kicked the door and stumbled in like a marching band, beaming at me brightly. "Rise and shine!" they shouted in unison, shredding my eardrums with flash bangs of happiness.

Lilith—yes, *that* Lilith who had refused to submit to Adam in the Garden of Eden—preferred to go by Lily, even though I'd finally gotten her to come clean on her real identity. When I'd first met her, she'd been in the form of a terrifying, giant, crocodile demon, chained up by my predecessor for the last hundred years.

She'd given herself a makeover, and absolutely everyone approved. Hell, even Adam would have called her back if he could have seen her now. Blasphemy was fun.

Lily was a tall, overly curvy, woman with bright red hair, reminding me of Jessica Rabbit. She was heart-throbbingly beautiful, and she was my doting godmother, even though she looked about ten years my junior. One of her favorite ways to annoy me was by calling me—

"Sulfur sugar!" she cackled, pouncing onto the bed to throttle me awake. Ryuu lowered his sword, running his hand through his hair as he shot Samael a meaningful look that seemed to say *knocking and waiting is courteous, knocking and assaulting is not.* My godfather was too busy laughing at Lilith's excitement to be bothered by such trivialities.

Samael was a maturely handsome, muscular man with broad shoulders and long dark hair past his shoulders. He radiated authority, and charisma oozed from his pores. He could have easily doubled as a Bond villain. His demonic form was entirely different from Lily, more of a demon with the skin of coins rather than scales. Thankfully, they both preferred their human forms.

Lily finally hopped off the bed and skipped over to Samael. She grasped his hand and batted her long eyelashes at him. The pair were sickeningly in love.

I licked my lips, trying to get enough saliva to make my mouth work. Maybe it wasn't sweat, but drool, soaking me, because my mouth felt as dry as a desert. I noticed Xylo standing in the corner of the room like a statue, the embers and sparks of his ligaments crackling as he leveled his smoky stare at my godparents.

Samael shifted from foot-to-foot, and I realized he was sweating like crazy. Lily and Ryuu seemed fine. As I studied my godfather closer, I realized that he looked rather sickly.

"Are you okay?" I asked him, struggling to wake my brain up.

He flinched as if I had slapped him, earning a startled look from Lily, who suddenly gasped. "Sammie! You're sweating like crazy!"

He shot her a crooked smile, using his forearm to wipe at his brow. "I'm fine," he assured her, obviously lying. "You're sweating, too," he accused, sounding desperate.

I nodded at the obvious fact, silently wondering what was going on here.

Lily turned to me. "I just came to say good morning—"

Samael dropped to his knees like he'd been shot. I jumped to my feet with a shout and called up balls of fire in my palms, searching for the shooter. Ryuu had half-drawn his katana and Xylo had snapped off one of his rib bones, holding it overhead aggressively. Lily was eerily silent, and I turned to see her staring down at Samael with a stunned look on her face.

"Lily, will you marry—"

"YES!" she shrieked, loud enough to send me stumbling back into the headboard and release my magic as I slapped my hands over my ears. Then she was pulling him to his feet and kissing him like she was trying to suffocate him. He wrapped his arms around her, kissing her right back and laughing between gasps of air—when she let him.

I turned to Ryuu with a baffled look and he shrugged, smirking faintly.

Samael finally extricated himself and grinned at me, chuckling as he wiped his brow again. "I don't know why I felt so nervous," he admitted, embarrassed. "We've waited so long to be together, and I wanted you to see what you gave us by saving her for me." He wrapped his arm around her waist, pulling her close. "You brought us together, so I wanted you to see me propose."

Lily was sobbing messily, resting her head against his shoulder. I smiled, unable to help myself. It was cute, and incredibly kind. Ryuu glanced over at me and abruptly averted his eyes. I froze, my smile slipping.

I was standing on top of my bed in a soaked white tee that barely covered my ass with no bra or panties on underneath! I sat down hurriedly, covering myself with the sheets. My cheeks felt as if they were on fire. Ryuu kept his attention focused on Lily and Samael, pretending he hadn't seen anything.

He'd definitely gotten a free show.

Lily was grinning at the two of us, looking entirely too amused. Xylo had reattached his rib and watched us thoughtfully. "You know..." Lily said slowly, drawing my attention. "Castle Dracula would be an appropriate place for the ceremony. The place that brought us all together for the wrong reasons could bind us all together for the right reasons."

Samael nodded his agreement. "My thoughts, exactly! This place could use a party!"

Thinking of actually planning a wedding gave me an instant migraine but imagining such a big event also made me grin from ear-to-ear. "As long as you don't expect me to plan it, that sounds like an excellent idea."

They cried out in unison and wrapped each other in a tight, hopping hug, thanked me profusely, and then bolted from the room. The door clicked shut behind them and I just stared at it for a few moments.

"Did that really just happen?" I asked, shaking my head. My good cheer rapidly faded as I recalled my meeting with Legion. At least Hell seemed perfectly fine with taking care of the arrangements for my anticipated wedding. Silver lining.

Ryuu grunted. "Samael asked me where you were at least three times last night, and then pretended it was nothing important when I told him you were out. Now I know why," he said, chuckling.

I knew Ryuu wasn't pleased about me being *out* last night, because I hadn't warned him about it ahead of time, and he took his bodyguard duties very seriously. Which was one reason I'd escaped in the first place—to get away from the constant scrutiny and pressure of being the boss.

I turned to Xylo. "You okay over there, buddy?" I asked, uncertainly, wondering why he wasn't speaking.

He nodded, casually. "I have been crowned the Bone Heir King."

I stared back at him for a few long seconds. I turned to Ryuu to find him nodding discreetly, fighting back a grin at the way *Bone Heir* had made it sound like he'd claimed to be the king of male erections. Was Cain playing another prank on him? I rubbed at my eyes and turned back to Xylo. "What does that mean, exactly, and who...crowned you?"

He approached me as if marching, his pirate boots thumping into the floor and his crimson cowl remaining perfectly still. He walked...regally. "The skeleton army nominated me, officially, to lead them under your banner. The Bone Heir army will stand proud under the banner of the White Rose."

I bit my cheeks to prevent myself from bursting out laughing at his phrasing. In all seriousness, I hadn't known there was an official title. There was no doubt that the other skeletons followed him without question, judging by the fact that he'd been ordering them about for the past few weeks without issue. "That's...amazing, Xylo. Congratulations. And thank you."

He nodded, self-importantly. "I am quite proud. It will help give me more credibility when we hunt down the rebels," he growled.

I looked up sharply. "Has there been another attack?"

Ryuu nodded grimly. "They attacked the Village last night. It's one reason I didn't hunt you down when you ran off," he murmured in a stern tone. "Three dead." He watched me closely, gauging my reaction.

"Is that so?" I asked in a frosty tone.

I noticed that a pile of blankets and a pillow rested on the floor at the side of my bed. Ryuu had been sleeping here on the floor to guard over me. "I checked in on you last night and found you sleeping on the couch with your nose in a book, shivering," he said, pointing to the sitting area. I blushed, remembering that I had gotten ready for bed and then sat down to read a bit of Bram Stoker's *Dracula* until it put me to sleep. Mission accomplished, apparently. "You were having a nightmare, but I couldn't wake you up," he said in a careful tone, not meeting my eyes. "I didn't know if something was wrong. If something happened last night...so, I carried you to bed and decided to remain close." He was clenching his jaw, and his shoulders were tense, showing me how concerned he had been. How angry he had been that something might have happened to me when I left him behind.

Forcing him to make a judgment call that would probably anger me. I sighed. "Thank you, Ryuu," I said, reaching out to touch his shoulder. His posture relaxed slightly, but I knew the situation was far from resolved. "I just needed some privacy. I went for a walk."

He nodded, not prying. "In the future, you can tell me that."

I studied him. "Would you listen?" I asked, smiling.

He smirked. "Depends. But probably not," he admitted without shame.

I hit him with a pillow, making him laugh out loud. "Out of the way. I need a shower. Or a bath." He obediently backed out of my way and approached Xylo so that he wouldn't see anything indecent. "And coffee. Anything with caffeine will do, actually," I said, slipping out of bed and hurriedly making my way into the bathroom. Xylo said something about Cain possibly having a stash of cocaine, but I had already closed the door behind me, and I was confident that Ryuu could educate Xylo on the differences between caffeine and cocaine.

Surprisingly, the Harkers had adapted to the times, and had installed a shower. Rather than demanding to know how it worked in a castle located in another realm, I had written it off as magic upon verifying that it *did* work.

Whoever the castle's plumber was would get a fat bonus this year. I looked up at my reflection in the mirror and winced. My hair was a bird's nest, but at least my shirt wasn't as transparent as I had feared. The slogan on the front made me smile. Claire had custom ordered it after I'd told her about becoming the new Dracula and invited her to move out of Starlight's cave to live with me.

That's QUEEN Bitchula to you.

I shrugged out of it, feeling slightly jittery from hunger, but that could wait until after the shower and the cocaine. Caffeine. Whatever.

I wasn't sure I wanted to hear any other news updates from my night off. So far, my godparents were getting married, I had rebels wanting to rip the crown off my head, my unknown demon fiancé was already making our wedding invitations, and Xylo had been erected the boner king.

7

As I climbed into the shower, I finally allowed my thoughts to drift to the events from last night. I'd been studiously avoiding them, letting them simmer in my subconscious mind.

And...I was suddenly realizing what a terrible idea that had been—to keep something so monumentally terrible bottled up inside.

My pulse steadily began to increase, and my breathing felt shallow and forced as I remembered my decision to pick a fight with an angel. I recalled my encounter with Legion, and I felt a twinge of panic creep into my shoulders, wondering if Ryuu had found the wedding invitation or legal contract. I'd wanted to ask Samael about Legion, but now I was having second thoughts. He had just proposed and had a wedding to plan.

Also, I was beginning to realize how damning it might be to tell anyone that a demon wanted to marry me. As quickly as that, I began to feel overwhelmed. What would Ryuu and my friends say about that? With no one to watch me and judge me, I began to crumble under the weight of everything. Lying to Ryuu about last night, needing to deal with the rebels, stressing about the wedding, my precarious relationship with Nate, the Sanguine Council, and visions of Kansas City on fire if I made a wrong move.

Dead Freaks were one thing, but helpless Regulars...burning...

Once I thought of it, I couldn't get it out of my head.

My knees almost gave out before I caught myself against the wall. I began to shake as the hot water scalded my skin. I slid down to the ground and hugged my knees to my chest, chastising myself for acting like a coward. But the anger only increased my frustration and I pounded my fist into the floor, crying harder.

Ryuu poked his head into the bathroom, drawn by the sound of me punching the floor. When I didn't reassure him fast enough, he clicked the door shut, locked it, and then walked into the bathroom with his sword drawn. Through the foggy glass, he saw me seated on the shower floor, silently crying as I hugged my knees, leaning my shoulder and the side of my head against the glass. My anger and stress turned to embarrassment and I froze.

Rather than fleeing for his life before I erupted on him for invading my privacy, he quietly sat down on the other side of the glass, pressing his back against it. He rested his black katana across his knees and sat there in silence, willing to risk my anger to let me know that I was not alone.

Surprisingly, I didn't hide my emotions like I'd instinctively wanted upon seeing him enter. I didn't shout at him or command him to leave. I also didn't hide the raw pain tearing me up inside. I let it all continue to come out, and Ryuu never said a word.

He just sat there, a boulder in the pond. Steadfast, concerned, and dedicated. At the peak of my meltdown, I pressed myself closer to the glass, taking a deep, calming breath.

His presence seemed to anchor me in a strange way. His silence was a lifeline, slowly pulling me back. He didn't demand to know what was wrong —even though I *knew* he wanted to. And that simple act of trust helped settle me. Simply knowing he was there was exactly what I needed to clear my thoughts.

"Thank you, Ryuu," I whispered. "I think I'm okay, now."

He nodded, and then spoke in a low, gentle tone. "Turn the water hotter and practice your breathing for a few more minutes. Xuanwu says that it is best to take a few additional minutes of thoughtful meditation once an emotional storm breaks or an existential crisis passes. He is usually right."

My lip trembled and I nodded. More than anything else, I found it unbelievably touching that he chose this moment to use third party credibility to help me get through my breakdown. Ryuu typically *told* me what I needed to do—when it was an area of expertise he knew he had mastered. Like this exact moment.

Yet he'd chosen a passive tone. Which meant he was very concerned and didn't want to risk challenging me for fear I might crack. This tiny sliver of compassion meant he was more concerned for me than he wanted to admit. Had he seen the wedding invitation?

Was that why he thought I was crying?

The thought of marrying a demon had started my tears, but only because it was one of many things on my mind. Sometimes, a woman just needed to cry. To embrace the pain rather than avoid it like men often did.

I realized that I was staring at the back of his head—inches apart, but a transparent wall away. Through a smear in the steamy glass, I saw that he was no longer holding his black katana, but the melted, warped trophy blade Nate had broken for him. "I'm sorry for letting my emotions get the best of me, Ryuu," I whispered, staring at it.

His shoulders stiffened. "You should not apologize for something like this...Callie," he said, testing out the word as if it was a foreign language. He was obviously uncomfortable because he usually called me White Rose. "Apologizing for something you cannot control is foolish."

I frowned, realizing he'd thought I was talking about my breakdown. "No. I meant the Nate thing. You're holding that stupid blade. I shouldn't have put you in that situation."

He was strangely silent for a few moments. And then he let out a soft chuckle. "Oh. I'd already forgotten about it," he said, obviously lying.

I sighed. I'd said it, at least. That was what mattered. I calmly reached up to turn the water hotter and settled in to take his advice, closing my eyes.

Ryuu did the same on the other side of the glass, not peppering me with questions or demanding explanations.

I could have kissed him for that.

Otherwise, I might have been forced to lie—I wasn't sure how involved I wanted him to be when I punched an angel in the nose or turned down a demon suitor. The denizens of Heaven and Hell knew how to harbor a grudge, and they had long memories.

So, for now, I could pretend we were both being honest with each other, and that there were no lies or secrets between us. All that might change when I left the bathroom.

Ryuu cleared his throat. "I am going to tell you a story, Callie Penrose," he said in a soft, deep tone that I could feel through the glass wall. My forearms pebbled at hearing him use my full name. I was sure he had done it before, but never in such an accidentally intimate setting.

"Okay, Ryuu Ninja-face," I said, smiling. I didn't know his last name. Maybe he didn't have one.

He chuckled, shaking his head as he repeated the last name under his breath. He was silent for a few more moments, and then he cleared his throat before speaking in a soft, lecturing tone, like we were two teens who had snuck out of the house in the middle of the night to tell each other ghost stories and drink soda without our parents knowing.

"Buddha was walking in the mountains one day, far from the nearest village and even the most reclusive of outlying farms. He came upon a flower growing out of a standing puddle of water on a lonely boulder. It was the most beautiful lotus blossom he'd ever seen. He could practically taste the nectar in the air, and it filled his nostrils with such a heady scent that he almost imagined he had taken a bite from it. He stared at the flower, imagining how soft it would feel against his fingertips."

I stared through the foggy glass at the usually silent ninja, transfixed, even though I could only see the back of his head. My overactive imagination tickled my own senses until I could almost taste the flower petals on my own tongue.

"After a time, he found himself sitting down in the middle of the path, weeping as he stared, unblinking, at the rare beauty growing out from the unusual puddle in the stone. He watched as the sun trailed across the sky—noting how the arc of the sunlight brought the radiant flower to life in various new ways with each passing hour. Then the moon came out, and the flower transformed into something hauntingly mesmerizing and maddeningly stunning. Beautiful, but in entirely different ways."

The steaming shower placed me in a humid world of fog where his words could more easily come to life, the scene unveiling before me like a movie.

"A traveler came upon him the next morning, saw him crying in the dirt, and rushed over, fearing that Buddha had been injured. *Why do you cry, Buddha?* the traveler asked. Buddha, so wrought with emotion that he could not speak, merely pointed at the lotus blossom," Ryuu said.

I realized I was holding my breath and that my lips felt numb.

"The traveler looked up, smiled in appreciation, and then turned back to

Buddha, his smile slowly shifting to confusion. *It is a beautiful flower, Buddha, but why does it make you cry?*

"*It is* too *beautiful*, Buddha whispered. *I can only sit here and marvel at it in wonder—nothing more. I watch it so that I may remember it and know it. So that I may think back on it during dark days and remember what it means to smile.*

"The traveler scratched his head, perplexed. *Why not just pluck it and take it home with you, Buddha? Plant it in a pond back home?*

"At this, Buddha exploded with anger, rising to his feet and threatening the traveler against doing any such thing. The traveler, now frightened for his life, backed away hurriedly, reassuring Buddha that he would not touch the flower—had not intended to touch the flower.

"After a time, Buddha regained control of his emotions and assessed the flower. *I could pluck this perfect flower and take it home with me. I could try to seize the beauty and hold it close to my heart. I could love it more than any other thing in the world, but I will never be able to love it as much as that puddle on that boulder that it is impossibly growing out from. The flower thrives in this wild, uncertain, and unlikeliest of terrains. It has strong, resilient roots that were not suffocated by this boulder nor the barest amount of water needed to make it grow. The wind cannot defeat it. The rain cannot wash it away. The sun cannot burn it.*

"Then Buddha slowly turned to look at the traveler. *But my love would destroy it. Plucking that flower would kill it. By the time I made it back home in a few days, it would lose its luster, and I would be left with a new image to replace the one I have right now. I would look upon it and only see the death my overpowering love had wrought. How I had destroyed something so precious by trying to make it anything other than what it was. My love would smother it. So, I shall sit here for a spell, and appreciate it for what it is, not for what I want it to be.*"

Ryuu's words trailed off, echoing softly in the foggy bathroom. My lip trembled and I blinked through misty eyes, staring at the back of the deadly and surprisingly poetic shinobi assassin's head.

I tried opening my mouth to speak, but it took me several attempts to produce any words. "Why did you tell me that story, Ryuu?" I whispered nervously, fearfully and, admittedly...

Hopeful, although I wasn't entirely sure why.

"Because the story finally made sense to me," he murmured. "Almost ten years after I heard it." Then, he climbed to his feet. "I'll be waiting for you in the bedroom when you are ready." Then he left on silent feet.

"*What?*" I demanded, reeling from the abrupt change in the mood just as much as from his comment.

He just laughed before closing the bathroom door.

I'll give you three guesses on what occupied my thoughts as I finished my shower.

It wasn't Buddha, as sexy as his belly was.

҈ 8 ҈

After my shower, Ryuu was waiting for me in my bedroom alright—with a duffel bag of training essentials over his shoulder, his black katana and his warped katana on opposite hips, and he was pointing at my ninja training outfit that was folded neatly on my dresser. "It's anger management time," he said, grinning sadistically. "I'll wait outside in the hall." He smiled the whole way to the door.

"Oh, I feel plenty of anger right now," I muttered before he closed the door. With a resigned sigh, I changed into the training clothes. We'd been doing this every morning for a week, but my eventful wake-up call had pushed it far from my mind. Ryuu had not forgotten. He got a twisted pleasure out of tormenting me in our daily training sessions—which was what we had started out calling them. After seeing how angry I'd been following our first workout, Ryuu had officially changed the name to anger management class.

Once I finished getting dressed, I called Ryuu back in and Shadow Walked us to Xuanwu's home in Kansas City. I had no idea what to expect for today's lesson, and that was entirely the point of Ryuu's training—to expect the unexpected.

I waved at a few of the resident monks and ninjas, receiving warm, familiar smiles in return, and then I turned to Ryuu. "Why do we always train here? We could easily train at Castle Dracula or anywhere else. This is just a garden." He knew I hadn't meant any disrespect. There were plenty of specific training tools and weapons here for martial arts enthusiasts. Except we never used any of those tools; we used what Ryuu carried in his duffel bag. Hence my question.

Ryuu nodded thoughtfully, turning his attention towards the house. "It is better to be a warrior in a garden than a gardener in a war." He spotted Xuanwu exiting the home and gestured for me to begin stretching on my own before approaching his master. I stared at him for a few moments, digesting his words. Although it had been clever word play, I wasn't sure if he'd intended some deeper meaning.

So, I sat down in the grass and stretched out my legs, mentally replaying the various training sessions I'd suffered in the past week and wondering what might be in store for me today.

The first day of training, Ryuu had told me that Xuanwu needed to speak with me about something important. Not wanting to get on Xuanwu's bad side, I had taken us to the courtyard behind his home via Gateway. Without warning, Ryuu had tossed me a wooden training sword from his duffel bag and attacked me with one of his own. Xuanwu had come out to watch, sipping a mug of tea and settling down into the grass for what might have been the worst four hours of my life. We ended up working on everything from sparring—where he had pulled exactly no punches—to sword forms with our wooden blades. We worked on cardio, endurance, strength, and ended in a brief meditation session before starting the cycle all over again.

Three more times. With what felt like five minutes—cumulative—of rest over the entire block. Upon finishing, I had dropped my sword, my hands throbbing and tingling, and I had desperately gasped for water, ashamed of how out of shape I apparently was.

Ryuu had tossed me a lukewarm bottle of water, zipped up his duffel bag, and then hefted the strap over his shoulder. Xuanwu had left at some point, so we were alone. "Do better tomorrow," Ryuu had said. "You can't afford to rely on magic or weapons. You are the weapon. This is our new morning routine. Consider it anger management," he'd added with an amused smirk, recalling some of the creative curses I'd thrown at him over the four hours.

I had guzzled the water, not even caring that it was warm, and too tired to argue. "You're Satan."

He had shrugged unconcernedly. "You are not that lucky." Then he had turned away, heading back through the house without a word.

That had been the beginning of our new routine. And no day had been the same since. One day, he had made me spar him while maintaining a magical ball of fire over my head. If it weakened or flickered out, I was forced to do fifty push-ups. I did a lot of push-ups that day. A fucking lot.

After about ten minutes, Ryuu finally finished speaking with Xuanwu, bowed, and then jogged over to me. "All warmed up?"

I nodded, climbing to my feet. "Yes."

"Good," he said, leaning closer so that he would not be overheard. "You have suffered a defeat of some kind, and it is wearing on you. I can read it in your body language and the tension in your face. And I'm not referring to the shower," he assured me in a softer tone. "I will help you reclaim your confidence. Center you during this storm."

I stared at him, stunned. What had he seen in my body language? I'd only woken up a couple hours ago. But...his hypothesis wasn't wrong. My meeting with Legion had not been a defeat, but it had left me feeling defeated and weary. Realizing Ryuu was waiting for some kind of response, I nodded. "Okay."

"We will focus first on inner peace. Meditation. Have a seat."

I narrowed my eyes since he had waited for me to stand before telling me all of this. He arched an eyebrow, daring me to dig a deeper hole. I relented and settled into a cross-legged pose, resting the backs of my wrists on my knees as I closed my eyes. If he wanted to see flawless meditation, I would show him.

Because I was no stranger to meditation. It was one of my favorite things to do. I quickly fell into the rhythm of steady breathing, feeling the familiar tranquility roll into my muscles and the tension roll out as my mind became blank and silent, free of idle thoughts.

Until I heard a hissing noise beside me. I opened my eyes right as a string of firecrackers exploded next to my hip. I jumped up with a shout of alarm to see Ryuu swinging a fist at my face. My sudden panic from the fire-crackers instantly evaporated, and I effortlessly deflected Ryuu's punch before countering with a punch of my own. Of course, he dodged mine, and we began to dance. Ryuu snuck in a few solid blows, but it was less than any of the days before. I even managed to catch him in the ribs one time, and I knew I had earned it because Ryuu didn't give anything out for free. He said it cheapened real victories to dilute them with fraudulent ones. False praise would guarantee death on the battlefield because it led a person to believe that they had mastered that particular skill, meaning they would rely on it when they shouldn't.

We sparred several rounds with thirty second breaks between each. Even though I fought better than I ever had against Ryuu, the shinobi still managed to show no apparent effort in his ability to make a mockery of my past training as a Shepherd of the Vatican. It was truly remarkable because it wasn't any one thing that he excelled at or relied upon. If you watched Ryuu fight three matches against the same opponent, you would see him fight three different styles. Because it wasn't winning the fight that Ryuu focused on. That was the foregone conclusion. Ryuu focused on mastering those nitty gritty details that no one ever seemed to think about, and it showed. He was fighting against himself every time he sparred. His opponent just happened to put himself in harm's way while Ryuu mastered his craft.

When we returned to meditating, I waited for the firecrackers, feeling my shoulders tense as I prepared my body to explode into defensive tactics and get him in an arm-bar or something. If I tried really, really hard. Except the firecrackers never came.

I sat, tense as a coiled spring, for twenty minutes before I finally surmised that he really had wanted me to meditate this time. *That* was the unexpected trick—

A wave of ice water splashed into my face and down over my body, cold enough to physically hurt and practically freeze my very soul. My pulse skyrocketed into double time as I leapt to my feet, prepared to spar Ryuu the moment he attacked.

Except I saw Ryuu calmly meditating in front of me. He, too, was drenched with water and surrounded by ice cubes—yet his breathing was calm and steady as if he'd fallen asleep. I heard a rumbling chuckle behind me. I turned to see Xuanwu shuffling away, carrying two empty pitchers.

Grumbling unhappily, I settled back down to the ground to resume my meditation, forcing myself not to shiver. Seven seconds after I closed my eyes, something struck my thigh like a whip, sending a flash of heat down my leg and causing me to yelp. Ryuu was running away from me with a bamboo shoot in his hands. I bolted after him, chasing him towards the ancient statue of Xuanwu in the forest behind his house. I found Ryuu there, seated in meditation rather than waiting to spar. But the fucker was smirking faintly.

9

I stood there, glaring at him for about ten minutes, watching his breathing pattern for the perfect opportunity. I dove, hitting him in a tackle, already positioning myself for a choke—

Only to find myself suddenly fighting back a leg-lock and eating cold dirt. I managed to slip out of it, but I wasn't able to get the upper hand. Instead, he pinned me in a full mount, breathing easily as he effortlessly countered absolutely everything I tried. The sudden feeling of a man mounting me so completely, gave me a whole new perspective on Ryuu.

Where his Buddha story outside the shower had introduced me to his heart and his soul, him mounting me so easily and completely introduced me to the entirety of his physical presence.

He was...*vast*. Committed. He was obviously dangerously lethal, but I felt safe beneath him. Protected. He wasn't going to give me an inch, but he wasn't going to let anything serious happen to me. Here, he was my enemy, but only so that he could make me into the best possible form of myself in the real world.

His chest radiated heat from beneath his cold, damp clothes, and his natural scent filled my nostrils as he bent over me, fighting to trap my arm above my head. He breathed steadily into my ear as I managed to slip out of his grip, and I was panting heavily as I tried to get him into a wrist lock.

In that moment, I realized that he had unintentionally attacked me with an entirely different and unexpected tactic. Distraction via confused and starving hormones. We were a man and a woman, sweating, panting, and rolling around across the ground with only two layers of wet fabric between us.

Which was when he slipped into another hold, sensing my distraction. I tapped out and he calmly slipped back into the mount, his face giving me no indication on whether he had noticed *what* had distracted me.

I shoved away the thoughts, feeling angry at myself for such an immature reaction. I gripped his lapels with both hands, gritting my teeth as I struggled to worm my hips into a better position. Ryuu fluidly moved with me rather than shutting me down with force. He let me burn away my energy and strength by giving me just enough rope to hit a dead-end after expending more energy than necessary.

When I saw the smirk on his face, I punched him in the ribs, annoyed that my eyes kept latching onto his exposed chest of their own accord. It made me feel guilty. As if I was betraying Nate.

Even though I was having very mixed feelings about Nate at the moment, it was no excuse for a wandering eye. Ryuu was being professional. I was the one making it into something else.

Except...

Ryuu carried around the stupid sword Nate had melted. Like he was proud of it and idolized Nate—which only made my guilt worse. I continued to struggle, but I found myself talking before I consciously chose to do so. "Why do you lug that melted katana around with you everywhere?" I hissed.

He met my eyes, looking strangely calm. He was sweating and breathing heavier than usual, but his mind was at peace, as if he weren't truly putting in any effort so far. "The blade is your baggage, not mine," he murmured. "I'll release it whenever you unshoulder it."

I froze as if he'd stabbed me in the gut. "My baggage?" I asked, breathlessly.

He nodded. "When you are willing to call it what it is, the blade can be tossed aside."

"*It?* What *it?*" I hissed, confused.

"Your relationship with Nate Temple, a man I deeply respect. That *it.*"

The strength left my muscles and I felt myself melt into the dirt, staring into his deep dark eyes from only inches away. I felt very, very small in that moment.

He calmly extracted himself, realizing that I was now worthless as a sparring partner. Then he sat down, crossed his legs, and settled into his meditation.

There was no more fighting after that. Just a long, silent, two-hour meditation. I didn't ask about the melted blade again, and it took me a very long time to clear my head and focus on my meditation.

Ryuu called our session in a soft, soothing tone, asking me to open my eyes. He gave me a few moments to fully slip out of my trance, and I felt like I was hovering about two inches over the ground.

Then he stood, pulled me to my feet, and motioned for me to follow him back to the house. I did so in silence. No matter how hard I tried, I couldn't shake off the feeling of him mounting me—how imposing his presence was when he was in his element. I'd been mounted by sparring partners much larger and stronger than Ryuu, and none of them had seemed as overwhelming as the ninja with the calm face.

Of course, the mounting was stuck in my mind for more...unprofessional reasons as well, if I was being honest. It had been a long time since this girl had been in such an intimate situation. Nothing inappropriate had—or would have—happened, but I still felt guilty at the errant thoughts.

The fact of the matter was that I had never trained with someone as casually talented as Ryuu. I was beginning to appreciate just how good he really was in all manner of martial arts, not just with a sword and a cloak that made him invisible. I was beginning to realize exactly what Xuanwu saw in him, and just how useful he was as my bodyguard—how much of an honor it was to have him volunteer for the role.

Surely, Xuanwu had more important things for Ryuu to be doing, but I never heard either of them mention it. I never saw any meaningful looks between the two. Never any doubtful or frustrated looks from his fellow ninjas. Never even a questioning look from them to their boss. They trusted him. Period.

They trained and they meditated, never growing bored or anxious of the repetition or showing any expectation to what it was all for. I began to realize that this *was* what they lived for.

To better themselves. Fighting monsters was just a perk of the job. I knew they were policing the streets in Ryuu's absence. They often gave him reports after we finished training—as I struggled to compose myself—but the reports never lasted more than a minute or two.

Whatever was happening in Kansas City was nothing to be concerned about, apparently. Even though I saw men returning with fresh wounds a few times. I even saw a dead body once, but Ryuu had refused to let me question anyone. Xuanwu had backed him when I'd tried going over Ryuu's head. It was one of the reasons I had wanted to walk the streets of Kansas City last night—to get a look for myself.

And what had I found? Legion.

Had Ryuu's men been fighting demons this whole time? If so, why hadn't he told me?

I didn't trust myself to bring up such a difficult question right now. Not after our training today. I needed to clear my head. So, I focused on my Legion problem.

How does one get out of an unwanted proposal? Get some dirt on the groom-to-be. And who better to hand over some dirt than one of his own brothers. An angel. Not a low-ranking angel, either. I needed a big brother. One of those *judgmental* big brothers.

An archangel.

But there were obvious pitfalls to asking an angel about his demonic sibling without drawing suspicion. I couldn't, for example, let anyone know I needed the dirt because the demons were trying to force me into a marriage. If they heard even a whisper of that, they would lock me up for even the potential chance that it was true. I would be guilty by association.

Also, my mother hadn't just hidden me from Hell. She had hidden me from Heaven, too. So, I couldn't trust them either. I needed to string them along just as much as I was stringing the demon-groom along.

I needed to carefully bring the family together and introduce a little Jerry Springer into their lives.

And hope I had enough bouncers on the stage. The more I thought about it, the more I realized how I might use it to wrap up my loose ends with the rebels and possibly even whip the Sanguine Council into the palm of my hand. But first, it was time to head back to Castle Dracula for some food, a nice long bath, and a lot of sleep.

Because tomorrow was going to be a big day.

🦁 I O 🦁

I returned to Castle Dracula via Gateway, rolling my eyes as Ryuu leapt
through ahead of me with his sword drawn. I released my magic, and
the portal puffed out, leaving us standing on the ramparts of an upper
balcony of the Keep—an area I had designated as the Drop Zone for Gateways. The full moon shone down on the Keep, bathing it in a pale glow. The
swift change from day to night always jarred me—scratching some primitive
instinct in my brain to seek shelter from nocturnal hunters.

Except I was one of those nocturnal hunters. And I was the queen of
every other nocturnal hunter here. Ryuu sheathed his katana, having found
no immediate threats, and waited silently. I thought about saying something
but decided against it, still slightly flustered from our wrestling and his
comments about the warped blade tucked into his belt.

Your baggage, not mine, he'd said. Was he upset at how I was treating his
new best friend? His face was too closed off for me to read him, although his
eyes watched me like a bird of prey, seeming as if they saw entirely too much
of my secret thoughts.

Had he accurately picked up on my body's instinctive attraction to him
when we'd been wrestling? What if *that* was what had made him admonish
me about the luggage I was carrying around? Was he displeased about how I
had subconsciously betrayed Nate Temple? He was too professional to

outright say anything, or accuse me of any impropriety, but Ryuu was a man of honor. Deep honor. It was his creed.

Like Nate Temple. I realized I was feeling just about sick and tired of honorable men and the headaches they provided. I was currently feeling a craving for a barbarian with a temper, a good head for his mead, and who knew how to take what he wanted.

Think quieter, hussy, Sanguina's words tickled my mind in a breathy whisper. *I'm trying to sleep.*

My cheeks grew flaming hot and Ryuu cocked his head curiously. *You can hear me? Where are you?* I thought back.

You are inside me. I hear all, even from the opposite side of the Keep, she replied, dryly.

I pursed my lips and hurriedly made my way through a nearby archway that revealed a long flight of zigzagging stairs that led three floors below. I firmly put a vault door on my thoughts, tuning Sanguina out, before I started down. I had no privacy. None.

To punctuate that fact, Ryuu followed me like a faithful hound, giving me no more than ten feet of personal space. I sighed, knowing that snapping at him would only lead to him giving me a shorter leash.

He meant well, and he wasn't wrong, but chains—even unseen ones— chafed me something fierce. Hence the random drunken barbarian fantasy.

I exited the stairs and stepped out into one of the main halls. Thick red carpets stretched down the center of the Keep's hallways, reminding me of veins or arteries that kept the place alive by delivering the necessities of life from one organ or limb to another.

To that effect, the Keep even had diligent antibodies who worked around the clock.

I counted no less than a dozen servants in the vicinity, all wearing black silk suits or dresses lined with red at the hems. They were all human. I had given them the opportunity to return to Earth, only to learn that all of them had been born and raised here, going back generations. None had taken me up on my offer.

Which had been baffling to me. They preferred a land of eternal night with monsters over Earth. At first, I had assumed they were all blood donors and addicted to their victimhood, but that wasn't the case at all. None of them had ever been bitten. Any who had desired such a thing had instead been turned into a vampire and moved out of the Keep. The Harkers had liked their housekeepers human and untainted, for whatever reason.

I hadn't spent much time speaking to them because they always seemed to scurry away in fear that I was going to eat them for not dusting fast enough or bowing and curtsying low enough. But I always tried to smile, say hello, and compliment them in some small way as I passed. I even said please and thank you.

And I wasn't actually sure of the proper term, but Sanguina called them all servants. I'd chosen to call the men valets and the women maids; they'd seemed surprised at the promotion. I knew they would come in handy for the big wedding.

As I made my way down the hall, I smiled and waved at each of them, even offering a few good afternoons if they didn't slip away too quickly. They bowed and curtsied back, murmuring a polite response before resuming their dusting, sweeping, polishing, or transporting of linens, dishes, and anything else needing to be moved from one section of the Keep to another. I also had runners to deliver messages outside the Keep.

I passed a window and noticed the Coliseum in the distance. I had shut that down almost immediately. Dracula had used it much like the Romans of old had done—to provide violent entertainment for his people. The only problem had been that he'd kept his inventory of victims full by abducting humans and monsters from Earth to fight and die in the arena.

Since violence was a main staple of my new home, I had known I'd need to make a compromise or incite serious unrest. So, I had tacked a sign on the front that said *Temporarily Closed for Improvements*. Then I had set a meeting with Asterion, the Minotaur, to discuss his interest in making my Coliseum a satellite hub for his St. Louis Fight Nights. Because the current place he used let people fight to the death, but not actually die in real life. If you died at the Dueling Grounds, you woke up in your bed the next morning.

So, warriors could literally cut loose and fight as crazily as they desired, with no permanent harm.

Something like that at my Coliseum...would be perfect—and quite lucrative.

Because Asterion's place only had benches and a couple of food carts, while I had a massive stadium and a hungry audience. I also had all sorts of new monsters to play with, like ninja baboons and skeletons, and the shifter bears were soon coming back to Kansas City. I had plans to invite them to live here with me, since they preferred a wilder, primitive lifestyle.

I saw a pretty brunette eyeing Ryuu sidelong as she cleaned a table, so I veered towards her, smiling as I spoke in a soft tone. "He is single and going through a difficult time. I saw him crying yesterday, so try to be nice to him. I think he's lonely."

The maid's shock at my direct conversation slowly shifted to piqued curiosity as I continued down the hall, grinning to myself. "Take that, Mr. Ninja-face," I breathed under my breath.

I spotted a tall, well-built valet with long, pale hair diligently dusting a vase, not even seeming to notice my passing. "Hello," I said, cheerfully. He jolted, knocking the vase off the table. I caught it with a tendril of magic and set it back in place with a reassuring smile. He paled, swallowing nervously between profuse apologies. I waved off his unease. "Sorry to frighten you."

He bowed stiffly, waiting for me to continue on before resuming his work.

Ryuu arched an eyebrow at me and I shrugged. "Just making friends."

He nodded, suspiciously, glancing back at the valet and the maid—only to catch her eyeing him thoughtfully. I bit back a laugh and continued on before Ryuu spotted the guilty look on my face. I skidded to a halt to find Xuanwu and Qinglong in a side room off the hall, speaking privately. I shot Ryuu a frown and he shrugged pensively, looking equally surprised.

I strolled into the room and their conversation cut off as they turned to face me with warm smiles. Xuanwu was holding something behind his back that he obviously didn't want me to see, but I let that go for now.

"Hey, guys. What are you doing here?"

Xuanwu smiled eagerly, as did Qinglong. "Samael summoned us here to tell us the good news about Lilith saying yes," he rumbled.

Qinglong bobbed his head, his catfish-like mustache bobbing at the motion. "He also mentioned a bachelor party tonight."

A slow grin split my cheeks and I nodded, excitedly, seeing multiple ancillary benefits. "That's just what he needs. You could head down to the Village and cut loose," I suggested. "When do you two ever get to have fun? Judging by Ryuu's permanent glare, I'm assuming it has been a few hundred years."

Ryuu smirked, rolling his eyes. I could tell that the suggestion appealed to him, though. Perfect.

Xylo walked by, wearing a cowboy hat and a leather duster for some bizarre reason, so focused on his destination that he didn't seem to notice us. Cain was keeping pace with him, speaking rapidly. "I'm telling you, Claire will think it's hilarious. Just put this in her shampoo..."

I groaned, shaking my head. Cain was incorrigible, and he loved talking Xylo into terrible pranks. Messing with a girl's shampoo was a great way to introduce yourself to excruciating agony. Since Claire was a shifter polar bear, I almost hoped Cain was successful. That way I could watch a polar bear rampaging through the Keep chasing the two brothers down. Cain must have bought Xylo the cowboy getup—which was actually sweet, because Xylo thought hats helped him fit in with us non-skeleton types, so he had begun collecting them.

I turned back to see Xuanwu and Qinglong smiling longingly at the two brothers. I glanced at Ryuu and he very discreetly shook his head, advising me not to pry. Which was probably good advice.

"Why the sad smile?" I asked anyway, pretending not to notice Ryuu's almost inaudible curse.

Xuanwu shrugged. "Family. They remind me of my sisters." Qinglong hung his head, nodding.

I was silent for a few moments. He was speaking of the White Tiger and the Vermillion Bird. I didn't know much about them, just that they were not around. "What really happened to them?" I asked, softly, walking laterally in a casual manner, wanting to get a look at whatever he was hiding.

Xuanwu hesitated, coincidentally turning with me to keep his hand hidden. I arched an eyebrow and he let out a sigh. "We were actually discussing them before you came in. Because of this," he explained. He brought out his claw to reveal—

I jumped back with a surprised shout. "Where did you get that?" I demanded, pointing.

Because he held a fiery lotus blossom in his claw—exactly like the one I had found last night.

❦ 11 ❦

He cocked his head warily. "I've carried this for many, many years. It usually only smolders at the edges, but it flared brighter once I came here. I got it the day they went missing." The flower emitted faint burps of sparks as a low flame flickered around the edges, never burning out.

Qinglong cocked his head, seeming to frown at me. "You have seen one before," he murmured.

I nodded, shakily, opening my mouth. Xuanwu shook his head meaningfully, and I glanced over my shoulder to see Lilith storming down the hall with an angry, distraught look on her face. Her cheek was covered with black soot, and her hair was a wild tangle. Samael jogged at her side, shooting us an anxious look from over her shoulder as he tried to appease her obvious anger. The two disappeared from view and I turned back to the Divines, shaking my head. "Trouble in paradise," I murmured. "Poor Samael."

Except Xuanwu and Qinglong didn't look amused. They looked thoughtful. "She excused herself earlier when Samael told us the big news. She looked distraught then, as well."

"But her face wasn't dirty, and her hair wasn't all...whatever that was," Qinglong added.

"Maybe she is embarrassed that she doesn't have friends to invite," I mused, feeling sympathy for the bride-to-be. She'd been locked up for one hundred years, so her circle of friends wasn't extensive. As far as I knew, it was pretty much just me. "Claire and I could take her out for a bachelorette soiree, but not tonight."

Xuanwu smiled. "That is very kind of you." His attention drifted back to the fiery lotus in his palm.

I realized I hadn't answered Qinglong. "I saw a flower just like that last night," I said, warily.

Xuanwu flinched, and Qinglong gasped. "What?" Ryuu narrowed his eyes at me, not looking pleased that I had kept this news from him. Especially now that it concerned his mentor.

I would have to deal with that later. I studied Qinglong with a bemused frown. He should have known about it. He'd lived in my mother's laboratory for decades, guarding it from intruders. "In my mother's laboratory."

He scoffed. "Impossible." Xuanwu frowned at his brother, looking troubled.

"It was inside a metal box," I assured him.

Qinglong stared from me to the flower and then snarled. "You will show us. Now." Ryuu stepped up beside me and rested his hand on my shoulder. Xuanwu and Qinglong did the same, making contact. With no other option, I Shadow Walked us there.

Qinglong immediately began searching for the metal box. "Where?" He demanded, sounding furious.

I walked up to the metal box and scooped it up. Then I opened it, holding it so that everyone could see. The fiery flower flickered within, and Xuanwu lifted up his own flower for comparison. The two didn't react to each other but they were definitely identical. The two brothers stared incredulously, and then shared a long look. "I've never seen that box," Qinglong finally said, frowning at it.

I gestured at the table with my chin. "It was sitting under a pile of books."

Xuanwu leaned closer, practically sticking his beak in the box. Then he snorted—thankfully not blowing out the flower—and jerked his head back. He studied me with a frown. "That looks like your Spear of Destiny on that card."

I nodded. "It's a spitting image. The breaks even line up. But I don't know what it means." I glanced inside the box. "Those rings seem to be paired together, but that's all I know."

Qinglong began pacing, muttering under his breath. "What were you up to, Constance?"

Xuanwu watched his brother nervously. "We now have two puzzles to solve. The flower and the Spear," he said, turning back to me. "Could you call up your Spear, please?"

"I already tried. Nothing happened."

"Humor me, please," he said, obviously anxious about something. I obliged, calling the Spear of Destiny into my hand. I thumped it into the ground and held the card up beside it. Qinglong rushed over, and the three of them marveled at it with awed looks. "What do you see, Ryuu? What do you *feel?*" Xuanwu asked.

Ryuu leaned closer, shooting me a questioning look. I nodded, leaning the tip of the Spear closer to him. He studied the card for a few moments, comparing it to the break marks in the Spear. Then he took a deep breath and closed his eyes. After a few moments, he reached out with a finger and gently touched the tip of the Spear. The haft abruptly became warm in my grip and I tensed. I held my breath nervously, fearing an explosion or something, but it did not grow hotter. Ryuu opened his eyes and pulled his hand back with a puzzled frown. The haft instantly cooled. I switched hands, studying my palm nervously, but there was no pain or damage.

"That...doesn't make any sense," Ryuu finally said, resting his hand on the hilt of the warped blade rather than his black blade. Xuanwu took note of that, looking thoughtful—as if Ryuu's action had just confirmed something else.

I glared at the two of them. "Start talking or I start stabbing. What doesn't make sense, Spear Whisperer?"

Xuanwu let out a shuddering breath, his eyes twinkling with excitement as he waited for Ryuu to answer. The ninja didn't look pleased about his nickname. In fact, he looked slightly embarrassed. "I can read auras, and that blade was meant to heal, not harm," he said, firmly. "It is not a weapon."

I frowned, doubtfully. "That seems like a stretch. Anything can be a weapon. It has a pointy end, so it can stab people. That makes it a weapon."

Ryuu shook his head. "Anything can be a weapon, that is true. But I can tell if it is supposed to be a weapon. If it was originally created to be a weapon. Those hunger for blood. Your Spear does not." He shrugged, back to looking embarrassed. "To be honest, it has never been a particularly useful trait."

Qinglong was studying Ryuu and me with an intense look in his eyes. "Except now it *is* useful. You begin working for the White Rose and, suddenly, your seemingly worthless ability has great significance."

Xuanwu nodded solemnly. "Agreed." The three of them turned to study me like I was some creature in a cage that they had never encountered before. Ryuu looked baffled.

"Why are you looking at me? He's the one who talks to Spears," I said, pointing the artifact at Ryuu. He gave me a flat, disapproving glare. "All I know is that it stabbed Jesus on the Cross, and both Heaven and Hell want it." I managed to keep my face composed as a fear drifted into my mind. Was this why my mother had hidden me from Heaven and Hell? Because of the Spear?

Xuanwu motioned for me to sit in the nearby chair and settled himself down to the ground as if to calm me. He motioned for me to set the box between us, and I obeyed. Whatever was on his mind seemed to have excited him.

"The Spear of Destiny is bound to your soul, correct?" I nodded. "And this box appeared only for you, never once for Qinglong in his many years guarding your mother's laboratory, so it is safe to say your presence, or perhaps even the Spear, unlocked it." I considered his theory and finally nodded. "Which means your mother—the only other person who regularly used this room—wanted you, and only you, to find this box. She considered the contents of this box so important that she did not tell a single soul, not even Qinglong. And I think I know why," he said, staring at the open box.

I had been nodding along, already having surmised that my mother had left it for me—obviously—until he'd mentioned knowing *why*.

Xuanwu lifted his palm to reveal his fiery lotus. "We found this fire lotus the day our sisters disappeared, and I have carried it ever since," he explained, tapping a leather pouch on his belt. "I've never seen another like it nor heard of anyone else seeing anything like it. Yet last night, I felt it burst into flame for the first time—the same time you opened this box and found a fire lotus of your own." I stiffened, my eyes widening. "I think your mother was trying to tell you how to find them," he said, his voice barely a whisper, and that whisper was brimming with hope. "And it has something to do with your Spear. One we just learned is a tool for healing. A tool for help rather than harm. Perhaps it is a tool for salvation, which would make perfect sense, all things considered," he added meaningfully. Because Jesus had died on the Cross for our sins—for our salvation.

But...Xuanwu wasn't Christian. He was a god himself, which meant his sisters were also gods. What did any of this have to do with Heaven and Hell wanting the Spear?

I realized I was still holding the metal card in my hand. I glanced down at it. "If you're right, her map is incredibly unhelpful," I said, softly.

Xuanwu nodded sagely. "That is the puzzle I was referring to."

Qinglong glanced about the lab, sniffing at the air. "Your mother knew her fair share of secrets, and it wouldn't be the first time she pulled a fast one on me. If she would have told me anything about my sisters, I would have abandoned everything to find them, leaving this place unprotected," he said with only with a slight twinge of shame. He turned to study the box. "That was definitely hers. Everything inside has her scent. She knew how I would react, and that our sisters wouldn't have a chance without the Spear. Without you," he amended. Then he smiled, excitedly. "They must be alive. This is almost proof, or she wouldn't have bothered setting all this up!" Then he slithered over to Xuanwu and wrapped him up in a tight hug. "They're alive, brother! Our sisters are alive!"

His excitement only served to make me more stressed out. There was absolutely no guarantee that they were alive. And even if they were, I had absolutely no idea where they were. Our only clues were the two lotus blossoms, the shitty map, and the three sets of rings.

I stared down at the metal card, shaking my head. "What are you trying to tell me, Mom?" I whispered, ignoring the concerned look on Ryuu's face. Pity would not help me find them.

But I'd found another reason to pester an angel—to ask what was so important about the Spear of Destiny. I looked up at the two Divines. "This stays here. Do not tell Samael. If my mother had wanted him to know, she would have told him. For whatever reason, she kept this secret above all others, refusing to even draw a map that was too easy to read," I said, holding up the card. "As well hidden as this was, if she'd thought it was safe, she would have written down the answer inside. Let me handle Samael, but I've got a few other leads, first. Deal?"

The two Divines looked slightly crestfallen, and I was suddenly glad I'd warned them, because it was obvious they had intended to share the good news with Samael. I didn't have a reason not to trust him, but my mother obviously thought her secret box wasn't secret enough.

They agreed, only slightly deflated.

"Good. I'm going to get some food and rest. Go ahead and join them tonight, Ryuu. I promise not to leave my rooms, if it makes you feel better."

He didn't confirm or deny, which was fine. I really was done for the day. But tomorrow morning was another matter entirely, and that I did want to keep secret.

12

I had woken up an hour before sunrise—using the clock on my phone since looking outside the window at eternal darkness was entirely unhelpful—to tell Sanguina my plan about summoning Archangel Michael. As I tugged on my white training gear, I listed the ingredients I would need for the summoning ritual. She knew Castle Dracula like the back of her paw, so she could help me find what I needed without raising a fuss.

She'd stared at me, scathingly, for about one full minute, until I wondered if she hadn't entirely woken up yet. "That is an incredibly stupid plan."

I frowned. "I didn't ask for your commentary, I asked for your help," I growled.

"No."

I narrowed my eyes, realizing that arguing wasn't going to get me any closer to my goal. "Why not?"

She hesitated. "Would my reason change your mind?"

I shrugged. "I doubt it. I need answers only an archangel can give, and Michael is the only one I know. It's better than summoning Legion."

She lowered her gaze. "What if I told you that my powers will be useless against the forces of Heaven or Hell?" she asked, softly, looking surprisingly embarrassed.

I stiffened in surprise. "*What?*" I hissed. "Since when?" This was not good. I'd been hoping she could help me vaporize Legion and his boss or something. Damn it.

"I do not make the rules, so I do not know the answer. Our powers cancel each other out in a direct conflict—resulting in a stalemate. It would be a physical fight, which I am ill equipped for," she said, indicating her tiny foxy frame.

"Is this just about archangels and archdemons?" I asked, anxiously. Something about this news nagged at me, but I couldn't quite pinpoint what it was. It seemed that neither of us were protected from Heaven and Hell, but at least she was immune to their wrath.

Her tail twitched violently, her embarrassment turning to anger. "All angels and demons. Why do you think Dracula was forced to chain up Lilith?"

I shook my head in disbelief. "But Lilith was terrified of you."

Sanguina growled. "Now you know the value of reputation. Perhaps she did not know this fact, but I fear an archangel might."

"Does Samael know?" I asked. He was a Greater Demon—slightly lower than an archangel or archdemon. If he knew, I would bet my ass that Michael knew.

She shot me a grim look. "It is not something that comes up in idle conversation. Also, I don't do idle conversation," she growled.

I studied her thoughtfully. The benefit to bringing her was the fear factor —keeping Michael honest and wary. But if he saw my sidekick as...impotent. That wouldn't be good at all. Now that I thought about it, she was also a symbol of my new job—Dracula. That achievement would not likely earn me any gold haloes for my Biblical report card from Principal Michael.

"Then...you can't go with me," I said, softly. Sanguina's ears wilted and I felt a flash of sympathy for the little monster. "But you do know how to keep Castle Dracula safe. I need that just as much as I need answers about Legion and my Spear. Hell, maybe you can solve the rebel problem for me while I'm away," I said, smiling encouragingly.

She slowly glanced up at me, looking thoughtful. "I could try to find the rebels and make a shrine of their fresh corpses in the Eternal Gardens." I nodded, uneasily. At least she sounded slightly uplifted—if a tad eager and excessively gruesome. "Although they have proven rather elusive so far."

It wasn't ideal, but it would have to work. "It will be fine. Now, about those ingredients?"

She sneezed, shaking her head so that her ears flapped loudly. "Why waste your time with a bag of strange, complicated ingredients and excessive hand flailing when the Omegabet has a rune for summoning archangels and archdemons?"

I blinked. "You're kidding. Your rune will bypass the freaking ritual? That means anyone could use it."

She nodded. "Hence the dangers of the Omegabet—much of it is effort-free magic. Big magic."

I nodded, uneasily, foreseeing the damage such power could cause. "And you know the proper rune?"

Instead of answering, she closed her eyes and I felt an image flare into my mind—a very curious symbol that seemed too complicated and specific for someone to accidentally doodle on their notebook. "Drawing it will do nothing," Sanguina said, dryly, reading my mind. "However, drawing it in your own blood, and then saying the name of an archangel or archdemon will summon them. The consequences are entirely on you. The rune is not... protective. Safety is for wizards. The Omegabet is for winners," she said, haughtily.

I nodded, soberly. If Michael didn't like my little summoning, he could rip me in half. I envisioned the symbol, seeing it in perfect clarity. "Just his name. None of his titles or anything?" I'd had to use a handful of titles with my original ritual.

Sanguina considered my question. "Yes, but make sure you say the *right* name, of course. Don't just say *archangel*, for example, or you might summon all of the archangels—or the wrong archangel." She eyed me askance, not looking very confident in my abilities. "Perhaps I should come with you—"

"No. If they don't already know about your powers cancelling each other out, I don't want them learning it today." I glanced around the room, verifying that I had everything I needed. I knew Ryuu would be coming in less than an hour to take me to our daily training, and I didn't want him panicking when he saw me gone.

I scribbled a quick note on a scratch pad.

Went to grab some breakfast at an old favorite coffee shop in the city. Will meet you at Xuanwu's house at our usual time.

I set the note on top of my pillow where it would be easy for Ryuu to see. Hopefully I would be finished before he had time to catch me in the lie. Last night, I'd promised him I wouldn't leave my rooms all *night*. Except now, it was technically *morning*.

I'd considered bringing him along, but I hadn't wanted him there in case the secret about Legion's boss wanting to marry me came to light. I didn't want anyone knowing about that, even though I was never going to let it happen. The news—whether true or not—would spread like wildfire and would be just as hard to put out. Also, Archangel Michael wasn't a fan of humans, so I hadn't wanted to risk adding fuel to the flames. Ryuu could be a tad overprotective, and Michael could be a tad overaggressive.

I'd tell Ryuu the full story once I had it all sorted out—which was seeming less likely without Sanguina.

I shook off the pessimistic thought and reviewed my priorities.

I wanted answers on the potential ramifications of marrying a demon—not that I had any intention of doing so, but I needed to know the worst-case scenario. Because if I couldn't find a way out of this, Legion had told me my city would be immolated.

I was entirely certain that marrying this mysterious demon would instead force *Heaven* to immolate my city, so I needed to find a middle ground. I needed to play Heaven and Hell against each other somehow.

And after seeing my mother's secret fire lotus—

I grimaced and blushed at the same time, horrified by my internal phrasing—it was getting worse. "Well, *that* mental image of my mother naked will forever be seared into my mind."

Sanguina stared at me dubiously, still not looking convinced at my chances. I waved off her concern. After learning about the possibility of my mother setting me up to save the last two Divines, I needed to learn more about the Spear of Destiny. The first time I had met Michael, he had been highly interested in the Spear. I'd ultimately convinced him I was worthy of caring for the blade.

But that had been a while ago. Now, I was Dracula.

One thing I did know was that Legion, and however many other demons, had snuck into Kansas City shortly after I'd given up Excalibur, thus removing my mother's protection. Michael should be well aware of demonic presence in my city, but no one seemed to be talking about it. The Shepherds hadn't been roaming the streets with Holy Water and Crucifixes, and I'd heard nothing about nephilim activity.

The only hint at demons—other than me personally running into Legion

—was Ryuu's wounded men, which he hadn't explained to me. Another reason I had opted not to bring him along this morning. He wanted to keep secrets; I could keep secrets too.

So, with my priorities aligned, I turned to Sanguina. "Wish me luck."

She didn't. It looked like she'd actually fallen asleep.

I glared at her for good measure, and then I made a Gateway to a secluded park I'd found years ago, since I didn't want to risk drawing attention. It had plenty of trees, little to no foot traffic, and plenty of meandering running trails. It was deserted at this...ungodly hour, and I saw an abandoned playground that would better suit my aesthetic and artistic needs. I approached the merry-go-round, deciding to use the flat wood as my canvas. I took a calming breath and cut my palm with a throwing knife. Then I wiped my finger in my blood and drew the strange rune Sanguina had showed me.

It was only after I finished that I realized I hadn't called up the mental photo to guide me. I shivered at the prospect of my natural talent for using the Omegabet rising to the surface, unbidden. Just to be safe, I checked my work against Sanguina's mental projection. Perfect. I let out another mild shudder and rose to my feet, glancing at the sky. It would be sunrise soon.

I retreated about ten feet and sat down on one of the swings. I called up the Spear of Destiny and rested it across my lap. Out of habit, I shuffled my feet back and began swinging, smiling at the small joy. Then I cleared my throat. "Archangel Michael!" My shout echoed through the clearing, scaring a flock of birds from the nearby trees.

It wouldn't be long now—

A meteorite slammed into my rune on the merry-go-round at a forty-five-degree angle, and physics immediately bitch-slapped Heaven's Mightiest Halo.

The merry-go-round spun as fast as a particle accelerator, sending Michael straight into a complex web of crisscrossing metal bars known as a jungle gym. The metal snapped and shrieked as it wrapped around him in a somewhat spherical cage, tearing free from the ground supports, and began to roll.

It finally slammed into a wooden watch tower, obliterating the supporting pillars in an explosion of wood fragments that sent the tower crashing to the ground. I continued swinging on autopilot, staring at the devastation in disbelief. And then...I couldn't help it.

I fell into one of those fits of giggles that were impossible to stop.

Michael roared and raged, tearing through the metal with a ridiculously large crystal sword. He rose to his feet, panting as he surveyed his surroundings for the next threat. He drop-kicked one of those plastic dragons on vertical springs, and it immediately bounced back, kneecapping him so hard that he fell, and head butted the plastic dragon into a bajillion pieces. He leapt back to his feet again, panting and looking mildly panicked at this devil-cursed arena of despair.

I was actually crying at this point, struggling to catch my breath. Archangel Michael latched onto the sound, looking up to see the Horseman of Despair giggling uncontrollably. He narrowed his eyes murderously and began storming my way with his sword bared.

13

I held up a hand, forestalling him as I tried to blink through my tears. "Wait," I wheezed, sucking down air between outbursts. "Please. I can't breathe—"

"Stop. Laughing."

I nodded and then held my breath as I looked upwards at the sky so that my peripheral view of the destroyed playground and humiliated archangel didn't send me into relapse-giggles. I still shook for a few moments, but I finally managed to regain my composure.

He clenched his jaw, his white eyes glowing with fire. "You did that on purpose," he snarled.

I shook my head adamantly. "No. I swear it on my power," I promised him, wiping at my eyes.

He frowned, looking uncertain. Then he glanced back at the chaos. "You mean...all that," he said, gesturing with his sword, "was by *chance?*"

I breathed in through my nose, biting back another tirade of giggles, and nodded. "Believe it or not, yes."

He grunted, turning to look at his original landing zone. The merry-go-round was still spinning at warp speed, and it was squeaking wildly. I was surprised it hadn't burrowed into the bowels of the earth or taken off into the sky. Michael calmly walked up to it, narrowing his eyes, and then he shot his hand into the spiral of death.

Metal warped and wood cracked, and unseen mechanisms snapped and popped as he stopped it cold, gripping one of the metal handrails. Of course, it had bent and snapped free into the adjacent handrail, so he was technically holding two of them. The point was, he'd stopped it without even remotely losing his balance or shifting his feet. My humor evaporated, as I was suddenly reminded of just how powerful archangels were. Michael knelt down to inspect the rune I had drawn.

Then he glanced over his shoulder sharply, his face ashen. "Where did you learn this?" he rasped.

I shrugged, coyly. "I like to read."

"Do you know what this is?" he hissed, glancing left and right as if fearing someone might overhear.

I nodded. "The Omegabet. There's plenty more where that came from," I said, tapping my temple.

He locked gazes with me as he stabbed his sword through the rune and twisted, obliterating the symbol. Then he approached me again, warily this time. Very warily.

"Why did you summon me?" he asked, guardedly.

He wore ornate crystal and diamond armor that looked utterly bulky, heavy, and impractical. Except I knew that it was entirely functional and weighed practically nothing to him. I heard a faint crackling sound and noticed the steadily extending and retracting spikes rising up and down from his armor, as if restless.

Because his armor was kind of alive, in a strange way. Much like my angel wings, the armor wasn't static. It was ever shifting, made from living energy that could not be restrained. I'd seen Michael's armor grow spines as long and sharp as swords.

Speaking of swords, he still gripped his massive crystal blade. I cast it a thoughtful look, and he fired back with a mirrored look at my Spear. I sighed, letting it wink out of existence. He sheathed his blade, and the two of us stared at each other for a few moments, gathering our thoughts.

He wore his perfectly merciless and beautiful mask to cover up the scarred version of his face. I was the only human he had ever shown that true face to, and it had made him extremely uncomfortable to tell me that all angels hid their scars, while demons flaunted theirs by showing off their monstrous forms—sporting scales, tails, fangs, and anything else they could dream up. I wasn't entirely sure Michael's claim was true because Samael didn't appear to have any scars. Then again, he could be wearing a mask of sorts since he preferred his human form. Same with Lilith. She was downright gorgeous with nary a wrinkle. But their beauty seemed natural, whereas Michael's Mask made him look sculpted and untouchable.

Michael radiated power and authority. He was tall, broad of shoulder, and sported medium-length blonde hair. I noticed he was wearing a chain necklace with two white feathers tucked below his armor. I hadn't noticed that during our last meeting.

"Do you want me to put my Mask on as well?" I asked, gently. He'd already been humiliated, so I decided to dial back the abrasiveness I'd originally intended to show him.

He took a measured breath, and then his hand flared with white fire. He touched the flame to his face and the Mask burned up like magician's flash paper. "Better?" he growled.

I opened my mouth to respond when I felt a surge of power flare at my hip, and then wink out of existence almost as fast as I'd noticed it. The only thing in my pocket was the pair of rings from my mother's box. The metal card was in a different pocket. I realized I was still staring at him with my mouth open, so I cleared my throat. "Yes. Thank you," I stammered. "I didn't think you would actually do it," I said, hoping to explain my strange reaction.

He nodded, calmly, not seeming to have noticed the flash of power. I kept my features composed, but my mind was still racing. What the hell had happened to the rings, and why? Obviously, they had reacted to Michael taking off his mask, but I had no idea about the why. What did Michael have to do with the Divines? And if he was a key to saving them, why had my mother warded me from Heaven? Every time I learned something new, I learned something that contradicted what I thought I had already learned.

I studied him thoughtfully.

His real face was a scarred, imperfect reflection of the mask—still beautiful, but in a rugged, natural, realistic manner. It was what he truly looked like after the war of the angels so long ago.

Michael was a big freaking deal. He was the Supreme Commander of the Heavenly Hosts, known as the sword in God's right hand, and often referred to as the Angel of Death. I'd expected a lot more rage from him, but I was blessedly relieved to see that his impromptu cannonball arrival had served to get a lot of anger out of his system. It could have done exactly the opposite.

Still, I could see that he was deeply troubled by something. He was wary and suspicious of me, and it had nothing to do with the playground.

I debated how to answer his question because he wasn't acting as I had anticipated. I'd expected either outright anger and judgment, or his version of a greeting between old friends. Except we were in the middle of those two extremes and speaking with Michael was typically an exercise in futility. Not all angels were as difficult to communicate with, because they were lower ranked and spent more time around humans. Like Eae, the demon thwarter. But Michael was an *archangel*, not a run-of-the-mill angel.

He was also a soldier. He knew war. Period. People were things you killed. You didn't talk to them. Before me, it had been thousands of years since he'd interacted with a human, and it had shown.

Emotions were difficult for him to comprehend, let alone express, because he was entirely ignorant of mankind. He saw us as cardboard cutouts and had never heard of pop culture of any kind. His thoughts were occupied by much bigger things that mankind could not comprehend. So, he would say something to me that I wouldn't understand, and then I would answer with a sarcastic comment that he didn't understand. A translator would be ideal, but that wasn't in the cards, so I would just have to make do.

"Why did you summon me?" he repeated, his patience obviously dwindling.

I needed to bring up demons without bringing up Legion. And I knew how he would react—angrily. Which would suit my purposes, if handled properly. "Samael proposed to Lilith, and I wanted to invite you to their wedding. They haven't picked the date yet, but I thought you should hear it from me." I smiled. "They are very excited."

He regarded me calmly. "I have been studying humans since we last met, Callie Penrose. I am no longer as ignorant in your manipulative ways..." he growled, leaning forward aggressively, "and no longer as tolerant."

Damn it, the fuzz was onto me. "What does that have to do with anything?" I deflected.

"I have bigger things to worry about. Tell me why I would care about Samael and Lilith," he growled.

I stared back at him, processing this new development. He didn't look like he was proud or pleased with his newfound knowledge. In fact, he looked...*disgusted* by it. His once composed and almost emotionless demeanor now seemed about a hair-trigger away from violent eruption.

Which did not bode well for my plans. Anger at the topic of their wedding was fine—disgust at my existence was...troubling. My original plan to nudge him over the edge was suddenly slapped with an apocalyptic warning label. Because whatever he was now, he didn't see me as a person.

He saw me as vermin.

I cleared my throat. "I wanted to ask what kind of ramifications their decision might have. I've seen them together. They have fought to find each other for over one hundred years and have finally succeeded. Their love is genuine. But...they are demons, and I don't know all the details of the... family history. Is their decision going to have consequences?"

He stared at me, looking incredulous. "Consequences?"

I nodded, uncertainly, unable to read into his reaction. "Yes. I have never heard of a demon getting married, and that seemed significant. They do call it holy matrimony," I explained, trying to keep my questions vague enough that they could apply to my own situation, giving me a double answer. Because I truly was concerned about Samael's decision, in addition to my own. Except their marriage was consensual.

He continued to stare at me. Then he glanced left and right as if searching for a witness. "This is some kind of sick joke, isn't it?" he asked, rhetorically. I tried not to focus on the fact that my mother had wanted to protect me from Heaven just as much as Hell, but it was really difficult with the almost wild look in Michael's eyes. He was acting more human than ever before—entirely different from our first encounter.

He'd practically been an alien from outer space back then. Was this a good or bad development?

"Okay," he finally said. "Let's play out this game, Callie Penrose," he said in a low growl. "Gabriel let us know about their *unholy* matrimony," he said, gauging my reaction just as much as I was studying his.

I didn't bother hiding my perplexed look. "Gabriel?" I asked. It made sense, in a way.

Michael was the Archangel of Death and War.

Gabriel was the Archangel of Revelation. I'd once read something about him being set over all the powers, which had sounded kind of boss-like to me.

But how the hell had Gabriel heard about Samael and Lilith? Did I have a leak at Castle Dracula or had Samael been blabbing about it where the wrong person could hear and report to the archangels. I remembered seeing

Lilith disheveled and out of sorts last night, and Samael trying to placate her or make her feel better. One—or both—of them had done something stupid, and Gabriel had heard about it.

Michael nodded, still studying me closely like this was some sort of interrogation. "Gabriel has taken charge of the current...*situation* until my particular skillset is needed."

I narrowed my eyes dangerously, his comment snapping me out of my racing thoughts. I slid off the swing and squared my shoulders. "I know very well who you are, Angel of Death," I said, "and if you even *think* about using your *particular skillset* on my godparents, I will—"

He waved a hand, cutting me off. But it wasn't the gesture that had made me comply. It was the puzzled look on his face. "I'm not talking about the wedding," he said, very slowly.

I blinked, my pulse suddenly ratcheting upwards.

"You truly do not know..." he mused, scratching at his chin. His shoulders sagged, as if he no longer saw me as an immediate danger.

Which was incredibly stupid of him, really. "Michael, I'm about to do something you are really not going to like if you don't tell me what is going on."

"The Seven Sins have escaped Hell. I thought you knew," he said, just as casually as I had mentioned Samael proposing to Lilith.

14

My knees buckled and my ass plopped back into the seat of the swing. I managed to grab the chains for support, but that was the extent of my motor functions.

Because all my blood was rushing to my heart, and I thought it might actually explode. "When?" I whispered, not even caring that my voice was trembling, and my hand was shaking hard enough to rattle the chain. Because I feared that Legion had already given me the answer—the moment I'd removed my mother's protection.

Legion...represented one of the Seven Sins. He wasn't just a powerful demon who thought they could marry me. One of the Seven had set his sights on me. I recalled Legion's parting comment about me picking six members for my bridal party, and it suddenly made sickening sense. Six brothers plus one groom equaled the Seven Sins.

The worst of the worst. The bachelor party from literal Hell.

Michael was studying me thoughtfully, as if gauging whether or not I was faking my surprise. "A little over three weeks ago, we believe, although they kept an extremely low profile. Gabriel thinks it is because they are plotting to make Kansas City their new home. Heaven will not stand for this. We already lost St. Louis to Nate Temple and his heathens."

I snorted indelicately, still shaken by my own dilemma. Hell had concocted a clever way to take over—marry the White Rose and blackmail her into handing over the keys to the city.

"I thought it was why you truly called me here."

"Isn't that a major dereliction of duties? Shouldn't you have sensed that kind of thing?" I demanded, trying not to panic.

"Yes. *I* should have. Which is one reason *Gabriel* has taken a more active role. I will run the war—if it comes to that—Gabriel will manage everything until that point." He paused, eyeing me warily. "He told me not to trust you. That you had been compromised. He is concerned about the Spear of Destiny."

"You have got to be kidding me," I muttered. It was a plausible concern for anyone who didn't know me. I was the new Dracula. I was goddaughter to Greater Demons. I was hosting their wedding—practically throwing a party to welcome the Seven Sins home. And when Heaven found out about Legion's offer...

Ho' boy.

I quickly comprehended that I'd been very cleverly put into an impossible situation. Legion making his master's offer had put me in the untenable position of looking guilty no matter what I did.

If Heaven found out I had been proposed to and had chosen not to tell them—guilty.

If I told them I had been proposed to—guilty by association. Lock her up just to be safe.

My city would be immolated one way or another—by Heaven or Hell really made little difference.

Is it wrong that I briefly sent up a prayer, hoping that my groom-to-be wasn't Sloth or Gluttony?

Sue me.

Michael stared into my eyes; they burned with hatred for his brothers, and compassion for me—which made the situation so much worse. "We're talking dozens upon dozens of demons, Callie. The Seven and their armies, all hiding in Kansas City, waiting for something big. The Seven are not like any demons you have ever faced, Callie," he said, pleadingly. "These are *real* demons. Not like Samael and Lilith who have been somewhat domesticated by their time on Earth. These demons are fresh from Hell. They will want to celebrate their newfound freedoms in a riot of debauchery, bloodshed, and terror. To make up for lost time. At. Your. Wedding."

I dismissed the instinctive shiver that rolled down the back of my neck. His words had been accidentally accurate—*my* wedding—even though he had meant Samael and Lilith's wedding.

My biggest concern was what had so drastically changed Michael from the last time I'd seen him. Sure, we'd butted heads, but we had ended on good terms. Somewhat. But he was acting more emotional than when I'd seen last time. He'd almost been robotic in his previous attempt to be human. Was he truly that frightened of the Seven Sins?

He was an archangel. Shouldn't he have been excited to finally polish off his sword and commence with the pokery? Michael was not the same man from the stories. He was not even the same man I had met in recent years. Which confirmed another thing. Gods from other pantheons were also acting erratically and fighting over Missouri real estate. Those other pantheons were not the only ones participating in this Omega War.

Heaven and Hell would have to pick a side as well. Some of their number might have already done so, already accepted the enticing bribes of the elusive Masters. It was the only explanation that made sense.

"You can understand my concern," he said, pouncing upon my silence, thinking he was proving his case. "The Spear of Destiny is too powerful to leave in your hands—where a demon might take it, or you. It might be the only reason your city still stands." He took another step. "It might be your city's only hope for survival, Callie. As your friend, I am asking you to make a gesture of goodwill so that I can keep your city safe," he said, holding out his hand.

It was obviously not a request. I shook my head and pursed my lips. "No." Then I squared my shoulders, knowing what my defiance would cost me—our friendship, for one, and that was the hardest part.

Because he wouldn't see that until much, much later. After the damage was done.

Yet it was necessary. The moment I had set foot in Kansas City, Legion had lured me into the encounter outside the ice cream parlor, which made me absolutely certain that he had eyes on me—especially now that he'd delivered his boss's marriage proposal.

If Legion or any of his cronies were spying on me right now, and saw me meekly giving in to Team Halo-riffic, the demons would destroy my city—or try to kidnap me—before Michael even knew what was happening. I had to keep both sides thinking I was allied with the other. It was the most dangerous option for me, but the safest option for my city.

The only way to make that convincing was to openly stand up to Michael right now—or run away.

"The answer is no. Come any closer and I'll dent your halo or die trying. Either way, you won't get the Spear. It chose me, not the archangels."

He clenched his jaw, looking torn. "Then you leave me no choice," he growled. "If you will not hand it over, I must take you away for your own good. Remove you from the board."

I slipped out of the swing, backpedaling a few paces. "You need to tell me why it's so important," I said, recalling Ryuu's comment about the Spear not being a weapon. Because complying with Michael seemed like the kind of thing my mother had wanted to prevent. Was this what my mother had been trying to protect? My right to keep the Spear?

Michael didn't chase me. He looked...troubled. Not necessarily guilty, but secretive.

"And don't give me the tired excuse about it being a Holy Relic. You missed that boat by two thousand years. It was already broken once, and no one seemed to care. As soon as I got my hands on it and managed to fix it, suddenly everybody starts freaking out. It's all rather suspicious. Especially when only *your* side seems troubled by the good news. No demon has *ever* cared about it. Only angels. Yet you guys act like Hell is two seconds away from taking it away from me. Give me the truth, Michael," I said. "What... is...this?"

He flung up his hands in frustration. "We do not know!" he growled. "That is the danger. And that is why you are coming with me—"

Half-a-dozen smoke bombs erupted between us, instantly clouding the air, and something long and tentacular grabbed me.

I struggled to draw my katana, but the scaly demon held me firm, whisking me away.

Before I had time to draw my magic, I heard a familiar voice in my ear. "We've got you, child," Qinglong murmured. "Do not fear." The Azure Dragon set me down and bowed his head respectfully, checking my body for wounds. I looked up to see the smoke dissipating, and Ryuu and Xuanwu squaring off against Michael. I groaned. How the hell had they found me?

"Daemons," Michael snarled, sounding furious as his hand rested on the hilt of his sword. I frowned to hear the term again, but it really wasn't the important part of the current situation.

Xuanwu held his frosty, sheathed sword in one claw, using it like a cane. He dipped his razor-sharp beak in greeting. Then his claw tightened on the hilt of his cane sword, and his beak stretched into a slow, challenging grin.

Michael snarled and drew his own sword at about ten times the speed of the slow-motion turtle.

"That is unwise," Xuanwu said calmly, the frost and ice cracking over his thick, leathery skin as he slowly shook his head. "We came to make sure she was safe. We did not know she had...company. Or that the company would be so...forward."

Ryuu grunted. "To me, it sort of looked like our friend was refusing your offer. No means no, archangel," he said, slowly drawing his black katana. "Perhaps I can enumerate the finer points of the word," he said, sounding amused. And parts of his body suddenly began flickering in and out of view as he called up his Shadow Skin.

This was a disaster. Even Ryuu and Xuanwu couldn't challenge a freaking archangel...

Could they?

If so, that might be even *worse* when Gabriel heard the news. Because, like the demons, there were seven major archangels. The war over Kansas City might just start in this playground.

"ENOUGH!" I shouted.

None of them looked at me. Probably because they knew how furious I was that they had managed to find me when I obviously had not wanted to be found. I was betting they were equally frustrated with me.

Michael and Ryuu finally lowered their blades. Xuanwu was the wild card, though. He could attack without anyone seeing him move—maybe even fast enough to kill Michael.

"I should kill you," Michael snarled, which was rather broad as far as targets went.

"You don't want to do that," I warned. "They are gods, and I have bonded them to me. They are also bonded to Samael," I added, not sure if I was enough of a deterrent at the moment. "How would the Seven respond to you attacking Samael's friends?" I asked, hoping to diffuse the situation.

"Samael's *Daemons*," Qinglong corrected, turning to look at me, "and for what it's worth, angels usually get a might worked up when you use the word god—"

"There is only *one* God!" Michael roared.

"See?" Qinglong said, dryly, winking at me.

Michael pointed his sword at me, and I could tell our friendship was in dire straits. "I should have listened to Gabriel's advice rather than standing up for you," he snarled. Then he simply disappeared.

I rounded on the trio, clenching my fists.

I was going to have to use my mom voice.

❧ 15 ❧

Ryuu shook his head sadly, surveying the playground. "The children will be devastated," he said, softly, sounding genuinely upset.

"We will pay for the damages, Ryuu," Xuanwu assured him, pointedly not looking at me so as not to cast blame. "It will be better than it was before."

Ryuu nodded, and then turned to walk towards me with Xuanwu. "Thank you, Master Xuanwu." His face was calm and determined, not guilty or ashamed about interrupting my meeting with the archangel. In all fairness, they *had* actually saved me. I'd been ready to Shadow Walk away, but there was the very likely possibility that he would have pursued me. Now, that was no longer a concern. Still, I wasn't pleased.

I settled my glare on each of them individually as they gathered closer. "Before I begin verbally abusing you, what—exactly—is a daemon," I asked, testing out the word on my tongue. It sounded like *day-munn*. "I've heard it before, but I can't quite place it."

Xuanwu nodded. "A daemon is a conscience. The term often gets misassociated with demon, giving us a bad reputation. A daemon is a familiar, a guiding presence. Like our trinity with Samael, although trinities are...more complex."

Qinglong snorted. "Significantly more." He turned to me. "Where do you think the story of witches and wizards having helpful familiars comes from? Even the Horsemen adopted the practice with their horses."

I frowned. "Is that why you are bonded to Samael? He needed you in some manner?"

The two Divines shared a meaningful look. "It is a rather...personal question. The simple answer is necessity. If you want something more, you may ask Samael."

"What of your Sisters? Were they bonded to anyone? Is it a requirement, like with Beasts?" I asked.

"It is not a requirement," Qinglong said, choosing his words carefully.

"And I do not know if our Sisters were bonded," Xuanwu added. "Though, I'm certain we would have heard of someone looking for them if they had been," he said, shrugging his shoulders sadly.

"Could...my mother have bonded them?" I asked, warily.

They shook their heads in unison. "They were already missing by then. No," Qinglong said, emphatically.

I sighed, not sure if that was a relief or not. Samael had bonded these two, and my mother had also bonded Qinglong in a way. Ryuu was studying me with a calm look, not shying away from the anticipated topic of conversation he knew would be directed at him.

"How did you even find me?" I finally asked, splitting my glare between the three of them.

"When you didn't show up to train, Ryuu grew concerned, thinking you had been taken," Qinglong said. "Turns out we arrived a little early for that concern," he said, shooting me a dry look.

Xuanwu gestured with his claw towards Ryuu. "It is difficult to hide from Ryuu, White Rose."

Qinglong chuckled. "Difficult? Hah! Try impossible!"

I glanced at Ryuu with a thoughtful frown, wondering at the cryptic comments. Who was he, really? He smirked, lifting both shoulders in a drawn-out shrug as if he'd read my mind. "You are awfully quiet, Ryuu."

"A headless queen can wear no crown," he said.

I narrowed my eyes. Okay. That was how he wanted to do this? With veiled criticisms? Fine. "I will not hide from danger, Ryuu. You, of all people, should understand—"

"I do not want you to hide from danger," he said, as smooth as silk, as if we were talking about fabric swatches. He continued in the same tone, not even remotely condescending or angry. "You want to piss off angels? Tell me when and where so I can observe," he said with an easy shrug. "What I will not tolerate is you stabbing me in the back with a paper blade while I'm sleeping," he said, pulling out the note I had left for him on my pillow, "because you think it will prevent an enemy from stabbing me in the heart. That was the job I signed up for, and it was dishonorable and cowardly to try and take it away from me with this." He crumpled up the paper, not breaking eye contact, and dropped it to the ground.

"I was trying to save your *life*," I sputtered.

"Yet you somehow put me in greater danger than if I would have been invited in the first place. And I am my own protection. It is disrespectful to presume otherwise. I know my limits."

I stared at him, feeling like my head was about to pop off with carbonated fury, but I was unable to formulate a response. I couldn't fault his logic, and I couldn't pair his maddeningly calm tone with his razor-sharp accusations. But he wasn't finished.

"I will not tolerate you being so proud that you kill yourself to prove your bravery."

My shoulders were heaving. "So, I should have let you come here to fight for me? To die for me?"

He shrugged, absently. "If that was the most beneficial option to keeping you and my city safe, then yes," he said, calmly. "But a straw man argument is not enough to make me back down. The real reason you chose to lie to me is because you thought I would stop you from coming here this morning."

I stared at him. "It was a thought."

"It was an incorrect thought, then. You would know this if you had spoken with me."

I stared at him, surprised. "You would have picked a fight with him. Like you just tried to do?" I said, pointing at the space Michael had recently vacated.

He cocked his head, and I saw the first flare of genuine emotion in him. His voice dropped lower, throatier, almost primal. "Do you mean the fight I tried to pick with the man who was about to forcibly abduct you and take you where I could never find you?" He took a bold step forward, resting a hand on both sword hilts—the warped blade and the black katana. "Yes, Callie Penrose. I *definitely* did that," he growled.

I was surprised to realize that I had taken a step back from those dark eyes.

"But that is not *picking* a fight. That was me preparing to teach him a lesson he would never forget."

Xuanwu nodded his agreement, and the way he looked at Ryuu...it was obvious that Xuanwu had no doubts about Ryuu's chance of success in besting Michael in a sword fight. Jesus. I knew he was good, but *that* good?

Ryuu cleared his throat, regaining his composure. "If you had instead told me of your plan to confront Michael, I would have brought up alternative options. I might have even argued with you or challenged you. It pleases me to see your nose scrunch up whenever you're angry," he grinned suddenly, "just like that." I folded my arms, ignoring my heated cheeks. "Debate strengthens or destroys initial positions. Iron sharpens iron. After our discussion, if you had still insisted on your plan, I would have joined you as a silent observer. I would not have stepped on your toes or interfered in any way—unless you were in immediate danger that I did not believe you could overcome on your own. So, you would have been safe, and Michael would have been safe. Your decision to leave me behind led him to temptation—grandiose thoughts that he could do with you what he pleased—and that put him in grave danger."

I frowned, uneasily, at his phrasing. Was he really saying what I thought he was saying?

"He fled for very good reason, Callie Penrose. I am somewhat of a camp-fire story—even to archangels."

I turned to the Divines, waiting for one of them to laugh or slap him on the wrist for bragging.

Except...Qinglong nodded sagely. Xuanwu looked relieved at the actual outcome, almost thankful. My mind was racing with possible explanations, but there was absolutely no denying the resolute look in Ryuu's eyes. He was not exaggerating. He believed, beyond any shadow of a doubt, that he could have taken Michael, and the two Divines agreed wholeheartedly. I had to admit...Michael had fled rather quickly.

Who the fuck was my sparring partner, really?

"What he says is true, Callie," Xuanwu said. "I trained him myself." Then he bowed his beak respectfully at his student. The pride was palpable.

Qinglong cleared his throat. "There is a reason Michael did not attack. A reason why he used the word daemon like a curse," Qinglong said. Then he calmly pointed at Xuanwu. "The Black Tortoise had a...wild youth. They may have crossed paths before."

Xuanwu snorted. "We were not speaking of me. Ryuu has more than earned his own reputation."

I studied the three of them, wondering exactly what I had gotten myself into. What my mother had gotten me into.

❧ 16 ❧

O kay. I knew Ryuu was good but come on. An archangel?

"I don't believe you," I said, meeting Ryuu's eyes. Qinglong let out a long whistle—I didn't know how—as if I had just sealed my coffin. "I know you are a great warrior, but you are human," I said, ignoring the Azure Dragon.

Xuanwu sighed.

Ryuu did not look offended at my rebuke. He looked...thoughtful. "Draw your sword, White Rose."

I narrowed my eyes, shooting a questioning glance at Xuanwu and Qinglong, but they said nothing. "Wait. What?" I asked, turning back to Ryuu. "We don't have time for training."

"There is always time for learning."

"In all fairness, I'm surprised it took this long," Xuanwu murmured to Qinglong, seating himself down on the ground with a crackling sound from his frosty skin. He sighed contentedly.

I turned back to Ryuu. "This is a waste of time. I have magic."

He shrugged. "Do you only trust in your magic?"

"I could just wrap you up in air," I argued, flinging up my hands.

"You are welcome to try that," he said, sounding utterly unconcerned.

I stared into those cold, dark eyes, seeing something dangerous lurking beneath the surface. "Go to hell, Ryuu," I finally snapped, angry that my voice had a faint tremor to it.

Xuanwu pulled out a small thermos from the belt at his midsection. He lifted it to Qinglong. "Care for some tea while we watch them try to kill each other?"

Qinglong nodded sagely. "Splendid, Brother."

"No one is trying to kill each other!" I shouted at them.

Xuanwu ignored me. "Sugar?" He asked, tapping a small pouch with his claw.

The dragon shook his head, walking in a circle like a dog who was searching for the perfect spot to sleep. "Thank you, no."

Xuanwu poured the tea into two cups—I had no idea where they'd come from—and handed one to the serpentine dragon.

I frowned, uneasily, and turned to Ryuu. I blinked to see that he had tucked his right hand behind his back and into his belt, and that he was holding the warped blade with his left—his non-dominant—hand.

He was mocking me. "This is insane. I'm not fighting you with real swords. And that one is damaged, anyway," I said, pointing.

He lifted the blade to inspect it in the pale gloom of dawn. Although the metal was warped and chipped in places, the edge was still razor sharp. "It is serviceable. And yes, you are. You made the claim. Now stand behind it." He stared at me, settling into a fighting stance as he lifted his warped katana in preparation for our fight. Knowing how fast he was, and that he would pull absolutely no punches, I drew my own Silver katana and held it out before me—if for no other reason than to deflect his attack when he made his move.

Part of me knew I could destroy him with my magic—no matter what he claimed. That I could whip him like a schoolboy, embarrassing him.

And...

Another part of me knew that I would only do so as a last resort.

He had already mocked my reliance upon my magic by asking if that was all I trusted. This was important to him, and I didn't have time to deal with it later. Starting off by beating him with magic would just delay the inevitable, encouraging him to continue on with a wounded ego until the matter was resolved.

I knew he was proud, but I hadn't been doubting his finesse with a blade. He was claiming that paper didn't burn. That the Angel of Death was scared of him. But...if that was true, how had Nate bested him to give him the warped blade in the first place? Judging by the sudden twinkle in his eye—as if I had asked the question out loud—I suddenly wasn't so sure Nate had beaten him at all.

Ryuu gave me a very slow nod, glancing at the warped blade as if to say *our little secret.*

Why would he have done such a thing?

No. That was just ridiculous. I was letting my imagination get carried away with me. I narrowed my eyes. "I do not have fucking time for this. The Seven Sins are here, and I need to get answers...right *now.*"

Ryuu nodded his agreement. "We are very busy, so you should stop stalling."

I gritted my teeth. "Stupid fucking men, thinking only with the hair on your chests—gah!" Ryuu's blade lunged for my heart as rapidly as a shadow retreating to a corner when a light switch was flipped on.

I batted it away as my breath suddenly thundered in my lungs. Three more strikes followed the first, all in rapid succession and with full force.

They were so fast and unexpected that I wasn't able to simply deflect them—I had to essentially attack *back* at them, resulting in crackling *clangs* that made my ears pop and sparks fly.

My fingers numbed from the vibration. Then Ryuu was calmly, slowly sidestepping, holding the warped blade out before him in one hand—his weaker, left hand, because his right was still tucked behind his belt in mockery of my skills. "It's like riding a bike," he murmured with a smug smile, rolling his wrists fluidly to twirl the blade in great swooping arcs.

"I'm not fighting you, Ryuu—"

Clang!

His attack almost sent my sword flying, forcing me to use both hands just to hold onto it. Xuanwu and Qinglong watched in silence, the only sound was them occasionally sipping their tea.

I realized, with a flicker of fear, that I might actually have to use my magic to have a chance. I would wait until the last possible moment, but—

Clang. Clang. CLANG!

I sucked in rapid breaths, settling into a more stable stance. "Okay. Fuck this, Ryuu. You asked for it." It was time for some magic.

He laughed delightedly. "I did, didn't I?"

I ripped open a small Gateway at my side and thrust my sword through the opening. A matching Gateway appeared directly behind him, and I watched as the tip of my sword stabbed out of it, inches away from his lower back. I reflexively pulled short, not wanting to actually impale him, but I needn't have bothered.

Ryuu had twisted his body and spun, swatting away my attack without effort. He did this so powerfully that I almost dropped my sword. I tugged it back from the Gateway and released the power before it could slice my blade in half.

Ryuu did not wait for me to get my bearings. In fact, he used my distraction to *press* his attack. He was already spinning in a full-strength, overhead blow before the Gateway had winked out. I gasped, immediately Shadow Walking behind him, struggling for a moment of reprieve.

His sword whipped through the space where I had been and continued right around in a full circle to lunge towards my new location. I twisted, allowing the blade to graze my stomach, hissing as his sword scored a searing line of fire across my abdomen. I felt the blood immediately seeping into my shirt and my eyes widened in disbelief. He'd almost fucking *gutted* me—the woman he had sworn to protect! A quick glance showed me that the wound was superficial, but it could have been fatal.

I realized, in that stark moment, that this was nothing like our earlier sparring sessions with wooden swords. That those infuriating sessions had been to prepare me for the real thing, not just to keep me in shape or let off some steam. That this was not about a wounded ego. He genuinely needed me to understand exactly just how dangerous he was—so that I could formulate better decisions in the future.

And that I had truly pissed off the ninja with the deceiving note I had left on my pillow.

I met his eyes, expecting to see a look of guilt at the almost fatal wound he'd given me...

And I was rewarded with him calmly flicking my blood from the warped katana with a calm, emotionless look on his face. Then he came at me in earnest.

17

A second and third attack screamed my way, and I batted them back with a furious snarl, no longer remotely fucking concerned with his well-being. I didn't even care about the lack of reaction from the two Divines watching from the sidelines.

All that mattered was the ninja before me.

His dark eyes glittered invitingly. "Now you are beginning to see what kind of man you earned respect from the night you claimed sanctuary at Xuanwu's home." My heart skipped a beat at his statement. The night before I'd fought Roland outside the church. The night before I'd invaded Castle Dracula with Samael. "Now you are beginning to see what kind of man has volunteered to risk a blade to his heart in order to safeguard yours." He wasn't even breathing heavily.

I was no novice at sword fighting. In fact, I was pretty goddamned talented, thanks to my decade of study under Roland's tutelage. But Ryuu...yeah.

He'd married his sword decades before I was *born*. In fact, I wasn't even sure how old he was. He was Xuanwu's most trusted disciple, and the Black Tortoise was a god. Had Ryuu been one of the first humans to master a blade?

Perhaps.

Or he wasn't as human as I believed. But none of that mattered right now. I wasn't *just* a swordswoman. At first blood, I realized that Ryuu would not hold it against me if I used every tool at my disposal. I felt guilty for using it earlier in the fight, but that had been an emotional decision. Now...

I had learned from Roland, and the code of the warrior was to use your every ability to the utmost to win. So, just like that, my magic was back in my toolbox if I saw an opening.

The only way to truly win was for both of us to hold nothing back.

Anything less was dishonorable, and I'd already made that mistake once.

Ryuu lunged forward to attack. Rather than defending or attempting another jolting parry, I evaded enough to take the strike across my arm, accepting a shallow slash—which he hadn't expected me to do—in order to break his follow-up attack. I immediately countered by lunging forward with my katana, and his eyes widened a fraction of a millimeter in surprise. His body reflexively leaned upon the use of his right hand—which was still tucked behind his waist—causing him to stumble ever so slightly. My blade scored his inner arm and then his inner thigh before he leapt back with a sound of approval.

He continued moving laterally, briefly checking his dripping wounds with a respectful nod. Then he calmly lifted his hilt to his lips and kissed it. As he lowered his hand, he now wore a black face mask that covered everything below his nose, and a black sash was wound around his forehead, tying his long hair back. Magic? The two ends trailed down his shoulders, seeming to shimmer like oil in the morning light, yet they moved as if underwater, following his movements like floating streamers intended to distract.

His feet began emitting tendrils of smoke, obscuring his movement. I narrowed my eyes, angrily. Yeah, he had other powers and he wasn't afraid to use them either. Not so human, after all. I'd always assumed he was mostly human, but with supernatural gifts. But this was something else entirely, and I suddenly realized why calling him human earlier had led to him telling me to draw my sword.

Part of me wanted to cheer at my small victory—that I had pushed him into tapping into his additional abilities. But, because I wasn't a psychopath, I tried reasoning with him again. "You have proven your point. Enough is enough. I'm sorry."

He shook his head. "Not just yet," he replied.

Before the calmly spoken words had even finished escaping his lips, he was whipping towards me in a whirlwind. I did my best to parry and block, gripping my sword as if it were a cliff and I was hanging over an eternal drop into inky obscurity. I clenched my teeth at the painful vibrations and the thunderous clanging, but I managed to block each of them—a feat in and of itself.

But he was a fucking bastard, because with each strike, he taunted me in a laughing jeer.

"She loves me!" CLANG! "She loves me not!" CLANG! "She loves me! She loves me not!" CLANG-CLANG-*CLANG*!

He even laughed between strikes.

"This isn't about *love*, Ryuu," I snapped, panting desperately as I tried to puzzle out the reason behind his choice of taunts.

He scoffed, laughing harder—which hurt more than deflecting his strikes. "It is what one says when plucking petals from a flower. Like *this*!"

My momentary distraction earned me three slashes. One across my forearm, another down my cheek, and the last across my thigh.

But I slipped in three of my own. One slashed across his chest—deeper than any other cut in our exchange, judging by his grunt and stumble. It also allowed me to dart close enough for two more. One struck his upper arm, and the other slashed away his face mask. Blood dripped down his jaw as he stepped back and calmly dipped his chin.

Then he sheathed his sword, smiled warmly, and gave me a respectful bow. "Good."

I blinked, panting and trembling—both from pain, raw nerves, and disbelief. I couldn't even feel my fingers and I was soaked to the skin with blood and sweat. "What, you don't know how to take a hit?" I asked, shakily pointing my sword at the wounds I had given him.

He smirked, shaking his head. "I won."

I grunted. "It was a fairly even fight. And my cut was deepest," I said, pointing out the deep fan of blood spilling down his chest and ruining his shirt.

"Have you counted? Because you're currently in danger of becoming indecent," he said, keeping his eyes slightly averted. "Twenty-one, by my count, but feel free to check my work."

I frowned, glancing down. My eyes widened to see that I was practically wearing rags, resembling a bloody mummy. There were cuts through the fabric all over my torso, my arms, and my legs. I stood there, stunned, lowering my sword. "How?" I stammered, still trying to catch my breath.

Xuanwu cleared his throat. "Because he is my student. The bloody slash to your abdomen numbed your pain receptors and gave you a shot of endorphins, preventing you from feeling the little ones. Those are much harder to deliver, as I'm sure you know. Cutting fabric but only grazing the skin."

I shook my head slowly, trying to process the flogging I'd received. "I still got you," I grumbled.

Ryuu chuckled. "You did," he said, lifting his shirt to show me his wounds—

"They're gone!" I gasped. Blood still marred his skin, but the slashes were healed.

He nodded, lowering his shirt. "And yours are not, which was the real purpose of this exercise."

I frowned. "To show me that you heal faster than a shifter?" I demanded.

"To teach you that some people are irreplaceable, and should be used wisely," Qinglong said, pointing a claw at me with a stern glare. "So how about you let the foolish man protect you and stop making things more difficult than they need to be. You've got bigger, harder battles to fight. Let him help you get to them in one piece."

I nodded, slowly. "Okay."

"Splendid. Let's go," he grumbled. The two Divines finished off their tea and Xuanwu began packing away his mobile beverage stand.

I hadn't actually eaten anything, and sparring with Ryuu had taxed me heavily, so my legs were feeling rather jittery. I tried sheathing my sword and one of my legs buckled, almost sending me to the ground. Ryuu caught me with an arm around my waist. "I've got you," he said, taking my sword and sheathing it for me.

"I'm fine," I assured him, embarrassed of my stumble. "Just running on an empty tank."

He shot me a wry look. "Huh. Maybe you should have *actually* gotten breakfast at your coffee shop this morning," he teased.

I sighed, resting my head on his shoulder in a gesture of peace. "I really am sorry, Ryuu. Even?"

Ryuu chuckled. "Of course. Let's commit to brutal honesty from here on out. I'm not going anywhere."

I nodded, smiling at Xuanwu and Qinglong to assure them that wobbly knees weren't an indication of impending doom. I was bleeding, but I'd taken dozens upon dozens of worse cuts over the years while training with Roland. That's what happened when you advanced to real blades.

Ryuu leaned closer, speaking in a low tone as Qinglong and Xuanwu wrapped up the last of their gear and made their way over. "For the record, I had a healer waiting on standby before I left to find you. I would never put you in real danger just to prove a point. My ego is not *that* frail."

"But you did," I murmured back, smiling.

Ryuu stiffened. "No, Callie. You were never in real danger. I swear it on my name."

I chuckled. "No. You did prove your point. You're a badass angel killer. Ginsu Ryuu," I said, tugging at my shredded clothes with a pinch of my fingers. "There are easier ways to go about taking a girl's clothes off," I quipped, dryly. Then my eyes widened, wishing I had the words back as my cheeks flushed red. "I didn't mean—"

Ryuu laughed loudly, drawing startled looks from Xuanwu and Qinglong as they huddled around us. "I know what you meant," he said.

Xuanwu rested his claw on my shoulder, and Qinglong reared up on his hind legs to complete our circle by extending his claws to Ryuu and Xuanwu.

I felt a gust of icy wind, and the world went dark as Xuanwu whisked us away from the ruined playground. A moment later, I gasped to find us standing in the training area behind Xuanwu's home.

A petite, remarkably pretty woman with straight, shining black hair was waiting for us. Since she was the only other person in the garden, I took a wild guess that she was Ryuu's healer. She wore an elaborate, black silk robe, and her hands were folded into the long, wide sleeves. She flashed me a warm, inviting smile as Xuanwu and Qinglong quietly walked deeper into the garden, speaking in low tones.

I kind of just stared at her for a few seconds, gobsmacked. It was the woman who had given me a sponge bath the night I had claimed sanctuary here. The same night Ryuu had mentioned when we had been fighting a few minutes ago—the night he had decided to become my bodyguard.

Ryuu cleared his throat, sounding amused, and I snapped out of my daze. "Hi," I said, awkwardly, realizing I'd been staring at her for entirely too long.

"Good morning, White Rose. If you would please come with me," she said, stepping to the side and gesturing with her hand towards the house. She kept her eyes downcast.

❧ 18 ❧

The healer led me towards a private section of the garden that butted up to the house. Then she silently offered me her hand. I placed my hand in hers with a curious smile, and the world flickered away.

Next, I found myself staring up at a twilight realm of royal purple skies with millions of huge, twinkling stars that appeared close enough to reach out and touch. We were in the cherry blossom fields beyond Xuanwu's home —that otherworldly plane I had seen from his garden. The gentle breeze was floral and pure, as if it had never known the stink of mankind. I spun in a slow circle with my fingers outstretched, mesmerized by the surrounding field of swaying, waist-high, bluish-gray grass, soft as feathers. I smiled as it tickled my fingers, and I watched it roll and sway in the breeze, awed by the tranquility of the place.

I spotted a bioluminescent tree less than fifty yards away that stood proud and tall, celebrating the fact that it was the only tree in this place, making it a mythical unicorn for that aspect alone. Its trunk and branches were a dazzling white with neon pink cherry blossoms. Hundreds of the psychedelic petals were swept away in the gentle breeze, but hundreds more replaced them, growing out from the branches of the tree so that it never seemed to change its pregnant vibrancy.

With the tree swaying and the blossoms floating up into the sky in an endless stream, it reminded me of a bonfire spewing up sparks but never dying down. Except these sparks were beautiful petals of life rather than burned husks of death.

The woman smiled at the joyful look on my face, and then guided me towards the glowing tree. We soon stepped out from the tall grass and onto a carpet of thick, spongy grass that led beneath the canopy of the other-worldly tree.

Except the grass was yellow. Not a sickly yellow, but a perfect canary yellow. And the tree looked older than anything I'd ever seen.

A rice paper, tri-paneled divider—like those used in dressing rooms—was literally rooted to the ground, looking as if the entire thing had grown up from the soil. About fifty yards farther on from the tree was a small pond with a low, hand-carved bridge that could have come from a royal palace in feudal Japan. One of those iconic bridges seen in almost every martial arts movie. Bright pink blossoms covered most of yellow grass in a thick, perfumed blanket of fallen petals.

The young woman gestured at the divider. "You may disrobe. We are private," she assured me in a soft tone, like we were in a library and she didn't want to get us in trouble. I found myself struggling to label the healer with the term *woman*. She looked young enough to barely qualify as an adult. Yet she also seemed wise beyond her years. She was not matronly, but she was...sagely.

"That's swell and all, but my mother always taught me *names before nipples*. I think she was referring to men on the prowl, but I never specifically asked her, so...what's your name?"

The healer smirked, bowed, and then left, disappearing around the divider in the direction of the pond.

I frowned, leaning out from the partition to see where I was supposed to go after disrobing. My eyes widened to see her black silk robe flutter to the ground behind her as the pale, petite woman continued walking without a care in the world, as if she hadn't yet noticed she'd suffered a wardrobe malfunction. But the carefree sway of her hips told me it had not been acci-dental and that the woman beneath had been released from the unseen binds of the restraining silk.

Like a caged bird suddenly flying free.

Like a woodland nymph entering the darkest depths of the forest.

Or she was an elite level nudist.

I realized that I was still staring at her, slack-jawed. Even though we had met once before, we hadn't actually communicated. She'd given me a sponge bath. To her, that had apparently set a precedent for *hey, we should hang out naked again!* I averted my eyes and leaned back to assess my own shredded, bloody clothes, feeling remarkably self-conscious about stripping down to my skin with her in another dimension—especially when she didn't want to give me her name. It certainly put a whole new spin on the phrase supernatural, turning it into super-*naturale.*

I was beginning to realize that most of my acquaintances seemed more concerned with getting naked or getting high on questionable plants than they were about helping make the world a better, safer place.

The air was soothing and warm, so at least I wouldn't be risking frostnip by taking off my clothes. I leaned out from the partition again to check on the voyeur healer as I set my weapons belt down and began untying the laces of my boots.

The woman was calmly wading into the pond, and I squeed excitedly as I noticed thick steam rising up from the water. Hot springs were *definitely* more my style, and skinny-dipping was better than skinny-walking. Even better now, thanks to my consistent training with Ryuu, at least I wasn't concerned about turning it into chunky-dunking or a cannonball calamity. However, compared to the petite Asian woman, anyone would look overweight. I felt like She-Hulk compared to the dainty creature.

I hurriedly emptied the contents of my pockets into my boots, hesitating as I picked up the rings I had found in my mother's lab. I'd almost forgotten about the surge of power I'd felt from them when Michael had taken off his mask. I inspected them warily, but I noticed no change in the physical or magical spectrum. They felt exactly the same as the first time I had seen them, so I tossed them into my boots.

I continued to undress, wincing as I peeled the blood-soaked fabric away from my wounds. When I tried sliding my arms out, both sleeves simply tore free from the garment, thanks to Ryuu's surgical slashes. The same thing happened when I tried tugging the jacket open. And the pants. Within moments, I had a pile of shredded strips of bloody cloth at my feet. There was no chance of wearing any of it again, so I would have to knock the healer out and take her robe if she hadn't thought to bring a spare.

That was on her. I would take no pleasure in it. But she hadn't even given me her name.

I inspected my wounds, confirming my earlier analysis that none of them were particularly concerning. I did count over a dozen red scratches that made me look like I'd gone streaking through the woods at night. Ryuu's unseen cuts. I shook my head absently, marveling at the requisite precision it had required. I slipped out of my underwear in an ungraceful stumble, but I did manage to catch myself before falling head-first through the priceless rice paper divider like the Kool-Aid man. That was a win.

Since my clothes now resembled a pile of used surgical pads after an off-the-books cartel surgery, the only things worth keeping were my boots, my bra, my panties, and my sword. All things considered, that was all a woman really needed to take over the world. I considered taking my boots with me to the pond since they now doubled as a purse for my stuff, but I knew Xuanwu's people were not thieves, so I left them.

I took a reassuring breath and stepped out from the divider, feeling uncomfortably exposed between one step and the next—even though I'd been just as naked behind the divider as I was now. I ignored the reflex panic and pressed on. The grass was ridiculously soft and spongy beneath my little piggies as I made my way towards the bank of the pond, and I realized I was smiling in anticipation of the warm soak. I touched my fingers to the wound in my side, grimacing at my imagined reflection. I probably looked like a terror. But the nameless woman was a healer, so she probably wanted to get me cleaned up in the pond before getting to work. Or maybe the pond was full of magical Koi fish that would heal me with playful nibbles.

I paused at the shore, my smile slowly fading into a frown as the woman turned to face me. A thick cloud of white steam hovered over the surface, but the water was as smooth as glass. Her movements hadn't caused even a single ripple or disturbance in the fog. She stood so that the water only barely covered her perky breasts. Then she smiled and dipped beneath the surface.

I felt a wave of goosebumps roll down my spine. Even submerging hadn't caused a ripple.

Maybe it wasn't water but some denser, healing liquid.

If Ryuu hadn't vouched for her, I would have been long gone by now.

I dipped my toe in and let out a sigh of relief to find that it wasn't just warm, it was invitingly hot. That perfect temperature for relaxation. I waded out into the steaming depths, wondering why she was still underwater. My muscles loosened up with each step through the hot muddy floor of the pond, and I was definitely causing ripples. I frowned, self-consciously, reassessing my chunky-dunk parameters. My wounds tingled pleasurably upon contact with the water, and I took a deep inhale of the thick steam, appreciating the privacy of the thick white fog. I reached the spot where she had submerged, yet I didn't see any telltale bubbles of air or feel her hiding beneath.

"Strange Asian lady?" I asked, trying to wave away the steam surrounding me. She didn't answer, and I found it difficult to prioritize my concern over the seductive pull of the water. "Mind doing some healing—"

I cut off as I felt a cool breath of air across the back of my neck, but a gentle finger touched my shoulder before I could turn or cry out. I gasped as an explosion of heat radiated outward through my body from the frisky finger.

And...I shuddered in relief. The fiery heat raced through my body, stretching from my fingers to my toes in a healing wave, and I felt a sharp tingle in my more serious wounds before the pain simply disappeared. I checked with my fingers and found only healed flesh. Then the finger broke contact and I spun dazedly to see the tiny woman smiling at me.

"Hi," she said, with one of those impossibly infectious smiles. The kind that made their whole face light up as if you were the most important thing in the entire universe and they didn't want to miss a single moment of your interaction. The kind of smile that made you feel their opinion might actually be true.

She was entirely different from the almost coy and reserved woman I had met earlier. As if she was safe in her natural habitat and could finally be herself. Yet through the kindness in her eyes, I saw a deep intelligence and a well of power within easy grasp. I couldn't define that power, but I could feel it.

"Um. Hi," I said, still trying to shrug off the abrupt tremors of relaxation rippling through me. "You've got quite the gift."

She giggled, the sound rolling over the motionless, steamy water like wind chimes. "I do," she agreed, obviously amused.

"What is this place?" I asked, knowing she obviously still didn't want to mention her name.

She smiled, glancing left and right. "This is the training fields. Where we die and are reborn. In this pool, specifically."

I gawked at her in disbelief. "*What?*"

She nodded, excitedly. "Rebirth. Here."

I pursed my lips. "I heard the words, they just didn't make any sense." I was swimming in zombie soup. Disgusting. "Are you immortal? Some kind of water goddess? Is that why you won't tell me your name?"

She smiled. "My name is unimportant," she said in a gentle tone. Then she scrutinized me like I was a patient with a particularly meddlesome parasite she hadn't quite figured out how to remove.

Time to nip that in the bud. "Thank you for healing me."

"Thank Ryuu," she said, fondly, grinning to reveal that perfect dimple. "You do understand that you are quite the enigma around here," she mused, assessing me thoughtfully. "Ryuu has never offered to protect someone before. Ever. He hardly even *likes* people. So, it shocked us all when he announced his intention to guard the White Rose."

Despite her sweet smile, there was a very surgical warning in her casual tone. "To be honest, it probably shocked me more," I admitted. "I wasn't given much of a say in the matter."

She smirked knowingly. "That sounds accurate."

I took a gamble since the ninja wasn't looking over my shoulder at the moment. "I honestly don't know very much about him, but I'm quickly learning that he is far more than the leader of the shinobi. I heard Ryuu was quite dangerous—and I heard it from people who I thought were at the top of the food chain."

She nodded, absently, not seeming particularly interested. "I once heard that orgasms feel nice."

I stiffened, and my eyes widened in confusion at her baffling comment.

She was smirking deviously. "*Dangerous* is an understatement. As is devoted, demanding, daring, dauntless, defiant, determined, and disciplined. And that's just using one letter of the alphabet." She stared deep into my eyes as if digging for something. "Who told you this?"

I shrugged. "The topic came up tonight with Ryuu, Xuanwu, and Qinglong. I thought Ryuu would downplay it, but he was very determined to convince me," I said, enunciating one of the words she had used to describe him.

She narrowed her eyes, looking more annoyed than angry. "*That's* why he set this up. So I could clean up his mess," she said, sternly, in the tone of someone who had known him a very long time. Which made her...equally as inhuman. Because Ryuu was definitely something more, judging by his fighting skills. She took a calming breath before focusing back on me. "I'm afraid we've only healed the easy part. Next, we get to fix your chakras. They are a hot mess, if I'm being blunt."

I smiled crookedly. "My chakras?" I asked, reeling at the rapid shift in topic—let alone the fiery independent dragon of a spirit that had been slumbering inside this petite little woman before she'd stepped into this pond. What the hell was in this water, and could I bottle it?

"Bodies are easy to heal. The roots of pain and injuries lie deeper in the soul, and those roots often force the lines from the chakras to take strange, inefficient detours."

"Oh. Well, if you insist," I said.

She nodded. "I do. Follow me," she said, and then she turned and began swimming back to the shore without disturbing the surface of the water.

I let out a resigned sigh, speaking to myself since she was halfway back to shore already. "Okay."

19

We sat beneath the cherry blossom tree on a bed of fresh petals, facing each other. The woman regarded me, but she seemed to be staring into me rather than at me. It was unsettling. We had not gotten dressed, because she'd absently swatted my hand the moment I'd tried to grab my underwear. And the effortless motion had struck me as hard as a wet, metal ruler.

"Why are we still naked?" I asked, folding my arms.

"So I can see your chakras clearly," she murmured distractedly, pursing her lips as if annoyed. "I am looking into your very *essence*. What it's wrapped in does not matter to me. Not in the slightest."

"What a relief," I grumbled. True to her words, she did have a vacant look on her face; her eyes darting around, looking over my shoulder or at specific points of my body like they were tracking a ping-pong championship.

"I see why he asked for me," she finally murmured, scrunching her nose up.

"What does *that* mean?" I asked, scowling. "He wanted you to heal my physical wounds."

Her eyes came back into focus and she blinked a few times. "Your entire soul is a tangle. It's all knotted up, as if trying to protect something."

I hesitated, eyeing her warily. "Like...a spear?" I asked.

She gave me a vaguely condescending look. "Is *that* what you think it is?" She resumed her study for a few moments, as if testing my theory. "It is not a weapon," she finally concluded, sounding intrigued.

I kept my face calm upon hearing her parrot Ryuu's claim. Knowing how concerned Ryuu was about my safety, I began to suspect that this had been his plan all along. He'd had the healer on standby long before we'd drawn swords. And getting a second opinion about my Spear also served to possibly benefit Xuanwu by giving us guidance on how to use it to save them. I couldn't fault him for that. I would have done the same in his shoes.

"Anything else buried inside I need to worry about?" she asked, dryly. "An axe, maybe?"

I frowned, giving her question serious merit despite her tone. "Well, not anymore."

She cocked her head and furrowed her eyebrows. "I was joking..." she said, and I watched as her puzzled look shifted to surprise. "But you were *not*. You really had an axe hidden in here? No wonder it's such a mess. You do know there are other places to hide things, right?" she asked, exasperated.

I rolled my eyes. "Thanks, doc. I'll keep that in mind. And it was a sword, by the way."

She studied me for a few seconds, shaking her head. "You are zero for two. It was a Name, not a sword. And a *big* Name," she added, her curiosity obviously piqued again.

I gritted my teeth at her utter lack of bedside manner. She'd been fun before putting her chakra-scope on, and it was unsettling to hear about scar tissue in my soul. "It was Excalibur."

She threw her hands up and let out a flustered breath. "You had them *both* inside you at the same time? Don't tell me you've had Ryuu's dark blade in there, too."

My cheeks caught fire at her phrasing. "You know," I growled in a warning tone, "I'm beginning to feel slightly awkward, sitting here in the nude with a stranger, getting judged for what I put inside my body, and at what times. I'm being soul-shamed."

She blinked, and then she suddenly looked just as embarrassed as I felt. "Oh, my. That *did* sound rather inappropriate, didn't it?"

"Exceedingly," I said.

"I'm sorry. When my mind is at work, I have a hard time focusing on social courtesies."

I waved a hand. "The phrasing threw me off, is all." But she had inadvertently brought up a good point. "What is the deal with Ryuu's black katana? You called it the dark blade like it meant something."

She nodded, soberly. "Some call it Angel Killer." The hair on my arms pricked right the hell up. But she wasn't finished creeping me out. "*And God saw the light, and it was good. And God divided the light from the darkness,*" she said, quoting the Book of Genesis—which made absolutely no sense. Ryuu wasn't Christian. "The Angel Killer was made from particles of that dark void, predating angels and demons. And that terrifies them," she explained in a sober tone. She let out a wary breath. "Ryuu does not call it that. He prefers to believe it was made from the ashes of a dead universe. That the sword was forged from the scraps no one wanted. The scraps the original gods feared to use."

I stared at her in disbelief, not knowing what to say or what to even ask. Rather than a question, I thought about Ryuu's personalized explanation for his sword. "Like the pond," I said, indicating the nearby healing pool. "The old is born anew. It suits him," I said, smiling faintly. "But how did he come to acquire—"

She was shaking her head adamantly. "I have probably already said more than I should. Ask Ryuu. I'm sure he will tell you, of all people, the story," she said, apologetically.

I smiled, nodding. "I understand. I wasn't trying to get you to break his confidence," I assured her. Questions were zipping through my mind, though. Was he bonded to it? Where had he gotten it? What was it really made of? Was it like my Spear of Destiny? Which only made me realize that it really was time for me to wrap this up.

"I'd really like to get this over with. I feel fine, so is this really necessary?" I asked, careful to not sound unappreciative. "I have very pressing concerns to deal with in Kansas City."

She nodded. "From what I can see, you are a ticking time bomb. You could keep going for either a year or for another five minutes, but at some point, you're going to have a major problem that will require major psychic surgery and extended recovery. Rather than that, I recommend a preventative realignment. I can do it now, and it will not put you in a figurative sickbed."

I leaned forward, staring into her eyes. "You are certain? Millions of lives will depend on your answer, and that is not an exaggeration," I told her, imagining the population of Kansas City stuck between the Seven Sins and the archangels. "Will it weaken or incapacitate me? I need to be at fighting strength."

"If I do my job right, which Ryuu trusted me to do, you should end up being a hell of a lot stronger," she said with a smug smirk. "But you might suffer mild side effects. Your magic could be more potent as a result of me streamlining your chakras. Things like that. Drink plenty of water and think twice before you cut loose."

Knowing that I was going to be confronting archdemons and archangels, I realized now wasn't the time to risk a breakdown, and it might be exactly the *right* time to put some nitrous in my veins. Ryuu trusted her, and Xuanwu and Qinglong trusted Ryuu. "Okay," I said.

She dipped her chin and smiled reassuringly. Then she drew a deep breath and closed her eyes, centering herself for the task ahead.

At some point in our talk, I had lifted my knees to hug to my chest as a sort of barrier between us, wrapping my arms around my ankles for added protection down low. I returned to my seated, cross-legged position, forcing myself to remain calm rather than fretting over my current nudity, but it was hard. Clothes were a sort of armor that allowed you to hide your most vulnerable bits from prying eyes. The only consolation was that she was equally as indisposed, yet she wasn't letting it hold her back. I could at least be as confident as her.

After a few moments, she opened her eyes and I noticed that faraway, almost dazed look to them. She scooted closer and knelt an inch or two in front of me, our knees almost touching. Then she lifted her hands and set the pads of her fingers down on my mid thighs.

The moment her fingers touched my skin, I gasped involuntarily, feeling as if she'd punched me in the soul. I sucked in a breath and realized I was entirely unable to move away from her, as if she'd anchored my ass to the ground, or put it to sleep. Electric tingles raced down my bones and ignited the blood in my veins.

I opened my mouth to ask what she had just done, and her fingers darted out like Mr. Miyagi catching a fly with chopsticks. Except my lower lip was the fly in this case. I stared at her incredulously, unable to move or speak for fear of her ripping it off with some chakra ninjitsu.

"Do not talk," she murmured distractedly, rising up on her knees to loom closer to me. "It disturbs your aura, and this is going to be difficult enough as is." Finally, she released my lip and I let out a breath of relief.

She lifted her hands and then trailed her fingers down the sides of my ribcage from top to bottom with a thoughtful frown on her face—as if she was using a stethoscope. I sucked in a breath as faint pops reverberated in my soul, as if she was a chiropractor adjusting each rib back into place, one-by-one. But the pads of her fingers were like hot velvet, both ticklish and euphoric, and exerted no physical pressure. Tension I hadn't known I carried cascaded down to my hips like water released by a dam.

She reached up to pinch my earlobe in a gentle but firm grip. She set her lips, looking on the verge of anger. Then she squeezed and I sucked in a breath, my eyes instantly watering at the sharp pain.

But...my mind spun with confusion as I felt an unpleasant fiery sensation rapidly building up within my right shoulder. The woman growled and immediately grabbed the shoulder with her other hand—in the exact location of the fiery pain—and squeezed her fingers in a tight grip.

Then she pinched my earlobe again—harder.

The fire instantly shot to my shoulder again—hotter than the first time —but immediately exploded outwards as if her other hand had dispersed it elsewhere. And...that painful heat dissipated with faint popping sounds in my shoulder blades, my left kneecap, and my right pinky toe.

I was shaking, blinking back tears of both pain and relief. What the hell was *that* all about?

"You will require more work than I thought, White Rose," she said, sounding almost offended about it.

I opened my mouth to demand an explanation, but all I managed to do was squawk as I was lifted into the air on unseen tendrils of power. I tried to scream but my voice did not work. I found myself hovering horizontal to the ground, staring up at the underside of the cherry blossom tree with my head hanging free and my limbs splayed out like a starfish.

My earlier guess that she was powerful had been spot on.

20

I sucked in a breath, reaching for my magic.

"That is just going to get in my way," she growled as she snapped her fingers. My power evaporated so completely that I momentarily wondered if I had ever *had* any magic at all. I wasn't shielded—she'd simply ripped my wizard's gift out of me and set it down on the grass like some bothersome, inconveniently-placed organ during a surgery.

Then she began to work. Dozens, upon dozens, upon dozens of unseen fingers suddenly poked and prodded me, caressed and pressed, pinched and pulled, at the unlikeliest of points across my body.

And I lit up like a switchboard as the woman calmly walked from my head to my feet, her hands clasped behind her back as she occasionally loomed over me with a studious look. Those unseen spiritual fingers continued their work despite her actual fingers not physically touching me anymore. Almost like she was using magic to keep up her poking and prodding, but I felt no magic from her.

I began to shake and tremble as ice, fire, pleasure, pain, numbness, heaviness, weightlessness, and electricity raced from my nose to my elbows. From my shoulders to my shins. Metaphysical touches that caused seemingly random sensations: flicking my forehead caused my hip to tingle, pinching my index finger caused my tongue to grow numb, squeezing my right hand caused my body to spasm in agony, brushing my collarbone caused the back of my knee to tickle.

But even as I tried to catalog these bizarre connections, she diverted them elsewhere. The second time she brushed my collarbone, my breasts grew painfully tight. The woman cursed, firmly grabbed my hips—with her actual hands this time—and then the next spirit finger caress to my collarbone released the pressure in my chest. The woman let out a satisfied murmur and released my hips. Then she loomed over me and used her finger to brush my collarbone—to check her work—and...

I felt it only on my collarbone.

Except it was more noticeable and rawer than anything I'd ever felt before. As if I'd never truly felt someone tickle that spot before. I let out a faint, unbidden whimper of relief. Dozens more interactions like that happened in the span of mere minutes, as if she was trying to set a speed record or something.

And all the while, my soul felt like it was roaring—angry and joyful—and growing, expanding to the point where it felt like it extended past my flesh.

At one point, my vision rapidly tunneled to darkness.

The woman was suddenly beneath me, and I felt her fingers playing the piano down my spine like a madwoman. My vision snapped back, blindingly bright, and my soul let out a sigh of relief as it shrunk back within my body, seeming to amass in the center of my chest in a tight, turbulent, glowing green knot of...

Well, not like a *painful* muscle knot.

This...well, it was slightly embarrassing. I'll admit that it gave me a smile, though. A huge one.

Although similar to a growing climax, it was spiritual rather than sexual, because I felt it reverberating throughout my entire soul like an echo. It felt like a harmonious hum that was resonating with the rest of my body, as if I was being tuned up. I tried not to think about it, knowing the mad doctor was just going to do something else to change it into a different sensation entirely.

She touched the base of my neck with her fingers and my Sanguina-vision exploded into action, making me gasp and arch my back as the world abruptly shifted to chromatic shades of gray.

I glanced down to see hundreds of golden lines crisscrossing my body in a crazy web of light—the only color in existence with my Beast vision activated. The woman chuckled. "Clever, clever, clever. But if I move this back over here..." she murmured to herself, sounding out of breath. She was sweating and seemed to be faintly glowing herself. The golden lines of light were bright enough to make me squint, although I was devoting all my energy to sucking in breaths.

She did something with the erogenous zone on my neck and Silver spikes exploded out of me, peppering the branches above and shredding millions of petals to send them floating down like rain over us. I cried out as a great weight suddenly slipped from my neck and shoulders. What felt like a steaming washcloth suddenly pressed over my upper back and face, making my toes curl, and my body go slack as my vision returned to normal.

The petals continued to fall, looking like fat, apocalyptic pink snowflakes. My ears popped and then seemed to open up for the first time, letting me hear the petals falling as if in stereo, and I'm not talking about them hitting branches.

I could feel the wind brushing their surface as they fell, as if my vision had been intensified on an entirely inhuman level. Something beyond even any supernatural senses I'd heard of.

I stared, stunned, unable to move anything but my eyelids. I could see each individual Silver needle that had exploded out of me. They coated the tree like quills on a porcupine, and then I watched as they slowly sunk into the glowing tree as if being consumed. I felt no fear, somehow knowing she hadn't stolen my powers or anything. The woman had removed some block on my Silvers, because I suddenly felt that my bond with Sanguina had strengthened.

I was no stranger to pressure points—on how to use them in combat, to relieve pain, to cause pleasure, or cause any other number of sensations. I knew many of these strange connections from Roland's teachings on chakras. If you had a headache, you could apply firm, almost painful pressure to the web of skin between the index finger and thumb to eliminate the headache. I knew how to wall away my pain so I could continue fighting—both in a mental practice and from a pressure point application. I could make my opponent's arm go numb or his leg not work properly. All that esoteric knowledge I'd acquired...

Apparently, I had only been a poorly trained field medic—the woman who the real surgeons cursed and hated for attempting such crude, detrimental, battlefield surgeries that only put the victim in greater harm, long-term. Who cared that the patient didn't have gangrene? I'd amputated his foot.

But magic spirit finger lady? She was the world's most esteemed neurosurgeon.

My eyes bulged as the resonating, pleasurable sensation returned with a vengeance. My whole body hummed in tune with it, more strongly condensed in my navel than anywhere else. It felt like I had one of those rubber hot water bottles on my stomach for particularly painful cramps, but no larger than a grapefruit and beneath my skin. It was yellow. I don't know how I knew that, but it definitely was.

And I began to panic as that almost forgotten, green knot of pleasure in the center of my chest condensed into a green ball of light, and slowly began to drift down like a falling feather, quivering more intensely as it drew closer to the yellow orb of heat beneath my navel. My panic grew stronger as the full-body humming grew more intense, because although the orb wasn't hopping the fence to take a detour to my happy place, I had a feeling that my body's response was going to be close enough for it to qualify.

It simply didn't know what else to do with the stimulus package.

I sucked in a breath, shaking my head in both frustration and embarrassment, knowing that if the green orb touched the yellow orb, I might die of shame.

It continued to fall lower, closing the distance.

I found myself panting, no longer feeling the woman's touches—spiritual or physical. The blood began to roar in my ears and my tongue swelled, salivating double-time. My toes curled and the insides of my elbows, the back of my neck, and my shoulder blades all grew uncomfortably hot.

The green orb touched the yellow orb in the *exact* right spot beneath my navel, emitting a faint chime that heralded the presence of God.

Reality exploded, and I became a supernova of euphoria, creating my own pocket universe. My full-body chakra-gasm knocked me unconscious.

Immediately.

21

I came to, opening my eyes languidly. I lay on the bed of petals again and I was wearing a black silk robe like the one the healer had been wearing when I first met her. Speaking of the healer, she knelt at my side, brushing my hair with a jade comb. She had donned her old robe, and was smiling down at me. "How are you feeling?" she whispered with a warm smile.

"I'm...exhausted," I admitted. My cheeks flushed darker upon remembering my encore departure. "And embarrassed." I sat upright, trying to mask my reaction.

She frowned. "Why would you be embarrassed for passing out? Everything went smoothly as rain."

I blinked. "Oh. I...guess I thought I screamed. It was all fuzzy at the end," I lied. If she didn't know about my chakra-gasm, I wasn't going to bring it up.

"You did scream, but that is a typical response when everything falls back into harmony. A cry of celebration." She studied me thoughtfully. "In fact, most patients cry after they wake up."

I grunted. "I cry on the inside," I said, smirking. Xylo had taught me that one. Accidentally. "Thank you for the robe," I said, studying it with a smile. "It's very well made."

She nodded. "Healers must have a deft touch with a needle. Sewing things back together again is a hobby of mine," she said, smiling. "Like I did with you."

I arched an eyebrow. "That sounds...concerning. I thought you were just realigning my chakras?"

She nodded. "A wound which required stitching afterwards. Especially to heal the wound left behind by tearing out Excalibur," she said. "I used to love to stitch it back together, since I sensed maternal love where the sword had been," she said, softly. "Your mother must have cared for you very, very much. I sensed sorrow in that love. It was a parting gift, wasn't it?"

I blinked rapidly, not having realized she would have been able to see something so personal. "Yes."

She smiled, reaching out to touch my forearm with her fingers. "That is why I used love for the thread, so the wound would not be forgotten. Love is very powerful. There is a reason mankind has always called a lover a soul-mate, or a cherished friend a kindred spirit. In both cases, love is the thread that binds these souls together to become something greater than the sum of the parts."

"So, did you put everything back?" I asked, recalling how she had plucked out my wizard's magic.

She smiled, nodding. "Your power is fine. You are fine. With plenty of water and physical activity, you will hardly notice a difference. But your magic might be...more explosive as your body adapts. Not uncontrollable or anything. Just more potent."

I let out a sigh, rolling my shoulders. That wasn't a bad thing. I experimentally reached out for my magic and let out an internal sigh to feel it back where it belonged. It did seem to respond quicker than usual, confirming her comment. It almost seemed hungry and eager.

My skin felt energized and I was as refreshed as if I had taken a long nap, but I wasn't hearing a huddle of monks chanting in my head, nor was I overcome by an aura of zen serenity. Harmonious Callie was kind of identical to hot-mess Callie.

"I'm actually relieved we didn't wait to address the imbalance," she said, eyeing me nervously. "Once I began working, I realized you had also bonded a Mask, and that you were harboring a Beast. Furthermore, that your Beast is somehow a biological part of you—something I've never seen before," she said, meaningfully. "That unique bond was the only thing holding your aura together. If not for your Beast, you would have been comatose weeks ago."

I shuddered at the thought. I wouldn't have even known what was wrong with me. "Thank you," I said meekly. "Forgot to mention those." She watched me thoughtfully, obviously wanting to pry. "Now that you've had a closer look, any idea what the Spear actually is? You said it is not a weapon, and Ryuu said it was made for healing, not harming."

She pondered that in silence, seeming to compare it to her own mental notes. Finally, she nodded. "That sounds accurate. It was not intended to be used as a weapon. Although it does have a sharp point, so..." she shrugged, smiling playfully. "Technically, it could be both."

I laughed. "That's what *I* said!"

She grinned, her whole face lighting up. "It fit you like a new key and needed to be broken in."

My good humor evaporated. "You filed down the Spear of Destiny?" I hissed, incredulously.

She frowned, shaking her head. "No. I fixed you, the lock. It will no longer disrupt your chakras."

I let out a sigh of relief. Her answer wasn't much better, but at least I wouldn't have to explain to anyone how the Spear had been whittled down for my convenience. I had tallied up enough reasons for Heaven to hate me, especially after my conversation with Michael. Speaking of, I needed to get back to the real world.

"So, am I all healed?" I asked, rising to my feet and dusting off my hands.

She shook her head, rising to her feet as well. "It will take time to permanently heal you. Your body might try to resort to old habits, so I suggest coming back to me a few times for a check-up."

I smiled, glancing at the hot spring pond. "To this dump? I'll think about it," I teased.

She narrowed her eyes in faux anger. "I'll try to spruce it up for you. Maybe put out some magazines."

I laughed, nodding. "Perfect." For the first time, I noticed about a bajillion Silver needles covering the ground all around me. I winced guiltily. "I'm so sorry. Were you hurt?" I asked, studying her nervously.

She shook her head with a smile. "Your Beast thought I was attacking you, at first, so she lashed out through you. I reassured her that I was helping you—and her, as it seems. She is also stronger now. As for me, my physical body was behind the tree. I worked on you from the astral plane.

That's where all the wild magic is. The...colorful sewing threads," she said, alluding to her comment from earlier.

I blinked, dumbfounded. "Your *soul* did all this to me?"

She nodded. "Of course. It takes a soul to fix a soul. I'll probably fall into a deep sleep here in an hour or so. Magic doesn't come from nothing," she said, shrugging. "The bane of a healer." She studied me thoughtfully, seeming to perk up. "As a matter of fact, I wanted to suggest something." I nodded, still struggling to process the whole soul doctor aspect to my chakra surgery. "You have the gift to become a great healer yourself, White Rose. It is quite rare."

I blinked at her, surprised. "Really?"

She nodded, spurred on by my reply. "Your body responded faster than any I've ever worked on. It practically sang beneath my fingers," she murmured, her eyes growing distant. I blushed uncomfortably, wishing she had considered her phrasing. Was that the explanation for my chakra-gasm? "It takes an intuitive person with a deep understanding of their own mind and body to heal maladies in others. It is a natural talent and cannot be taught to just anyone," she said, staring deep into my eyes.

"What makes you so sure?"

She arched one eyebrow in a frank look. "What I just fixed in you would have killed most people."

I nodded, uncomfortably, trying not to think about that last part. "How... long would it take to learn?"

She waved a hand. "Oh, time isn't relevant. We have the immortal pond. A few hundred years and you could be as talented as me. Possibly even stronger. Who knows? Perhaps your Spear is your sewing needle," she said, grinning mischievously.

I frowned, thoughtfully, considering her words. Obviously, I wasn't going to take a sabbatical for a few hundred years, but I was thinking about her comments on a more personal level, assessing them for truth. "I am definitely not a healer. I'm a destroyer," I told her.

That wasn't me pitying or judging myself. Analytically, I was a fighter, not a healer. My traits were geared towards breaking opposition that I deemed harmful or detrimental. It wasn't the only thing I did, but it was the majority of it. Someone needed to do it so people like this woman could clean up the mess after.

She was relentless. "And what do you think a healer does to parasites and poisons? We destroy it," she said with a violent, merciless grin. Then she leaned back. "Just think about it," she said.

I smiled, nodding. She made a fair point. "I don't have a few hundred years to learn. But thank you for the kind words," I told her, walking over to the base of the tree where I found my boots and weapons belt, untouched. I sat down to take out my personal items—the white metal card, the rings, and my phone—and then tugged on my boots. With a smile, I scooped up one of the apocalyptic pink petals as a memento.

"Aala," she abruptly said, causing me to look up from tying my laces. "My name is Aala." She was obviously self-conscious about it, because she wouldn't meet my eyes.

The name wasn't familiar to me—I couldn't place it with any goddess or anything. "It is a beautiful name," I said. "Thank you for sharing it with me, and it's a pleasure to officially meet you, Aala."

She smiled, still not meeting my gaze.

I bent down to pick up my weapons belt—which had survived Ryuu's beating—and slipped it on over my silk robe, accepting the fact that I looked ridiculous. I had enough pockets to tuck my stuff away, at least. I slipped my katana into its sheath and straightened my belt.

I would see if Xuanwu had any new clothes for me because I wasn't going to wear a silk robe into a battle with angels and demons. He was paying for a new playground, so he could afford to replace the ninja outfit that his student, Ryuu, had shredded.

"How long have we been here, Aala?" I asked, smiling at the ability to finally use her name.

She considered my question. "Less than an hour."

I let out a sigh of relief. At least there hadn't been a time delay between this realm and mine. "Good."

"I'm sure Ryuu is anxious by now," she said with an amused grin.

I pretended my heart hadn't dropped into my stomach at her comment. I even managed a faint laugh.

"I'll take you back," she said, walking up to me and extending her hand, "but this will be our goodbye. I must go for a swim to recover and replenish. I expended a lot of energy on a very inconsiderate patient, and now I must feed my soul before I pass out," she murmured with a mock frown.

I narrowed my eyes. "You're welcome," I said, dryly, biting back a grin as I accepted her hand.

She chuckled, squeezing my hand tightly. Without warning, the twilight realm winked out and we were back in Xuanwu's courtyard. I turned to look at her. "Thank you, Aala. I look forward to seeing you again."

She smiled warmly, squeezing my hand again. "Me as well, Callie." She didn't let go, looking as if she had something else she wanted to say, so I waited patiently, knowing she had a shy streak in her. She let out a sigh and finally met my eyes. "Trust will save the world. To get trust, you must first give it." She let out a breath as if she'd had to force herself to say it. "My mother used to tell us that," she said, looking embarrassed. "I have never told anyone before, but I thought you should know it. From one healer to another."

I smiled compassionately, touched by her extension of...well, trust. "Thank you, Aala. That is a very difficult thing to do, so your mother must have been very wise."

She nodded, awkwardly. Something about her comment nagged at me, but she released my hand, snapping me out of my thoughts. "Be safe, Callie. I will see you soon."

I opened my mouth to reply and she promptly disappeared, leaving me facing a Buddha statue. My mouth clicked shut and I stared at the plump god for a few moments. Then I sighed, took a step forward, and bent down to rub his belly. "Wish me luck," I told him.

He was too kind to respond with a lie.

❧ 22 ❧

I sighed, accepting Buddha's judgment, and turned to go search for my
ninja. I only took five steps before I stopped in my tracks with a
frown, wondering if Aala had taken me from the twilight realm to the
Twilight Zone.

Because the Black Tortoise was grilling corncobs on a charcoal grill, and
he had a tarp wrapped over his chest as a make-shift cooking apron. But I
hardly noticed the grillmaster ninja turtle. I was staring at something much
more...rewarding.

Ryuu was chopping wood.

A simple chore. Nothing magical or particularly lethal about it.

But I suddenly felt a buzzing sensation across my skin, and a fluttering
lightness in my stomach.

Ryuu was chopping wood.

And...god...*damn* he looked good doing it!

I shot a quick look over my shoulder at the Buddha statue to pay my
respects. *Thank you.*

Then I turned to resume my ogling of the ninja since neither of them
had noticed my appearance and the yard was otherwise empty. He worked
like a machine. Set, swing, chop, discard. Ryuu had obviously chopped a lot
of wood in his days. Two tall, orderly stacks of freshly quartered logs marked
his progress, but there was still a large pile of uncut logs. More than fifty of

them, if I had to guess. He was stripped to the waist, and I couldn't seem to peel my eyes away. He was slick with sweat, and the early afternoon sunlight highlighted the sharp curves of his muscles like he was made of gold.

I had known Ryuu was fit, but I hadn't known his body fat percentage was so low. I could make out the individual striations to the muscles in his back as he lifted the axe high overhead and slammed it down, his sweat-damp hair whipping about wildly.

He scooped up another log with one hand and turned to bring it back to the stump. I could make out the veins in his neck as rivulets of sweat rolled down his broad chest and onto his six-pack abs, his torso forming that perfect V shape from his shoulders to his waist. His hip bones were prominent, and his oblique muscles rose above his pants with a pleasant *hello!*

He noticed me for the first time since turning around, and he stiffened, staring out at me from beneath a curtain of wild, sweaty hair. I noticed him noticing me and I feigned surprise, turning to Xuanwu.

The Black Tortoise noticed something for the first time, too—a lull in the wood chopping department.

He turned away from the grill to glare at Ryuu not chopping, then shifted his glare to the neat stack, and finally turned back to his grill with an audible sigh. "Hello, Callie," he said, not bothering to look back at me, somehow knowing I was there. "I don't care if she is stark naked and dancing, Ryuu. You're only halfway finished," he said, sternly. "Or I could start counting at the beginning again. Your choice."

Ryuu clenched his jaw, and set the log down atop the stump. Then he hefted his axe and set back to work.

I stared at the pile of logs he still had to cut. That was half of the original number? Good lord. That was insane. "He will find you when he is finished, White Rose," Xuanwu said, sensing my lack of movement. "I hope you aren't truly dancing naked behind me," he added, dryly.

I let out a laugh. "I'm decent. Why is he chopping wood?" I asked, walking towards him and his grill.

"Do you want to become part of the problem?" he asked, "or part of the solution?"

I halted, still a few paces away. Then I scowled at his spiked shell. Someone was in a *mood*. "I need him," I said firmly. "Now."

Ryuu slammed the axe down into the stump harder than he had before, sending the two quarters flying. He panted hoarsely, hunched over his axe, his muscles quivering. Then he released the handle, stormed over to pick up the two pieces, and carried them to the stacks of finished wood. His gaze shot up to me for a millisecond and he subtly shook his head before bending to scoop up another log and carry it over to his stump. He was no longer breathing heavily like a moment before.

"I already explained that he is all yours. Once he is *finished*," Xuanwu said in a warning tone.

"What is he being punished for?" I pressed.

This time, Xuanwu turned to look at me, and there was nothing pleasant about his glare. "He insisted upon visiting the pond after a mere ten minutes of pacing back and forth like a lost puppy, so I gave him something to do to keep him occupied. One hundred and twenty somethings, to be specific," he added smugly. He turned back to his grill, using the long claws of his only unburdened hand—the other hand obviously gripped his sword cane—to roll the corncobs over.

I turned to stare at the tall stacks of quartered wood that hadn't been there earlier. Over one hundred logs. He was going to kill Ryuu. But as I studied the sweating ninja, I realized that he was moving faster now, with no signs of slowing. He'd been doing this for an hour already, yet he looked like he had the energy of just starting out.

"Do you have any spare sets of gear for me to wear, Xuanwu?" I asked.

He glanced back at me, looking slightly guilty as he noticed my robe. Apparently, he'd forgotten about my shredded clothes. "None that would fit. I can have some made or ordered," he suggested.

I waved a hand dismissively. "That's fine," I said, pulling out my phone to buy some time. It was obvious that Xuanwu wasn't feeling conversational, so we weren't going to talk about the Michael thing. To be honest, I didn't really care to talk to him in his current mood. I would find my own answers.

To that effect, I knew just where to go. Darling and Dear were notorious information hounds, and Legion had claimed they made his shoes. If anyone knew about demonic activity in Kansas City, it would be them. Or maybe Dorian Gray, but I didn't have the energy or patience to deal with him right now. He'd make me commit to a party before he said a word, and the angelic police would likely shut that down early and hard, giving them another reason to accuse me of being evil.

And wearing a flashy silk robe and a sword was just the kind of thing to make Darling and Dear—the perverts—salivate. If they didn't have anything useful to tell me, I could head back to Castle Dracula to interrogate Samael while I waited for Ryuu to finish. At the playground with Michael, Qinglong had hinted that Ryuu could find me anywhere. Their arrival had been proof of it. But just in case that had been a fluke, I continued pretending to read my phone. "I'll be out of your hair in a minute, Xuanwu," I muttered, seeing him in my peripheral as he used his long neck to swivel his head and check on me. He grunted, turning back to his grill. I waited until Ryuu was retrieving one of the split halves and carrying it back to his stump. He risked a brief look up at me, silently telling me to leave before I got him in more trouble.

I pointedly lifted my foot and tapped my boot with my finger in a significant gesture. Ryuu frowned, and then a flash of recognition crossed his face. He gave me a subtle nod before setting down the wood on the stump. I treated myself to another eyeful as he scooped up the axe, telling myself it was to make him feel uncomfortable under my scrutiny.

With a powerful heave, he buried the axe into the stump and, in a slightly exaggerated motion, bent over to pick up one of the quartered logs. I blushed, realizing that he was eyeing me with a shit-eating grin, catching me red-handed. But he was straightening back up to toss the pieces onto the finished pile by the time Xuanwu turned with a suspicious narrowing of his eyes.

Backfire.

But I don't regret it—

I froze at a new thought. Nate. I hadn't thought of him in some time.

I'd found myself thinking of Ryuu more often than Nate in recent days. I no longer found myself absently smiling about Nate. I no longer found myself absently *thinking* about Nate, as a matter of fact.

Instead, I was thinking of my lumberjack barbarian ninja who'd almost killed me earlier. How messed up was that?

The continued promises of pursuing romance with Nate—later—were growing stale. Forced and hollow, like we were both placating the other rather than truly meaning it. I shrugged off the thoughts for...later.

I Shadow Walked to my favorite purveyor of retail therapy. Darling and Dear. Armorers of the Apocalypse.

23

I stood on the steps of Darling and Dear in my silk kimono robe with my hand on the hilt of my katana. I didn't see an army of nephilim or demons patrolling the streets, so I let out a sigh of relief. I really wasn't dressed for that sort of thing at the moment. I hadn't bothered changing my boots into something that might better match the robe—like fuzzy slippers. Long story short, I looked like a billboard for the walk of shame, stumbling home at an ungodly hour after an all-night bender and banger. I took a deep breath and knocked on the door, my thoughts drifting to Ryuu and his axe.

I blushed just as the door opened, and a bedraggled Darling stared at me with wide, red-rimmed eyes. He had a necktie wound around his head, a dozen violet lipstick kisses all over his neck, his chest was bare, and around his waist was a Greek war skirt, like he'd been cosplaying as Achilles sacking Troy.

Dear stepped out from behind him wearing a Spartan helmet, a man's unbuttoned white dress-shirt, and knee-length sandals. Both looked manic and agitated, their hair disheveled and their skin glistening with sweat. I had to hand it to them, they had a healthy sexual appetite. Gluttonous, some might say.

Which kind of killed my amusement since Gluttony was one of the Seven Deadlies.

Darling and Dear were both in incredible shape, sporting well-toned physiques and impressive curves. They stared at me, blinking slowly. "Unless you're here for a ride on the Bony Express, come back some other time," Darling finally said. Dear apparently agreed because she was already pushing the door shut.

I stuck my boot into the doorway, preventing them from locking me out. "You *know* why I'm here!" I snapped meaningfully. There was only one reason they would try and kick me out so fast. They were hiding from me and didn't want me asking questions about Legion. If it had just been me interrupting them having sex—which was always—they would have bantered back and forth, inviting me inside in a dozen inappropriate ways.

They froze. Dear stared at me, her eyes dilating within milliseconds as her frustration changed to something animalistic and feral. She licked her lips and gripped my arm. Her fingers were feverishly hot. "Finally!" she hissed, yanking me inside.

"Best. Day. Ever," Darling growled, chuckling excitedly as he slammed the door shut behind me and ushered me into the darkened corridor that led deeper into their shop. "Get undressed quickly. I hope you're hydrated."

I blinked in confusion. Then I mentally replayed my earlier demand and instantly let out a frustrated groan. I skidded to a halt, slapping away their grabby hands. "No! I'm not here for sex!" I snapped, rounding on them.

Darling eyed my robe—and what he envisioned beneath—with a crest-fallen look. "Could have fooled me," he muttered, pinching the silk fabric with an annoyed sound.

I swatted his hand away. "Focus! Tell me why you made shoes for Legion. Tell me about his *pals*."

Dear's face paled and she shushed me loudly. "We sell to *anyone*, and we weren't given much choice."

Darling looked even more annoyed. "You interrupted us for *him*—and dressed like *that*?" he snapped, sounding personally offended. "I'd sell to the Devil himself for the right price," he said, haughtily.

"You are a cruel woman, Callie Penrose," Dear agreed, playing with my hair fondly. Sadly.

I slapped her hand away. "You two really need to get your priorities straight. This is my city. Of *course* I'm here for the demon invasion. Not everything is an opening scene for an adult film."

They stared at me, looking utterly ridiculous. "Well, that was just rude," Darling grumbled.

Dear cocked her head, the helmet slipping to the side. She muttered an echoing curse from within and tugged it off. She flung it behind her without even a glance. "Do you have *any* idea what you interrupted?"

"I'd rather not know the details, so how about you tell me about the demons."

She stared at me suspiciously, even sniffing at the air. "Something is different about you, White Rose..."

Darling assessed my face curiously. Then his eyes widened, and he took a step back, eyeing my silk robe with a wicked grin. He began to slow clap, flicking his head to the side so the hanging tie flipped over his shoulder and out of his face. "I don't know what the man did to you, but he did it well."

"Someone had a spectacular morning," Dear mused with a devilish grin.

"Your aura is literally *glowing*, child," Darling agreed. "Brava."

"Was it that Temple boy, or have you already gotten that out of your system?"

I scowled at the pair of them, realizing they could somehow read the effects of my experience earlier. The unexpected mention of Nate made my face pale—which they took for proof of their accusation, of course. "It was a woman, and it wasn't sex. She was fixing my chakras."

Dear rolled her eyes, pinching my silk robe with a leering smile. "Darling used that line on me recently, as well. I had no complaints."

He smugly polished his knuckles on his sweaty chest. "Any port in a storm. Like that evening in Buenos Aires with the pirates—"

She swatted at him, annoyed. "I want to hear about *her* lotus blossom, not *mine*."

I took a calming breath. "I forgot how much I missed you two," I said, deadpan.

"You could *show* us," Darling suggested. And for some inexplicable reason, he was holding a yellow rubber duckie in his hand—I don't know how and didn't want to learn from where. He squeaked it with a mischievous grin. "Best two out of three?"

I stared at the squeaking, yellow bath toy, knowing he meant something inappropriate, but I literally couldn't think of a single thing to say, let alone imagine *any* possible bedroom scenario. Best two out of three? What the hell did *that* mean? If that made me a prude, thank God.

"I'm going to pretend that didn't happen, and I want you to know that I will never be able to look at a yellow rubber duckie again. Period. Thanks for that."

"You are welcome," he said, actually taking it as a compliment.

"I don't have time for games. I just want answers. Then you two can get back to playing Spartacus."

"They came, they hid, and one of them came to our shop, threatening to burn the place down if we didn't fulfill his order," Dear said, glancing over my shoulder distractedly. "No, we don't know where they are, and we don't want to know. Just like we would tell anyone else if they came asking about *you*," she said, adamantly. "Now, go."

I sighed, promising myself that I would come back to burn their shop to the ground if they were lying. I hadn't risked my dignity standing outside their door like this only to be lied to so they could get their rocks off. "Great. It's been a pleasure."

"No. *Alfred* would have been a pleasure," Darling said, squeaking the rubber duckie again.

I rolled my eyes. Alfred? He'd named the creepy thing? What had he meant by best two out of three? I squashed the thought, stubbornly. I didn't need to know. Alfred was the gateway sex toy.

I was about to turn away when another question came to mind. "Why is Phix so scared of you."

They froze as if I'd stabbed them in the hearts. "She was scared? Of *us*?" Darling asked, softly.

Dear looked heartbroken. "That...doesn't make any sense. We adore Phix. I would risk my life for her."

And for the first time, she sounded entirely truthful. In fact, she looked downright devastated.

I nodded, uneasily, realizing that I should have kept the question to myself, but knowing it was too late to take it back. "She was hurt during the siege on Kansas City before I took over the Sanguine Council. I suggested taking her to you and she freaked out. I've never seen her so scared before."

Silence stretched between us. "Did she put you up to this?" Darling finally asked, smiling strangely—as if he had caught me in a prank.

I shook my head, unable to pick up anything but genuine confusion on their faces. There was no middleman to have given me wrong information because Phix had said it directly to *me*.

So...

What could have made the Sphinx fear Darling and Dear...if it hadn't been them who incited the fear?

Ironically, I faced a riddle—not *from* the Sphinx, but *affecting* the Sphinx. As if I didn't already have enough crap to deal with. At least I knew she was currently safe at the training camp with Death and Grimm.

"I'm not asking this on her behalf. She'd probably gut me for bringing it up, but I want to know what's really going on here. And why you left Kansas City before the barrier went up—when I heard it was impossible for you to do so."

They shared a long look, discussing their answer internally. "Who told you this? About us being trapped here." Darling's voice was no longer playful. In fact, it was downright chilling.

"I heard it from someone else. Anubis told a friend of mine who told me."

Darling abruptly burst out laughing, his aura of danger evaporating like smoke. "Oh, you're speaking about when we ran into the Temple boy in his lover's bar," he said, dismissively. "Misunderstanding. Don't worry yourself over Anubis. He won't matter much longer."

I stared at him, my mouth hanging open, and feeling quite puzzled—detached, even—as if I were having an out of body experience. Darling took a step back from me, shooting a wary look at his wife.

Dear looked concerned. I watched her lips move, silently repeating Darling's statement—as if trying to decipher the cause behind my reaction. "You look pale, White Rose. Would you care for some water?"

I shook my head, numbly. I *did* need water, according to Aala's post chakra surgery recommendations, but I wasn't about to put anything from Darling and Dear in my mouth.

In any way, shape, form, or clever implication, thank you very much.

"The Temple boy's lover?" I asked, softly. I'd heard about her—a Valkyrie named Kára. I'd even drunk Gateway'd to her bar in St. Louis one night, but I hadn't summed up the courage to actually enter, realizing that it would have only made me look crazy.

But...it wasn't jealousy that made me feel like an abstract observer to the current moment.

It was that I did *not* feel any jealousy. I did not feel anything at *all*.

I'd heard Darling's words, told myself that I was supposed to be jealous, and...

I had felt a strange *popping* sensation in my shoulder blades, of all things —tension, sloughing away.

And I realized that Darling had said something else about Temple. He'd asked if I had *gotten that out of my system already*, or something along those lines. He'd said it with casual certainty—like he already knew the future.

He was licking his lips anxiously. "Slip of the tongue. You know how I like that, right, Callie?" he asked with a nervous laugh that cut short too soon. Darling didn't mess up dirty one-liners. Ever. Whatever he saw in my face or heard in my tone...I'd scared the living shit out of him.

I slowly shook my head. "No. It was not. What did you mean by it, Darling?" I asked, calmly, taking a step closer and staring him in the eyes. "And that other thing about getting him out of my system?"

He looked as if he'd seen a ghost, unable to respond. Dear looked suddenly anxious, reaching out to rub my upper arm affectionately. "He didn't mean anything, Callie. Just teasing you like usual. But speaking of the Temple boy, how was he in bed?" She asked—again, sounding too forced.

I slowly lowered my gaze to look down at her hand touching my arm. She yanked it back with a startled sound. I opened my mouth to answer her pointless question with the truth.

"Leave us," a calm, authoritative, woman's voice purred from behind me.

I spun to see a figure saunter out of the shadows at the end of the hall. She moved with a confident sway to her hips—a motion that would have looked forced and unnatural from anyone other than her. She was breath-lessly stunning with long dark hair, and she wore a purple silk robe that looked more suitable for pleasure than decency—the kind that had only been designed to barely cover the lingerie worn beneath.

"Listen, lady. Go back in the other room and wait. They will join you in just a moment, and I'll make sure to tell them to give you a nice tip."

The woman smirked wryly. "Oh, he already...*tipped me.*"

I felt my cheeks heat up at her smoky tone, and inflamed further by her suggestive comment. She made no move to leave. "Well, the first part still stands. Go wait in the other room. We're busy," I said.

"Is that so?" she asked, looking as if she was struggling not to burst out laughing. "I like to get busy."

I arched an eyebrow at her complete lack of shame. "Have some *dignity*, woman—"

"I am Aphrodite, child," she interrupted smoothly. "And I heard you mention a very important name." Her eyes seemed to glisten with golden light for a fraction of a second. "Nate Temple."

24

I froze upon hearing his name, suddenly seeing her in a very different light. It's also when I noticed that Darling and Dear were quiet. They watched the goddess of sex in complete, adoring silence. Aphrodite had bewitched them. That was why they'd looked so frantic when they answered the door. They were strung out.

The weirdest part was that I didn't think it had anything to do with her powers. Because Darling and Dear were mysteriously powerful in their own right. They might also be gods. Perhaps they were just overjoyed to finally play with someone who qualified to perform on their level in the Sexual Olympics.

I studied the goddess warily. I could feel the alluring pull of her aura, so soft but unrelenting, like an underwater current. A whisper of freshly baked brownies in the air. I fought it, pursing my lips defiantly. Aphrodite assessed me with a growing smile, nodding appreciatively.

"Leave us," she told Darling and Dear in a firm tone. "We will pick back up where we left off with Alfred once I am finished with Miss Penrose. Best three out of five, this time," she added in a competitive growl.

The yellow rubber duckie squeaked twice in response. My grim glare shattered, and I burst out laughing. Some twisted part of me *really* wanted to discover Alfred's purpose. I heard a door open and close from somewhere down the hallway, and then it was just me and Aphrodite.

She clasped her hands before her, smiling politely. We stood that way for almost a minute before I began to grow curious. If she had meant me harm, she would have tried by now. She also could have mocked me, taunted me, shown me disdain, or threatened me. Instead, she looked...well, slightly nervous, actually.

Hesitant. And I could tell it wasn't an act. The commanding air she'd shown Darling and Dear was gone.

"How do you know my name?" I asked.

"Everyone knows your name," she said, simply. "The White Rose. Dracula. And your long white hair is rather distinguishable—and quite fetching," she added with a grin. "Reputation is a powerful thing."

I grunted, letting my anger fade. "Reputations can do more harm than help." I wouldn't be cruel or rude, but I would be on my toes. I could be clever without being confrontational.

She nodded her agreement, and then motioned for me to follow her through a door into one of the shop's many sitting rooms. She went in first, so I followed. I entered to find two loveseats facing a crackling fireplace. A leather ottoman filled the space between them, doubling as a coffee table. She stood behind the far loveseat, as if to reassure me that a barrier stood between us. By the look on her face, she might have been more nervous of me than the other way around.

"Do you trust me?" she asked, dry washing her hands in a nervous gesture. It wasn't feigned.

I considered the question. "I met you two minutes ago. I know you like competitive games involving kinky rubber ducks." I glanced at her robe, ignoring her sudden grin. "And you like the color purple. You may or may not enjoy threesomes," I said, indicating Darling and Dear's departure. "That's all I know about you, lady," I said, choosing my words very carefully.

She was still stifling her laughter, obviously wanting to maintain a serious, more formal tone. "Is that *all* you know about me—*Aphrodite*?" she asked meaningfully, holding her arms wide to show off her body.

I considered the question for about a minute. "That is all I *know* about you."

She studied me thoughtfully, looking intrigued. "How interesting. Explain."

I shrugged. "Any story I might have heard about the goddess, Aphrodite, is just conjecture and fable. I don't know any of that to be true. What I *know* is what I have *seen*, firsthand."

I had heard many stories about Aphrodite, and I knew how detrimental it was to rely on rumors or stories written by other people. But one thing I had read about Aphrodite was that she wasn't just the Goddess of Sex—she was the Goddess of *Love*.

Real love.

She valued family, affection, and all facets of love—not just the minimum-wage three minutes of sexual bliss she was so often celebrated for. And Aala had told me love was powerful healing magic.

Aphrodite regarded me with an amused smile, propping her chin between her thumb and the knuckles of her index finger. "Clever, clever. The question still stands. Do you *trust* me?"

I hesitated, recalling Aala's parting comment about trust. "I don't *distrust* you." She arched an eyebrow and gave me a flat look. I decided to take Aala's advice and see where it led me. I took a deep breath and finally nodded, not bothering to hide my own smile. "Yes."

Aphrodite lowered her hand and beamed happily. "Thank you." Her eyes seemed to glint with golden light again, but only for a moment. She gestured at the ottoman.

I looked down to see she was pointing at a box with a purple ribbon. "What is this?" I asked, warily.

"A gift."

I stared down at it. I was trying to trust her. I really was. But how did she have a gift for me when I'd only decided to come here in the last half-hour? Secondly, why did she want to give me a gift at all?

"Open it," she murmured, encouragingly.

I tugged at the ribbon and lifted off the lid of the white box, feeling a twinge of excitement to receive a gift from the goddess of sex. Unless it was Alfred 2.0. Then I was leaving. Period. I'd take Alfred with me, but only to see what all the fuss was about.

Aphrodite had taken a seat in the chair and had lit a clove cigarette. She gestured at the box, leaving a trail of dark blue smoke, seeming impatiently eager for me to see the contents.

I slowly turned back to see a folded set of white clothes inside the box. I pulled them out and shook them. I gasped as they unfurled to reveal a white outfit that was almost identical to my shredded ninja garb, but these felt much lighter. Almost like lace. I quickly checked to make sure they weren't lace—a lingerie version of my ninja gear. But they weren't. The fabric was thick and tough, but it also felt slightly elastic—it simply had no weight. I dragged a fingernail across it and grunted. It felt as tough as metal.

"More resilient and even stain-proof. It's almost as strong as Kevlar, but as light as the faintest of lace because they were woven from moonbeams and starlight. If they become damaged, leave them out at night during a full moon and they will be repaired by morning. Given your new residence at Castle Dracula, I thought this an appropriate design requirement" she said with a wink. Aphrodite's voice hung in the room as thick as the pungent smoke. "Put them on. I'm certain they will fit—perfectly."

I dropped them on the ottoman and quickly slid out of my boots. Then I unclipped my weapons belt and untied the sash around my robe. Without a flicker of hesitation, I let my robe fall to the ground. I'd spent enough time in the nude this morning to make me a pro. Or maybe Aphrodite's very presence served to lower inhibitions. Either way, I began tugging on the pants she had gifted me, and grinned as they slipped on as light as silk and just as easily. But once donned, they suddenly seemed to constrict, hugging me like yoga pants. As I stretched out my leg, I noticed they didn't constrain me at all, seeming to stretch *with* my movement. I flung on the coat, noticing the same qualities, and hurriedly buttoned it up. I twisted and tested my movements, somehow feeling like I was still naked.

I stared down at the final result, grinning stupidly. "This is beautiful," I said, awed. It felt like I was wearing air itself, but the fabric had a faint shine to it, and I could tell it really would hold up well against a bullet, and maybe even a blade. Ryuu rematch! "Why?" I asked, turning to the goddess.

"Because you are *worth* it," she said, compassionately, smiling at me. Was that a tear in her eye?

"We've never even met before," I said, frowning.

She nodded. "Yet you trusted me rather than vilified me. You didn't rely on the countless stories you've heard. You treated me like...a woman," she whispered, obviously touched by my decision. "It has been some time since I've received such a warm welcome."

Had Aala somehow foreseen this? Was that why she had told me her mother's anecdote about trust? Another possibility was that Aphrodite had read my mind. Gods could do that, and I hadn't been protecting myself.

Rather than silently suspecting her, I brought it right out into the open. "Can you read my thoughts?"

She smiled. "So forward," she said, relaxing her shoulders and exhaling a plume of smoke. "No, I cannot read your thoughts. You are too strong for me to mentally manipulate. Not since you became the new Dracula. Now *that* must be a fun story," she said, flashing her teeth in a dazzling smile.

I grinned back. "Something like that." I felt relieved that my thoughts were safe.

The Goddess studied me appraisingly. "You look positively lethal," she said.

I sat down on the chair opposite her and gathered my resolve. "What is all this, really? I appreciate the gift, but I find it troublesome that you just happen to be here with a gift for me. I didn't know I would come here until less than an hour ago. So, how did you?"

"Oh, I didn't. I've been looking for you, but I only came *here* for a little R & R. I knew they might also have information on how I might find you when we were finished...catching up," she said with a dark grin.

"R & R," I asked, dubiously. "Rest and relaxation? Here?"

She cocked her head, looking puzzled. "Is that what humans think R & R means? How...innocent," she mused. "Anyway, I had intended to leave your gift here for them to give to you. I was going to set up a separate time to meet you. Then I happened to hear you mention Nate's name in the hallway, so I came to look who had stopped in. Imagine my surprise. Imagine your suspicion," she added with a smile of understanding. "I get it. I assure you I have the best of intentions—for you—in mind. I don't go around looking for trouble. I have enough on my plate as it stands. Nate Temple is at the center of that storm, although he is as much a victim as me."

I had been watching her face for any signs of deceit, but I saw none.

She cleared her throat, staring off into the middle distance for a few moments, collecting her thoughts. "I fear Nate Temple is not doing very well right now," she said, cautiously. "I comforted him last night, but his morning will be the exact opposite of yours. Pleasure and friendship for you," she said, pointing at me, "pain and enemies for him. Two sides of the same coin."

25

I swallowed my instinctive anger and fear, forcing myself to take a calming breath. "Where is he?"

"He is in the process of escaping," she assured me. "Nate Temple will survive the day—I am seeing to that, personally. Which brings me to the purpose of my visit. Matters of the heart."

I pinched the fabric of the outfit she had given me, tugging at it so she could see. "This is the closest path to my heart right now." She frowned, looking heartbroken at my claim. I sighed, feeling guilty. "Okay."

A smile slipped back into place, as bright as the sun. She leaned forward. "Tell me about you and Nate Temple. And be honest with me. On matters of the heart, I *can* read your mind," she warned with a reassuring smile.

I reached into my pocket instinctively, only to suddenly panic. My Horseman's Mask! I didn't remember grabbing it when I'd taken off my shredded ninja gear—

I let out a gasp of surprise as my fingers settled over a metal figurine in my new pants.

Aphrodite grinned. "With that outfit, anything bonded to you will always be at hand. You don't seem like a purse kind of girl. Unlike Nate," she added with an amused chuckle.

"Satchel," I said on reflex, smiling at Nate's never-ending argument about his man-purse. The one I had gotten him.

"Oh, don't get me started on Temple's satchel," Aphrodite chuckled. "Talk about a man in denial! My brother, Hermes, is *exactly* the same about his ridiculous purse."

I grinned, nodding my agreement. But my smile slipped to see Aphrodite's rapidly fading radiance upon mention of her brother. I held out the figurine, still excited about my magical outfit. "Nate gave me one like this a long time ago. A symbol of our feelings for each other," I admitted. "It is very special to me."

Aphrodite arched an eyebrow. "*Special* is so overused that it has become increasingly banal. I am speaking of the heart, girl. Do not hide behind seemingly pretty but hollow words like *special*."

I sighed uncertainly. I wasn't sure what to say, or what she was digging for. She had asked for the truth. After her incredible gift, didn't I owe her that much? She claimed to be helping Nate, but I wasn't sure how me airing my dirty laundry was going to help. It would probably only make things worse, wouldn't it?

"How is this going to help Nate?" I asked. "I need to know."

She smiled empathetically. "Oh, child. I misspoke. I've already been helping Nate. Right now, I am here to help *you*," she said, meaningfully. "By doing so, I can help you both. I am the goddess of love, after all."

I stared at her, feeling suddenly anxious. Her words rang true. I did need to talk about this, and with someone who wouldn't be put in an awkward position as a result. I closed my eyes and took a deep breath, gathering my courage. If I couldn't talk about my love life with the goddess of love, who the hell could I talk to about it? I opened my eyes and let out a breath.

"Neither of us has made a move," I finally said. "At first, I waited for him to do so. Then I wondered why I hadn't done so. We are both always busy with our...work," I said, lamely, trying to come up with a term for our ongoing wars against monsters. "We always choose work over each other."

Aphrodite nodded. "Has another man taken up space in your heart?" she asked. "Evicting Nate?"

"No!" I growled, dismissing thoughts of Ryuu—because the two men weren't mutually exclusive.

I'd come to a conclusion about Nate well before Ryuu started occupying my thoughts. This wasn't me trading in Nate for a newer model car. With or without Ryuu in the picture, my Nate relationship remained static. And that was the problem.

"It's not another man. It's just...the more time we spend apart, the more I find myself rationalizing and making excuses to justify our decisions. I haven't lost my feelings for Nate, but they have *changed*." I frowned at her suspiciously because she had been nodding subconsciously. "You already know this."

Aphrodite crossed her legs, inhaling her cigarette thoughtfully. "Matters of your own heart are not something someone else can tell you. They must be discovered, not heard."

I folded my arms stubbornly. "I know! But it sounds so childish and petty. Woe is me; I'm not getting paid enough attention. I've fallen out of love! Boo-fucking-hoo."

My words echoed in the room like a guillotine blade slamming home and my eyes widened in surprise.

"That's not—"

"It is *precisely* what you meant, child," Aphrodite said in a calm, but significant tone. "You cannot deny your own feelings. You have simply never said it out loud. You have fallen out of love." She studied me, letting her words hang in the air like a thick fog. "But accepting that fact is not enough for inner peace," she said, softly. "You must also discover why you fell out of love—why you didn't make each other a priority."

I nodded, feeling numb, but knowing she was right. "I already know," I whispered.

"Oh?" she asked.

I nodded, speaking on autopilot. "I'm speaking for myself, but I think my feelings are reciprocated, whether Nate knows it or not." Aphrodite nodded, expelling another stream of aromatic smoke. "I want someone here, by my side, in Kansas City," I whispered. "And Nate can never be that man because he is already that man for *St. Louis*. I admire and adore how much he cares for his city, and I want a man who feels that way about me and my city."

She nodded. "That is a fair desire."

I nodded, woodenly. "To get what I want, I would have to take him away from what he loves—his city, his family history, and the hundreds of people who love and depend on him. Over time, he would grow to resent me for it. My love would *destroy* him," I whispered. "Which would destroy *me*."

"You love Nate Temple too much to break him," Aphrodite said, softly.

"You know that what you require of him would break the very qualities you respect and value."

I nodded. "And I think he wants the same thing from me—something I cannot give him."

"Neither of you are wrong in this desire. And neither of you should feel guilty. Love is a choice."

"Maybe I just need an Alfred," I grumbled. "He's a Kansas City man, through and through."

She grinned, nodding—only making me more curious about the rubber duckie. "I will have one delivered to you." My eyes widened and I opened my mouth to object, but Aphrodite cleared her throat. "It is done. You will thank me later. Now, I am a goddess, first. I, too, have duties that interfere with the dictates of my heart. Perhaps you have heard of my husband, Hephaestus," she said, softly. I looked over at her, thoughtfully, her comment dashing thoughts of Alfred from my mind. I had heard of the two—and how Aphrodite spent more nights sleeping around with practically everyone else but her husband. Top of her list was Ares, the god of war. But I didn't understand how it related to our conversation—and I had specifically chosen not to rely on old stories to judge her.

I nodded. "I have heard of Hephaestus," I said, carefully. "You are unable to be with him?"

She nodded ever so slightly. "That is exactly what I am saying, although I was not expressly forbidden from doing so. I voluntarily chose my actions in order to attain a greater good."

I frowned, confused. The only beings who could *make* Aphrodite do anything were probably her parents, Zeus and Hera. But Zeus was the one who had arranged her marriage to Hephaestus in the first place. "Why would the goddess of love deny her only true heart's desire—if that's what Hephaestus is to you?"

A single tear rolled down her cheek. "He is," she whispered. "But there is something he loves more than me, and the only way I can help him get that is by hiding my true emotions from public view."

I stared at her, horrified. "Another woman?" I asked.

She laughed, shaking her head. "Yes, but not in the way you are thinking."

I pondered her words. A woman, but not in the romantic sense? Then it hit me like a lightning bolt. "Pandora. You're talking about his daughter, Pandora."

Aphrodite hung her head and took a deep breath. "Yes. Her safety is directly correlated to my distance from Hephaestus. The farther away I am from my soulmate, the safer she is."

"That's...terrible," I whispered.

She grunted. "They don't call it Greek Tragedy for nothing."

Pandora was a target, and the closer Aphrodite got to her husband, the more danger Pandora would be in. Her love for Hephaestus would get his daughter killed. "How do you two stand it?" I whispered.

Aphrodite slowly lifted her chin to look at me, and she stared directly into my eyes with such an intense gaze that I felt like curling up into the fetal position. "You misunderstand, Callie Penrose. Hephaestus does not know."

26

Her words were resolved and committed and full of pain. "Men are not as strong with certain things. They wear their emotions on their sleeves or act out with direct violence at the institution. Women are wiser and can often find indirect ways to achieve a better solution—at the price of personal pain. Hephaestus would lash out publicly, getting himself, Pandora, and me, all killed or tortured. But I can work behind the scenes with none the wiser, allowing myself to be painted in an undignified light by my fellow Olympians as a wonton harlot. In fact, it is better to proudly embrace my disguise for all to see, throwing my cloak of shame to the wind, and wildly fucking my way through every barrier between me and my ultimate goal." Her eyes were feverish, and her skin was flushed. "The goal is to reunite my husband with his daughter—over my own dead body if needs be. The harlot is the hero in my story—in *his* story. If that makes me a monster, then *rawr*," she said, curling her hand into a claw.

I stared at her, stunned. Aphrodite was...a *boss!*

"I...had no idea."

She was silent for a time. "Neither does my husband. But the thought that strengthens me is the gift I will ultimately give him—the look on his face when I manage to reunite him with his daughter. The men and women complicit in her abduction and extortion will become the wrapping paper for my ultimate gift."

Well. That was better than a Hallmark card.

"Our situation seems even more childish now," I said with a faint smile.

She shrugged. "All love seems childish from the outside. It should. Children are carefree and light-hearted," she said with a smile.

I nodded, unable to make myself smile. "I fear that telling him this will push him over the edge. That he might think I'm rejecting him when he's been waiting to start our relationship. We can't afford for a man like Nate to feel heartbreak. He might even see it as betrayal. The Horseman of Hope would lose hope because the Horseman of Despair took it from him. We would destroy more than just each other."

Aphrodite nodded. "To be fair, he would do the same to you if you were to abandon Kansas City for St. Louis. You would be equally murdered. Whoever moves will slowly wither away and die."

I nodded, shakily. "How do I tell him without hurting him?"

Aphrodite smiled. "Can you handle a harsh truth, and promise not to tell anyone—especially Nate?"

I nodded, curiously this time. "Yes. Of course."

She hesitated, considering her words carefully. "Nate Temple is in love with another over you."

I frowned at her, confused. "What?"

She nodded, soberly. "He does not even know it. That is the cruel irony. He does not even realize that his heart yearns for another. Your analysis was more than just an awareness of your own feelings, Callie. You were reading his. I ask you to be patient and gentle with him until he accepts the truth."

I stared at her, struck silent. Nate had the same reservations as me? "I don't understand."

Aphrodite pursed her lips. "Nate Temple is in pain. Has been in pain. Enough for two lifetimes. He has very few happy moments, and that is what has made him the Catalyst. He will pay almost any price to feel happiness—often by making sure his friends find happiness in his stead."

I nodded, knowingly. My lip trembled and my eyes misted slightly at Nate's surprisingly vast self-sacrificing moral fiber. "I love that about him," I whispered, not caring that my voice cracked slightly. I was still struggling to process the fact that he might not be in love with me as much as I'd thought. It hurt, in a way. Yet...it was liberating. I would not have to hurt him—like so many of his loved ones often had.

Her words, although they cut deep, rang of truth. But to hear that he loved another? "How can he love someone and not know it?" I asked, doubt-fully. The only reason I hadn't laughed in her face was because of her heart-felt story about her husband. That the goddess of love had sacrificed her own love in order to get him what he desired above all—his daughter.

I frowned. "Wait. Didn't you say you comforted Nate last night? What the hell did *that* mean?" I demanded, suddenly feeling protective of my friend. Had she used Nate as a notch on her bedpost—a chess piece on the board for her to get Pandora for her husband?

Because Pandora belonged to Nate. She was the librarian for his Armory, and she referred to him as her host and master. Was Aphrodite angling to use Nate in order to acquire Pandora? Was I sitting with my enemy? "Are you using Nate for your own ends?"

Aphrodite stiffened, as if my words had cut her to the bone. "Never," she whispered. "I cannot destroy love, even if I wanted to. If Nate were single and happy and I wanted to get in bed with him, I could do so with the crook of a finger," she said without hesitation. "Betraying or being complicit in the betrayal of a man's love—helping him commit romantic suicide—is quite literally not possible for me. And utterly contemptible, morally speaking. I would lose my powers in an instant, and everyone—including Hephaestus—would know what I had done. Even if I were willing to sacrifice my own powers to get Hephaestus his daughter, I would forever poison their reunion, defeating the whole purpose. So, no. I did not fuck Nate Temple. You idiot."

I felt very, very small under her glare. "Sorry. I'm just—"

"Protective of your friend. I get it," Aphrodite said, letting out a calming breath. "Now, regarding your first question about Nate not knowing his own heart's desire," she continued. "What he truly seeks is a lover he lost long ago. He does not know he lost her, and he does not know she is still within his grasp, but I am determined to help him realize it. Because the poor bastard was deceived. The more I think about it, the more certain I am that it is an insidious attack. That the Carnage hunts his very soul."

I cringed instinctively at the word, even though I had never heard it in such context. "The Carnage?" I whispered.

She nodded. "You do not need to fear the Carnage. You already defeated it in the Doors. You were never even aware of it, but your godfather helped you defeat it. Nate Temple faces a similar crucible now, and I will save him from it."

I stared at her. "I could help—"

Aphrodite held up a hand, quieting me. "No. Your involvement, at the wrong time, would only tip the scales the wrong way. With you shining in his sight, he would continue down his path of denial."

I nodded in understanding. "He would avoid his inner pain in favor of me."

Aphrodite nodded. "Not because he is a coward, but because he does not know he is at war. He does not even know he has been at war—for years, now. That he was lied to," she growled, clenching her fist. "And you are the desirable young nurse fixing up his wounds—a dangerous distraction when his life has been a battlefield of lost friends, pain, and betrayal. He seeks you out to maintain his sanity, not knowing that you are merely his doom. No disrespect intended, of course. He is equally your doom," she reminded me with a small smile.

That sounded like Nate. Focusing so much on keeping everyone else safe that he overlooked his own problems. As arrogant as he was, he was alarmingly altruistic. I realized I was smiling. "I need a Kansas City Nate."

Aphrodite shook her head firmly. "No. Never *need*. Love is not need. That is desperation."

I considered her words, surprised at her sudden vehemence, but understanding what she meant. "I desire someone at my side who is not divided. But I don't want a sycophant to grovel at my feet. I want someone to stand beside me, not below or behind me. Someone as commanding as Nate. A man willing to shove me back when I make a mistake and hold me accountable for it. A man who values my city as much as me."

Ryuu, I thought to myself with a faint blush.

Aphrodite nodded knowingly, as if sensing my thoughts on Ryuu. "Yes, Callie Penrose. I hope that you one day find such a person. There is no guarantee, of course, although I think you are in luck," she said, cryptically. I wondered if she had the answer and was prevented from telling me. That the act of hearing his name from her lips would kill some of the magic in discovering his name for myself. Which made sense. Was it...Ryuu? My heart fluttered nervously at the thought. Aphrodite noticed my suspicious gaze and shook her head. "I will say no more. When I want to, I can clam up so tight that no one may enter." She shot me a wry look. "And no, the irony is not lost on me. The goddess of sex can be just as closed off as she is opened wide."

I burst out laughing.

Aphrodite abruptly stiffened, and her eyes darted to the far wall. Then her gaze shot to my weapons belt. "Is that sword the only weapon you have on you, child?" she asked nervously.

I jumped to my feet at her tone, following her gaze. "Yes. Why?"

"Because something very terrible is about to happen," she said, softly. "Right outside." She pointed at the wall. "I can sense the raw hatred. It is the exact opposite of me," she whispered. "A demon. A very, very powerful demon," she said, slowly rising to her feet.

I strapped on my weapons belt and rested my hand on the hilt of my katana. My heart pounded in my chest, knowing that the demon wasn't here for her. One of the Seven Sins was here. For *me*.

Where are you, Ryuu? I thought to myself. *I could really use the Angel Killer right now.*

"No, Aphrodite. I will handle this myself."

She turned to me with a confused frown. "By yourself?"

"Someone needs to go save Nate Temple," I said with a smile, not wanting to draw her into my problems. It sounded like she had enough on her own plate—even without Nate. "I've got this."

Aphrodite studied me appraisingly. Finally, she nodded. "He is not here for me, is he?" she asked.

I shook my head. "No. He is here for me."

Aphrodite nodded slowly, staring down at my ring. "I think the world might not be ready for you, Miss Penrose," she said. "You are no Catalyst, but perhaps you are something equally dangerous. We could do great and terrible things together, I think."

I studied her, trying to read the look in her eyes, but they were strongly defended.

"Give Alfred a squeeze for me," I said. She choked on her laughter. "My city is calling me."

I turned to walk towards the front door and meet the demon but had one last wish for Aphrodite. "And good luck with your love life," I said, smirking back at her.

She nodded. "You as well, child. You as well."

As I left down the hall, I thought I heard her murmuring to herself.

"Great and terrible things..."

27

I stepped out onto the street, checking over my shoulders for ye old sucker punch ploy. Demons weren't the only guys hunting me on these streets. The nephilim wouldn't be far behind—either hunting me or the demons, and they would kill whichever of us they found first.

But the streets were empty, and my boots did not tingle in the slightest. I angled them towards the alley leading around to the back of Darling and Dear's shop, and the tingling sensation started. "Of course it's an alley fight," I muttered, imagining the scene from *Anchorman*—just with less LOL's. If the nephilim showed up, it really would wind up like that insane brawl.

Although foreboding, a discreet, out of public view fight was better than one in the middle of the street in broad daylight. Part of me considered leaving and returning with backup, but what if the demon wreaked havoc in my brief absence? He most certainly would if he felt me leave. He had come here for me, after all.

I made my way into the shadowy alley, silently appreciating the craftsmanship of Aphrodite's gift. The armored fabric stretched with each step, yet it still managed to hug me tightly, reassuringly. Had Hephaestus made it? He was the blacksmith god for the Olympians, and I couldn't think of anywhere else Aphrodite might have gotten it. I realized that Aphrodite had helped me in other ways. My shoulders felt more relaxed and my heart felt lighter after our talk about love.

I would always love Nate, just not in the way either of us had thought. And knowing that it was actually the best solution for the both of us—not just me—I felt downright amazing. Like I could hover over the ground rather than walk. That dark cloud of guilt and anger had hung over my head for far too long.

Today was a new day.

I took a measured breath, focusing on the danger ahead as I flexed my toes inside my tingling boots. A very powerful demon, Aphrodite had said. It had to be one of the Seven. Given that the entire block wasn't on fire and no one was screaming, I presumed he wanted to talk. I thought about all the buildings around us—most of them commercial retail—and wondered how many people slept in the lofts above. At least it was Sunday and early enough in the morning for very few stores to be open for business.

Perfect time for me to have a date with a demon—while a large number of innocents were safe at church.

Maybe I could lead the demon out of the city entirely. I could Shadow Walk him from this area, at least, since it had so much potential for collateral damage. Maybe go to a warehouse area since they didn't typically work on Sundays.

Due to recent events, it was no longer so unbelievable to the residents of Kansas City that monsters existed. The majority still doubted, of course, but too many had seen the vampires taking over the city, walling it off from outsiders with a glowing red dome in the sky. Those people did not buy the flowery reassurances given by the politicians and news pundits on the evening news.

People were scared. A lot of them. Enough to draw national attention, perhaps. We were rapidly approaching the day when monsters and magic would no longer be a secret. The epicenter of that awareness would be either Kansas City or St. Louis.

And, unfortunately, fear only served to *attract* demons. I gritted my teeth, frustrated. How had the Seven Sins managed to enter my city with none the wiser? Who was helping them? If Darling and Dear had no answers, the only other person I could think to ask was Dorian Gray, and that was an exercise in boundaries.

Maybe my date would give me the answer. The homeless population had nominated this dark alley as a premium latrine, so it smelled sharply of ammonia and death. Dumpsters overflowed, disgorging their contents onto the wet pavement, adding to the stench. I hesitated before an intersection where the alley split to the left and right, forcing me to choose.

"Hello? I'm just a scared little girl walking down an alley," I called out in an overly frightened tone in hopes that it would draw my prey out. My fingers drummed on the hilt of my katana as I waited.

To the left, I heard a commotion from deeper within the warren of intersecting alleys. I rounded the corner with my blade raised, ready for an immediate attack. Instead, I saw a familiar man leaning against the brick wall. I narrowed my eyes suspiciously, ignoring the alarm bells suddenly ringing in my head.

Legion puffed on a pipe, emitting a pleasant-smelling cloud of dark gray smoke that lessened the stench of decay. He pointed at the fork in the intersection. "Seemed too obvious to stand there," he said, smiling.

I grunted. "Of course. Crossroads—"

I cut off abruptly, noticing three dead ninjas crucified to the wall about ten feet past the demon. I didn't recognize any of their faces, but I was sure I had crossed paths with them a few times at Xuanwu's home. They hardly spoke and were always bowing reverently when I approached. They liked me —I knew that much—but they were a tight, close-knit group, and it would take time for me to get into their circle.

Still...they were my people. I clenched my jaw and lifted my blade. My magic crackled within me, seeming to purr just beneath my skin, anxious to be let out. In fact, it was more of an effort to contain it than it was to call it up. Aala's work on my chakras had brought my magic so close to the surface that I felt like a quick draw gunman, the fastest spell-slinger in the Midwest.

I glared at the crossroads demon. "You will pay for that, Legion," I promised.

He gestured with his pipe towards the three crucified ninjas, leaving a trail of smoke so dark that it almost looked blue. "That wasn't us. We're desk-demons," he said, indicating his suit and pointedly not looking towards the corpses—as if he might successfully will them away by doing so. I'd almost forgotten about his use of the plural. I kept my eyes sharp in case he chose to turn into a dozen replicas and demonpile me. "Remember, you asked for this," he said, gently. "Unless you're willing to sign?" he asked, almost sounding hopeful as he nudged a suitcase sitting on the pavement. "We brought a fresh copy with the changes you requested."

I shook my head. "No. I am not signing. We agreed on one week. I have a few days left."

He nodded, morosely. "Time is not the only thing you asked me for, White Rose," he said, jerking his chin past the dead bodies and further into the alleys. "Proceed at your own peril." He took a deep puff from his cigar and then exhaled it in a long streamer of dark smoke. I jumped back a step as his actual body faded into smoke and then merged with the cigar's dark cloud. Within seconds, it had dissipated, leaving me alone.

I stared at the dark alley, seriously reconsidering further exploration. Not out of fear of danger, but at the prospect that Legion's boss was ahead—the demon who wanted to marry me. After my conversation with Aphrodite—my revelation about my heart—the irony of meeting an archdemon who wanted to force me into marriage hit me deeply. It was revolting and frightening and...entirely unfair. Aphrodite had helped teach me what my heart truly desired, and now my choice was to abandon that chance at happiness or risk my city being destroyed.

"Then you'll just have to kill him, White Rose," I told myself out loud—my own private cheer squad.

I forced myself to press on, murmuring a silent prayer as I passed the dead ninjas and the pool of blood beneath their bodies, which had collected into one large mass that was slowly creeping across the pavement. I felt a faint resistance in the air as I passed the ninjas, like I had stepped into a steam room. Then it was abruptly gone. I reached out to my magic and was relieved to find that it still worked. So, it hadn't been a ward. I didn't bother masking the sound of my steps—Legion had already made me, so stealth was off the table. And...stealth hadn't saved the ninjas. But why had they even been here? Had Ryuu sent them to guard over me while he finished chopping wood?

Right now, the why didn't matter. They were dead either way. I *wanted* the demon to hear me approach. To hear the sound of his own death coming. Legion had said I'd asked for something more. Was he talking about a traditional proposal? Was I going to find a kneeling demon up ahead, holding out a sulfur diamond?

It was almost laughable.

I hoped that my swim with Aala had washed off any potential archangel stink. If not, it was possible that I had lured the demon out of hiding, leading him directly to the leather shop. Yet Legion was already a customer of Darling and Dear. Had...the kinky leathersmiths sold me out?

After several more turns, I stepped into a wider convergence of alleys that formed a hub large enough for delivery trucks to turn around. A small loading area branched off from the alley, leading to a brick wall with a single door—the back of Darling and Dear's shop. Luckily, the alley was long and curved, so it was concealed from the main streets on either end. As long as no trucks entered, we could fight without anyone seeing us.

The space was utterly empty. No groom waiting to profess his undying love, and no more dead ninjas. I made a slow circle, leading with my katana. "What is this?" I murmured, my boots still tingling—in every direction.

As if summoned by my question, six demons suddenly appeared out of thin air from the alley to my right. They were taller than me, and about as stereotypical as you could imagine—red-skinned with horns and hooves like goats. In fact, they looked like half-assed cosplayers. They even had black, single-handed pitchforks and their scaly tails had those little leaf shapes on the ends. Except they were ridiculously chiseled, as if their favorite place in Hell had been the prison yard.

And their eyes were entirely red. I stared at them in mild disappointment. "Really? Horns and everything?" I asked, tapping my temples—where they each sported a pair of horns. They could have been cardboard cutouts of one another. They hissed, revealing black, pointy teeth.

A sound to my left made me glance down the opposite end of the alley to see *another* gang of six identical demons.

A dozen demons. Against one Callie.

The air now positively reeked of sulfur. It was time to put Aphrodite's armor to the test and answer the age-old question—did wearing protection halt the spread of HTD's—Hell-Transmitted Diseases.

On that note, I absently patted a pocket on my weapons belt to check the two rings I had been carrying around. They had not tingled or given off any magical sensation in response to the demons like they had with Michael. Were they only for angels? My boots were working perfectly fine, though, so I dismissed them from my mind.

"Which one of you assholes killed the three ninjas back there?" I growled, pointing behind me.

One of them sneered and pointed over my shoulder. I spun to see six more demontuplets lurking only ten feet away from me. I tried to keep all three of the squads in my sights as I slowly spun in a continuous rotation. The demon who had pointed out the six new arrivals thumped his chest proudly. "We killed three as well," he rasped, pointing his trident behind him. A demon from the last gang said something similar, pointing over his own shoulder. "It's how we set the ward and trap. None may cross it, so don't even consider fleeing, little human," he sneered.

Not three ninjas. *Nine* ninjas had been murdered and put on display.

Not twelve demons. *Eighteen* demons had forked up and come out to play.

As proposals went, Legion's boss could have used some pointers for my very special day.

Then again...it wasn't all that bad.

I smirked back wolfishly, feeling a rush of adrenaline hit my bloodstream. Despite the sudden boost of endorphins, I was raging on the inside. These demons had set a trap for me. They thought to ensnare me, and they had used Ryuu's men to do it. Ryuu was going to be livid. He wouldn't show it, but he would feel it in his heart and soul. Out loud, he would say something brave about the fallen ninjas all knowing what they had signed up for. But I didn't agree with Ryuu on that.

They'd signed up to keep my city safe, not to die and then be put on display in a macabre demon ritual.

As an extension of Ryuu's will, I would make sure the ninjas hadn't died in vain. I would avenge them and teach the demons a lesson—don't fuck with the shinobi or the White Rose. Since the demons had outnumbered the shinobi two-to-one, I considered the idea of killing each demon twice in memory of Ryuu's men—to set a precedent. After I killed them with magic, I could manually go around and behead them all as a symbolic gesture—like a cat leaving a dead bird on your doorstep. Maybe it would show Ryuu how much I cared about him.

Lone swordsmen didn't last long against almost twenty-to-one odds, so I'd have to use magic to prevent them from swarming me all at once.

I studied the two demons who had spoken up. "You two die last, so you can tell me how to nullify this supposed ward. You're welcome. I'll give you a minute to say your goodbyes," I said, lowering my katana.

They sneered at me, clenching their pitchforks tighter. Then they rushed me simultaneously, craving a little Callie sandwich. Time to teach them what happened when you tried to eat your food too fast.

But first, a tribute.

"The Redgoats are coming! The Redgoats are coming!"

28

I opened myself up to my magic, allowing it to do more than just rest beneath the surface of my skin. I screamed in delight at the euphoria that instantly hummed throughout my body. My soul ignited with magic much faster than ever before, and power rushed out of me like I'd taken the kink out of a kinky garden hose.

It wasn't my proudest metaphor. Or was it a simile? I could never remember the difference.

My magic was *way* more potent than usual. Aala had warned me about my powers being more combustive, but she had severely understated it.

I flung my hand towards the demons on my right and left at the exact same time, and I used entirely different magic for each, laughing as the power ripped out of me like the final, glass-shattering note of an opera singer's solo.

The demons on the right screamed as living vines of inky black thorns erupted through the pavement and exploded out of the brick walls surrounding them. The vines struck like a thousand vipers, tearing into and through a handful of the demons, wrapping back around to tirelessly impale a second and third target—often multiple times—until the area resembled a black spider's web with a fresh catch of demonic flies.

The demons on the left screamed as a wall of liquid white fire about twenty feet tall and as wide as the alley hit them in a tidal wave of dripping, splashing flame. It stuck to their flesh and sizzled like salt poured on a slug, replacing the rotten stench of sulfur with bacon and char. The surface of the pavement baked and crumbled to fine dust beneath their feet and the mortar of the brick walls did the same, sending the two walls of now white-hot bricks crashing over them.

I stood in the middle, one hand blazing with an orb of white light and the other an orb of pure darkness.

I released my magic, staring in awe at the results of my attack. The white fire and black thorns were not common magic, as far as I'd been told. I knew Nate had access to them as well, but I'd never actually learned or practiced them. They'd just come to me over time.

But the two seemed to negate each other; or maybe complement each other. They were connected in some way, like yin and yang.

The gang of demons behind me roared in outrage. I spun, tapping into my Sanguina-vision.

Time froze as I assessed the six demons standing motionless before me —the first of them only a foot away. The static image was pure chaos, but frozen in limbo.

Ribbons of crimson light showed me the upcoming lines of the dance. I studied it, memorized it, and then I perfected it so that it was beautiful and inspiring. Dances were supposed to be beautiful.

I added order to the chaos of their bloodlust.

I gripped my katana and smiled as time resumed to normal speed. I hadn't wanted to slaughter them while they were defenseless. Where was the fun in that? The first demon lunged at me with his barbed pitchfork.

I intercepted it with my katana, stabbing up between the prongs to trap it rather than parrying the haft to the side—like shoving a stick through bicycle spokes. Then I continued my arm's momentum in a circular, rotating motion that twisted the pitchfork from his grip. He was so focused on losing his pitchfork that he hadn't noticed my fist sailing for his throat. My punch crushed cartilage, making him gag and squeal, clawing at his neck for air. I caught his pitchfork and used a burst of magic to slam the butt of the weapon down into the pavement like a flagpole. Then I swiveled and hip tossed him, back first, onto said flagpole.

He screamed and thrashed, kicking his hooves, and clawing at the three tines poking up from his stomach, only serving to drive himself further down the wicked barbs.

The other demons stared at his plight with outraged looks, and I capitalized on the opportunity to grab one of the horns of the second demon and drive my katana through his eye and out the back of his head. His instant scream cut off just as abruptly as it had begun. I released his horn and held onto the handle of my katana with both hands as the demon's knees buckled and then gave out. His weight slowly pulled him off my blade with a sickening sound before he thudded to the ground, twitching.

"Anyone want s'mores?" I asked as I lit the screaming, impaled demon behind me on fire like a marshmallow. In response, his hoof kicked out and hit me right in the back of the elbow...

On the funny bone. You know, the unfunny one.

My arm spasmed and shot forward, sending my katana clattering and skidding across the pavement amidst the four surviving demons.

I was so relieved to learn that Aphrodite's fancy ass armor could block bullets and blades, but not protect my goddamned funny bone. "Give me my sword, please," I said, holding out my hand.

The four looked up and I saw something strange come over them, almost seeming to possess them. Their eyes danced with manic bloodlust as if they were suddenly beyond all rational thought. They roared at me in a sputtering, mindless rage, and then they rushed me, thinking I was weaponless.

Except they were wrong. Ryuu and Aala had agreed that the Spear of Destiny wasn't a weapon, but I kept on thinking of that pointy bit. And I had to admit...

I was mighty curious about playing with it.

The Spear crackled to life in my palms and filled the darkened alley with blinding light that burned the eyes. Well, *their* eyes, not mine. As the Spear's caretaker, I must have had some default form of protection that banned the bright rays from harming me.

You might say I had Ray-ban protection. Or, better yet, *Son*-glasses, since the Spear had first become a Holy Relic after stabbing God's son on the Cross.

Blaspheming was fun.

The demons cried out, squinting against the antithesis of their existence. I somehow managed to dim the light with a thought—the Spear responding as if an extension of my will—because I wanted to savor the ebb and flow of battle rather than picking off the blinded, blighted bastards one-by-one. I lunged forward, right into the thick of their squad, and stabbed the Spear through the closest Redgoat—the only one who looked like he could still actually see.

One of them managed to trip over his own hooves as he tried to skewer me. I twisted my shoulders reflexively and my angel wings exploded out of my back, deflecting the blow with a metallic clang and a sizzling hiss. A choking gasp and a wet splat told me that my wings had actually sliced him in half, sending his upper body crashing to the ground. His lower body continued trotting around, kicking and clomping like it was in a dance audition, drawing the attention of his allies. Well, two of his allies.

I was too busy staring at the third demon who currently had my Holy Spear through his throat. I watched, fascinated, as the scaled red skin around the tip of the Spear crackled and burned away like an old newspaper. Then, picking up speed, that white fire surged through his body, burning him alive from the center out until curling fingers of burnt flesh floated up into the air with a sickening, sulfuric stench.

Which was when one of the two remaining demons hoofed me in the... well, the term for what he did to me was *also* known as *hoofing*, funnily enough.

He kicked me in the lady bits with Hellfire horseshoes, and I felt like my pelvis bone should have shattered. The blow sent me sliding to the side, gritting my teeth in anger as I doubled over, leaning on the Spear for support.

Which was when his fellow kicked me in the jaw—likely having aimed for a double-whammy hoofing, but I'd been doubled over, so I blocked it with my face.

Stars exploded across my vision and I instinctively slammed the butt of the Spear into the ground like an anchor. My ears rang and I shook my head, already feeling my jaw swelling. I'd been too distracted by the smoldering demon—my first experience using the Spear—to keep an eye on the other two.

I noted the demons' locations in my peripheral vision as I forced my pain down into my body.

The pain took a strange detour without asking my permission.

The Spear seemed to slurp it down like the last dregs of a smoothie, magically converting it to nuclear power. The Spear let out a soft, unassuming chime and then exploded, whipping my hair back and almost sending me cartwheeling as I fought to hold on.

I opened my eyes, staring at the Spear in wary disbelief. It had done that all on its own, wanting to show off for its debut, I guessed, apparently annoyed by the student driver behind the wheel—me.

I glanced left and right, deciding to worry about it later. It hadn't broken —which had been my biggest fear. I frowned, blinking a few times as the Spear dimmed, seeming to power down entirely. The alley was noticeably different than a few moments ago. The red brick walls and the greasy dark pavement were now perfectly white.

And the six demons were...

Gone.

All of them.

My eyes widened to notice that the only things marring the pristinely white surfaces were two sooty silhouettes seemingly burned into the wall upon vaporization. I spun in a slow circle, noticing that all remains of the other demons were also gone, leaving behind black silhouettes of the demons.

The white surface formed a perfect circle around me—even on the walls. Like a bubble of white paint had popped, painting everything in its radius white but leaving everything beyond untouched.

I reached out to touch the sooty smear on the wall and realized I couldn't wipe it off. The demon's silhouette was *permanently* burned into the white surface, and there was no denying it had been anything but a demon. It wasn't a humanoid silhouette because it still held the pitchfork, had horns and a demon tail.

It looked like a painting.

One of my wings scraped across its surface with a loud, scratching sound, but they didn't leave a mark. I grunted, letting my wings evaporate. Whatever the Spear had done to the wall, it had apparently fortified it—making it strong enough to withstand angel wings. I eyed the spear warily, before walking out into the center of the insanity, spinning in a slow circle. Eighteen demons. All dead. If I hadn't lost my focus, I wouldn't have even taken a hit. I glanced down at my new, armored clothes, surprised to find that the fiery hoof hadn't burned a hole in my crotch. The fabric didn't even have a dirty scuff. I rubbed at my jaw, confirming that it wasn't broken—although it did hurt like hell. I retrieved my katana, surprised to find that it hadn't been melted to slag or vaporized, and shoved it into my sheath.

The burned shadows of three bands of six dead demons surrounded me, forming a triangle with me at the center. I studied the glowing spear, wondering what the hell had just happened. I hadn't even had to resort to my Horseman's Mask.

Then, from the darkness, came a slow clap.

I spit out some blood and lifted my head with a bloody grin.

"I'm all warmed up!" I said, thumping the Spear into the ground at my side as I tried to spot the source of the clapping.

29

Legion shuffled into view with a notepad in hand, scribbling on the page with a pen that looked to be made from finger bones. Yuck. The clapping sound continued for a few moments, telling me Legion had a friend with him. I shifted my boots in each direction but only detected a tingle when pointing at Legion. I frowned, warily, wondering who the non-demon clapper was.

Legion studied the pile of black ash where the thorns had been, looking annoyed and muttering under his breath. He made a notation on his notebook. Then he turned to look at the white areas I had made. I watched, smugly, as he absently lowered his notepad to his side, his mouth falling open in disbelief. He quickly shook off the incredulity and resorted to counting the silhouettes. Then he shrugged, disappointedly, scribbling on his notepad.

"All eighteen are accounted for, my Lord. Six, six, six," he said, chuckling at his little joke as he pointed out the pile of dead demons and the two incineration zones I'd made. "The temporary barrier is down," he said, likely referring to the ward created by the dead ninjas. Then he turned to assess me with an awed look on his face, noticing my clothes were pristine and that I only had what looked like a bloody lip. His eyes flicked to the Spear, but his face remained blank. After a moment, he dipped his hat at me and disappeared in a puff of smoke.

I took a moment to collect myself, making sure my face showed nothing

—not surprise or pain or concern. Whoever Legion's Lord was, he needed to think that the Spear and I were old pals—not that the outburst of power had been as much of a surprise to me as it had been to my foes.

I scowled in the direction Legion faced when he had been speaking and waited. A new figure calmly walked into view from out of the shadows, and I squinted, trying to make out anything other than his silhouette. My boots still didn't tingle, even though Legion had called the stranger *Lord*.

"Eighteen of my demons and you're not even breathing heavily," the figure said, in a rich, sophisticated voice, his body still cloaked in shadows.

"The poor dears tripped down some stairs," I said with faux innocence.

He chuckled good naturedly and I finally got a good look at him.

Like all of the worst kinds of men, he was inhumanly beautiful— emphasis on inhuman. And my boots *still* weren't tingling, although the man had said the demons belonged to him. Which made me very nervous. His smile told me he knew it—glancing down at my boots and then winking at me was overkill.

He moved in a confident, lazy stroll as if he didn't have a care in the world. His tan skin was unblemished, and he had long, dark hair that looked professionally styled. His face was perfectly sculpted, and he had just the right amount of stubble to make his impossibly pale—almost white—blue eyes shine like ring lights. He looked to be perpetually smirking, but in a kind manner rather than a cruel, cynical one. Even more surprising was that his whole demeanor was not spiced with arrogance, as so many of his type— those handsome, imposing, successful, and confident elites—were. He looked like the kind of man who found no interest or pleasure in rubbing anyone's face in his good fortune. Just a happy, carefree man. I didn't get a sinister vibe from him—not in any way whatsoever. And I was actively looking for one.

Because I knew he was obviously bad news. The fact that I wasn't picking up on it only made him more dangerous. He was several inches over six feet, making him quite a bit taller than me. But he wasn't a fifty-foot-tall devil of scales and fresh scalps or anything.

He was obviously a regular at the gym, judging by the strain his thighs and biceps inflicted on his skinny black slacks and his expensive white dress shirt—which was open to mid-chest to reveal a black chain necklace with two black feathers hanging from the base. They looked excellent resting there on his tan, well-defined pecs.

Objectively speaking, of course.

Michael had worn a similar necklace—but with white feathers.

Were they from his angel wings, or some status symbol for archangels and archdemons?

Strangely enough, he wore no shoes, like he'd been caught walking on the beach on a balmy summer day. But his Miami Vice wardrobe didn't scream playboy or lady-hound; rather, it looked natural and genuine, like he'd been hot and had chosen to let loose a few buttons.

Who was this guy? He couldn't be a demon, or my boots would have been giving me toe cramps. But he owned demons and Legion had called him *Lord*. Legion had also admitted to working for the Seven, so I had anticipated this stellar gentleman to be one of them. *Perhaps Pride or Envy*, I thought, assessing his overall demeanor. He probably wasn't Gluttony or Sloth. That left only Lust—which would make sense—and Wrath—which did not. He was entirely too chill to be angry.

He assessed the dead bodies, nodding absently, but his grin stretched wider at the destruction to the alley itself, especially as a brick fell from a wall, almost right onto his toes. He glanced at me and the Spear in my fist, arching one eyebrow. "You made a bit of a mess," he teased, gesturing at a few flickering fires.

"I repainted, too," I said, gesturing at the pristine white areas. I realized that I had been smiling—subconsciously infected by his cheer—so I forced myself to suffocate it. I studied his eyes and realized that I actually felt inferior in his presence. And it had nothing to do with power because I sensed none from him. I felt inferior because of the raw intelligence burning in those pale, pale blue eyes.

Those startling eyes locked onto the blood on my lip. "You're hurt," he said, observationally.

"Who are you?" I asked with forced calm. "And what are you doing here?"

"Picking up a package," he said, pointing a long finger over my shoulder. I'd almost forgotten that the rear entrance to Darling and Dear was behind me. What kind of package was he picking up? "They are quite good, as you well know," the strange, barefooted enigma continued. "But I'm sure you've surmised that many of your...accoutrements simply do not work around one such as me." His gaze latched onto my boots and Spear, and I suppressed a shudder. He assessed my ninja garb with an approving smile. "Excellent choice, but Constance's slaughtering suit would have fared you better. It carries a mother's protection, especially against demons. It is a crime they were lost to the decay of time," he said. "Your mother paid a heavy price for them." There was no mockery in his tone. No insidious subtle jab or anything. He meant it. And he thought the outfit had been lost for good. That was a benefit.

I stared at him, unable to speak. He casually spoke of my mother in such a familiar manner. He'd known about her hunting clothes, but not that Lilith had passed them down to me.

He gestured at my current garb, cocking his head appraisingly. "That would work best against angels, on the other hand, so now you have an outfit for each group of feathered fiends." He smiled, showing me his perfectly straight, white teeth.

"And how do you know of my mother and her slaughtering outfit?" I asked, feeling brittle and fragile—not from fear or sorrow, but from anger at the fact this person knew my mother better than me.

"I am Wrath," he said with a casual shrug. "We all knew her. Good woman. Highly respected."

I stared at him, feeling poleaxed. This...*was* one of the Seven Sins? So why weren't my boots working? How had he known they weren't working? And why was he so...non-demonic?

Wasn't Wrath supposed to be...well, angrier? This man oozed chill.

I gripped my Spear tighter, suddenly fearing that he might be using some unseen power to deceive me or lure me into his control. I willed the Spear back into my soul, not daring to hold it out in the open where he might grab it. Especially when I couldn't sense a lick of evil about him. Not even a lick of *power*.

No wonder he looked so perfect. Archangel Michael had looked much the same—when he was wearing his mask, of course. Michael had told me that demons openly wore their scars and grotesque transformations to flaunt their difference from their hallowed siblings. Except...Wrath looked pretty god-damned beautiful.

Pun intended.

Yet there was a difference between Wrath and Michael's haunting beauty. Although Wrath still had that eerie perfection, he looked more rugged and real. His face showed emotion.

And Wrath had even shown sarcasm and dry humor. He was much more human than his archangel brother. Was that because he had fallen? And what was hiding beneath this beautiful facade? If demons openly wore their scars...where were the freaking scars?

I eyed him up and down, pursing my lips. "You expect me to believe that you are Wrath," I said, deadpan, trying to get a better read on his power because Michael had almost scoured my mind clean with his aura.

The man smiled at my obvious doubt. "I am not used to repeating myself," he mused, grinning wider.

I did not smile. "And what lies beneath?" I asked, gesturing at his body with my hand. Samael had been a monstrous demon covered in scales made of darkened coins, and Lilith had been an incredibly strong crocodile-demon hybrid.

He arched his eyebrows and gently pressed his fingers to his chest in mock embarrassment. "Well, *that* was forward of you. We are not even officially betrothed yet. I came here to propose, just like you asked Goodmen Legion."

I blinked. "Wait. *You*...are the one wanting to propose to me?" I whispered, instantly hating myself for subconsciously eyeing him up and down in an approving manner. *All that healthy male for me—*

I mentally dumped a cold bucket of water over the errant thought.

His eyes twinkled appreciatively at my wandering eye. "I must admit that I've never done this before, and I find myself at a loss. Are you absolutely certain that a proposal is necessary for us to get married?" he asked me in an utterly serious tone.

Was it terrible that I instinctively wanted to coach him on exactly how to propose? Like seeing a lost puppy and instantly *needing* to care for it as if your whole life abruptly revolved around the dog you hadn't known existed two seconds ago. It only took a fraction of a second for me to murder the thought, but I did have it. I would have liked to say that he was manipulating my mind with some demonic power.

But he wasn't. He gave off no demonic aura that put truth to his claim.

And...I could sense the honesty in his question. He might be a devil and terrible, but he was genuinely annoyed with the whole proposal development. Which was fucking bonkers.

"Well, you can start off by not sending close to twenty demons to murder me. That would have been better," I finally said, folding my arms.

He scratched at his stubble with a bemused frown. "I...see. I meant it as a compliment to your skills—so you could have a chance to impress me. I had no doubt of your victory," he said, shrugging—and having absolutely no clue how misogynistic it had sounded. All I could do was stare at him in disbelief. "Our first introduction required...fanfare. Is that the right word? A grand display. That is what the YouTube showed me about marriage proposals."

A laugh almost bubbled up at his mention of *the YouTube*, but I managed to squash it. I checked again on my mental defenses, wondering if he really had managed to brainwash me with those pecs of his. They weren't as appealing as Ryuu's muscles when he'd been chopping up all that wood—

I blushed, lowering my eyes at the errant thought. *Get your shit together, girl!* I chastised myself.

Wrath took my blush as encouragement and beamed happily, flashing his pearly white teeth. I held up a hand, shaking my head *no* to correct him. "My mind wandered. That was not what it looked like."

His smile slipped and, for a fraction of a second, I thought I saw a flicker of blind rage flash in those icy blue eyes. But it was gone so swiftly that I couldn't be sure I hadn't projected his namesake onto him.

Maybe a change of topic would be safer.

"What about the rest of your crew?" I asked. "Are the rest of the Seven Sins like...you?" I asked, gesturing vaguely at him.

My question had an immediate impact. He curled his lips into a snarl and glared at me with a dangerous gleam in his eyes. "There are *none* like me," he said in a frigid tone, his chest suddenly heaving.

No more Mr. Nice Guy.

30

I remained silent and completely motionless, hoping the storm in his eyes would blow over.

It did not blow over.

"I am finished playing these foolish games," he snarled. "I am Wrath, First of the Seven. You are the White Rose. We will do great and terrible things together, so let's just get married and forget this proposal nonsense," he growled.

My eyes might have widened at his abrupt change in tone, but they practically popped out of my head when he echoed what Aphrodite had said right before I left Darling and Dear's shop.

We could do great and terrible things together.

I knew my answer already, but did I really have the guts to say *no*, right here, right now? I needed to string him along and figure out why he was so transfixed on this idea of our marriage.

"Why, exactly, are you so fixated on marrying me?" I asked.

He grinned eagerly, his eyes growing distant. "Because of the prophecy, of course."

I almost peed a little. If that was true, Michael's decision to try and abduct me suddenly took on a whole new meaning. Wrath certainly believed it. "What prophecy?" I asked, hoping he would answer vaguely, proving that it was idle boasting or an outright lie to get him what he wanted.

Wrath cleared his throat, smiling wistfully before he took on a lecturing tone. "And the Seven shall come to the City of Fountains, where the First shall lay claim to the White Rose. Her love will rock the pillars of Heaven and rattle the foundations of Hell, burning away all that once was in a purifying bridge of Anghellian fire. Her Wrath will do great and terrible things," he said, finishing.

He had emphasized the *H* sound in the word *Anghellian* with a proud smile. I'd never heard the term before, but that was the least of my concerns.

I felt like the wind had been knocked out of me, and my hands were shaking. Thankfully, Wrath was staring up at the sky, breathing in through his nostrils as if to embrace every sense available to him so that he could later recall this pivotal moment. I managed to get my hands to stop shaking so as not to alert him.

Some of his earlier comments suddenly took on deeper meaning, and it was obvious that he had bought into this prophecy wholesale. I needed to find ways to pick it apart—to cast doubts about its meaning.

Think! I told myself. I began to break the prophecy down in my mind.

It had referenced *her wrath*—which could have meant my own anger, or my partner who was named Wrath. I dismissed it for now.

The *First shall lay claim to the White Rose* could imply a competition rather than a guaranteed win for Wrath—as in, the first of the Seven brothers to catch my interest.

The only other thing I could think to use as salvation was that the prophecy hadn't explicitly said that I got married. Although, I couldn't think of any way to spin it at the moment.

I was now certain that my mother must have known about all of this. That was why she had tried to hide me. To keep me as far away from this crazy prophecy as possible.

Wrath finally turned to face me with a hungry smile, and I knew that the pleasant man from earlier had been a courtesy. He'd tried it my way, and it hadn't worked as he'd intended. Now it was time to try his way.

"You will be my wife," he said, determinedly.

I stared at him, frantically searching for the best way out. His hungry smile began to fade at my lack of response, and I felt myself panicking. I had to stall him. Buy time. My mind raced, reviewing the critiques I'd found and then weighing their chance at success. A different angle came to mind, and I pounced on it.

"The prophecy said *her love*," I said hurriedly. His smile returned, and he nodded, eagerly. I gathered my courage, hoping I would survive the crazy plan that was slowly materializing. I was in uncharted waters, but I had to keep paddling. I folded my arms stubbornly. "I am not the type of woman who can just fall in love. I must be...courted," I said, choosing my words with exceeding care. His smile stretched wider.

"And what does courtship mean to you, Callie Penrose?" he asked, expectantly, seeing that his way was already working better. "Because courtship could mean me taking you with me right now. To take care of you properly where I know you will be safe."

I realized that I would need to do more than merely cast doubt on the prophecy's words. I needed to get inside his head because he was his own worst enemy. He was intelligent, but he was also emotional—it was in his freaking name. Wrath was bold, and everyone he met probably feared him. Which had to get boring after a while. He craved something new and exciting. It was why he'd broken out of Hell and come to Kansas City, after all—to have an adventure. A challenge. A prophecy.

So...I needed to be bold. Defiant. In control of myself. Independent. Wrath would crave those traits because they were qualities he *never* encountered. Luckily, I was pretty good at being a pain in the ass.

Of course, there was a chance that I would be wrong, and he would blow a fuse. But even if that happened, I was somewhat safe because he *needed* me —I was integral to his adventure.

I decided to call his bluff. I scoffed and rolled my eyes. "You can't possibly be that stupid."

His smile slipped and he stared at me without moving. For about ten whole seconds. "Go on," he finally said, seeming to surprise himself with the words.

I obliged him, trying to hide the feeling of triumph I felt at accurately guessing his desires. "If it were as simple as kidnapping me and taking me for yourself, the prophecy wouldn't have used the word *love*—which is a feeling that must be reciprocated and earned. That's the challenge in it—to *convince* me to go along with a demon, voluntarily. Otherwise, there is no love, and there is no prophecy. So, make it worth my time, devil boy."

His eyes danced with sudden excitement. "Devil boy," he mused. "And what if I disagree with your analysis on the prophecy?" he said, circling around me as he studied me from head to toe.

It was time to flex, because he had a cat who ate the canary look on his face, making me suddenly relieved that I hadn't tried to debate him on technicalities. Messing with his head on an emotional level seemed to have worked like a charm, though.

He'd complimented my prowess earlier. I could use that. I cleared my throat and shot him a wicked smile. "I'm an enigma. The daughter of a dark wizard and a nephilim, and my DNA is fused with a Beast. I am one of a new breed of Horsemen when there are already Four Horsemen. I am wanted by both Heaven and Hell—both want to reclaim and control their missing daughter. I was a Shepherd, yet I became the new Dracula and I now control the world's vampires. I am, dare I say, quite formidable, you see."

He smiled, delighting in the danger. "Ah. Then I should be quite terrified of my betrothed," he murmured, circling behind me like a hungry panther.

I shook my head. "That's just it. I have not said yes. You haven't even asked, if we're getting technical. And you seem like the kind of man who likes to get technical," I said, swallowing the reflex bile that rose up into my throat.

He let out an animalistic growl from behind me.

And, for the first time, he let slip a bit of his power. I felt a solar flare of heat bloom against my back—so hot that I thought my hair had caught fire. It was gone a fraction of a second later, but it made my heart race and my fingers go numb. Confirmation received. Wrath was legit, and easily as powerful as Michael. Enough to kill me six times over if he so chose. Even if I tried using the Spear against him, I wasn't sure it would do much harm. It was shockingly humbling.

I somehow managed to keep my composure rather than Shadow Walking to safety—because it would have only encouraged him to *chase* me. "The question is just a formality," he argued.

I shrugged unconcernedly. "Are you willing to bet your prophecy on it? Because without me, you might as well go marry an actual white rose—the flower—and cross your fingers," I said with a smirk.

31

W rath stepped back into my peripheral vision and came to a halt, studying me with those icy eyes of his, trying to determine whether I was bluffing or if I truly did have a valid point. Whatever he saw on my face must have been convincing because I saw multiple personalities suddenly flit across his face in the blink of an eye—rage, fear, disbelief, and then forced calm. "You have no reason to cooperate with me—"

"I will do anything to protect the City of Fountains," I interrupted him, speaking the truth.

His lips tugged into an eager smirk. "That is simple enough—"

"I was not finished," I interrupted him again, scowling at him for good measure. He arched an incredulous eyebrow and then laughed. He motioned for me to proceed, folding his arms with an amused grin. "I need to meet your brothers. All of them. Privately."

His humor shifted to suspicion and then anger. "That is a dangerous request. We do not all get along very well. They would try to do you harm. Private is not possible."

"Private is *required*, Wrath. I can take care of myself in case you've forgotten. And I have the Spear."

He scoffed. "The Spear is worthless against us. Go ahead and stab me with it if you doubt me."

166

He spread his arms and calmly walked within striking distance, inviting me to test his claim. What if attempting it destroyed the Spear? Or allowed him to take it for himself? Finally, I shook my head. "I already had my suspicions about the Spear, otherwise the archangels would have killed me for it long ago."

He lowered his arms and studied me thoughtfully, looking intrigued by my words rather than doubtful. I wasn't sure what that meant, so I arched my eyebrow and showed him my resting bitch face.

Wrath smiled, nodding. "Princes of Hell can only be killed by Princes of Heaven," he said, gauging my reaction. "Archangels can only be killed by archdemons. Opposites attract, and only opposites can negate the other."

I saw a faint flicker of hesitation in his eyes, as if he'd briefly recalled a fact that contradicted his claim. Then he dismissed it with a faint grunt, shaking his head. Whatever it had been, his reaction told me that it had nothing to do with my current tool belt—not my Mask, my Seal, or my Spear.

So...what had it been? Why even think of it if it wasn't viable?

Had he been thinking of Ryuu and his Angel Killer dark blade?

"You intrigue me, Callie Penrose," he said, snapping me out of my thoughts. "I will admit that I was anticipating our union before I even met you, but now...I think I am quite madly in love with you. Your defiance is..." he trailed off, taking a deep inhale through his nose and then an exhale out of his mouth, "so *refreshing*! I truly look forward to seeing you again. And soon."

With that, he bowed his head and then made his way towards the back of Darling and Dear's shop. I followed his movements and noticed a black, gift wrapped box with a white bow on top sitting on the ground just outside the door. It hadn't been there earlier. Wrath picked it up, drummed his fingers on the top, and then smiled at me. It was about the size of a Monopoly box.

"What is that?" I asked, warily.

Wrath smiled. "You will find out soon enough, my beloved," he said with a wink. "Do you recall where you first powered up your precious little Spear?"

I frowned, caught off guard by the question. "Yes."

"Good. You will find one of my siblings there. He is not expecting you," he added with a macabre grin. "You have my permission to murder him, of course. He's been a pain in my side for quite some time. Remember that your typical weapons will be no match for one of the Seven, so I recommend sending one of your archangel friends. Michael is an obedient little guard dog. He won't be missed."

"Michael is not my friend. I made him quite upset this morning. In fact, he ran away."

Wrath cocked his head curiously, obviously not having known this bit of news. "Is that so?" he mused.

I nodded. "He was upset about Samael and Lilith's wedding, and he threatened to destroy my city if I consorted with anymore demons," I said dryly. Then, realizing I didn't want Wrath knowing about Ryuu's ability to potentially kill archangels, I scrambled for an answer as to how I managed to make Michael flee. "I threatened to break the Spear if he didn't back the fuck off."

Wrath burst out laughing. "Well. That ought to do it." His laughter slowly faded, and he stared deeply into my eyes. "You've obviously met Samael's Daemons, judging by the ninjas my men killed." I nodded. "What about Lilith's pair? I heard they went missing," he said in an overly casual tone.

My blood instant froze, but I managed to shrug with an annoyed groan. "Not you, too."

He frowned. "What?" he asked in a dark tone.

I sighed. "Michael asked about them, too. He didn't like my answer."

"And what was your answer?"

"I. Don't. Know." I shrugged, disinterestedly. "I don't see why anyone cares."

He nodded, slowly, reading my face. It was all I could do not to fidget under his scrutiny. "I think I would like to visit my dear siblings, your godparents. Congratulate them on their special day."

I grunted. "You can just pump the brakes, devil boy. We're not far enough into our courtship for you to meet them. I'll pass on your regards," I said, dryly.

A slow grin split his cheeks. "You intrigue me, White Rose. How about a goodbye kiss?"

I scowled. "How about no?"

He chuckled. "Worth a try. I look forward to hearing about your visit with my dear brother, White Rose. Don't delay. I have a feeling that things will begin moving very quickly, soon. And I would prefer you meet the rest of my brothers without delay. So we can get down to the matter at hand." He winked.

With that, he simply disappeared. I stood in the alley, not moving, for a full minute, making sure Wrath didn't return for any reason.

Then I fell to my knees. "What the hell am I going to do now?" I whispered.

Wrath's absent comment about Lilith having her own pair of daemons had almost broken my resolve. Why hadn't she told me? Or had Wrath been lying? He wasn't exactly the epitome of honesty and goodwill. More importantly, what did I do with the information? I definitely couldn't go to Xuanwu and Qinglong until I had proof. Which meant I needed to confront her.

More importantly, it was another reminder of my mother's webs. She'd gotten the two Greater Demons to be my godparents, efficiently tying me to all four Divines. But...why?

I debated whether to confront Lilith or to go meet the next member of the Seven Sins—the one who Wrath casually encouraged me to kill, even though he knew I couldn't. Unless I took Ryuu and his dark blade, the Angel Killer.

It didn't take me very long to convince myself that I needed answers before I picked any new fights. Maybe Samael could confirm some of Wrath's claims before I confronted Lilith—

Something moved in my peripheral vision and I hurled a dozen blasts of fire on reflex, blanketing the area in flames. "Fuck off, creep," I snarled weakly, not hearing any cries of pain.

"Creep?" a familiar voice growled at my side. I flinched, looking up to see Ryuu staring down at me with a concerned look. The rest was of his body was invisible, cloaked in his Shadow Skin.

I let out a sigh of relief, which turned into a sob of frustration. "Ryuu," I whispered. "Take me home."

He scooped me up in his arms and held me horizontal across his chest. I leaned into him and closed my eyes. Without looking, I lifted my hand and ripped open a Gateway back to Castle Dracula. I felt Ryuu moving, but I was more interested in his scent and the steady beating of his heart against my ear.

"Ryuu?" I murmured sleepily.

"Yes?"

"You didn't say anything about my new clothes," I mumbled, frowning unhappily.

"I was more interested in your lips," he growled. My breath caught and I grinned widely as I felt his pulse quicken beneath my ear. "They are bloody—"

"Quit while you're ahead, Ryuu," I growled, nuzzling my cheek closer into his chest and letting out a long, contented sigh. His grip tightened around me instinctively, making me feel safe and protected. I didn't know where he was taking me in Castle Dracula, and I didn't care, but I was asleep long before we got there.

And I had some pretty good dreams...

32

I glanced back at Ryuu, smiling. "You ready for some fireworks?" I asked, squeezing his callused hand.

"Once you finish drinking your water," he said, smirking as he indicated the full glass of water on my nightstand. I scowled at it with a resigned sigh. "Aala told me you needed to drink plenty of fluids."

"Fine," I muttered, releasing his hand with a pang of frustration. I scooped up the glass and started drinking. He had only made me drink about four of them in the past hour.

After picking me up in the dirty alley, he'd carried me to my rooms and tucked me into bed, and I'd been so tired—or relaxed by the deep, rhythmic thumping of his heartbeat in my ears—that I hadn't stirred the whole walk back. So he'd made the executive decision that lil' Dracula was all tuckered out and needed some rest.

I had woken up hours later in my darkened room to see a candle burning on my nightstand. I'd risen up to a seated position in my bed to find Ryuu sitting on the floor, facing the door, with the stupid warped blade resting across his knees. A few more candles illuminated the shadowed areas of the master suite, but all-in-all it was dark, and warm, and...romantic. Sensing I was up, Ryuu had glanced back at me with those arresting dark eyes of his, making my breath catch. He hadn't asked me any of the hundred questions on his mind. He hadn't needed to.

Because I had wordlessly reached out with my hand to pat the foot of my bed, inviting him to join me on Dracula's big cushy mattress. There, together in the candlelight, and with no one to interrupt us, some beautiful magic had happened.

Raw, naked honesty.

I told him the truth and nothing but the truth. Everything on my mind. About the Seven Sins, the murdered ninjas, and Wrath's foreboding prophecy. All my suspicions and fears, all the things I had learned, and probably even things that didn't actually matter to the present situation. But I had not wanted to hold anything back from him. I didn't want any more secrets between us. The only gray area, ironically, was in regard to my budding *personal* feelings about Ryuu—as a man, not my bodyguard. I held those comments back because I needed to personally end things with Nate before I did anything else. I did tell him all about Aphrodite, and what I had discovered about myself.

I even came clean about Nate—my epiphany and the weight it had taken off my shoulders.

To that, Ryuu had wordlessly climbed off the bed and poured me a glass of water from a nearby pitcher.

After I'd accepted the glass, feeling somewhat confused by his response to my unburdening of my personal baggage about Nate, Ryuu had walked over to the nearby balcony and drawn the warped blade in an aggressive but silent motion. I'd been startled by the sudden aggression, almost spilling my water. But...he hadn't attacked anything. He'd stared down at the warped blade for a few moments, before calmly hurling it out into the night sky like a javelin.

My mouth had fallen open as I stared at his silhouette in the moonlight. He let out a breath and then turned back to me with a tranquil smile. Our gazes had locked together, and I knew that something deeply significant had just happened. I also knew that if I asked a single question about it, he would answer me in any number of deliciously unpredictable ways—none of which I could currently entertain.

Not until I had spoken with Nate.

So, I'd dipped my chin with a small smile of acknowledgment. He'd done the same, and the moment had been a conversation in and of itself. We both learned what we needed to know without a word uttered, and that had been good enough for now. For once, *later* had felt honorable and genuine.

Soon after, we'd worked together to formulate a plan, leaving my bedroom to pick up a few necessary items and get some food. We'd dined together on my bed, treating it like a candlelit picnic, as we ironed out the finer details of the plan. I smiled, now, recalling how he had suggested that we make the picnic a regular occurrence. That had been as close as we came to the unspoken tension between us.

But I had agreed.

I finished my glass of water and set it down. "Okay. Let's go," I said, grabbing his warm, much larger, callused hand in mine. I scooped up a metal box in my other hand, and Shadow Walked us to the hallway outside Lilith's rooms.

I knocked on her door, waited two whole seconds, and then I strode inside. Ryuu followed behind me, as silent as a shadow. Lily faced me with her mouth open and a wine glass in hand, on the verge of either inviting me in or telling me to wait a moment.

Since she was stark naked, I took a gamble that she had intended the latter.

Ryuu swiftly averted his eyes and closed the door behind us with a soft click.

"Lilith," I said, sweetly.

I opened the metal box from my mother's laboratory, reached inside to grab the fire lotus, and then lobbed it to her in an underhanded toss. "We need to talk," I said, shutting the metal box with a click.

She caught the fire lotus with a sharp gasp of recognition, verifying Wrath's claim that she had a relationship with the missing Divines—Xuanwu and Qinglong's sisters.

She stared at the burning flower in her palms and I watched as a single tear spilled down her cheek from one eye. Then she looked up to meet my steady gaze, and her shoulders sagged wearily, knowing that it hadn't been a request. "Of course," she said. "Have a seat, sulfur sugar. I'll just put something on."

I chose not to acknowledge her social ploy of trying to establish us as trusted confidants. I didn't have time for games, and I felt somewhat betrayed by her actions. I was hoping she had a good excuse or there were going to be problems between us. I still needed to talk to Samael to see if he had been complicit in her secrecy. And, more importantly, what the Divines had to do with my Spear.

Once I squeezed the information out of my godparents, it would be time for me to go meet the next of the Seven Sins and try my best not to get killed while gathering information about Wrath's prophecy.

The mansion owned by Circle Seven Holdings didn't hold too many fond memories for me, and I was very suspicious about Wrath encouraging me to go there. He couldn't really think I would try to kill his brother, because he knew I had no weapons to accomplish such a task. So, why had he suggested it?

Lilith slipped into a red silk evening robe and motioned me to join her near the fireplace. I sat down on the couch, appreciating the warmth from the flames, and she sat down on a chair across from me. She placed the fire lotus on the table between us, staring at it nervously. Ryuu remained near the door with a stoic look on his face, as if the world consisted of two types of people: those who were friends with Callie Penrose, and those who needed to be horribly murdered. And judging by the look on Lily's face, she was not very confident on which camp she had been relegated to.

"I heard some interesting news today," I said, crossing my legs and leaning back into the couch. It was hard not to smile at the firelight's reflection on my armored ninja gear—the flickering flames turned it into a shimmering orange hue, like I was on fire. Aphrodite had truly outdone herself.

Lilith's body language told me how anxious she was, but she was doing an exemplary job of hiding it. I had gotten pretty good at reading people, though. "Interesting how?"

"Interesting in that it's something I should have heard from you. Weeks ago. Pretty much the moment I freed you from your shackles."

She continued staring at the flower. "And who told you this? Because I feel like I'm being accused yet I still don't know exactly what I'm accused of."

I nodded, deciding to go for the throat. I watched her face very closely as I spoke. "Wrath told me you knew the two missing Divines—the Vermillion Bird and the White Tiger. Before I say anything further, I know he's an asshole and I don't trust him. So, why don't you tell me everything you know about them. Now. Wrath had quite a bit to say, so I would advise against holding any information back. And you obviously recognize the fire lotus, godmother. I no longer have time for games."

She had turned alarmingly pale.

She closed her eyes nervously and took a few calming breaths. "I knew them," she whispered, her lower lip trembling with fear. "I did not hold anything back from you for my own benefit. I kept my secret in hopes that it would keep them safe," she said. Tears spilled down her cheeks, but she didn't cry.

"Go on. Who were you keeping them safe from?"

"I was commanded to kill them, but I...refused." Her hands were shaking and her eyes darted around the room as if expecting the news to earn her an instant death.

"Who commanded you to kill them?" I asked, hearing Ryuu move away from the door to check the bathroom and closets further back in the suite. He'd picked up on Lilith's obvious fear and had gone into seek and destroy mode.

"Wrath," she whispered, flinching as one of the curtains leading to the balcony shifted.

I stared at her, frowning. He certainly hadn't told me that part. The more I thought about it, I couldn't wrap my head around the timeline. "You were locked away in Castle Dracula for one hundred years, so this happened before your imprisonment." She nodded, fidgeting uncomfortably. "You're telling me they've been hidden for that long and no one has found them? Do you have any idea how much pain Xuanwu and Qinglong are in right now? Did you know they also have a fire lotus like mine, and that they can hardly think straight, fearing for their sisters?" I demanded, glaring at her.

33

She nodded, miserably. "Y-yes. I saw Xuanwu's flower yesterday when we were telling him about the upcoming wedding," she whispered. "It startled me. I didn't know anyone else had one."

Which told me why she had been so distraught yesterday. "Where could you have hidden them for so long?" I asked, leaning forward. Her eyes danced about wildly, and she was panting in fear. "Tell me, Lilith. You owe me."

"The Neverwas," she whispered, barely loud enough for me to hear. "It was the only place to keep them safe from their hunters. Even Wrath and his minions cannot survive long in the Neverwas."

I leaned back, my mind racing. "Why would Wrath want them killed that badly?"

She laughed involuntarily, but it was a dark, cynical laugh. "Because they are bargaining chips. The four Divines can make someone strong enough to face an Arch." She studied me as she said it. "Demon or angel. But you obviously knew that. So, you know why I was told to kill them."

I hadn't known that, actually, but I wasn't going to correct her. Inside, my mind was racing at the revelation. The four Divines could make me strong enough to kill an archangel like Michael.

Or an archdemon like Wrath.

No wonder Wrath had wanted them murdered. And no wonder Michael had been so disgusted by Xuanwu's presence at the playground. It hadn't actually been disgust. It had been *fear*. I felt a small flicker of hope inside my chest. If I could save them, I could stand up to the Seven Sins. I wouldn't need Ryuu to do the work all by himself.

More than anything, I needed to figure out how to get to the Neverwas, and find the two Divines. My mother had obviously thought I stood a chance at saving them, and it had something to do with my Spear. But I couldn't risk Wrath finding out, which meant I still needed to go see his brother. I couldn't just disappear, or he would come looking for me, and I wasn't able to stand up to him right now.

The groom-to-be was very anxious to get to the altar.

But I needed Lilith to confirm Wrath's claim. He'd called them Lilith's pair, which was more involved than simply helping them escape. "What I don't understand is why you didn't obey Wrath. Why you let them live."

She scoffed. "I sent them to an uninhabitable wasteland of despair. Another name for the Neverwas is Purgatory. I sent them to a limbo where every inhabitant is permanently starving, and the only food is each other. Yet no one can actually die in Purgatory because everyone slowly recovers their health over time, and the most that can be eaten from you each day is half of what you are. So, every day, the ravenous inhabitants leech power from the strongest souls they can find, until one day, they are the strongest soul and everyone else turns on them. It is a madness far worse than anything down in Hell," she snarled, clenching her fists. "*That* is how I saved my fucking friends. And *that* was better than killing them for Wrath!" she roared, panting desperately. And then...

She broke down in tears, hanging her head in her hands. I stared at her, horrified. Purgatory did sound worse than any version of Hell that I could imagine. I wanted to vomit, realizing that I had walked through such a place with Samael. We'd been on a giant crystal bridge high above, but I'd had no idea how vile the place was until now.

"Some friend I am," she whispered. Ryuu had finished inspecting the adjoining rooms and had moved onto the first of three balconies.

"How did you end up a prisoner here?" I asked, entertaining a new thought that made my stomach writhe.

She lifted her head to stare at me with bloodshot eyes. "I was tricked. I have no proof, but I believe it was Wrath punishing me for my failure to kill them. The timing makes sense."

I cursed under my breath, clenching my fist.

And that's when Samael stepped out from the last balcony, staring at Lilith with bloodshot eyes. "What?" he rasped in a voice as cold as the oldest glacier on the planet. His fists were clenched so tightly that his arms shook, and his knuckles were white. Ryuu slipped out of the second balcony to find the large, imposing man's back to him, unable to see his face. He instantly drew his sword.

Samael didn't break eye contact with Lilith as he flicked a hand dismissively, sending Ryuu flying across the room to crash into the bed's headboard with a splintering, cracking sound. My godfather's face was unnaturally calm, and he didn't appear to be breathing.

"What?" he repeated in a lifeless tone, "did you say about Wrath?"

Lilith had turned to stare at him from over the back of the couch. She trembled in absolute terror and shame. "I think he arranged for my imprisonment here."

Samael stared at her, unblinking, and long black claws slowly ripped out of his fingers, glistening with fresh blood. "I...will kill him," he whispered, quivering with fury.

"I had to protect them. We were a trinity," Lilith whispered, desperately, as if afraid he meant to kill her.

Samael stumbled back a step, his eyes widening in surprise. "You formed a trinity, too?" he breathed, clutching at his chest as if he was suffering a heart attack. He had once mentioned forming an unholy trinity with Xuanwu and Qinglong. I'd taken it as a figure of speech, but it sure as hell sounded like a legitimate thingamabob.

Lilith nodded frantically. "It was the only way I knew to keep them safe. They were my friends, Sammie," she croaked in a heartbreaking sob. "Please don't be upset with me. I couldn't tell a *soul* without risking their lives. Even you," she croaked.

He nodded, stiffly, taking a moment to clear his head. "I understand, and I would have done the same, my dear," he breathed. "I am not angry with you," he whispered. Then he shifted that murderous glare my way. "Tell me you know how to kill an archdemon. Tell me right fucking now, goddaughter."

Ryuu had hopped off the bed but he hadn't sheathed his black katana. He moved laterally, keeping his eyes on the two Greater Demons as he crept closer to me.

Samael blinked at him. "When did *you* get here?"

Ryuu froze, cocking his head to the side. "You just swatted me across the room, big guy," he said with a puzzled frown, pointing his blade at the broken headboard. "I have been here the whole time," he said, warily.

Samael cocked his head, glancing over at the bed. He harrumphed at the headboard. "Huh. I didn't even realize I'd done anything." He turned back to the ninja, eyeing him up and down. "That headboard was oak."

Ryuu's lip curled up on one side, and he lowered his sword. "I noticed. Very sturdy."

Samael smirked faintly. "Well, don't stand there whining about it. And put on a goddamned bell or something. Creeping around all the time," he muttered. Ryuu chuckled darkly as Samael turned back to me. "Now, what is the plan? That son of a bitch is going to pay. I love Lilith, and no one fucks with the people I love. So, I'm going with you, no matter what you say. Yes, it's irrational. No, I don't care. Let's proceed from there."

Ryuu murmured his agreement, dipping his chin at Samael as he sheathed his black katana—another weapon capable of killing an Arch, as Lilith had called them. I nodded, rubbing my hands together. "Have a seat, godfather." Samael joined Lilith on the couch, clasping her hand in his. Ryuu returned to his position by the door, even though he'd failed as a security guard for not finding Samael. I was totally going to give him shit for that— for as long as possible. "First, do either of you know how to get to the Neverwas?" Samael had taken me there when we'd first come to Castle Dracula, but that had been with a huge spell that involved a year's worth of preparation.

They both nodded, and Lily cleared her throat. "I already tried finding them," she whispered. "Yesterday, when we bumped into each other in the hall."

I frowned, suddenly remembering the strange encounter. "You had soot on your cheeks!"

She nodded. "I couldn't find them, though. The place is too vast, and I felt my soul slipping away the moment I entered. Not even counting the fact that the tide of inhabitants caught my scent almost instantly. Without knowing where the Divines are, no one could survive long enough to find them. An archangel or archdemon would last longer, but not long enough. And even they would fall under the weight of hungry souls."

Samael shifted in his seat, frowning. "I once heard that an archangel and an archdemon, working together, could survive for longer. But good luck forming that partnership."

I grunted. "Never going to happen," I agreed. "But my mother thought I stood a chance, and it has something to do with my Spear." I smiled at them. "Not sure if you knew this, but my mother was one clever bitch. She got us this far," I said, holding out my hands. "It's time for us to see it through."

Lilith smiled, resting her cheek on Samael's shoulder. My godfather smiled, dipping his chin. "Okay, Callie," he said, setting his palm on Lilith's thigh. "But I still want Wrath to pay."

I nodded. "I will see to it personally. But I could use your help on something if you have some free time."

His lip curled up into a darker smile and he nodded. "So let it be written. So let it be done."

34

Samael and I stared at the mansion in silence. It had definitely seen better days. I'd tasked Ryuu with giving Xuanwu and Qinglong the good news and setting up a broad watch on Kansas City. I needed to know what Wrath was up to, and the possible locations of the other Sins. His ninjas would be invaluable. He hadn't argued with me about my decision to confront another archdemon, which I had found incredibly refreshing. He'd simply made me promise to get the hell out if things went sideways, since I quite literally could not win a fight against one of the Seven. I had no intention of dying, so I had also agreed without argument. This whole trust and truth development had been easier than I had thought.

Lilith and Sanguina would watch over Castle Dracula in my absence.

I'd agreed to take Samael as an olive branch to the archdemon. A mutual acquaintance to unruffle any feathers, figuratively and literally speaking. Also, Samael was liable to go pick a pointless fight against Wrath if I left him unsupervised.

"Is he inside?" Samael asked, looking doubtful.

I scanned the estate, averting my gaze away from the edge of the cliff where I had hung suspended on a Cross so long ago. Good times. I didn't see an army of demons lurking about, waiting to ambush us, so I started walking towards the front door. "Let's go find out."

Rather than knocking, we opened the door and walked inside. I kept my hand on my katana. Even though it would be as helpful as a butter knife against an archdemon, it worked swell on lesser demons. Samael wasn't strong enough to kill one of the Sins, but he was strong enough to shield me from instant death.

The place was furnished with the most beautiful and bizarre collection of sculptures, paintings, furniture, and knickknacks I'd ever seen, making me feel like I'd walked onto a movie set for a scene with a billionaire treasure hunter. Actually, it reminded me a lot of the Croft Manor in those *Tomb Raider* games. I was so transfixed by the casual display of extreme wealth that I failed to notice we weren't alone. A man was standing before a tall, gilded mirror. He wore silk pajama pants and nothing else. He had long blonde hair and he was flexing, admiring his oiled muscles.

Which, to be fair, were definitely worth admiring.

He had a chain that matched Wrath's, complete with two black feathers hanging down his chest. So, it was some kind of symbolic token. Arch-class demon, most likely.

I sensed no power from him, much like Wrath, but Samael's body language was tense and respectful. Wary. Maybe this guy was just as bipolar as his brother. He saw us in the reflection, made a vague sound of acknowledgment, and fixed a few loose strands of his hair. Then he smiled, checking his teeth, before turning around to graciously share that smile with us.

"Feast your eyes," he said, holding out his hands and planting his legs wide so we received the full scope of his awesomeness and a clear outline of his package. I was pretty sure I knew which of the Seven Sins this was —Pride.

I felt a sharp flash of power from the rings tucked into my weapons belt. They reacted *exactly* the same way they had when I'd spoken with Michael. It was just as brief, and just as startling, but I managed to keep my face composed. Whatever it meant, I didn't have time to worry about it now.

Because I felt like the floor had suddenly dropped out from under me. I knew him. "Whips and chocolate," I whispered under my breath, quoting something he had said. Because Pride was the blue-eyed hipster I'd seen at the ice cream parlor before I'd bumped into Legion. The one with the harem of college girls clawing all over him.

Pride's lips curled up into a grin. "I truly am unforgettable," he said, sagely. "Looks like I didn't miss my shot, after all," he said, alluding to his pick-up attempt on me from that night.

I rolled my eyes, shaking my head. Was this a good development or a terrible one?

I leaned towards Samael, speaking out the side of my mouth. "I thought you said he was better looking?"

The archdemon narrowed his blue eyes. "Ha. Ha."

"Why were you following me?" I asked.

"If you recall, I was there before you," he said, dryly. "I don't do *following* —professionally or personally." He tapped the feathers on his necklace, "As proven by my job title." Then he shifted his fingers to his oiled chest in a little drumming gesture. "And these spectacular pectoral muscles."

I grunted. He hadn't followed orders well in Heaven, so he had fallen, and women chased *him*, not the other way around. "Okay. Then why didn't you introduce yourself to me, properly?"

"Properly..." he mused, scratching at his stubbled chin. "Because a proper introduction would have taken hours and hours of sexual intercourse, and I couldn't afford to have you fall in love with me. That, and I already had my hands full, if you recall," he said in a low, smoky tone. "One of them was named..." he squinted thoughtfully, "it was something funny. Give me a moment. Ah! Chastity!" he hooted, grinning.

I burst out laughing at his unashamed narcissism, unable to help myself. "Wow. Okay."

He waved his hand dismissively. "I used the fallen from Heaven pick up line. You had your chance to get the hint. And Legion was lurking about. I didn't want him nosing into my business, reporting to his boss." He shifted his scowl to my godfather. "What do *you* want, Samael?"

"Blood and vengeance, Lord Pride," Samael growled. "I want to eat Wrath's heart."

Pride arched an eyebrow, his anger slowly morphing into a dazzling smile that made the sparkling chandelier above look drab and dull. "Oh. How delightful! May I ask why?"

Samael took a calming breath. "For mistreating Lilith. My fiancée."

Pride rubbed his hands together excitedly. "*Finally*, Samael. Do you know how long I've been waiting for this moment?" he asked, gesturing for us to join him on a pair of leather Chesterfield couches facing each other with a glass table between. He sat down on one and we took the other. He stared at Samael with almost hungry fervor. "Catch me up on your problem."

I held out a hand, forestalling Samael. "Wait. What if he's lying?"

Pride chuckled. "For the record, I haven't actually made any claims yet. Samael knows me about as well as anyone," he said, gesturing at Samael to vouch for him.

Samael nodded firmly. "Out of all the demons, I would trust Pride the most. And if there's one thing I know for sure, he hates Wrath more than most angels, and that's saying something."

Pride nodded, his eyes flickering with fire. "That is putting it mildly," he said in a low growl.

"Why?" I asked, still suspicious. Even though he might hate Wrath, that didn't necessarily put us on the same side.

"He thinks he's better than everyone else, and that is categorically false." He pointed a thumb at his chest. "Hello? Pride. I am the fairest of them all."

I nodded, still not sold. Delusions of grandeur and personal vendettas weren't anything particularly useful to me. I needed something real—something I could use.

Pride leaned forward, studying my face curiously. "I can see that you are not convinced, but remember that you came to me, not the other way around. Why are *you* here? Because if this is about Wrath wanting to marry you over that ridiculous prophecy, I think it's a terrible idea and I wish you the worst of luck."

I narrowed my eyes. "Gee. Thank you. I have no desire to marry that piece of trash, but you begin to see my concerns. And for what it's worth, he basically asked me to kill you." He shrugged, not seeming particularly concerned. "Why do you call the prophecy ridiculous?"

He snorted. "*All* prophecies are ridiculous. And it wasn't about me, so I don't very much care. Let him have his fantasies if it makes him feel important enough to leave me alone."

"That fantasy is *me*," I reminded him, "so I do *very much care*."

He frowned. "Fair point," he admitted. "So, hating him and wanting to stop him are great starting points for a lasting friendship. But without an archangel on board, he isn't dying any time soon."

Samael glanced at me with a questioning look. I nodded, giving him the go ahead. He turned back to Pride. "We have found the location of the last two Divines."

Pride stiffened. Then he leapt to his feet excitedly. "They *are* alive! I knew Wrath hadn't found them, no matter what bullshit claims he made! Ha, asshole!" he crowed, flipping off the chandelier. "Eat a demon dick!"

Samael opened his mouth to say something, but Pride adamantly lifted a palm in the universal sign for *stop*. "Hold on. I need a moment to savor this," Pride said, closing his eyes with a malevolent grin, and then he took several deep breaths in and out through his nose. Finally, he opened his eyes and looked at Samael. "Okay. Where are they? We can go get them right now. Before that knuckle-dragging cock-gobbler even knows what is happening!"

I let out a startled laugh at his adept use of curse words, committing them to memory.

Samael held up a hand, dampening his enthusiasm. "It's more complicated than that."

Pride's excitement waned and he frowned at Samael. "Why?" he asked, his suspicion shifting to me. "Does this have something to do with you?"

I shook my head. "Absolutely not!" I snapped, indignantly.

Samael swallowed audibly, knowing that he couldn't take his next statement back once it was uttered. So, this was the ultimate act to prove how much he trusted Pride. "Much like I formed a trinity with the Black Tortoise and the Azure Dragon, Lilith formed one with the Vermillion Bird and the White Tiger."

Pride abruptly sat down on the couch like a puppet with his strings snipped. "Shit," he whispered, staring at the table with a blank expression. I studied the two of them, eagerly wanting to know what this trinity nonsense was. But Samael had made me swear not to talk about it until we recovered the last two Divines. Something about putting the demon before the horns —which I translated to putting the cart before the horse.

But whatever this trinity issue was about, it had definitely shaken Pride.

I had my own reservations. "I don't get any of this. The Divines have nothing to do with Christianity."

Pride slowly turned to look at me, eyeing me up and down with his warm blue eyes as if looking for something. "But they have something to do with you. The girl who is powerful enough to hold the Spear of Destiny in her soul. The woman whose heart is a literal forge to fuse it back together," he said.

I blushed under his intense scrutiny. "That was an accident."

He snorted. "Much like all of creation," he mused sagely. "I imagine my Father probably said something similar, but it was taken out in the editing stages." He chuckled before continuing on in a dramatic voice. "And on the Eighth Day, the Lord said *I have an alibi!* But he did not."

I winced, but I couldn't help laughing. "Fine. Point taken," I admitted. "But why did Wrath want the Divines killed?" I asked. I already knew the answer, but I wanted to see if Wrath's most hated enemy had any additional details. Archdemons were likely privy to classified information.

Pride grunted. "Gabriel was making a play for them. Wrath didn't want Heaven getting their hands on them, of course, since—" He cut off abruptly, glaring at me suspiciously.

"Yeah. I know. They can help counter arch-class power, putting everyone on equal footing."

He gave me a slow, hesitant nod. "Wrath didn't want Heaven getting the Divines. None of us did. Likewise, Heaven didn't want us getting our hands on them. Same shit, different day," he said with a bored shrug. I nodded, thoughtfully. He turned to Samael. "So, where are they, anyway?"

"Lilith hid them in the Neverwas," Samael said, not meeting Pride's eyes.

The archdemon blinked a few times, and then he cursed. "Well, that's just fucking *great*. What was that, one hundred years ago? I'm sure they're fine—probably not that psychotic yet. Nothing a few Xanax couldn't resolve. We can just make a picnic out of it. Bring a megaphone with us and shout loud enough for everyone to hear us, hoping that the residents don't eat us alive before we find them. Excellent plan," he said, dryly. "Thank you so much for getting my hopes up."

I climbed to my feet, dusting off my hands with a can-do attitude. "Perfect," I said, pretending not to pick up on Pride's obvious sarcasm. "Samael told me you had the biggest set of balls in Hell, and that if anyone were brave enough to help us, it would be you. I have to admit that I had my doubts," I said, purposely not meeting his eyes. Instead, I scanned the paintings on the wall, spinning in a slow circle and nodding appreciatively until my back was facing him. "You have great taste, by the way."

Psychology had worked on Wrath, so I was hoping it would do the same with his brother. I was also thinking about the rings, and how they had responded to both Pride and Michael. What did that mean?

There was a tense, confused pause. "Thank you," Pride finally said, seeming to draw it out into four syllables. I allowed myself a brief smile of victory, careful to keep it hidden from Pride.

Then I let it go and turned back towards the archdemon. "So, Mr. Big Nuts, you in? I can't do it alone." Samael had told me that Arch-level demons could last longer in the Neverwas. I had zero chance of getting

Michael to join my gang, but Pride's assistance would help buy me the time I desperately needed, so it was better than nothing.

Pride grinned wolfishly. "Flattery will get you everywhere, Miss Penrose," he said, seeming to read through my tactic—or at least wanting me to think he had.

"So, you're not just a pretty face," I said with a disappointed sigh. "Pity."

He laughed, glancing at Samael with a nod of approval. "Godfather, eh?"

Samael studied me up and down. "I've aged a million years in our brief acquaintance," he grumbled. "No. More," he added with a smile.

I rolled my eyes and Pride chuckled. "If it means taking down Wrath, then hell yes, I'm in. But the logistics will require a bit of brainpower."

I sat back down and propped my elbows on my knees. "Why?"

"Us getting into Purgatory is fairly simple. Us finding them before my power fails or we're eaten alive by the inhabitants is practically impossible. But getting them *out*..." he trailed off, pursing his lips, "we would need a miracle. Literally."

So that was the issue. The White Tiger and Vermillion Bird were somehow anchored to the place. "Then why did Lilith take them there?" I asked, frowning. "There has to be a way to get them out. Something no one has thought of."

Pride shrugged, shooting Samael an apologetic glance. "No offense, Samael, but maybe Lilith just fucked up and made a bad call," he said, gently. Samael's lips thinned, but he didn't argue Pride's point. The archdemon turned to me with a sigh. "Those in Purgatory are supposed to be stuck in stasis for eternity. They didn't qualify to go to Heaven or Hell because they lived such an apathetic life in the first place. Second chances aren't given to those who lazily squandered their first chance. Once you set foot in the Neverwas, you become part of the environment. And if you stay too long, they give you a set of keys, because you are now part of the eternal food chain."

I nodded, grimly. "But if we're making a Gateway in, why wouldn't a Gateway out work just as well?"

Pride pinched the bridge of his nose as if searching for an explanation. "This isn't very accurate, but the concept applies," he forewarned, clearing his throat. "From inside Purgatory, making a Gateway back out is kind of like trying to run while floating in space. You can see Earth right in front of you, but no matter how fast you pedal your legs, you're not going anywhere.

There's no friction for you to grip. There's nothing for you to anchor *to*, which is why you have to leave the Gateway you used to get *into* Purgatory open—and then hope you're strong enough to keep it open or you're fucked. That's where the Arch-level power comes into play. I have more endurance than my fellow demons. No offense, Samael," he said with a dry grin.

Samael rolled his eyes, but nodded at my inquisitive look, backing up Pride's claims.

His analogy actually did make sense to me. The Gateway into purgatory would act like a lifeline thrown down a well. An archdemon was a stronger rope, figuratively speaking. And archdemon and an archangel together would be even stronger, but that wasn't an option. I pondered the puzzle, wondering how my Spear might fit into the equation. My mother had certainly seen a chance at success, even though no one else did.

Even with the proper team in place, I had no idea how to even find the White Tiger and Vermillion Bird once we arrived. Lilith hadn't given me any clues either. Probably because the two Divines were constantly running for their lives—or actively hunting down other souls.

The whole situation sounded fucking insane.

"What else do you know about the inhabitants? These hungry souls?" I asked, letting my frustrated thoughts simmer in the background.

He met my eyes and they were haunted. "Apathy. The only food in Purgatory is your fellow souls. Only problem is that you can't *die*, per se. You just grow weaker—forever. Your existence is to be eaten by your own people, slowly regain some of your essence, and then get eaten again. Forever." He saw the disgusted look in my eyes and nodded very slowly. "They don't call it *never was* for nothing," he said, enunciating the two words individually. "Never was anything worthwhile in life, so why afford any of those squandered luxuries in death? Spend eternity suffering the very creed you embodied on Earth. Be forgotten and seen as nothing by your peers. Just a thoughtless, mindless, eternally hungry parasite sucking off those around you and being sucked off in return—which is nowhere near as fun as it sounds."

I turned to see Samael staring off at nothing with a disgusted look on his face. "Why would Lilith send them there?" I mused. "To keep them safe by making them part of the menu?"

Pride cleared his throat. "In Lilith's defense, women have always made poor choices when it comes to food. A certain apple comes to mind..." I shot him a murderous scowl, but he was grinning without shame. "Bazinga."

Samael grunted. "That was Eve, asshole. Not Lilith," he muttered, somewhat proudly.

I knew they were only teasing, but Samael's comment actually got me thinking. What might the world have been like if Adam hadn't been too insecure to occasionally let his first wife, Lilith, be on top during sex? His requirement to always be on top was, debatably, just as damning as Eve and her apple had been.

Pride nodded. "I agree, Callie." I flinched, not having realized that I'd spoken my thoughts out loud. My cheeks flushed, wondering exactly which part I'd verbalized. Pride grinned. "What's not to love about a woman straddling your hips and riding you into the ground, while you lay back and enjoy the view? Tits or tats, I don't care which direction she faces, because I'm a gentleman. The view is great either way."

I burst out laughing. "Boobs or tramp stamps?" I hooted. "Is that what you're saying?"

He grinned and then pinched his thumb and forefinger together in a circle as he made a kissing sound. "It's glorious either way. And I'm going to ask to bend her over in the next day or two, so what do I care? Share the wealth. Sex is all about variety and trying new things. The fun is in the experimentation."

"Are you two quite finished talking about my fiancée?" Samael asked, folding his arms.

I flashed my godfather a guilty wince, having forgotten he was present. Pride shot me a discreet wink before turning to face Samael. "Women in general, old friend. No offense intended."

"Offense?" Samael repeated, looking confused. "Lilith would have been laughing right along with you. I meant that we have more important things to discuss—like how to get the Divines back out."

I let out a sigh, focusing back on the topic. "And to keep Wrath unaware of this whole thing. If he wanted them dead a hundred years ago, and saw fit to imprison Lilith for disobeying him, I can only imagine what he'd do if he learned where they are, or that we are attempting a prison break."

Samael nodded grimly. "He also knows I'm your godfather, and that my Daemons are alive and well. The only reason he hasn't gone after them is because the other two Divines went missing. I just didn't know where they were before today," he said, shaking his head. "So we can't afford to make Wrath angry."

I scoffed. "Keeping Wrath calm is going to be a little difficult."

Pride was studying me, tapping his chin thoughtfully. "Well, we already know what he wants," he said, miming a finger pistol at me and then pulling the trigger. "You as his wife. That would stay his anger."

I shook my head angrily. "No way am I marrying a Prince of Hell. I have no power over him as it is. If I marry him, I'll be his slave."

Samael nodded. "She's right. Neither option will get us what we need—which is him preoccupied."

I held up a finger, rising to my feet at a new thought. "When we met earlier today, I stood up to him. I was careful not to push it too far, but...he really liked it. I could keep stringing him along for a very short while. Emphasis on very short."

Samael let out a nervous breath. "I don't like it, but I don't see any other way. Either you marry him—a loss. You deny him—starting a genocide in Kansas City. Or you can try to buy us enough time to figure out a plan to save the Divines—who you can then turn around and use as armor to destroy him. So, you'll have your payback."

I nodded, uneasily, gathering my resolve. Then I glanced at Pride. "You can't keep him busy for me? You're both arch-class. Couldn't you punch him around or something?"

He shook his head. "I already told you. We're the same. Only an archangel can take out an archdemon. Otherwise I would have killed him millennia ago. Or vice versa."

"And there's Michael to consider," Samael said with a frown. "He's adamant about Callie joining Heaven before she turns to Hell."

I hung my head in my hands. "I'll just have to keep stringing him along, too. But we still don't have any answers on how to get the Divines out of the Neverwas."

Pride nodded. "Facts," he said, leaning back into the couch.

I studied him, thoughtfully. "Why is one of the Seven Sins not a complete and utter asshole like Wrath?" I asked, genuinely curious. "I understand why you hate him, and that one demon is different from another," I said, indicating Samael. "But you're one of the most feared demons."

He locked eyes with me. "Are...you *flirting* with me, Callie Penrose? Because that would be *super*."

I scowled. "Nevermind. Case dismissed."

He chuckled good-naturedly, and I found myself wondering how much of it was an act. Was he playing his own game here? I decided to err on the side of caution and assume that he was. Still, there was something different about him. I had no misconceptions that he could be just as evil as Wrath if he saw the need, but his default setting didn't seem as cruel as Wrath.

"The only difference between us and angels is that we didn't like the status quo. We rebelled, and we lost. People forget that we all had different reasons for rebelling—some noble, some decidedly not so noble. Similarly, how we handled that loss spans a wide spectrum of responses from bitter to vengeful to apathetic to relieved. I'm much too beautiful to be angry for eternity," he admitted with a shrug. "This face was made for swooning, and you can't swoon with a frown," he said, flashing me a brilliant smile.

He made a fair point. It was a really good smile. And...it made sense psychologically as well. My premise had simply been flawed—that the Seven Sins were different from humans. They were, but they also were not.

In fact, in some ways, they were more similar than different. Michael had been an asshole to me, as had Wrath. Eae had been somewhat skittish, but loyal in the end. And Pride...well, I could have grabbed a few drinks with him if I hadn't known he was a demon. Wrath had even seemed slightly bipolar, in my limited diagnostic capacity for mental disorders.

Pride was studying me curiously, taking my thoughtful silence as agreement.

"Demons can be cruel, but so can angels. They are just as broken as us—they just chose the winning side on that fateful day outside of the Garden of Eden. Once you accept the fact that most of religious doctrine is propaganda, everything starts to become much clearer. The angels are not the heroes from your precious Bible. Check the Old Testament because the originals are always better. Angels are heartless killers just as often as demons are. The main difference is that we choose not to deny or defend it. Because we know white robes don't hide bloodstains, haloes don't hide hate, and a black feather weighs just as much as a white one," he said, tapping one of the black feathers on his chest and then pointing at my white outfit.

I stared back at him, unable to blink. That...had been beautifully poetic.

I wasn't putting on a team jersey or anything, but this was the most honest conversation I'd had with a powerful angel, and I found it ironic that Pride had convinced me of his point with a touch of humility on his own side's failures. Samael was studying me curiously and gave me an appreciative smile when our eyes met. Then he turned to Pride with a respectful nod.

And I couldn't blame him. Demon of the Year went to Pride. Of course, I wasn't going to tell him that. He already had a healthy ego.

I leaned forward, locking eyes with the archdemon. "I'm curious. Why *do* you hate Wrath so much?"

He considered my question for a few moments. "Wrath and I share the balance of power with the Seven, although he is more popular because anger works better in a mob. Pride is more...individual. The system we had in Heaven was broken, and I was too proud to watch it continue to deteriorate, so I left. Since then, I've learned that walking away did not solve the problem—it only gave absolute power to those who had proven they could not handle it wisely. People like Wrath and others. That is why I hate him so much. He took something I was proud of and soiled it. He and others made the system worse," he growled. Then, he leaned forward, staring deep into my eyes. "So, Callie Penrose, I want to burn it all down."

Samael was watching our exchange with a concerned look on his face. I leaned back in my seat, studying the archdemon with a thoughtful look. "Why the hell would Wrath send me to talk to you?" I asked, flustered. "It's no secret that you two are polar opposites."

Pride laughed. "Everyone knows of our feud. It's only lasted a few millennia, after all."

I tapped my lips, frowning. Why would Wrath send me here, then? What game was he playing?

"CALLIE PENROSE!" A voice roared from outside the mansion, making the glass panes rattle. "COME OUTSIDE! NOW!"

I jumped up from the couch, drawing my katana on reflex as I scanned the room for points of ingress and egress. Samael and Pride gave each other shocked looks. Rather than join in on their staring contest, I raced for the front door, wondering why the voice had sounded familiar. I hid my body as I risked a quick look through the glass and—

I froze.

Then I slowly turned to see Pride and Samael standing behind me with grim looks on their faces.

"Um. Your brother, Michael, is here," I whispered.

Pride folded his arms and shook his head at me. "Well, he didn't ask for me. I didn't stay this pretty by being brave. Get your ass out there, toots."

✵ 36 ✵

After verifying that the archangel was alone, I opened the door, but kept myself out of the opening to make sure Michael didn't send an introductory blast of holy fire my way. Nothing happened, so I stepped out onto the porch, glancing left and right to make sure there wasn't a hidden welcoming party lying in wait.

But we were entirely alone.

Michael stood with his feet shoulder-width apart, and he held his fiery sword out rather than tucked into his sheath. His eyes flickered with white flame and his chest was heaving with outrage. I drew my katana, and carefully descended the front steps, keeping my eyes focused on him while using my peripheral vision to make sure a gang of nephilim weren't hiding in the trees or around the side of the mansion.

As I approached, I was very aware of the rings in my pocket, realizing halfway across the yard that the two people they'd responded to were present—Michael and Pride. But Michael didn't look very open-minded at the moment, so there was nothing I could do about it until I calmed him down.

Samael and Pride remained behind, knowing their involvement would only make the situation worse. Especially since Michael had only called *my* name. I came to a halt about five feet away from him.

"What is the meaning of this, Michael?" I asked, guardedly. "How about we put our swords away—"

"I had to see it for myself," he snarled, venomously. "When I heard you met with Wrath, I refused to believe it. Then I heard about the handful of demons you slaughtered, and I convinced myself that you had been *attacked* by Wrath, not that you voluntarily *met* with him."

I narrowed my eyes at his tone. "There were eighteen demons, not a *handful*," I growled. "And I didn't have tea and scones with Wrath. He found me and *trapped* me."

Michael gritted his teeth. "And did *he* find you, too?" he asked, visibly shaking as he pointed his blade at the mansion. "You can't claim victimhood for your second Sin of the day."

I swatted his sword away with mine, not appreciating how close it happened to be to my neck. His eyes widened in momentary surprise. "They were having a two-for-one special," I snarled. "And what business is it of yours, anyway? I didn't see any of your associates showing up to save me, so I rolled up my sleeves."

His eyes flared brighter. "And is that what you're doing here? Rolling up your sleeves? Because to me, it looks like you are *consorting* with him."

"I'm killing him with kindness," I said sarcastically. "Let's pretend I *was* consorting with him. So what? Let's make it even better. Pretend we were actually in the middle of a romantic engagement." I stepped forward, right up into his face. "It is exactly *zero* business of yours, because you only show up *after* the action happens."

He glared at me, clenching his jaw, and squeezing the hilt of his sword as his face purpled.

I calmly stepped back, sheathing my sword. "Now, buzz off. I didn't get my happy ending yet."

And I turned my back on him, internally cursing my inappropriate comment for multiple reasons. Something about Michael's holier-than-thou attitude always got under my skin faster than any demon's arrogance. My intended point was accurate—that Michael only seemed to show up too late or when a tangible asset was up for grabs. But that last jab...it was probably going to cost me.

A wall of white fire erupted before me, cutting me off from the mansion. I halted, closed my eyes, and then took a deep breath. *Focus, Callie*, I told myself. *His righteous wrath is toxic and contagious.*

"You absolutely sure you want to end your story like this, Mikey?" I asked in a calm, detached tone.

"You cannot defeat an archangel, so there is only one story in danger of ending," he growled.

I laughed softly, drawing my katana, and approaching the white fire. "Not only are you picking a fight with a girl, but one who is admittedly weaker than you," I said, calmly and clearly, as I extended my Silver katana into the wall of flame. My katana was not made of steel but my bond with Sanguina —the Eternal Metal, as I'd heard it called. Although not strong enough to kill an archangel, it was strong enough to make a good showing. "What a brave and noble archangel!"

Pride's words emboldened me as I watched my sword somehow catch flame.

I turned back to Michael, my face utterly blank and expressionless. Then I began to advance, and with each step, my angel armor crackled into place —first, my gauntlets, and then my boots, and then an ornate breastplate, seemingly made of glass.

Michael suddenly looked less certain about his decision, eyeing the fire on my blade in disbelief.

"All you know how to do is swoop down when you see birdseed on the ground, pigeon. You hear children laugh and convince yourself that it is their adoration for your magnificence when it is so much simpler—children will laugh with joy at the most simplistic of nature's wonders. Even a pigeon," I said, my voice cold and brittle as paper-thin crystal.

His mouth worked wordlessly, staring at me in stunned outrage.

"And you are blind to the fact that those of us on the front lines see you for the vermin you really are—rodents with wings." He stepped back with a hurt look on his face. I shook my head in disappointment. "As a little girl, I grew up *dreaming* about seeing an angel one day. I thought you would be magical, pure, inspiring beacons of light in a cruel, dark world." I lifted my sword and my wings exploded out the back of my armor, stretching out to their full magnificence. "Just goes to show...you should never meet your heroes. It's time to dance, rodent. Dance with the child of broken dreams, archangel," I spat. "Or be the role model she once thought you were and lower. Your. Fucking. *Sword*."

I knew my fight was hopeless. But I was comfortable with Despair. After listening to Pride's recollection of events about his fall from grace, I'd had enough. I was calling Michael out, once and for all. Sometimes, it wasn't about winning or losing. It was about setting an example. Sacrifice.

Something an angel was supposed to do—not an orphan at the end of her rope.

I lifted my katana upright before me and swept out my wings, fanning the flames behind me. "Decide."

Michael set his jaw. "I do not want this, Callie."

"Then don't *do* this, Michael," I said.

"You risk breaking the Spear."

I shook my head. "No. *You* risk breaking the Spear by swinging your sword at it—at me!" I fired back.

"Why are you here if my suspicions are unfounded?" he hissed, exasperated. "You see how this looks and you try to paint me as the guilty party?"

I shrugged. "You assumed the worst in me from the moment you arrived. In your shoes, I would have asked you the question before passing any judgment. When have I *ever* given you reason to assume my intentions were in any way nefarious? You keep forgetting that the Spear chose ME!" I roared.

The Spear is not a weapon. Aala and Ryuu's analysis whispered in the back of my mind. But I wasn't using it at all, let alone as a weapon, so I ignored it.

Michael gritted his teeth, obviously torn. "I told you what was at stake. The Seven must not take Kansas City," he rasped, his eyes desperate. "Yet you are here, talking with Pride! What am I supposed to think?"

"If you knew he was here all along, why are you only just now coming by?" I asked, hitting him with the hard questions. If he wanted to talk about the potential for an all-out war between archangels and archdemons, I would totally understand and even accept it. But his track record was consistent. He always showed up with his sword when a prize was on the line—never when an innocent life was on the line.

"I follow orders, Callie. I can't just swoop in whenever I wish," he whispered.

I cocked my head. "Orders? Gabriel sent you here?"

He nodded. "Yes. To protect the Spear."

I frowned. "Protect it from what, exactly? It's not in any danger. No one can take it from me without my permission, and surprise, surprise, the demons don't even care about it! So, tell me, what exactly is Gabriel so concerned about?"

Michael was silent for a few moments. "He did not say," he said, sounding slightly troubled.

I scoffed. "And how did Gabriel suddenly know Pride was here? The timing is incredible. If he knew Pride's whereabouts, why didn't he send you here earlier to chase him away?"

"I do not know."

"And how did he know *I* was here?"

"I do not know."

"I'm sensing a theme, Michael."

He nodded, woodenly. "If an archangel came into direct conflict with an archdemon on earth, there would be open war. Kansas City would become an angelic battlefield, and no human would survive."

I nodded. "And your boss still sent you here, knowing an archdemon was inside. He isn't giving you the whole story. You came here, willing to kill me with your sword of justice, clad in armor of ignorance. Even while knowing one of the Seven was here. I'm just spit balling, but don't you think you should have been given some backup? Confronting me and one of the Seven Sins does not require a buddy?" I asked, shouting. My words rang out over the hills, echoing.

Michael slowly lowered his sword and the white fire surrounding us began to dim. "I...do not know," he whispered, looking as if his wings had suddenly been ripped from his back. Case in point, they began to droop as he stared down at the ground, his eyes dimming in time with the fire. "It doesn't make any sense," he murmured, agreeing with me, and not sounding relieved by the revelation. "Why would—"

"RPG!" a voice shouted. I heard the telltale thump of a goddamned rocket propelled grenade and my eyes widened in alarm.

Michael looked up sharply and his eyes widened as his gaze shifted to something over my shoulder. The light of the sun winked out between one moment and the next, and I felt a concussive *thump* about two feet away from me—like I had been standing too close to a Fourth of July artillery shell when it went off.

It should have incinerated me or obliterated my eardrums, but something had muffled it. I still heard the roar of flame, but it sounded muted.

I checked myself to find that I wasn't a burning, smoldering corpse, but I did begin to cough and choke at the cloud of smoke filling the front lawn. "What the fuck is happening?" I shouted.

I looked up at the sky, wondering why it had grown so dark, and I flinched to find a canopy of inky black feathers sheltering me. In fact, those feathers created a defensive wall to my side as well.

And it hadn't just protected me. Michael stared at our savior in disbelief. "Pride," he whispered, sounding both awed and horrified. Pride grunted, lowering his massive black wings enough to peer over the top and assess our apparent attackers.

"Who the *fuck* just shot a rocket at me?" I demanded.

Pride turned to look at me from only inches away and I sucked in a breath, physically jolted by his haunting, nightmarish beauty. Those devilish blue eyes promised long, sensual nights and even longer, bloodier battles against anyone who tried to interrupt us. I realized, in that singular moment, that Pride had been heavily muting his aura from me when we'd first met.

But out here, under attack...

Hot. Damned.

His power radiated off of him like an open oven. I felt him dial it back down, and I let out a shuddering sigh of relief, blinking rapidly to get my bearings.

"Dozen nephilim," he growled. Then he winked at me. "You're one bad ass broad, Callie. Has anyone ever told you how sexy crazy looks on you?" He asked, indicating my earlier exchange with Michael. I grinned in spite of myself and nodded smugly.

Michael sputtered, sounding as if he was short-circuiting. "What is the meaning of this?" he demanded. I couldn't tell if he was angry at us or the nephilim.

"Easy, brother," Pride told him with a roguish grin. "Maybe they were trying to protect you from this prickly little rose," he said, swatting me firmly on the ass.

37

I squawked in surprise, but it was mixed with laughter.

Pride cackled as I swiped my sword at him, easily dancing out of range as he buffeted his thick black wings, forcing me to shield my eyes from the blast of air.

Michael sputtered at the world in general.

Then the three of us turned to face the nephilim as Pride finally lowered his wings.

Two of us were smiling. The other one was Michael.

Rather than a virtuous army of nephilim, I saw a dozen scared as hell young men. But they weren't looking at us. They were looking about twenty feet over our heads.

The three of us glanced up to see Samael in complete demon form—a monster of truly epic proportions. Instead of skin, he had scales made of darkened coins, and his horns were at least ten-feet-long each. His eyes blazed with red fire. His wings blocked out the sun. I slowly turned back to the nephilim with a shit-eating grin on my face.

"You guys ever met my godfather?" I called out, releasing my angelic armor and calling my wings back in now that my godfather was here to keep me safe—

One of them dropped his rocket launcher, and the damned thing misfired straight at Samael. I gasped in fear but Samael lurched forward to catch it in his mouth like a dog catching a frisbee—where it exploded. He abruptly sneezed, spewing flames into the air. He shook his head, his face on fire, and chewed up the metal fragments as he let out a bone-chilling laugh. Then he spat the metal glob onto the ground in front of the nephilim hard enough to create a small crater.

One of them grabbed his crotch with both hands, obviously peeing his pants. Others drew swords in shaky gestures, making the sign of the Cross over their faces. I'd give them that much. They wouldn't die bravely, but they were willing to die holding their ground—

Two of them took off running and I burst out laughing.

Michael stormed forward, pointing his sword at the lot of them. Pride gripped my shoulder and gently squeezed. "I don't like this," he said, shaking his head, and there was nothing humorous in his voice.

In fact, he sounded downright troubled.

"Stand down!" Michael shouted, indicating both parties. To his credit, the glare he shot Samael was equally as fierce as the one he shot the nephilim. Samael didn't impress him, which really put things into perspective for me.

What the hell would an archdemon such as Pride's full form look like if Michael was so unconcerned about the giant, Samael? I risked a glance at Pride from the corner of my eye. He was still in human form, wearing only his silk pajama pants and no shirt, but regal, black feathered wings grew out of his back, looking startlingly majestic rather than horrifying or monstrous.

Samael grumbled something and I felt it in my boots, even if I couldn't translate it into a word. But he didn't antagonize the nephilim further. After taking a rocket to the molars, I would have let him play with the nephilim for a few minutes as fair compensation. I glanced down to see that the fire on my katana had finally extinguished, so I sheathed the blade and folded my arms.

Michael rounded on the nephilim, now that he was certain no one was going to escalate the fight. He absently snapped his fingers, and the two nephilim in the distance—almost to safety—suddenly tripped and ate dirt. They did not get back up. Michael grunted disgustedly. "What is the meaning of this?" he growled, singling out one of the lead nephilim—a gangly, strawberry-blonde, twenty-something who looked like he had qualified for the job by beating his sister at *Call of Duty*.

"Lord Gabriel sent us, sir," the nephilim said, obviously conflicted.

"Did Lord Gabriel command you to introduce yourselves with a rocket?" he asked in a chilling tone.

The nephilim—startling everyone on my side of Archangel Michael's DMZ—nodded affirmatively. "Yes, Lord Michael. Anything to take out Callie Penrose."

The front lawn grew as silent as a tomb. I blinked, slowly turning to look at Pride. He looked just as startled as me. But I watched as the demon within stared out through Pride's dreamy blue eyes, and he took a subconscious, protective step closer to me, curling his lip at the nephilim.

I felt my heart flutter with both fear and...

Appreciation. Pride had almost lost his ever-loving shit after hearing Gabriel's shoot-to-kill order on me.

Michael glanced back at me with a grim look. In his eyes, I saw a great leviathan stirring just beneath the surface. I sucked in a sharp breath as I finally caught a glimpse of the legendary archangel I had wanted to see ever since I'd been a pig-tailed brat doodling in the church hymnals on Sundays. I could see the truth in his face. He was just as livid as Pride. He had not been told—and would not tolerate—Gabriel's order.

Michael rounded on the nephilim, making them flinch. "Gabriel sent me here ten minutes ago," he said in a foreboding tone, "and he gave me no such order. You expect me to believe he so drastically changed his mind in such a short span of time?"

The nephilim suddenly realized the situation he'd been put in, looking like he now envied the two who had fled. He licked his lips nervously. "She has agreed to marry Wrath."

"The *hell* I have!" I shouted, outraged. "He hasn't even proposed yet—" Pride groaned beside me, slapping his forehead with his palm. I closed my eyes. Damn it. That hadn't sounded the way I'd intended.

I opened my eyes to see Michael glaring at the nephilim. "In the last ten minutes, she agreed to marry Wrath?" he asked, his voice dripping with cynicism. "I see Pride and Samael, and everyone knows Wrath despises them."

The nephilim stammered, obviously not having an answer. "I have a picture of her signing the contract with Legion earlier this morning," he said, pulling out his phone hurriedly.

I shook my head angrily, ignoring the curious look from Pride. "I absolutely did *not*!" I told Pride under my breath, unwilling to take my eyes off Michael as he took the phone and began flipping through pictures. "I did see Legion, and I refused to sign his contract—for the second time," I hissed.

Pride turned to look up at Samael, speaking in a strange tongue. Samael replied in a low growl, making the ground rumble beneath me. I turned to shoot them both a furious glare. "Would you two shut up?"

I turned back to the nephilim in time to see two of them on either edge of the line lifting assault rifles and setting me in their sights. "For God!" they shouted in unison.

And then they opened fire.

Michael let out a roar and a pair of massive, white-feathered wings ripped out of his back, blocking off all the nephilim from me, even the two gunmen. But he wasn't quick enough to stop all of the bullets. I felt three sharp impacts hit me in the chest, and then I was sitting on my ass, staring at Michael's back in shock. The guns continued to unload and I saw Michael's feathers quiver as his wings were peppered with impacts, even producing a faint trickle of bright red blood in two places. I saw his hips swivel ever so slightly and all sound abruptly ceased.

Then he collapsed to his knees. There were no more nephilim in front of him.

"Where did the nephilim go?" I mumbled, wincing at the painful throbbing sensation in my chest. Pride pulled me to my feet without asking and then began fondling my boobs.

I swatted his hands away, wincing in pain, but he ignored me, redoubling his efforts, so I relented. He let out a stunned breath and finally ceased his groping—much to the relief of my bruised girls. "What the *fuck* are your clothes made of?"

"Why?" I asked, peering past his black wings at Michael.

"Because they saved your life," he breathed, shaking his head. I barely heard him.

Because I was staring at the kneeling archangel in sudden understanding. I took a stumbling step, biting back the pain arcing across my bruised chest. "No," I whispered. "Michael saved my life."

I couldn't take my eyes away from the crimson stains in his wings, even as they sagged low to the ground in abject shame. As I shambled closer, Pride ducked under my arm to support me, expediting our travel time as we approached the archangel.

And that's when I saw the headless nephilim—ten bodies oozing blood across the dying grass. Michael had stabbed the tip of his sword into the ground and knelt before it, holding the hilt with both hands as if it was the only thing supporting his weight.

The blade was painted bright red with the hot blood of the nephilim.

And the archangel wept.

I sucked in a breath and Pride froze in disbelief.

Michael had just fallen from grace.

And it was all my fault.

"Why?" I whispered to Michael. "Why would you risk everything to save me?"

Michael rested his forehead against the hilt of his blade. "So Pride wouldn't have to save you," he whispered.

Pride stared at his brother, a look of pain and regret tearing him in half— and through it all, love.

Love for his brother.

38

The area was silent, and I knew it wasn't my place to speak.

"You don't even *like* me!" Pride snapped, sounding disproportionately angry.

A faint laugh bubbled up from Michael's throat. "I don't have to like you."

Pride was staring at him in disbelief.

I cleared my throat gently. "I don't understand," I said, softly.

Pride curled his lip, sounding like he wanted to bring the nephilim back to life so he could kill them all over again with his bare hands. "In saving you, I would have instantly retaliated by killing them all."

"Which would have started an open war on the streets of Kansas City," Michael said. "I did it for him so that all those deaths would not fall on his shoulders. They were my responsibility. My burden."

"And now you will fall. You fool," Pride growled, and I saw that his eyes were brimming with angry tears. He folded his arms, averting his gaze from his brother.

Michael just nodded, accepting the price without shame.

Samael stepped up behind me, back in his human form. He checked me over with a concerned look on his face, and then let out a sigh of relief. "That's some armor," he said, shaking his head at Aphrodite's gift.

Then he stormed past me and hoisted Michael to his feet. "You fool!" he

said, shaking his brother by the shoulders. "You blind, stupid, sanctimonious
—" And then the greater demon was pulling the archangel in for a tight,
brotherly hug, forcefully slapping him on the back as he continued his angry
tirade in a low growl.

Michael smiled absently at the affection, but his eyes were very far away.

They finally separated and we stood in silence, staring at Michael, and
waiting for...well, I don't know what, exactly. For him to fall. Whether that
meant losing his wings or suddenly turning into a demon of some kind, I
wasn't entirely sure.

Pride began to fidget and Samael was tapping his foot worriedly. Michael
hung his head, occasionally alternately glancing over his right or left wing—
both still dripping blood.

Nothing happened. Except for Pride getting twitchier, Samael getting
tappier, and Michael almost giving himself whiplash by checking each wing
every half-second.

"Okay!" I finally snapped. "This is kind of like how men hate asking
anyone for directions, isn't it?" I asked, frowning at their impatient tics. "I'll
just say it out loud. Why hasn't Michael fallen?"

Pride and Samael exchanged meaningful looks, but didn't speak. Michael
finally lifted his head to stare at me, and his face was pale. "It means," he
whispered, staring at the dead nephilim, "that I was in the right. That their
order to kill you was either a lie, or that Gabriel had no authority to make
such a command."

Pride sighed. "You guys ever seen an archangel have an existential crisis?
Because you're about to see an archangel have an existential crisis," he said.
"Been there, done that. I'm going to go see if there is a Starbucks around
here. Their Frappuccinos are like mouth sex without the sin, and I think
Michael is going to need one." Then he was walking back to the mansion,
muttering under his breath while angrily punching his fist into his palm. His
black wings evaporated after only a few steps.

I blinked, trying to process his comment. I turned to Samael, arching an
eyebrow in hopes he would explain. "I'll go keep an eye on him," he said.
"You deal with..." he gestured vaguely at Michael, "that."

"Gee. Thanks," I muttered, as he jogged after Pride. "We probably need
to get out of here. The place is burned!" I said, cupping my hands around my
mouth to make sure they both heard me. Samael flashed me a thumbs up
without turning around, and then he was striding up the stairs and into the

house, where I heard the sounds of crashing glass—as if Pride was breaking every fragile thing he could get his hands on.

I turned to Michael, realizing I could only deal with one meltdown at a time. He was staring at the blood on his sword, and occasionally forcing himself to look at the bodies. I did the same, shuddering at a new thought. My father had been one of them. An elite version, judging by how everyone spoke of him, but he would have died just the same as these rookies. "Thank you, Michael."

He nodded, numbly.

I glanced at the blood on his pristine white feathers. "Are your wings okay?

He nodded. "I'm fine. But what does this mean? I would *know* if Gabriel had fallen."

I didn't even want to think about that chilling thought. "How about we come up with a cover story? I know! I blackmailed you into helping me. You only saved my life to protect the Spear of Destiny."

He slowly turned to look up at me. "That is a lie."

I held up a finger. "Only if you know the truth."

He narrowed his eyes. "Which I do."

"Fine. A better one, then. If you wouldn't have saved me, I would have destroyed the Spear."

"Also a lie," he said with a frown. "You do understand that the story isn't the problem, right? It's the lie."

I grumbled an affirmative response. The goodie-two-shoes definitely hadn't fallen.

"Were you really going to marry Wrath?" he asked.

"Of course not!" I snapped, throwing my hands up into the air. He stared at me, waiting. I let out a frustrated breath. "But he did ask me," I admitted. "And I might have decided to string him along until I came up with a plan to stop him," I said, cringing at the fuse I'd just lit.

Michael's eyes almost bugged out of his head. "You did *what?*"

Pride came sprinting out of the house tugging a tee on over his head as he ran. He'd changed out of his pajamas and thrown on some jeans and military boots. Samael was hot on his heels, and both of them looked anxious. Pride tugged his shirt down and pulled his hair back into a ponytail before slipping on a pair of aviators. I stared at his shirt and burst out laughing.

Blasphemy is a victimless crime.

With a picture of Jesus riding a dinosaur.

He skidded to a halt, grinning at my reaction. "Okay. Good news and bad news," he said.

Michael opened his mouth with an emo look on his face so I cut in. "Good news."

"Okay. We get to drive a convertible."

Samael leaned towards me with a disgusted grimace. "It's a Mazda Miata—"

"It's a *convertible!*" Pride snapped, glaring at him. "And now *you* get to drive." He tossed the keys to Samael, and I swear to God there was a little disco ball on the keychain.

I bit back my smile and nodded. "And the bad news?"

"No sin-free mouth sex for Michael. There isn't a Starbucks for twenty miles—"

Samael swatted his arm, discreetly shaking his head as he gauged Michael's body language.

Pride sighed in resignation. "And we don't want to be driving around those extra twenty miles because we *both* have a price on our heads, now," he said, pointing at Michael and then himself. "Congratulations."

Michael stood as still as a statue, looking numb. The other two were just as helpful, as if they were waiting for a motivational speech to kick off the family road trip.

I clapped my hands together, pleased that they all flinched. "Let's go! They already know about this place, so there's no point standing over the evidence."

Pride led the way, jogging ahead and motioning for us to follow him around the side of the house towards a detached garage. I glanced back to where Michael had taken down the first two fleeing nephilim. "Think those two ratted on us?" I asked him, thankful that he wasn't too shell-shocked to move.

He met my eyes for a fraction of a second and shook his head. "I killed them, too. It all happened on reflex," he murmured. I winced, reaching the garage just as the door began to rise, revealing Samael trying to fit his large frame into the cutest little red sports car that had never heard the words *male dignity*. Pride was grinning in the passenger seat as I guided Michael towards the smallest backseat ever.

I shoved him in before pausing long enough to think of the obvious. "Wait. Why don't I just make a Gateway?"

"No!" the three frantically shouted in unison, swiveling their attention to me, revealing horrified looks.

I froze, holding up my hands in an appeasing gesture, and then I climbed into the backseat beside Michael. "Mind telling me why?"

"They might be using a tracker," Pride said, turning to look at me as Samael turned over the engine. "They can pick up the scent of magic and follow it. We need to go old school until we know we've lost them."

Samael turned the key in the ignition and the toy car revved to life like an ambitious lawnmower. The stereo kicked on, blaring *Yeah!* by Usher, of all songs. And then we were racing away at sixty-six horsepower. Apparently, Pride was a self-proclaimed karaoke king, because he was soon belting out the lyrics at the top of his lungs. It wasn't long before I was singing right along with him, laughing at the ridiculousness of the entire situation—three angels and Dracula cruising down the backroads in a convertible Miata.

Michael began blushing uncomfortably as soon as he started paying attention to the lyrics, which only made me laugh harder.

"Where are we going?" Samael shouted, looking at me in the rearview mirror.

"Wherever the music takes us!" Pride crowed, fist-pumping the air. Then he lifted his phone to take a selfie with miserable Michael in the background. "Hashtag road tripping with my bros!" And he actually posted it on Instagram. Because, of course he had an account. He was Pride, after all.

Rather than wading into that cesspool of a conversation, I leaned closer to Samael. "Let's take them to church!"

He glanced back at me with a grin, and then nodded.

Roland was going to be so pissed.

39

I opened the doors to the church and ushered everyone inside as quickly as possible. We had parked the car a few blocks away, and left the keys in the front seat, before hurriedly fleeing down a back alley. Because Pride had informed us that he'd stolen the car two days ago, and that it hadn't actually belonged to Circle Seven Holdings.

He told us this only *after* we saw our first police cruiser.

I closed the doors behind me and let out a breath of relief. No sirens. We were in the clear. The church was dark since Roland had blacked out most of the windows for his vampires. The last time I'd set foot in here, I'd fought Roland almost to the death. It was where I'd first officially met Samael. Putting it into context, that hadn't happened all that long ago.

I turned around to see Pride pointing a finger pistol into the church. "Pew! Pew! Pew!" he said, miming trigger pulls with each sound effect. I groaned upon noticing each shot had been aimed at one of the church pews Roland had kept for aesthetic reasons. He grinned at me from over his shoulder. "I've always wanted to do that."

A new voice interrupted us from the shadows near the altar. "What do you think you are doing—"

Pride deftly spun, suddenly wielding a Desert Eagle .44 Magnum, and pulled the trigger. A concussive *boom* made the air shudder, and I felt a pulse of magic from Pride's target.

I dove forward and snatched the gun out of the archdemon's hand before forcefully shoving him back. "Are you insane?" I snapped, popping open the cylinder and ejecting the rounds into my palm. "What part of low profile did you not understand?"

Pride cocked his head, looking confused. "He's a vampire. Just make another one, Dracula."

I stared at him for a few seconds, seriously considering pistol-whipping him. Instead, I flicked a round at him with my fingers, hitting him right above the eyes with a solid thunk. He slapped a hand over his forehead, cursing at me. "Pew!" I said, mimicking his sound effect from earlier. I shook my head and turned towards the altar, shoving the revolver down the back of my weapons belt and pocketing the four rounds. "Sorry Roland!" I called out.

Pride shot me a glare, and I grinned smugly at the red mark on his forehead. He muttered unhappily as he turned to stare into the darkness with an impressed look on his face. "You're fast, vampire," he murmured. Then he suddenly took notice of the silver statue in the corner of the room—the angel I had trapped the moment he fell from grace. "Hey! I *know* that prick! Selfie time!" he crowed, strolling over to the statue to pay his disrespects.

Michael and Samael had seated themselves on the nearby pew and were speaking in low tones, seemingly unaffected by Pride's childish curiosity, the gunshot, or the vampire preacher. Roland walked up to me, his crimson eyes flicking between each of my new friends with a mix of anger and trepidation. "A word?"

"That's *The Word* to you, heathen swine!" Pride jeered, snapping a selfie with Nameless.

I sighed, turning to my old mentor. "Ignore him. He's drunk," I said, gesturing at Pride. "And yes, it's about as bad as it looks," I admitted under his scrupulous glare. I was very familiar with the look, because I'd made him practice it for ten years.

He nodded, facing me but keeping his eyes on the others. I hadn't spoken to Roland recently, but we were on the mend since our momentous fight. The only reason he lived was because Samael had blocked my sword from killing him in this very room. Roland's ruby red eyes settled on Michael and I saw a flicker of compassion cross his face, replacing the tension. "He is hurt," he said.

I nodded. "He said his wings—" I coughed into my fist, realizing I'd almost said more than I should. Wings meant angels, and Roland would fangirl over an angel. I rephrased my comment on the fly. "He said he would wing it. Just a minor flesh wound."

Roland eyed me suspiciously. "I was speaking of his heart—figuratively. He's in pain. Internal pain."

I smiled at my old mentor, deeply touched by the genuine concern in his voice. He had been a pastor, first. A Shepherd of the soul before he'd become a Shepherd of the blade. Roland had the heart of a teddy bear, but the claws and fangs of a sleuth of *actual* bears. "Yeah," I agreed, following his gaze to assess Michael's situation. "That's putting it mildly. He had to make a choice between two terrible outcomes. He's torn, fearing he made the wrong call while knowing he made the *right* call."

Roland smiled empathetically. "Like a Shepherd choosing to become a vampire?" he asked, gently.

I felt a smile creeping onto my face. "You know, it's almost *exactly* like that."

"Maybe I could talk to your friend," he suggested, "if you think it might help."

I didn't want to spoil the surprise. If Roland managed to cheer up Michael without realizing who he was actually talking to...it would be the greatest gift I could possibly give him—to help his hero.

Because Archangel Michael was Roland's Michael Jordan.

"You might be the only man who could," I admitted honestly. "We won't be here long," I assured him.

"This is your sanctuary, Callie," he said, squeezing my hand in his. "Take all the time you need."

Then he was walking past me on silent feet. "How did you dodge that bullet?" I asked. "I felt magic."

Roland turned and lobbed something at me. I caught it, frowning. "Something I learned from you...the last time we were in this room," he said. Then he continued on, leaving me to feel guilty all by myself as I stared at the bullet slug in my palm. When we'd fought here, I had used orbs of power to catch lightning bolts he had thrown at me, freezing them in mid-air.

He'd used one to catch Pride's bullet. I shoved it into my pocket as a keepsake.

With nothing else to do, I made my way over to Pride, who was speaking to Samael in hushed tones near the Nameless statue. My ears grew hot as I picked up the tail end of their conversation.

"Did you just say assassination contracts?" I hissed, interrupting them. Michael and Roland were already deep in conversation, and Michael was smiling faintly. His shoulders looked less rigid, which was a good start. "I thought you were being hyperbolic when you said you two had a price on your heads."

Pride turned to me. "What did you just call me?" he asked in a low growl. "Hyper-what?"

I took a calming breath. "I didn't know you meant a real assassination contract, earlier. Talk."

He held out his hand. "Give me my gun back and I'll talk."

"Talk or I'll make this statue a new friend."

He grinned brightly. "I like you, Callie." He shoved his hands into his pockets and leaned against the statue without remorse over his brother's plight. "I tuned into archangel radio and it was all anyone was talking about. Apparently, Wrath put a hit out on me for conspiring with Michael to help kidnap his betrothed, Callie Penrose." I bit back my instinctive snarl, and Pride nodded knowingly. "Dick move, right? Get this—Gabriel put a hit out on Michael for murdering nephilim and then attacking me and Samael, risking a war. But both are claiming it's to prevent an all-out war before the other side does something foolish. I think we all know both are just covering their asses, because whatever Michael was doing at my house, he was *definitely* set up."

"Agreed," Samael said. "If his orders were genuine, Michael should have had a flight of angels as back-up. In which case, Gabriel wouldn't have been able to send a second crew of nephilim to kill Callie without it looking suspicious."

I grunted. "Are you two really suggesting that Gabriel is...what, fallen? Or just incompetent?"

Samael shrugged. "He gave conflicting orders within a ten-minute window. If he had wanted you dead, he wouldn't have sent Michael to you, first. He needed a scapegoat. We all know incompetence is a joke."

Pride stared into the middle distance, thinking. "But everyone would have known if Gabriel had fallen. And yet it's the only logical explanation. Except he hasn't fallen. And Michael hasn't fallen. It quite literally makes no sense." He shot me a look. "And I'm not being hyper-whatever."

I rolled my eyes. "Could someone have pretended to be Gabriel?"

Samael shook his head. "No. Michael would have easily seen through it. Even the nephilim would have."

"And we're sure they were nephilim, right?" I asked.

The two looked at each other and shrugged. "Michael was convinced," Pride said. "He spoke with them as if he knew them. He didn't demand to speak with their commanding officer or anything, like he probably would have done if he didn't know them." He grunted. "Which means Gabriel sent those guys to their deaths. Add that to the list of his crimes," he muttered. "And I didn't sense any illusion or concealment magic. They smelled like Heaven to me."

I sighed. "Well, Michael couldn't have been in on it, because he's now the target of this assassination contract. Also, I don't think he has a deceitful bone in his body."

Pride grinned. "Every man has at least *one* deceitful bone in his body, and I can show you where—"

"Message received," I interrupted, holding up a hand to cut him off. I risked a discreet glance at Michael to see that he was now facing Roland openly, and talking back just as much as he was listening. He was also smiling openly.

"That's one hell of a vampire," Pride mused, impressed. "How is he able to stand in a church?"

Samael butted in, telling Pride all about Roland. I was surprised at how much he seemed to know, and at the level of praise he gave my old mentor.

Once Samael was finished with his baseball stats version of Roland's biography, Pride stared at the two in disbelief. "From vampire hunter to master vampire, and *now* he's counseling an archangel."

"Let's not interrupt them," I urged. "Whatever he's saying has worked better than anything we've tried."

Pride nodded distractedly, not seeming to realize that he was smiling at his brother—as if seeing him in a new light. As if brotherly love had been rekindled—

"He has no idea, does he?" Pride asked, his smile stretching into something mischievous. "That he's talking to an archangel. He doesn't know."

I stepped in front of him just as he made a move to ruin Roland's ministering. I shoved Pride back into the statue—hard. "If you fuck this up, I will shove the Spear of Destiny so far—"

He grinned toothily. "Give me back my gun and I'll drop it."

I narrowed my eyes. "Why? An archdemon doesn't need a gun."

He held out his hand. "Because it's not right to steal, and it makes me feel cool." I waited for the real answer. He sighed. "If I kill a nephilim with a gun, there is a lower chance of them pinning the murder on me—precisely *because* an archdemon wouldn't use a gun. If I use my wings or claws or anything even remotely demonic, it's easy to point the finger at me. And just like that, their assassination contract gains credibility. Why do you think the nephilim used guns rather than their blessed blades or whatever holy weapons the kids use these days?"

"Plausible deniability," Samael murmured, nodding. "That actually makes a lot of sense."

I stared at Pride, impressed by his logic. I'd horribly underestimated him. "Wow. Okay. But only if our lives are at risk. No more shooting at shadows."

He shrugged. "Sure thing."

⚜ 40 ⚜

I handed him back the gun and bullets, and then turned to Samael. "We should get a few more guns. Roland can probably help us with that." I glanced down at my phone, wondering if I had time to check on Ryuu and Lilith in hopes that they'd found something useful. Maybe it was safe enough for us to head to Castle Dracula instead of hanging out here. "Is there any way to prove your case and get the contracts retracted?" I asked Pride. "Isn't the term *assassination* misleading since arch-class can only kill their counterparts, not their allies?"

Pride furrowed his brow unhappily. "No on the retraction option, and you are exactly right about assassination description. It makes zero sense. I haven't even heard of it before, but it's literally futile to aim at an archangel or archdemon. Unless both sides agreed to take out the other's trash."

"Maybe it was just the quickest way to turn any potential allies against you. No one wants to touch a pariah," Samael suggested.

Pride nodded. "Either way, we're going to have nephilim, angels, and demons crawling all over the city, searching for us. Both sides want us dead, but at least no one seems to realize we're working together. And that's what it's all about, my friends. There is no *I* in team."

"There's one in assassination," I said, dryly. "Two, actually. One for each of you." Pride laughed, and I found myself smiling back at him, shaking my head. I could tell that he used his sharp sense of twisted humor as a shield to deflect, but only because it came easily to him. Pride was a very carefree demon. Wrath had pretended to be that way, but had quickly resorted to posturing when the tactic didn't immediately get him what he wanted—me.

Despite the deflections, I could see that Pride really did have a big heart. He wasn't a softie or anything, but he was kind of two-sided—casually socio-pathic and willing to shoot a stranger at the slightest perceived provocation, but he also loved Frappuccinos, karaoke, and convertibles.

But the look on his face when he realized that Michael had risked his own reputation to protect him...

That had hit a deep, deep nerve. Possibly one that Pride had forgotten he even had. So, I was keeping a close eye on him.

In a darker way, Wrath had been similar—split between two warring personalities. There had been no sunshine or rainbows in his other half, though.

Even Michael had exhibited a drastic dichotomy in personalities. From judgmental and pious to self-loathing and morose.

I absently fingered the rings I had tucked away in my weapons belt—the ones that had sent up a flare of power when in proximity of both Michael and Pride. I'd checked them a few times on our drive here, even going so far as to discreetly touch Pride with it when I tapped him on the shoulder, and Michael when I'd patted his back reassuringly. There had been no reaction—from the rings or the two brothers.

Sensing Roland and Michael were wrapping up their conversation—judging by the louder laughs and casual tones in their speech—I spoke quickly to the demons. "To summarize, Gabriel and Wrath are covering their asses. Wrath sent me to speak to you, suggesting that I kill you," I told Pride, "and then he immediately puts a hit out on you when I don't kill you. Gabriel sent Michael to find me, and then immediately put a hit out on me, knowing it would put Michael in a trap. When that failed, he openly put a hit out on Michael. That's either the universes aligning or we're looking at some sort of collaboration effort. Either way, you two have been taken off the board. If you rear your heads, you will be instantly targeted. If you do anything to cross a line, you immediately corroborate their accusations, turning their paper-thin assassination contracts into ironclad proof. Oh, and Kansas City will burn no matter what happens. The war everyone claims to want to avoid pretty much already started."

They stared back at me with hard faces, nodding.

Samael abruptly cocked his head, his grim countenance switching to suspicion. "Fuck."

Pride looked over at him with a frown. "What?"

Samael pointed at my face. "That's her scheming face, and I don't think any of us are going to like it."

Roland and Michael joined us. Roland was smirking, having heard Samael's accusation. He nudged me with his elbow. "Callie probably had a plan two hours ago. She's just been perfecting it and letting it simmer, psychologically prodding you like horses to water so that you would drink when she later brought it up." His words had an instant effect on the three other men. They slowly turned to look at me with questioning frowns.

I smiled guiltily. "Only for the past hour, not two. But the rest is accurate." I shot Roland a glare. "Jerk."

He smiled at me like a proud father. Then he turned to Samael and dipped his chin. "Good to see you again, Samael." He turned to Pride and extended his hand. "My name is Roland. Welcome to my church."

"Pride," the archdemon said with a bright grin, shaking his hand energetically. "Thanks for having me. It's been a while, if you know what I mean."

Roland's smile slipped and, for the first time, he seemed to notice Pride's t-shirt. He licked his lips uneasily as everyone watched him.

Pride indicated Michael with his chin. "In all seriousness, Roland, thank you for talking some sense into Archangel Michael. He's as stubborn as a rock, but he's still my brother." Roland noticeably stiffened, looking as if he'd been zapped with a cattle prod. Pride could have rubbed Roland's nose in it, but he didn't. Instead, he gave Michael a warm, genuine smile, and there was nothing mischievous about it. "I know exactly what he's going through," he said, empathetically, "so I know exactly how hard it is to shake off and remember who you once were. Thank you for helping my brother, Roland. You've got a friend in me."

The church was dead silent. Samael was biting his knuckle, and I couldn't tell if he was nervous or if he was fighting not to burst out laughing. Roland's face was gaunt and pale, looking as if he was ready to self-destruct in humiliation as he slowly turned to his newest friend, Michael.

The archangel shrugged with a guilty smile. Then he draped his arm around the vampire's shoulders. "You truly are a good shepherd, Roland Haviar. Your own story was deeply moving. I don't think any other story could have picked me back up from where I had fallen. And I don't think I would have been wise enough to properly appreciate it until a little over an hour ago."

Pride lowered his eyes bashfully, pretending to look at his boots.

Roland stared straight ahead, trapped under his hero's arm. Or...sheltered under an archangel's wing. He was speechless and mortified and...*afraid*.

"If anyone should feel humbled, it is me," Michael continued. "You helped me open my eyes, and for that you have my gratitude. You gave me the courage to keep my chin up, and that's all a man needs in this world. Well, courage, endless stubbornness, and a little splash of pride," he added with a mock glare for the archdemon—who was *still* pointedly looking at his boots.

Roland nodded stiffly, licking his lips. "Thank you," he whispered, his lower lip trembling. "I feared...that you would strike me down if I ever had the honor of meeting you," he breathed, barely audible. And I watched as tears spilled down his cheeks.

I blinked through my own tears, wiping them on my sleeve.

Michael sighed. "How could I strike down the man who has lifted me back up?" Roland hung his head, overcome with emotion.

I couldn't take it anymore. I snatched Roland away from the archangel and cupped the sides of his head in my palms. He stared into my eyes, tears trailing down his cheeks as he blinked rapidly, and I could feel him quivering. I planted a fat kiss on his forehead and then leaned back with a sob of my own. "I *told* you, Roland. You're still a good man. And now you owe me one."

He hung his head, and let out the faintest cry I'd ever heard. Then he pulled me in and hugged me hard enough to almost hurt. I buried my face in his shoulder and squeezed back. Moments like this were what carried me through the tough days. This.

And one more thing.

I peeled myself away from my old mentor and gripped his wrist so he couldn't escape. Then I turned to Michael. "Can you sign a Crucifix, or something less blasphemous, for him? You're his childhood hero."

Roland's face purpled and he sputtered wordlessly.

"Well, if he won't, *I* will," Pride said, turning as if to go nab a Crucifix off the altar. I shoved him back into the statue, laughing.

"I think I need some coffee," Roland said, looking as embarrassed as I'd ever seen and desperate for any excuse to escape. Then he sighed, and a slow smile turned into a full-on shit-eating grin. "And I would love that signature," he said, deciding to own his humiliation.

Michael laughed. "For pulling me back to my feet? Of course, Father Roland."

The Master Vampire of Kansas City squeed.

On the inside. Because he had an image to uphold. But his eyes danced like a million stars, and I felt like at least one good thing had come of this kerfuffle.

The two of them made their way towards Roland's office.

"So, what is this scheme of yours?" Pride asked. Samael just shook his head, muttering under his breath.

I told them.

Pride burst out laughing. "We're all going to die!"

❧ 41 ❧

R oland paced back and forth, stroking his chin pensively. Pride was snoring, using a stack of bibles as a pillow. He had put his aviator sunglasses back on for absolutely no discernible reason. Michael was scribbling an inscription into an old bible that I'd bought for Roland after my first year as his student. After he'd saved me and Claire from vampires in an alley as teens. I'd scraped up every penny of my allowance money that summer to buy it for him. I had later doodled and sketched on at least a third of the pages within.

When Roland had offered it up for the archangel to sign, I'd almost broken down into tears all over again. Roland could have chosen any of the ancient, priceless bibles from his personal collection, but he'd chosen *mine*—complete with doodles and sketches, and worth all of thirty dollars in babysitting money. The scars between us were fading, and I finally admitted to myself how much I'd missed him after our big fight.

I sat beside Samael, staring through the old stained-glass window as night fell over Kansas City. I toyed with the apocalyptic pink cherry blossom petal I'd picked up from the training fields where I met Aala. She had told me I had a natural gift for healing and, looking around me now...I couldn't help but feel some small measure of pride at how I'd brought the five of us together.

If that wasn't healing, I didn't know what was. Maybe Aala had been right about me.

I'd caught everyone up to speed, sharing the initial plan I'd formulated with Samael, Lilith, and Ryuu, and factoring in the new knowledge I'd gained from Pride. The manhunt currently taking place outside for the archdemon and archangel only served to emphasize the importance of finding the last two Divines—the White Tiger and the Vermillion Bird.

Michael and Pride had been equally concerned about me gaining access to all four Divines, knowing that it would give me the ability to stand up to an archangel or archdemon. But now that their own people had seemingly set them up and were now gunning for them, there really wasn't any other choice. We all wanted answers, but we had different names for it.

Pride called it vengeance.

Michael called it justice.

Samael called it salvation.

I called it a reckoning.

Because if I could get the power to square off with Wrath or Gabriel...

I wasn't beholden to their family commitments. I could prevent a war. At least a war between Heaven and Hell. Instead of trying to kill each other, they would focus their efforts on me. And my ultimate defense was that the Spear of Destiny was inside of me, which would give both parties reason for pause.

Or so I hoped.

But none of that mattered if we couldn't survive Purgatory. Or find the Divines before we were eaten alive by the billions of cannibalistic soul-eaters living there.

I cleared my throat, drawing everyone's attention—except for Pride. He continued snoring away. "We still don't have a way to find the Daemons, though," I said, holding out the figurines for Xuanwu and Qinglong that I'd stowed away in my pocket before confronting Lilith. I'd almost completely forgotten about them in my haste to corner her on her deception, and I'd only remembered having them when I'd been absently searching for the cherry blossom petal a few minutes ago.

Michael clicked his pen and gently closed my Bible before turning to face me. He eyed the figurines with a frown. "What are those?"

One thing I'd definitely overlooked was that I could use the figurines to summon the Divines.

"Check this out," I said. I nicked my finger on the edge of my katana and then pressed my blood onto both figurines before murmuring their names. Qinglong and Xuanwu abruptly appeared, looking startled. Michael leapt to his feet and Roland snapped out of his daze to see the two Divines suddenly standing in his office. Michael scowled at Xuanwu, recalling their last encounter at the playground, and set his hand on the hilt of his sword.

Then his legs were invisibly swept out from underneath him and he shattered the wooden chair on his way down to the floor. "Don't," the Black Tortoise said in a calm, rumbling tone. I shot Xuanwu a discreet grin but he pretended not to notice it as he sat down on the floor. "I take it this has something to do with the sudden activity on the streets of Kansas City? I hear there are two different manhunts in progress—Pride and Prejudiced." Pride grinned, as if it had been a compliment. "I'll admit that I was more surprised to not hear of a third contract, since I know Callie Penrose must have infuriated some powerful people since I saw her this morning."

I shot him a dry look. "Nice to see you, too, Xuanwu. I'm relieved to see that you're not being a grouch anymore." I turned to the others. "Don't upset him or he'll make you split wood."

He chuckled softly, causing his frosty skin to crack and creak.

Roland helped Michael to his feet, and I was surprised to see the archangel shaking his head with a humbled grin. He dipped his chin at Xuanwu, acknowledging his defeat. Xuanwu did not appear to classify it as a match, but he politely dipped his wicked beak back at the archangel.

Qinglong sat down beside his brother, staring at the figurines in my lap. "Still feeling okay?" he asked me, seeming to stare into my body like a doctor with x-ray vision. "No concerns about Aala's treatment?"

I shook my head. "I'm fine, although I am feeling a little temperamental."

"You can thank Eve for that," Pride murmured loud enough for everyone to hear. I shot him a nasty glare, only to find him grinning with his eyes closed. Michael crashing into the wooden chair must have woken him up.

Samael nodded. "It's a fair point," he said with a smug grin. "Lilith is the best."

I rolled my eyes and turned back to Qinglong. "My magic is definitely more potent, but I haven't really tested it out much. When I did, it was a doozy. Other than that, just a little more...temperamental," I repeated, shooting a withering warning glare at my godfather and Pride—who both smirked openly.

Pride got up and stretched. Then he strolled over to the desk, checking his phone—a mirror application, judging by how he fixed his hair with meticulous care. Then he pocketed his vanity tablet and sat down next to his brother, yawning.

Xuanwu leaned my way. "Ryuu informed us of your plan to find our Sisters," he breathed, so softly that no one else seemed to overhear. "He takes his commitment to keep you safe very personally and, if you don't come collect him soon, I may be forced to build additional storage for all my new piles of split wood. He is growing rather irritable coordinating watches for the city."

I chuckled. "We will be there soon. Tell him he only has to wait a little longer. Tomorrow morning."

Qinglong growled anxiously. "Why have you summoned us?"

"I found a way to safely traverse the Neverwas," I said, pointing at Michael and Pride.

Pride grunted. "And by *safely traverse*, she means we can *survive* a tiny bit longer before we are overrun and eaten alive."

I shot him a scowl before turning back to the Divines. "But I don't know how to find your sisters once we get there. I don't know where their figurines are."

Xuanwu and Qinglong stared at each other with looks of unanticipated hope. "You said Lilith banished them?" Xuanwu asked. I nodded. "Have you asked her about the figurines?"

I blinked at Xuanwu. Then I frowned. "Of course I asked her."

"She definitely didn't ask her," Pride murmured, leaning closer to Michael.

Michael smirked boyishly. Then he abruptly realized that he was agreeing with his brother, the demon. His smile faltered and he frowned with a confused look on his face, as if not knowing which reaction he should entertain. He scooted a few inches away from his brother, focusing on the Divines.

Samael was frowning at me. "You didn't ask her. I'm certain of it."

I clenched my jaw. "Does anyone else want to criticize me or can we move onto finding some solutions?"

"We probably have time for both," Pride suggested, scratching at his jaw, pensively. I reached for a nearby book and threw it at him. He didn't even look at the inbound projectile as he casually leaned to the side, letting it whip past his head to hit the wall.

Qinglong eyed the archangel and archdemon, cocking his head as he assessed their auras. Whatever he saw troubled him, but he didn't comment, and they didn't seem to notice his attention.

Samael cleared his throat. "If we're finished staring at each other, I'm sure I can book an appointment with my fiancée to ask her about the figurines. Castle Dracula is safer than the streets right now—"

"The hell it is," Pride scoffed, frowning at my godfather. "Envy has been living there since day one. Who did you think was inciting the rebels?"

42

I froze and my stomach squirmed like I'd swallowed a live eel. "What?" I hissed.

Pride hesitated at my tone, realizing that it was not a safe time to poke fun or say something inappropriate. "Envy is living at Castle Dracula. Since a day or so after we broke out," he said, slowly. He glanced from face to face with a frown. "You guys are pulling my feathers, right? How did you think we've kept such a low profile all this time? Envy tracked her every move and sent out *daily* fucking emails with her known itineraries so the rest of us would know when it was safe to explore the city."

No one spoke.

Pride turned to Samael. "We got the idea from you living there! Sanguina can't keep us out just as we can't shut her down. It's the perfect stalemate."

I felt very cold all of a sudden, and the only solution was fire. Which was probably why a ball of white fire was suddenly hovering over my palm and I was standing up, glaring at Pride. He cringed uneasily and Michael had a concerned look on his face—torn between permitting a demon earned punishment and defending his brother.

"Callie," Roland warned in a calm tone. I let out a shuddering breath and released my magic. It had come so easily that I'd barely even had the thought before it responded.

Pride let out a nervous laugh. "I thought you knew," he mumbled. "Pretty obvious. And before you ask, I have no idea where he is. I just know he's keeping tabs on you and firing up the rebels as a distraction."

And...it *was* obvious when I thought about it. I'd put too much stock in the innate abilities of angelic beings, assuming they just *knew* things and were always seven steps ahead. After fleeing the scene of a mass homicide in a stolen Mazda Miata with a playboy archdemon and a self-loathing archangel, I'd subconsciously come to the conclusion that angels and demons were not even remotely omnipotent. But I hadn't actively applied that awareness to the current situation.

I clenched my jaw. "I'm *really* starting to hate your family."

Xuanwu cleared his throat. "Openly heading back to the Castle might actually serve to throw off their scent. If everyone is looking for the brothers here and then Envy reports that Callie is suddenly back at Castle Dracula without them, your enemies will have to reassess the situation. Best case, they will assume these two are independently on the run and that Callie has nothing to do with them. If you make your return look exceedingly mundane and ordinary, all Envy will have to report is that you returned, had dinner, and went to bed. He would have no reason to think you are working with Michael or Pride."

Qinglong nodded. "Leaving you open to set a trap to find out where Envy is. Send out some breadcrumbs and see who bites. And you can collect our sisters' figurines from Lilith, since you forgot to ask her."

I grunted at his attempt for levity. "If she even has them. Why wouldn't she have simply given them to me when she came clean?"

Samael looked troubled, having the same thought. I hoped she had a good answer.

"I can keep these two safe in the catacombs," Roland said. "They are heavily warded from detection, as Samael well knows. He hid there for a year with none the wiser."

"That is true," my godfather assured Michael and Pride. The two brothers did not look particularly pleased with this development. I wasn't sure if they were more upset about being left out of the action or having to spend quality time together. It was almost comical how hard they worked to deny their curiosity in catching up and reestablishing their brotherly bond. They'd spent so long working against each other that they didn't know how to act in a moment of peace.

Except I could tell that part of them was desperate to explore it. They were just too chicken-shit to be the one to make the first move.

"We could get to work on how to secure the Gateway to the Neverwas," Michael suggested.

"What about Sanguina?" Pride asked. "She's strong, and she could keep it anchored from this side while we go on safari." Xuanwu grumbled warningly and Pride rolled his eyes. "Sanguina could buy us time."

I frowned, leaning forward. "I thought your magic cancelled each other out? You literally just said that."

He rolled his eyes again. "Our magic can't work in *opposition* to each other, but it can *coincide* with each other just fine. Teamwork makes the dream work."

Michael snorted, eyeing his brother sidelong at the last comment. But he was nodding. "That could work," he agreed. The two brothers began talking in low tones, discussing the strategy of working with Sanguina. Samael and Roland were reading the Bible together—well, the inscription Michael had left, at any rate. I left them to it.

I turned to Xuanwu and Qinglong. "Okay. I guess I'm going home for a relaxing evening," I said.

Xuanwu met my eyes. "Perhaps I could send Ryuu to keep you...entertained," he said with a knowing twinkle in those all-seeing, obsidian eyes.

Qinglong burst out laughing and my ears burned. "What is this, an escort service?" the dragon hooted.

I smirked guiltily. Did everyone sense the tension between us, or was it because Ryuu was Xuanwu's student. "No matter how...entertained I would like to be, it's probably a better idea to keep him at your home. He has work to do—"

"And it's so exhausting to bat too many eyelashes and sigh longingly," Qinglong wheezed, still laughing.

I tried to narrow my eyes at him, but I was smiling ruefully. "Remember who is saving your sisters tomorrow. I need to be focused. And it is exhausting," I said, folding my arms.

Xuanwu rested a claw on my shoulder. "We will make sure all is ready for the Gateway. It was a good idea to use the training fields. They will need healing after you save them," he said, wistfully, obviously imagining seeing his sisters again.

I nodded, numbly, hoping I wouldn't let him down. "I will give it everything I have," I promised.

Xuanwu nodded proudly. "You always do, White Rose."

"Except with Ryuu!" Qinglong jeered. Xuanwu and I both elbowed him at the same time, but he evaporated to safety before contact, earning growls from both of us.

Xuanwu met my eyes. "I believe in you." And with that, he was gone.

I sighed, clenching my fist. I mentally reviewed my plan, knowing there were a few variables I hadn't been able to determine. My mother had obviously believed I had the ability to save Lilith's Daemons—her trinity, whatever that meant. But the fire lotus she had left me had been with the sets of rings and the metal card. So...what did my Spear and the rings have to do with saving the Divines. I had plenty of wild guesses, but absolutely none of them were rooted in facts. Perhaps my night in would give me time to clear my head.

I turned to the room and cleared my throat. "It's time for Samael and me to leave. I don't know when we'll be ready to make our move—either late tonight or early tomorrow morning, so be ready to go on a moment's notice," I told Michael and Pride. "I want to stick around long enough that Envy has a whole lot of nothing to report to Wrath for his stupid email updates. Leaving too soon will make him suspicious."

The pair nodded. "We'll be ready," Michael assured me. "Be careful, Callie."

Pride turned to Roland. "Is there a Starbucks nearby? My brother has never had a Frappuccino, believe it or not," he said, sounding as if it was a crime.

Michael shrugged, smiling. "True."

Roland chuckled. "I can make that happen."

And just like that, I saw magic happen. The real kind. Healing magic.

Two brothers setting aside their differences for the pursuit of commonalities. If these two could do it, anyone could. Even if their first step was a Frappuccino, it was still progress.

"Sleepover time!" Pride cheered. "Oh! We can play confession or dare!"

Roland shot me an anxious look and I shrugged, ripping open a Gateway. "Good luck!"

43

The Gateway opened on the upper balcony of the Castle Keep's Drop Zone.

Samael hopped through behind me and I let it close before Pride got any bright ideas. I turned to Samael. "Go get Lilith and meet me in the Feast Hall for drinks. Don't rush. Take your time and share pleasantries with anyone you pass on your way to get her. Basically, just be you—the love-struck fool," I said, teasingly.

He nodded, glancing around the empty balcony. "This would be a great spot for the wedding," he mused, smiling down over the sprawling grounds below. All of Castle Dracula spread out before us, and there was a small courtyard large enough to host an outdoor wedding or reception.

I smiled, nodding. "Then you have ample reason to make sure this works."

"Will you be okay up here? All by yourself?" he asked, obviously thinking about Envy.

I didn't answer immediately. I leaned my elbows down on the railing, staring down at the Timber Forest where the Master's Library was tucked away. Then my gaze continued to sweep over my estate. The Observatory. The Infernal Armory. The Coliseum. The Eternal Gardens. The Clocktower. The Village. So many places to hide the rebels, and so little time. I wondered if Envy might be working in the Keep itself, hiding in plain sight.

"Do you remember what I almost did to our good friend, Mike, outside that house earlier?" I reminded him, softly.

He grew quiet, obviously recalling my almost fight with Michael. "Yes."

I glanced over at him. "I'm sure I'll be fine, godfather. I've been in a few scraps before."

He grinned, lifting his hands in a surrendering gesture. Then he bowed dramatically at the waist, and left. I waved a hand to my left and right, igniting the braziers lining the railing. They roared to life with red flame, bathing the balcony in a bloody glow.

A beacon, to let anyone watching know that Dracula had returned. I'd turned on my porch light.

"Come and get me," I murmured, surveilling the property.

A flight of gargoyles screamed as they soared overhead on their patrols. One of them peeled off, noticing the flames and seeing me all alone. He slammed down onto the balcony ten paces away from me, kneeling and lowering his glowing crimson eyes. "Master Dracula," he said in a rasping, reverent growl as he tucked his massive wings back. "How may Captain Hoggle serve?"

I smiled at the name, thinking of the grouchy dwarf from the movie *Labyrinth*. "It is nice to meet you, Captain Hoggle. Rise," I commanded.

He obeyed, thumping his moss and lichen coated trident—the points were needle sharp—into the floor. I was still getting used to the various factions that made up my new home, let alone the factions within the factions. Gargoyles came in infinite shapes, sizes, and combinations of various hybrid monsters. Hoggle was one of the more traditional looking gargoyles—an impossibly colossal bodybuilder with the head of a bat. He had long, pointed ears and a perpetual snarl. He was at least seven-feet-tall, and his arms were as thick as my waist, with claws long enough to poke entirely through me—both on his hands and his enormous reptilian feet. Simply put, he could rip me in half with his bare hands.

"Impress me, Hoggle," I said with a smile. "Show me what you and your men can do in the air."

He smiled devilishly. "As you command, Master Dracula." He thumped his fist to his heart with a loud cracking sound, and then his wings unfurled and he took to the skies. He flew towards his unit, sweeping his massive wings to hover beside them and pass on my orders.

I gasped as they scattered. Then they formed lines and raced towards each other in aerial combat, clashing stone blade against stone blade, shouting and snarling as they danced in the skies. I grinned, watching as they switched from combat to elaborate aerial feats that included climbing high in the sky and then plummeting to the ground to see how close they could get before opening their wings. They did it in pairs or alone, performing acrobatics and dances that made me clap giddily. It was like watching falcons or other birds of prey during their elaborate mating rituals. It was truly breathtaking.

Twenty minutes went by before I heard boots behind me. I glanced over my shoulder to see Claire staring at me uneasily. Sanguina trotted over to me, obviously having led my best friend here—like I'd asked her to do while I'd been watching the gargoyles. "Hey, Claire," I said, smiling warmly. "You have to see this," I said, patting the railing with my palm.

Sanguina watched us in silence, just like I had asked her to. We would talk later when I retired to my rooms for the night.

Claire joined me, staring at the dancing gargoyles with a smile. "Wow," she breathed, shaking her head.

I grinned. "Right?" I could sense that she was troubled. Her body language was tense and awkward. "Everything okay here?"

She started, nodding hurriedly to cover her jittery reaction. "Weird, but no weirder than usual. Until now, that is," she added, eyeing me sidelong. "You okay?" she asked, guardedly. "I've hardly seen you since I moved in."

"I'm fine," I said with an easy shrug. "Things are a little dicey, but I'll manage. Any news on the rebels?"

"No change," she said with forced calm.

I nodded, distractedly. "It's beautiful up here. From far away, it's easy to forget that a monster is lurking behind every tree or door. That rebels hide in plain sight, pretending to be who they aren't."

She nodded, slowly, obviously wondering why I was acting so nonchalant and hanging out on the roof by myself. "You sure you're okay?" she asked, resting her fingers on my forearm. "You look tired."

I smiled. "I am exhausted. But I promised to have a chat with Lilith about some of the wedding plans. I'm not going to lie, it would be great if the rebels chose to attack to get me out of it."

Claire's smile slipped, not entirely sure whether I was joking. "Xylo and his men have the Keep pretty much buttoned up. A rebel attack would be laughable."

I pursed my lips. "Damn. Mind walking me down to the Feast Hall? I promised to talk to them both before I crashed for the night." Sanguina trotted towards the door that led to the long, spiraling flight of stairs that would deposit us back in the main halls. Claire had been watching the fox thoughtfully, likely wondering why she'd been led here. I cleared my throat and held out my elbow to Claire. "I meant right now. Before I fall asleep on my feet."

Claire smirked guiltily as she slipped her arm through mine. I walked at the slowest pace possible towards the door. We ducked inside and reached the top of the long, deserted staircase. "We can walk a *little* faster, you know—"

Without warning, I opened a Gateway to a park in Kansas City and tugged Claire through. Sanguina obediently remained sitting on the stairs, looking amused.

Same pace I just used, I told her. I let the Gateway wink out and spun to face my startled best friend.

"What the fuck is going on, Callie?" she demanded.

"We only have a few minutes before our absence will be noted—exactly as long as it would have taken us to walk down the stairs back there. So, I need you to shut up and listen. Afterwards, you need to play it cool and *discreetly* let Xylo and Cain know what I told you without drawing *any* attention. Raise. No. Alarms."

She nodded, looking oddly relieved. "Good. I've been bored to tears," she growled.

I gave her a rapid monologue of my recent adventures, feeling like Luis from the movie *Ant-man*—who was arguably the best storyteller ever born. Claire began breathing faster as I spoke, but I squeezed her shoulder reassuringly until she calmed down. Once finished, I smiled. "Hold your shit together, woman. I trust you more than anyone."

She closed her eyes and took a deep breath to center herself. When she opened her eyes, even I couldn't read anything suspicious on her face. I grinned approvingly, ripped open a Gateway to the base of the stairs we had just left, and tugged her through. Sanguina calmly walked off the last step and joined us as I let the Gateway wink shut.

Perfect timing, she said in my mind.

"So, have you let Kenai officially move in yet, or are you still dangling that over his head?" I asked, grinning as I stepped into the main hall. I saw a few servants working here and there. One was carrying a tray of folded linens and another was dusting a side table. They saw me and bowed, going out of their way to make sure they weren't a nuisance to Master Dracula. Same faces I'd seen the last few days, and I had casually spoken to each of them at one point or another. Even if only to say hello and scare the living hell out of them by doing so.

Claire chuckled. "He is only permitted to visit, for now. I can't let him get too comfortable or he'll start acting uppity and bring a toothbrush, or something equally dreadful."

I chuckled, nodding along. "Up to you, but he's welcome. Don't give him a complex or anything."

"Speaking of, he promised to take me on a walk through the Eternal Gardens tonight. If you're going to be boring and go to bed like an old woman, then maybe I'll take him up on it."

I rolled my eyes. "These wedding plans are going to be the death of me. Thanks for helping Lilith. You know this isn't my kind of thing," I admitted. "Once I put in my time with bridezilla, I'm off to bed."

She gave me a tight hug and then let go. "You have to stop leaving me here alone. It's boring and weird and creepy without you here." She scrunched up her nose. "I guess it's like that when you are here, too, but at least it gives me someone to laugh about it with."

I gave her a thoughtful look. "How about you come with me tomorrow? I'll swing by your rooms late morning to pick you up. Let's say eleven."

She grinned excitedly. "That sounds amazing. What are we doing?"

I shot a wary look down the hall, noticing maids and valets studiously attending to their duties. "I...can't talk about it here, but I think I found a way to kill our big-league feathered friends," I said, in a loud whisper. As if I had no concern about the workers overhearing me, but that I had wanted to make sure no one important heard. In reality, I was tossing chum into shark-infested waters. Because if I was Envy, I would be using the servants to get me intel. Or...I would pose as a servant myself.

So I discreetly took note of each face—even though all of them seemed to be pointedly ignoring us so as not to bother us. If my secret trip with Claire became not so secret, the most likely culprits would be one of these diligent workers.

Claire stared at me anxiously, sensing that I was up to something. "Are you sure that's wise?" she asked in a loud hiss, sounding nervous. "To kill one of them would be—"

"Keep your voice down," I hissed. "I'm going to kill one tomorrow, and you're going to help me!" I snapped, scowling at the hall in a broad, sweeping manner. Servants jumped and dusted or polished more fervently in the wake of my ire.

Claire nodded uneasily. "Okay."

"I'll see you at eleven tomorrow morning. Get some sleep tonight. You're going to need it." She nodded, clamping her lips tight as if bottling up her fear. I gestured down the hall. "Samael and Lilith are probably waiting for me. I'll see you at eleven tomorrow morning."

"Okay. Good night, Callie."

Then she was walking down the halls, clenching her fists open and closed, her shoulders trembling.

What was that all about? Sanguina asked me, making me jump.

I motioned for her to follow, eyeing the servants as we passed.

I debated not answering, but I didn't want Sanguina causing problems. So I told her in my head. *A trap. To see if one of the servants is a spy.*

I'd counted at least a half a dozen servants close enough to overhear us, but it was entirely possible that none of them were rebels working for Envy. It wasn't perfect, but it might at least help me determine which servants not to suspect.

I opened the door to the Feast Hall and ushered her inside.

I closed the door behind us to find Lilith and Samael seated at the table, sipping glasses of wine. Judging by the expectant grins on their faces, Samael's request for the Daemon figurines had given us a favorable answer. I shook my head minutely. "No toys until after drinks," I said, cryptically. Then I mimed zipping my lips shut so they didn't say anything damning. Who knew if a servant would walk in at any moment?

"Then...let's plan a goddamned wedding," Samael said, wearily.

Lilith clapped delightedly.

44

I sipped a glass of wine, listening to Lilith talk away about food, decorations, flowers, guests, and possible dates. Samael had caught the wedding bug, and was soon making as many suggestions as Lilith, which was cute to see. Most men couldn't care less about the details. To them, weddings were military missions—to survive long enough to claim the hill after the smoke cleared, and plant their flags in victory.

The bursts of cork-fire, the screams and cries of loved ones, and the frantic chaos of the dance floor battleground were all things a competent soldier must learn to overcome.

I soon found myself coming down with a mild wedding fever, caught up by their contagious excitement. Granted, recent events hadn't revolved around fun, happy moments, so it was a breath of fresh air to plan a different type of battle.

Samael was halfway through selling Lilith his suggestion on using the upper balcony for the ceremony when there was a loud knock on the door to the Feast Hall. I glanced at Sanguina. *Hide in my rooms.* Thankfully, she didn't argue my command. She disappeared between one moment and the next.

I gave Samael and Lilith a reassuring look, careful to keep my own composure. After planting my seeds about a secret plan with Claire tomorrow, I had considered a dozen or more scenarios resulting from a spying servant passing the information off to his or her boss, Envy. Reactions ranged from an outright rebel attack on the castle, to armies of angels and demons tearing through Kansas City, to any number of visitors showing up here, at the Feast Hall—since I had made it no secret I was coming here for a long chat with my godparents. The problem was, I didn't know which scenario was on the other side of the door, and battle plans typically went to hell the moment the first shot was fired.

"Come in," I called out in an officious tone.

The door opened and Xylo walked in. He bowed at the waist. I had no way of knowing whether Claire had caught him up to speed, so all I could do now was hope for the best.

"There is a...man outside who wishes to pay his respects to Lilith and Samael in regards to their upcoming wedding," he said. The way he had paused at the word *man* sent a shiver down my spine, but I kept my composure. He looked troubled. That's when it hit me. I hadn't even considered talking to him through our mental connection.

Trust me, Xylo. Talk to Claire.

The pools of shadow in his eyes flared. *I already did. Can I help you kill this angel or demon?*

I choked on my wine, almost dropping my glass. Samael and Lilith looked suddenly concerned by my bizarrely delayed reaction since they couldn't hear my internal conversation with Xylo. I managed to suck down some air between coughs, waving away their concern.

Don't worry about that, Xylo. Just do what Claire told you.

He gave a subtle nod before speaking out loud. "He is unarmed and claims to have brought a gift."

"He may enter," I said calmly, and then I took another sip of my wine to try and wash down the last of my coughing fit as my mind raced with who this man might be. It seemed my rumor about having the power to kill an angel or demon had reached the right ears, causing one of the archdemons to make a move.

Demon. Powerful demon, Xylo told me through our mental connection.

I suppressed a shudder. A minute later, Wrath swept into the room with a regal air. He still didn't wear shoes, and had opted for tight jeans and a startlingly white collared shirt with a satin finish. It was unbuttoned like the last time I'd seen him, showing off the two black feathers on his chain necklace. He bowed, formally, flashing me a dark, amused grin.

I dipped my chin ever so slightly. "Leave us," I told Xylo. "This is a family matter."

Thankfully, he didn't hesitate in obeying me. I hadn't wanted Wrath to see my own guard questioning my commands. It also served to subconsciously warn Wrath that Xylo had enough confidence in my abilities to leave me alone with the new guest. Wrath would think he'd been underestimated.

Good.

Overconfidence was a ruthless killer of men—human or otherwise.

The door clicked shut and I used my magic to retrieve an empty wine glass from the cabinet. I set it down before an empty seat and gestured for Wrath to join us. In my head, I flipped through the rolodex of servants and valets who had been within earshot of my talk with Claire, careful to ward Xylo from my thoughts to prevent him from going on a murder spree.

"Don't mind if I do," he said, smiling and taking a seat. He set a rolled piece of parchment down on the table and I had to force myself not to hiss. Had he really brought Legion's wedding contract? But I managed a polite smile, permitting only a curious glance at the paper. Thankfully, even in the best of situations, a visit from Wrath was enough to cause IBS, so it wasn't suspicious that Lilith and Samael were noticeably perched on the edges of their seats, looking like they wanted to bolt.

"You look well, brother," Lilith said, managing not to squirm—because she was seated before the man who had likely sold her to Dracula.

Samael nodded. "It's been a long time," he said, carefully, and I knew he wanted nothing more than to rip Wrath's smiling lips off with rusty fish hooks.

Wrath smirked, shooting Lilith a meaningful look. "Oh, I don't know. Longer for some than others," he said with a chuckle, obviously alluding to seeing Lilith more recently than Samael. When he'd commanded her to kill her Daemons. But only Lilith was supposed to know about that, so Samael and I feigned curiosity as Wrath continued. "I had the privilege of meeting Miss Penrose recently, as I'm sure you well know." The pair nodded. "She told me you had opted to become her godparents, and that you were getting married. I am so very happy for you," he said, and the level of sincerity was so thick it bordered on syrupy.

"Leave them alone, Wrath," I said, dryly. "It's already awkward enough without you laughing at your own jokes."

He chuckled, and then chose one of the three open bottles of wine on the table. He poured himself a glass and put the bottle down. "There is always time for a little fun and sibling rivalry."

I sipped my wine. "Samael and I already had our fair share of sibling rivalry this evening," I said. "As *you* well know, so let's just cut to the chase." Wrath sipped his wine with a contented sigh, smacking his lips as he turned to me, gesturing in a way that came across as him granting me permission to continue.

Which pissed me right the hell off. This was *my* castle.

I turned to Lilith with a warm smile. "Oh, before I forget. You simply must have lilies on the centerpieces. I know an excellent florist—"

"Hey!" Wrath growled. "I'm feeling slighted."

I slowly turned to him, giving him a puzzled, somewhat pestered frown. "Then feel free to leave, or bite your tongue until I'm finished speaking with my godmother."

Samael hid his smirk by guzzling his wine, but I kept my face blank as I held Wrath's glare as carefully as a baby bird—tight enough to control but not hard enough to crush. He was completely motionless, not even seeming to breathe. Then he let out a grunt and leaned back in his chair, sipping his wine as if it hadn't been worth getting upset over in the first place.

But those eyes bored into me like hot irons—furious yet infatuated with the puzzlingly defiant creature whom he intended to marry and form a new world order with. His prophecy was not far from my mind.

I turned back to Lilith and smiled, clasping her hands in mine. "Now, where were we? Ah, yes. I know an excellent florist." Then I squeezed her hand, turned back to Wrath, and sipped my wine as I pompously motioned with my hand, granting him permission to speak—in the exact same way he had tried with me.

I saw a vein throbbing near his temples as the skin around his eyes tightened. "You didn't add anything. You literally repeated the same thing from a moment ago."

I nodded. "How astute. Perhaps I was making a point. That in these halls, I wear the crown and you kiss the ring," I said, holding out my limp hand to show off the Seal of Solomon—the ring that trapped demons in a metaphysical prison. "How is your wine?" I asked, dryly.

That vein in his temple looked about ready to erupt and his shoulders visibly shook before he took a calming breath, and a truly wicked smile split his cheeks. His eyes danced with lust at my stubborn refusal to give him an inch of control.

He. Fucking. Loved. It.

And it was all I could do to maintain a confident, dismissive air. Because we both knew I was bluffing.

"I seem to have overstepped my place," Wrath said in a surprisingly calm tone, and he deftly leaned forward to gently grip my hand before I could retract it. His fingers were hot and tingled with power. "I humbly kiss the ring, my queen." And then he leaned forward to kiss the Seal of Solomon. His lips touched the demon prison, and there was a crackling pop, but he continued pressing his lips to the metal, ignoring the pain and power burning his flesh. After a few long seconds, he pulled away and released my hand. "Perhaps I could help you find a new ring. Soon." I managed not to recoil and hiss like a doused cat. Barely.

Then Wrath gave me a subtle bow and sat back down. His lips were slightly inflamed from the crackling burn of my ring, but they began to heal even as I stared at him. It was a steady flex of power—that my demon prison was a joke to an archdemon like him.

I nodded, politely, acknowledging the gesture as an expected social grace. "As I was saying, we can save some time by getting right to the matter at hand." Everyone nodded. I stared directly into Wrath's eyes. "I told you I would meet Pride—and the other Sins—in private. What happened this afternoon was the exact opposite of private. I don't know or care how, but you had something to do with the shit show Samael and I ran into. What I do care about is that you tried to use me for your own ends. And you need to know that I will not be used. Ever."

I leaned back in my seat, letting the point of the figurative nail sink in as I swirled my glass absently. He hadn't denied his involvement in the events outside Pride's house. Did that mean anything?

I decided to hammer the point home a little harder, since he wasn't reacting. I chose a sledgehammer. "You need me more than I need you. So if you want to play games, you better start believing in a different prophecy. I don't need the dead weight. Or the headache." I eyed him up and down. "The reward simply isn't worth the risk."

The room was eerily silent. "Is that why you came back home?" Wrath finally asked in a cold tone. Still not showing any denial or any shame.

"I knew you'd come crawling back when you realized how utterly your plan had failed. You broke your word *and* you disappointed me. I wanted to tell you, to your face, that your petty games only served to permanently dry up one of my ovaries."

Samael and Lilith both choked on their wine, flashing me horrified looks in my peripheral vision.

I remained calm, staring down the archdemon. Wrath gripped the table, his shoulders trembling. And the wood began to smolder beneath his fingers. He opened his mouth to speak.

"Let me guess at what you were going to say," I said, cutting him off with a bored sigh as I set my wineglass down. "Blah, blah, blah, don't you dare disrespect me or I'll hurt people you love. Blah, blah, blah, I am Wrath. Rawr!" I mock roared, lifting my pointer fingers to my temples so they resembled horns.

He stared at me, and I noticed one of his eyes twitching dangerously. Except he was licking his lips.

"Wrath, I feel my second ovary drying up just *thinking* about your excuses and justifications. Man up or go home. I gave you my terms. I will meet the rest of the Seven with no more interference from *anyone*. If I'm sitting down with Lust and I hear so much as a doorbell ring, our arrangement is finished. Period." Then I leaned back in my seat again and took a sip. "Your move."

Samael and Lilith were absolutely motionless, and their eyes were as wide as saucers. I hadn't really planned out my little speech, so they'd been given no warning. To be fair, I'd probably gone way overboard. But it was the only hand I had—to keep him reeling on his heels. I was so far outclassed on the power spectrum that I had to keep him thinking that my back was against a wall and that I would rather die than give in. Him using force to try and push me around was not going to work like it did on everyone else.

The only thing he didn't truly understand was someone without any fear whatsoever. I could fake that.

Wrath was a bully. It was his power.

So, I popped him in the mouth. Not enough to do any real damage, physically, but to destroy any semblance of control he thought he held—which had been made apparent by his arrogant entrance. Someone had gotten word to him that I had a plan up my sleeves tomorrow with Claire, and he had decided to come visit me personally to feel me out. But I wasn't supposed to know that.

He closed his eyes and I watched him shake with rage and...desperate need. Because he was broken, and encountering someone who didn't tolerate his shit was exciting to him. The fact that I was apparently crazy enough to commit figurative suicide rather than be used as a puppet made him fall deeper in love with me, in his own twisted way. I was the Harley Quinn to his Joker.

At least, that's what I needed him to think. It was the only way to control him. Until I got me some Divines tonight. But I wasn't supposed to know about their secret power, either.

He finally opened his eyes and stared at me. "Okay. I will not interfere again," he croaked.

Lilith made a faint strangled sound and he whipped his head towards her with a snarl, instantly infuriated that she had witnessed his humiliation. "Lilith," he hissed. "I brought you a gift," he said in a sadistic tone. He turned to me. "This is an internal family matter and has nothing to do with *us*."

Not really having any other choice, I gave him a faint nod of permission. In a way, he was seeking my approval, or at least acknowledging the fact that he didn't want to upset me more. I could meet him halfway.

He slid the rolled parchment to Lilith and downed his entire glass of wine. I squinted suspiciously. I had thought the rolled paper was Legion's wedding contract. What was he up to? He was already pouring another glass of wine as Lilith tugged at the string and unrolled the piece of paper. She began to read with a curious frown, and then her face went slack and cold. She dropped it to the table.

Samael snatched it up and gave it a cursory read. I saw the veins at his temples begin to throb and I discreetly kicked his ankles under the table, willing him to hold himself together. Lily was staring at Wrath, but with that concerning, blank expression on her face. She reached out to rest her fingers on Samael's wrists in a calming manner, making him flinch in surprise.

Wrath was grinning at the two of them, inhaling the bouquet of aromas in his glass before taking a sip.

"You were right to have done so," Lilith murmured in a soft, distant tone. "I would have told everyone that I bested you."

Wrath's humor evaporated and he let out another snarl, causing some of his wine to slosh onto the table.

❧ 45 ❧

I flung up my hands before anyone did anything stupid. "Everyone calm down and fill me in," I growled. "What is that?" I asked, pointing at the paper.

Wrath took a calming breath and turned to give me a thoughtful look. "I told you about her Daemons."

I nodded, warily. "She told me earlier," I said, choosing my words very carefully. Because under no circumstances could I let him know that I knew exactly what the four Divines were capable of. It would risk my entire plan. "She said they were dead."

Wrath scoffed. "Dead. Well, it's not that simple, is it, Lilith?"

I discreetly shot her a wink while Wrath wasn't looking. Luckily, she noticed it. "What is he talking about, Lilith?" I demanded in a stern tone, knowing that we were on thin ice. I couldn't dismiss the conversation without looking suspicious to Wrath, but I couldn't look like I was favoring Lilith for deceiving me, either. Especially about a topic I wasn't supposed to fully understand.

She folded her arms. "Let him tell you the truth," she said, emphasizing the last word. I hoped she wasn't about to say too much and ruin everything. Samael shot me a nervous glance and I mirrored it right back.

Wrath took a drink of his wine, staring at Lilith warily. "I commanded her to kill them. Rather than obeying me, she sent them to the one place even I cannot endure for any measurable length of time. I sold her to Dracula as punishment," he said with a casual shrug. "That is my copy of the contract," he said with a cruel grin. "Rather than granting them a swift death, she committed them to eternal misery. Even I have to admire the cruelty in that, so I gave her a reduced sentence. What's one hundred years of imprisonment to an immortal?"

I stared at him, grimacing disgustedly. "Why Dracula?"

"Seemed like a good idea since the Harkers had found out that Lilith's Daemons hadn't been killed like I led everyone to believe. And they were rather desperate, at the time, hiding a secret of their own. I agreed to keep their secret about Mina being the real pants of the Dracula operation, and they agreed to keep my secret that the other two Divines were vacationing in Purgatory. I gave them Lilith as collateral that I would keep my word—"

"But that's not the *entire* truth, is it?" she snarled venomously, leaning forward to stare directly into Wrath's eyes. "You and I know *exactly* why I doomed my Daemons to Purgatory."

Wrath narrowed his eyes in a warning glare. "Okay, Lilith. You're upset with me, and want to take out some aggression. It's in the past, so why not air it out?" he said, sounding entirely too calm. "I told Lilith to give me her Daemons for safekeeping. I wanted to be like Samael," he said with a humorless grin. "I was jealous of his pet turtle and dragon. When she refused, I ordered her to kill them instead. If I couldn't have them, she wasn't allowed to have them either."

Lilith leaned back in her chair, nodding one time.

And it suddenly made sense to me—why Lilith had sent the White Tiger and Vermillion Bird to the Neverwas. Because it was the only way—other than killing them—to keep them safe from Wrath. He had wanted them for himself, and he would have likely set his next sights on Samael's daemons so that he could control all four and guarantee his own safety, forever and ever, amen.

In a way, Lilith's sacrifice had also saved Samael and his Daemons. I wondered if the White Tiger and Vermillion Bird had known their eternal punishment was actually saving their brothers' lives. Because without them on the board, Wrath had no need to go after Xuanwu and Qinglong.

But I wasn't supposed to know about any of that. I could not afford for Wrath to think I had *any* interest in the Divines subject, or else my entire plan might go up in smoke. Although Lilith had given me an answer I needed in order to fully trust her again, she'd chosen the absolute *worst* time to do it.

She'd seen my wink for crying out loud!

So, I cleared my throat. "Not to be a coldhearted bitch or anything, but is there a reason it even matters right now? I understand that they were your friends, Lilith, and that you are upset by what Wrath did, but...they are dead all the same, right?" I asked her, gently. "Why dig skeletons out of the closet? Let's just move on," I said, firmly.

She nodded, stiffly, wiping at her nose. "It needed to be addressed just the same as this," she said, pointing at the rolled parchment. "I paid one hundred years of my life for my choice, and he couldn't even be honest with the world that it was out of shame for me outmaneuvering him."

Wrath snarled. "You impudent little—"

In a superman tackle of irony, Samael saved the day by choosing that moment to defend the honor of the most independent woman in history—his fiancée, Lilith—the bane of overcompensating Adam's existence.

He leapt over the table and tackled his bigger, stronger brother with a meaty thud, sending Wrath's chair and wine glass flipping through the air. Samael got in one good punch before Wrath hurled him across the room where he destroyed a glass cabinet of priceless china. Before I even had time to jump up from my seat, Wrath was already straddling him, screaming as he punched his brother in the face again and again and again.

I flung magic at Wrath in an attempt to knock him aside, but it only served to make his shirt flutter. I cursed, grabbed an empty bottle of wine from the center of the table, and then sprinted towards the two brothers. Lilith was pleading on her knees, begging Wrath to stop, but he couldn't hear her over his own incoherent yelling.

So, I smashed the bottle of wine over the back of Wrath's head as hard as I could. It shattered and Lilith gasped in horror. Wrath ceased shouting and punching the moment I hit him. Then he just sat there, eerily still astride Samael. I could see blood spatter on the floor near my godfather's head, but I couldn't move to get a closer look until I knew how Wrath was going to react. As the seconds ticked by, I began to wonder if I had actually managed to knock Wrath out.

Then he slowly turned to look at me, his face utterly calm. His hair was a mess and his face was spattered with blood. He had a deep gash on his lip and blood was dripping from his chin. He stared from my face to the broken bottle neck in my hands, and then back to my face. He blinked, looking momentarily confused. And then he calmly stood up. He turned to face me and I tried not to stare at the bloody spatter staining his shiny white shirt. He walked past me without a word and grabbed a fresh wine glass from the cabinet. He held it up, inspecting it to verify that it was clean, and then he walked back to the table, righted his chair, and sat down. Then he crossed his legs and poured himself a glass of wine from a new bottle at the center of the table.

And he took a sip. The hair on the back of my neck stood on end, wondering what kind of psychopath we were dealing with here. Hit him in the head and he turns into the calmest son of a bitch in the world?

I risked a glance at Samael and cringed. His face was a bloody mess, but it wasn't as bad as I had feared. His nose was broken, his lip was torn and swollen, and one of his eyes was purple and bloody. He was breathing, and that was all I really cared about. His demon power would heal him just fine. "Get him to his feet," I told Lily. "We're not finished with our drinks yet," I growled.

He groaned, trying to do it himself, but my tiny, curvy godmother pulled him to his feet with one hand before draping his arm over her shoulder. "I should take him back to his rooms," she said, not bothering to hide her tears. Tears of relief that he was alive and guilt for what she had wrought. She wanted to get Samael as far away from Wrath as possible.

"You're both going to sit your Greater Demon asses at that table and you're going to keep your wits about you like you were supposed to be doing this whole time," I growled.

Samael nodded firmly, but Lilith gave me a startled, almost indignant look. "But—"

"It was not a question," I growled in a warning tone, poking a finger into Lilith's chest hard enough to shift her posture. "*You* put us in this mess." I turned and jabbed Samael's chest with the same finger. "*You* let your emotions take over. Wrath did what Wrath does. You poked the wolf and it bit back. That's on both of you."

Samael nodded stoically. "She's right," he rasped. "I'm sorry, Callie—"

I got right up in their faces, snarling even though it was no louder than my breath—like hearing a dagger drawn from a sheath when you were alone in a dark, empty, silent house. "You could have killed your Daemons with that little stunt." Then I stepped back, nodding at the pale, chagrined looks on their faces. "Go sit down. And shut your mouths. Now," I commanded at a normal volume.

And then I stormed back to the table, still clutching the broken tip of the bottle in my trembling fist. I sat down and topped off my glass of wine—which amazingly hadn't been knocked over in the mayhem. I focused on my pulse, willing it to slow, as Samael and Lilith joined us back at the table. Wrath stared into his glass with a distant look on his face.

After a few moments of silence, I slid the broken tube of glass over to Wrath. "You're not a very good listener, so I had to raise my voice. Potential husbands should be seen, not heard." I glanced over at Samael. "That applies to both of you. Morons."

Samael chuckled, nodding. He spit a gobbet of blood into his broken glass and it made a clinking sound, letting everyone know he'd lost a tooth. Hopefully, Hell's immortality package had a good dental plan.

Wrath slowly lifted his head to stare at me, blinking a few times. "Potential husband..." he mused. "So, is that a *yes?*" he asked, his bloody lip stretching into a faint smile.

I scoffed. "An old track coach of mine once told me that saying *you have potential* is a nicer way of saying *you haven't done shit yet.*"

Wrath's lip curled up ever so slightly at one corner. "I like that." He bobbed his head up and down, not breaking eye contact. "My apologies. I got a little carried away. Forgive me?"

"I'll consider it," I said, slowly, "if you two apologize to each other and hug it out."

Lilith's eyes bulged and Samael grew still. Wrath grinned, shaking his head wondrously. "You never cease to surprise me, White Rose—"

Samael cleared his throat, cutting off the archdemon. "I swung first. I am sorry for punching you in the mouth, and making you bleed," he said with a cold, bloody smile. "But I won't deny that it felt great."

Wrath chuckled softly, and then he promptly burst out laughing, pounding his fist into the table. He wiped at his eyes when his laughter finally died down. "I knew I liked you for a reason, Samael. I must admit, it's been eons since anyone made me bleed. It felt...*good*," he said, fervently. Samael smiled, nodding his agreement. "I apologize for making your face look better than it did ten minutes ago." Samael rolled his eyes and spit some more blood into his glass. "You're welcome for the upgrade, Lilith," he said, turning his smile on her.

She smiled icily, having regained her fire despite my threat. But Samael's tactic had worked better than anything. Maybe calm and apologetic was not the right tactic, after all. "The Divines *asked* me to send them to Purgatory. An eternity of torture was preferable to one minute of your company. I can appreciate the sentiment." And then she lifted her glass of wine to Wrath in mock cheers.

Wrath grinned back at her, nodding. "Fair is fair."

I clapped my hands. "Great. Now that we've all had our fun, it's time for you to hug it out so I can go to bed. I'll need my sleep if I'm going to meet more of your brothers tomorrow."

Wrath turned to look at me. "Of course. I expect your future visits to be made privately. Not with Samael at your hip—or anyone else for that matter. It would be quite dangerous for them, I assure you. We do not want a repeat of this afternoon."

I stared him in the eyes and gave a brief nod. He hadn't mentioned Claire, specifically, so I couldn't ascertain whether he was referring to the rumor I'd started. "Agreed. And you won't interfere. At all. Because we don't want a repeat of this afternoon."

He brushed his hands together as if the matter were settled. "We have a deal." He nodded, stiffly and then rose to his feet. He scooped up the broken neck of the wine bottle with a smug grin. Then he slipped it into his pocket. "Souvenir of our first date." I managed not to vomit. He turned to Samael. "Let's get this over with, you big brute."

Samael climbed to his feet with a grunt and the two exchanged the most awkward, overly macho hug I'd ever seen. Then Wrath turned to me and repeated his formal bow from earlier. "By your leave, Master Dracula," he said, smirking.

I dipped my chin. "Thank God," I said, dryly.

He chuckled, shaking his head. And then he was walking away.

I waited until he was almost at the door. "You never said where the next Sin is."

He halted, and then glanced over his shoulder with a knowing look. "I think we both know where he is. How else did I know to find you here, White Rose? Envy always loved the finer things in life. He will reach out to you tomorrow to arrange a meeting."

I narrowed my eyes, as if upset that he'd caught me. "Afternoon at the earliest. I'm sleeping in."

He studied me with a knowing grin that cried bullshit, and then gave the barest of nods. He hadn't mentioned anything about my trip with Claire, so there was every chance that Envy had thrown up the Wrath Symbol in the sky the moment I'd returned, before he'd even had time to hear the gossip I'd started. I still had no clue which—if any—of my servants were spies. Perhaps even Envy himself, although that seemed unlikely for an archdemon to pretend to be a servant.

But that was the fun of the game. The not knowing. Like his prophecy, which he had not mentioned in front of my godparents, even after I'd tried goading him with it. Why? Pride hadn't seemed like it was any big secret. More like water-cooler talk among demons.

Wrath left the Feast Hall, and we let out a collective sigh of relief after the door clicked closed.

❧ 46 ❧

I turned to Lilith. "What the *hell?*" I demanded. "Did you not see my wink?"

She straightened her spine defensively. "I saw your wink, but he lied and then tried to rub my face in it." She stared me in the eyes. "And now, all he will be thinking about after tonight is how he got bullied around by two women. He will be too angry to entertain any conspiracy theories about the Divines, which buys you time. If I had sat there and taken his shit, he would have felt victorious and might have even decided to come calling on you for another surprise visit. Now, he has suffered a minor humiliation and will not return until he has something to brag about."

I blinked. "You're telling me that it wasn't an overreaction on your part, and that it was purposeful?"

She hesitated, and I saw her shoulders droop in slow motion. "No. I am... justifying my overreaction," she admitted sheepishly. "But I'm not wrong about the accidental benefits." She stared down at the paper, blinking slowly. "I'm sorry, Callie. I lost my cool when I read the paper, seeing confirmation of what I had suspected for so long." She glanced over at Samael, and her shame slowly stretched into quite the opposite as a growing, entirely inappropriate, smile split her cheeks. "But my Samael...just punched Wrath in the mouth, and he lived to tell the tale."

Samael puffed out his chest, looking ridiculous as he tried to act macho while focusing his single functioning eye on his fiancée. "I did get in a good swing, didn't I?" he asked, boyishly.

I sighed, unclenching my fingers and biting back a smile. "You're both crazy," I said, shaking my head.

When I'd sent Samael to fetch Lilith earlier, the plan had been for him to ask her about the figurines in the privacy of their rooms where no one could eavesdrop. And if she did still have them, I'd told Samael keep them safe and not hand them over to me until I expressly asked about them. Because I'd wanted to see what my gossip with Claire rustled up before risking bringing them out in the open.

So, when I'd first arrived in the Feast Hall, Samael and Lilith had both been antsy, expecting me to ask for the figurines, but I'd steered the conversation to their wedding instead. And that's when Wrath had arrived.

But now that my enemies had played their hand...

I turned to Lily, snapping my fingers to distract her from eating Samael with her eyes. "Do you have the figurines?" I anxiously whispered.

Lilith nodded, and then walked over to an armoire in the corner of the room. She opened it to reveal stacks of folded linens. "I put them in here just before you arrived," she explained, lifting a pile to remove two small figurines. She scooped them up, straightened the linens, and then closed the door of the armoire before bringing them over. I accepted them with a sigh of relief, inspecting them in a cursory fashion before slipping them into my pocket. A servant could walk in at any time and see them in my hands. And if that servant happened to be Envy or one of his moles...the gig would be up.

I noticed that neither of them looked particularly victorious or uplifted. "What's wrong?" I asked, warily.

"I don't think they work anymore," she whispered. "I tried using them when I went looking this morning," she said, morosely. "I can't feel them inside anymore. It's been like that ever since they left. I kept them as mementos, more than anything else. Pretty paperweights," she sobbed. "That's why I didn't give them to you earlier. I didn't want to get your hopes up."

I sighed, hoping she wasn't right. "Then why try summoning them?"

She shrugged. "Hope," she admitted sadly. "Guilt. I don't know. When I saw Xuanwu's flower this morning, I thought that maybe they were reaching out to me after all this time. But I still felt nothing when I tried. I used to dream about what would happen if I happened to enter in the exact right spot where they resided. I tortured myself with that dream for one hundred years. Now that I am free, it eats at me during the day, too."

I nodded, squeezing her arm gently. "I'm sorry, Lilith," I said sympathetically. A thought came to mind. "How long were you able to stay in the Neverwas this morning?"

"Same as usual. It's usually less than a minute before I feel my Gateway slipping and my soul being drained." I nodded, thoughtfully. In my mind was a question, but I didn't want to get her hopes up.

What if she simply hadn't waited around long enough for them to answer her call?

Hopefully, that's what Pride and Michael and Sanguina would help me with. Buy me those crucial extra minutes. "Were you telling Wrath the truth when you said that your Daemons chose to go to Purgatory?"

She nodded, sobbing. "They made me," she whispered. "They wanted to save their brothers." I felt my heart break to hear that my suspicion had been correct. That they'd opted to go to Purgatory, knowing it would buy their brothers' freedom, since Wrath would no longer have reason to get his hands on them.

I reached out and lifted Lilith's chin. She stared at me, her eyes red-rimmed, and in that moment, she didn't look much like a demon. She looked like a scared young woman. "What are their names?" I all but whispered. "Because I'm going to be shouting them as loud as I possibly can, and as long as I possibly can, until they hear me, Lilith."

She nodded, happily, her lip trembling. "Use their nicknames. They used to hate me butchering their real names, so forced me to stop. If they hear those pet names, they'll know I sent you."

I smiled. "Okay."

"The Vermillion Bird is Zoe, and the White Tiger is Bai."

I arched an eyebrow judgmentally. "You must have truly fucked up their names if they reduced you to the use of one syllable." She laughed, nodding guiltily. "All right. Zoe and Bai. That's easy. Once I find them, you'll have your first two bridesmaids." She gasped, looking as if the thought hadn't occurred to her. I grinned. "Three, if you ask me."

Her excited, happy smile abruptly froze and died, and that's when I knew I had overstepped. She began dry-washing her hands, shooting nervous glances at Samael. "I-I..."

I held up my hands, embarrassed by my faux pas. "No problem. That wasn't my place."

Samael cleared his throat. "Well. She would love you to, but she can't ask."

I arched an eyebrow, not sure I wanted to continue the conversation. "This is why I hate weddings. I don't understand any of the rules. Except for the *I do* part. That one is fairly straightforward."

Samael took a deep breath. "You can't be in her bridal party, because...I need a best man," he said, hurriedly, projecting the words onto my face like an assault.

My eyebrows almost climbed off of my forehead. I bit back a smile. "I'm...well, I don't know how to tell you this, godfather, but I'm missing the necessary tools. I thought that was apparent, since I'm your goddaughter—not your godson."

He scowled. "You're Dracula. I dare anyone to tell you what you can or can't do. And everyone else I know is an asshole. Plus, who *wouldn't* want Dracula as their best man? You kidding me?" he asked, grinning excitedly—which looked hideously painful on his currently battered face.

"What about Xuanwu or Qinglong?" I asked, trying to think of any other excuse.

He shook his head and stepped forward to poke me in the chest with a finger. "A best man needs balls, and you've shown more balls in the last few hours than I've seen other men show in a lifetime."

"Thank you?" I asked, not entirely appreciating the compliment. Lilith had her hands clasped together in front of her face as if praying, and she was nodding encouragingly. I let out a defeated sigh. "Fine. I'll be your best man, but only if you two put it in writing that I don't have to help plan the wedding—at all."

Lilith beamed, nodding even as she squealed with happiness.

Samael hooted excitedly. "Now you *have* to survive or you'll ruin our wedding!"

My smile slipped. "Wow. That...is impressively manipulative, even for you."

"Grow a pair!" he jeered, grinning from ear-to-ear.

I sighed, shaking my head, and throwing my hands in the air in surrender. "I'm going to bed. Keep an eye on the castle while I'm gone. Remember, if anyone asks, I'm around the Keep somewhere and I don't plan on leaving until late tomorrow morning. Annoy the hell out of everyone with your love and excitement to keep them distracted."

Samael was nodding seriously, staying his eagerness for the moment. "Good luck, Callie," he said, wrapping his arms around Lilith in a reverse hug. "Rescue her girls. Consider this a trial run for your right to carry our rings on the big day."

I nodded. "I will," I said, waving one last time before I turned around. That last comment had reminded me of the strange rings from my mother's laboratory. And as I left the Feast Hall, I was tapping the pocket that held them, thinking dark-wizardly thoughts. What had my mother been trying to tell me, and why had they responded to Michael and Pride?

47

O n my way to my rooms, I decided to swing by the private dining hall for the castle workers. They had a servants' lounge that was adjacent to the kitchens, and I was famished. Perhaps I could pick up an apple or something to snack on. And it would give me a chance to check up on my suspects from the hallway earlier.

When I entered the room, it was a hell of a lot busier than I had antici-pated. There were about a dozen maids and valets seated at two long tables, and they were all huddled over their plates, chowing down in soft conversa-tion. I spotted every single one of the maids and valets from my list, but I kept my face blank, never settling on one longer than any other so as not to arouse their suspicion that I might be on to them. They almost immediately leapt to their feet in stumbling bows and curtsies, averting their eyes and apologizing for...things. They all spoke at once, so I had no idea what any one person confessed to, and I didn't actually care about whatever mistake they thought they had made. Or maybe they'd been apologizing for eating some damned food. Christ.

The Harkers must have been unbelievably cruel.

I waved a hand, reassuringly. "Relax, guys. I just wanted to make sure everything is running smoothly. I've been away for some time and didn't want you to think you're not appreciated."

They murmured meekly, reassuring me that all was well.

"Good." I hesitated. "I'm...embarrassed to ask, but do you guys have any food?" I asked, smirking. Several heads peeked out from the adjoining kitchen and their faces paled with fear before they ducked back out of sight.

One woman, older than the rest, strode out of the kitchen, looking as if she was on the verge of chastising everyone for standing around rather than eating the food she'd made them. She was about my height, with strong shoulders, pale hair, and light eyes.

Then she noticed me and she froze with a gasp, dropping her wooden spoon. She straightened her apron self-consciously and curtsied. "Master Dracula! Has one of my staff caused you any trouble?" she asked in a tone that promised physical violence to any offenders. She was obviously in charge, and I recalled seeing her around the Keep a few times in my brief tenure.

I shook my head. "Of course not. I just came by to thank everyone. I'm afraid we haven't officially met," I said. "I've been a little distracted lately. My name is Callie Penrose."

She blushed even further, averting her eyes. "I am Constance, Master Dracula," she said, curtsying again.

I froze, my knees buckling as I stared at her with my mouth hanging open.

She began nervously fidgeting with her apron, and I heard a collective murmur of concern. "Master Dracula?" Constance asked, looking terrified. "Are you well?"

I nodded, stiffly. "Y-yes. I...I must be hungrier than I thought," I stammered, studying her.

She had pale hair just like mine, and she could have passed for my mother if I applied twenty-something years to my mental vison of her. But... of course she wasn't my mother. That was ridiculous. My mother hadn't been the only woman named Constance, and this woman would be acting very differently if she were meeting her long-lost daughter. My mother was dead. It was just a name.

...right?

I felt all the eyes in the room on me, so I took a calming breath. "Could you have something brought to my rooms, Constance?" I asked, trying not to stumble over the name. "Nothing fancy. Just meat, cheese, and crackers. Maybe a salad or some fruit, if you have any."

Constance bobbed again. "Of course, Master Dracula." I nodded as the beginning of an idea came to mind. This could actually turn out very, very well...

"Please send one of the valets," I said, as if at an afterthought. "I have some furniture that needs moving, and I believe it is spelled against magic or I would do it myself." I glanced around the room at the ten men. "Any of you with a decent pair of arms or legs will suffice," I said, turning back to Constance. "Oh, and have him bring fresh towels, please," I added. "I fancy a long soak."

"I will see to it myself, Master Dracula," Constance promised. "I am quite strong," she said with a bold smile. "I can wash your back and do your hair before you retire for the evening."

"No!" I said, louder than I'd intended. She flinched at my tone, licking her lips nervously. "Thank you, but no. I prefer you to stay in the kitchens where you belong. Just because you can do something does not mean you should," I said, managing a warm smile. "A general does not take the field of battle, and the House Mistress," I said, making up a title on the spot, "manages her staff, not the day-to-day duties. That invites chaos."

"It's no trouble, Master Dracula," she said, desperately, looking as if she was facing the guillotine.

I walked up to her and grasped her hand in mine, squeezing it reassuringly. "Constance?"

"Y-yes, Master Dracula," she stammered, sweat popping out on her brow.

"If you insist on bringing me dinner yourself, you're going to have to bring it to the guard post." She cocked her head, looking confused. "Because I will stand guard all night with the lowliest soldier. Which means I will not get my long soak in the tub."

She gasped, affronted at the very concept. "No, Master Dracula. What would people say?" she hissed.

I smirked. "*Exactly*, Constance. What would people say to see Dracula guarding the gate or the House Mistress delivering towels? We all have our duties. Mine is to lead and protect the people of this castle. Yours is to manage those who keep everyone fed, clothed, and cared for. Let's each focus on our strengths, shall we?"

She nodded, thoughtfully. "Yes, Master Dracula."

I curtsied to her—just as low as she had curtsied to me—even though Aphrodite's clothes consisted of pants and jacket. She blanched, making me smile wider. "Thank you for your hard work, Constance. I would entertain the concept of picking a personal attendant for such matters regarding clothes and hair," I admitted. "I have never considered the thought until you mentioned it. Perhaps we can discuss it in the near future."

"Of course, Master Dracula," Constance agreed, happily. "We have several girls who would be perfect for the role.

I turned to every other bug-eyed face with a warm smile plastered on my cheeks as I wondered which one of them might possibly be Envy or a mole working for the archdemon.

"And thank you all for taking care of the rest of my people. Don't hesitate to let Constance know if you need anything from me. You will not be reprimanded for voicing your opinions or offering suggestions for improvements around the Keep. I encourage it, in fact." And then I curtsied to them, too, making everyone about as uncomfortable as possible.

I turned to leave.

"Master Dracula?" Constance asked, sounding as if she'd been goosed.

I turned back around. "Yes, Constance?" I asked, trying not to flinch at the name.

"You are not anything like the Harkers," she whispered, lowering her eyes.

I nodded. "That is because I killed them, Constance." There was a sharp intake of breath from everyone in the room. And another when I allowed myself to smile. "I killed the Harkers because they were cruel. Castle Dracula is a very different place than it once was. I will expect much from you, but you can expect appreciation and respect in return. From me and the other residents of the Keep. I expect to be informed if that courtesy is ever abused or neglected. I will personally correct the offense and you will receive an apology and compensation. We are all in this together, after all. We keep you safe, you keep us healthy and strong. Deal?"

Constance stared at me, her mouth hanging open. Then she started, realizing she hadn't answered. "Of course, Master Dracula. Of course. A gentleman will be right up with your supper and towels, and to assist you with the furniture. In your rooms, not at the guard post," she added, emphasizing the difference in a stern, no-nonsense, motherly tone.

I grinned. "Yes, ma'am."

I left the kitchens, wondering how much water I would have to splash around to get Envy's attention. Because this next plan was already making me blush.

It was going to be much harder than challenging an archangel to a fight or breaking a bottle of wine over an archdemon's head.

48

I stood in the sitting room of my master suite—which consisted of four different rooms, technically. Mina and Jonathan Harker had spared no expense on clothes, jewelry, and shoes. Claire had boxed up all of his things, but Mina's clothes had remained in case any of it fit me. Claire was hoping none of them did so that she could swoop in for the kill and haul everything to her own rooms. In her short residency, Claire had also managed to acquire the keys to the locked suites of the other three Brides of Dracula—the Weird Sisters Xylo and I had killed. She had raided those rooms of all dresses, jewelry, or anything even somewhat shiny, and then brought it all over to my rooms—without warning—so that I could help her pick over the remains. Like vultures over fresh carcasses.

The bathroom was larger than any bedroom I'd ever had. In fact, it was larger than my old apartment. The closet and adjoining dressing room were the same, and it was currently a mess of boxes from Claire's kleptomania. The number of extravagant dresses, shoes, coats, and accessories from the four women was mind boggling. But in that collection, I had found exactly what I needed for my next battle.

An alarmingly short, red silk robe that had definitely not been designed for warmth. It had been designed for unveiling, and it would have made Aphrodite grin. Because I didn't have any furniture that needed moving. I had wanted to divide the suspects between men and women, so had decided to focus on the most likely suspect—the valets. If Envy was a servant in disguise, I doubted he would try to pass for a woman. Then again, he would have to be in disguise because angels and demons were hauntingly beautiful and would have been spotted a mile away.

So...the sex of the spy might not matter at all.

But one thing I knew for sure. Master Dracula had asked for personal help, and if Envy or one of his minions wanted actionable information on whatever I had planned with Claire tomorrow, it was more than likely the servant coming up to my rooms right now would be my guy.

And I knew how to make men uncomfortable. Little bit of skin, little bit of privacy, and a special something that might appeal to Envy, personally.

The giant claw-foot tub was still filling up with hot water, so I was standing before the massive mirror in the sitting room, sorting through boxes and ornate chests of extravagant jewelry that would have only belonged to literal royalty on Earth. There had to be millions of dollars' worth of precious metals and gems spread out across the vanity. Earrings, necklaces, pendants, brooches, rings, bracelets, anklets, and everything between.

Priceless treasure. For the demon who coveted anything of value, it was a buffet table.

I hefted a thick necklace of white gold that was wider than my finger. A deep blue sapphire as large as a robin's egg was fitted into the thick pendant and surrounded by diamonds—some of them as large as my fingernail. I lifted it up to my neck and smiled at the display of it nestled in my cleavage, contrasting with the blood-red silk. It matched the elaborate diamond studs in my ears.

There was a polite knock at the door. I took a calming breath to gather my resolve, telling myself that I wasn't to be judged by this wanton act. If Aphrodite could be a harlot to be a hero, I could wear a cute robe to make a valet squirm. I had knives tucked into a garter I'd found in the closet, and my magic was always readily available for a quick escape if I crossed the line and found Envy himself behind the door.

"Come in!" I called out as I reached up behind my head to clasp the necklace on. The door opened and I stepped back from the mirror, pirouetting on my toes as I inspected myself in the mirror, checking every angle.

Jewelry like this would make any girl look sexier. The robe was almost overkill.

There was a shocked gasp from the door and I turned to face the young man staring at me in stunned disbelief. It was the tall, well-built valet with long blond hair that I'd startled earlier today—the one who'd almost broken the vase when I said hello. He'd also been in the hall when I'd started my rumor with Claire. Was that a coincidence, or had my hastily thrown together fishing net actually netted me the mole? Or...Envy himself. Wrath had blatantly said Envy was here in Castle Dracula, and that his brother *always loved the finer things in life.* Even if this valet wasn't him, he would report to his boss about my collection.

The man's face was the color of some of the rubies on the table to see Master Dracula so indecent and looking directly at him. I smiled invitingly. "What do you think?" I asked, gesturing vaguely at my necklace, in a manner that only served to emphasize everything else on display for the young man. I had to fight not to blush myself, but I knew he would only take my reddened cheeks as an altogether different kind of reaction.

He stammered awkwardly, sounding as if he was choking as he tried not to gawk at my current state of dress while still obeying my command to comment on the jewelry. I could practically read the thoughts racing across the surface of his brain. Maybe I hadn't meant the jewelry at all. Was he supposed to comment on my body, my jewelry, make a romantic gesture, or run away screaming?

Pick a door, kid, I thought to myself.

"Mistress Constance mentioned furniture," he croaked through gritted teeth, looking so uncomfortable and nervous that he almost looked angry.

I smiled, gesturing for him to come closer. He remained firmly rooted in place, his shoulders quivering with frustration. Hell, maybe I had actually netted Envy, and he was having trouble thinking straight at the casual display of wealth before him. "I won't bite," I teased, reaching out to grasp him by the wrist and gently tug him towards the table of jewelry. I really cheesed it up, pointing at a ruby necklace consisting of three blood red orbs that were even larger than the sapphire I was wearing. "Is red a better color on my skin?" I asked, holding it up beside the sapphire with a thoughtful frown.

"I..." he stammered. "I c-can't be here," he croaked. "I mean, I shouldn't linger. Mistress Constance will be expecting me back," he choked, averting his eyes, and puffing out his cheeks. I caught a momentary flicker of anger in his frantic, darting eyes. "The f-furniture?"

But I had to be sure.

I reached out and lifted his chin. "Pick one," I said, flashing him my brightest smile. "There is no wrong answer," I said, lowering the jewelry as I stared into his eyes, looking for any telltale sign. He truly was handsome, but not perfectly so. Then again, I knew an archdemon would use a disguise to hide that inhumanly beauty or everyone would notice him.

Sanguina leapt up onto the vanity, and the valet let out a sharp gasp, not having noticed her until now. With all the bling on the table, her molten silver eye sockets had been overlooked. She sniffed at the air as she drew closer to the servant.

He is hiding something, but I cannot tell what, she told me. *I cannot sense whether he is Envy, much the same as I could not sense anything unusual with Wrath*, she added, almost angrily.

The valet twisted his head as if I was fitting him with a noose, gasping for air as his nostrils flared. He took an instinctive step back from Sanguina. "Furniture?"

I sighed, pointing at a small ottoman. He stared down at it, and this time I definitely could see a flash of anger. A child could have moved it. I pointed to a spot a few feet away, against the wall. "Over there is fine. I keep tripping over it. I have no idea why it's spelled."

He hurriedly shoved it to the new spot, slamming it into the wall. "There." He made as if to go, not bowing, or apologizing for his behavior.

I grasped his elbow, halting him, and he tensed. "Which one?" I asked, softly, close enough to lean in and kiss his ear.

"R-ruby," he finally whispered in a strangled cry. Then he practically sprinted for the door. He gestured at the rolling table beside him and almost knocked over the plate of food in his haste. He practically tore the door from the hinges in his desperate attempt to escape. Then he slammed it closed behind him without a word.

I frowned at the door thoughtfully. "Would a valet leave without bowing, or slam the door?" I mused out loud, tapping my lips with a finger.

Definitely the sapphire, Sanguina said in a dry tone. I continued staring at the door for about five minutes, thinking and scheming and waiting to see if anything happened as a result of my fishing net. Finally, I turned to the mirror, pursing my lips.

"Definitely the sapphire," I agreed. Then I unclasped it and set it inside the chest. I slowly removed the earrings, feeling as if I was peeling away a part of my soul.

Then I made my way over to the cart, grabbed the plate of food and a towel, and carried my stash to the bathtub, smiling to myself. Sanguina hopped up onto the bed. *I sensed nothing suspicious, but my assessment is not helpful with their kind*, Sanguina said.

I nodded. "Your move, Envy," I muttered.

Because if Envy was walking around disguised as a valet, he would have fought tooth and nail to be the one to deliver my food and towels after my show in the kitchens. If, on the other hand, Envy had a few servants on his payroll, they would have been desperate at the chance to get him some potentially helpful reconnaissance. And showing off my jewelry to Envy seemed like the safest way to piss him off. Because the Seven Sins were overly emotional. Their namesakes seemed to actually be their weaknesses. Envy didn't just *like* nice things, he *coveted* nice things. Lounging around my rooms in a sexy robe, having food brought up, and obviously preparing for a long bath meant I wasn't going anywhere anytime soon. Buying me time.

Of course, the poor valet could have been totally innocent and not even remotely involved with the archdemon. I shrugged, picking up a chunk of cheese and popping it in my mouth. "Then you got a free show, kid. You're welcome," I said out loud, grinning an evil grin. Sanguina's dark chuckle echoed in my mind.

I slipped into the tub and let out a long, relaxing sigh. As I soaked, I caught Sanguina up on Pride's suggestion that she help be our anchor for the Gateway to Purgatory. She'd agreed, sounding almost eager to use her powers after being cooped up in the Keep without me for so long. She saw merit in Pride's argument that their powers could work together without issue, which made me feel a whole lot better.

In fact, she seemed impressed by the plan in general, and she was one to poke apart anything not suggested by herself. That didn't mean we were guaranteed a win, but it sure helped boost my confidence.

I pondered the metal card, the two rings, and the intricately carved wooden phoenix and tiger figurines that I'd placed on the edge of the tub, occasionally inspecting them or testing them with tendrils of my magic—all to no avail. I thought about my Spear, but I came up with no new insights on how they were a part of saving the Divines. I had a few hours to kill until I was certain the Keep was quiet and news of my extravagant night in had reached Envy's ears.

Only then would it be safe for me to leave for Purgatory to try and save Bai and Zoe.

So I went back to the beginning, pondering the metal card...

What was my mother trying to tell me?

I stood in the twilight field, admiring the cherry blossoms trailing up into the purple sky. The bluish-gray grass swayed back and forth like rolling waves. I'd meditated in my suite at Castle Dracula for two hours after my bath. Then, in honor of my mother, I'd donned her black slaughtering outfit. I'd also tucked away the pair of rings and the metal card in my weapons belt, hoping to channel whatever psychic energy I could. Maybe if I brought enough of her with me, I'd have a better chance of success. The black pants were snug and sleek, and the seemingly simple black top felt like weighted silk, hugging my body much the same as Aphrodite's gear. The weapons belt went on last, and then I was ready to go.

I'd scooped up Sanguina, and Shadow Walked to Xuanwu's home. I had told the Black Tortoise that it was time to go collect Pride and Michael from Roland's church while I caught Ryuu up to speed on my plan.

Xuanwu and Qinglong had been less than courteous in dropping off the archangel and archdemon at my feet in this adjacent realm to his backyard—the two Divines had quite literally *dropped* them off from ten feet above the ground. I had wanted to be off the Earthly realm in case anything went wrong, and I hadn't wanted to do this at Castle Dracula—not if Envy was watching my every move.

And with the rebirth pond, the two Divines I intended to save would have quick access to healthcare, which they would sorely need. We might all end up needing it, in fact.

I glanced over at Sanguina to see her staring at Pride and Michael. She seemed to be muttering under her breath, but in her mind, repeating the same three words over and over.

Torn. Severed. Split…

I frowned, hefting my Silver katana in both hands. "You okay?" I asked her.

She jumped two feet, snarling in multiple directions. Then she promptly sat down as if she hadn't just suffered a stroke. *I am excellent, as always.*

I frowned. *It's just that you kept repeating—*

She curled her lip at me in warning. *I. Am. Excellent.*

Right. Touchy subject. If it had been relevant, she would have said something. She wanted a success here as much as anyone. I was her only family.

"Okay. You sure you are ready for this, Sanguina?" I asked out loud, gesturing at the area I had picked for our Gateway.

You need an anchor, she said. *I will keep the Gateway open from this side.*

"And the Purgatory souls won't be able to crossover?" Ryuu asked her dubiously, striding up beside us. Aala remained close to Ryuu—making me a tad jealous—and staring at things no one else could see. Especially when her eyes drifted to Pride or Michael, who were studiously silent as if something had happened during their sleepover that they didn't want to talk about.

Why was everyone staring at them? Was I just so jaded that I wasn't impressed by the archangel and archdemon, but everyone else was terrified?

I listened to Sanguina's response in my mind and then translated for him. "Not unless they have a body to ride. Sanguina the Silver is playing a foxier, scarier version of Gandalf the Gray." He stared at me blankly. "None shall pass? Heathen," I muttered.

"Hey!" Pride grumped, finally deciding to break his vow of silence. "I resent that."

Ryuu sighed, dropping the topic as he gave me a resigned nod and handed me a familiar scarf—as if he was concluding an errand I had asked him to do for me.

I stared at the scarf in silence, smiling. Then I slowly looked up at him. "When did you get this?" I asked.

"In your mother's laboratory. It's one of your Templar scarves that protects against magic. You left it there one night last week," he said, casually. "I wanted to make sure you are safe."

I hugged it close to my chest, deeply touched that he had done this all on his own without saying a word. Then I rose up on my toes and kissed him on the cheek. "Thank you, Ryuu."

He froze, staring straight ahead. Then he nodded, stiffly and walked away, checking the field for...I don't know. Rocks or something. Aala giggled at the two of us, and then left to follow after him. A looped, segmented chain hung from her belt, and one of the ends was affixed with a wicked spearpoint. I shuddered. Chain whips were no fucking joke.

I sighed forlornly at my ninja, wondering if he was just shy, or if it had something to do with the fact that I hadn't personally, officially ended anything with Nate yet. I tied the Templar scarf around my neck, and then I focused on the matter at hand.

I knelt down to the ground. "You up for this?" I asked Sanguina in a soft, concerned tone, glancing pointedly at the archangel and archdemon. The rings in my pocket hadn't reacted to their arrival, seeming about as inert as the first time I had seen them. "You're sure your magic won't nullify each other? Because we can't afford for you to fizzle out at the worst possible moment—which is when it *will* happen if it's *going* to happen, according to Murphy. Can you hold on?"

I was born in magic that would melt your mind. Just because you dominated me does not mean I can't dance circles around you in the realms of power. You do your part, I'll do mine. I smirked at her, relieved by her feistiness. It was reassuring. *Do you know how to do what I asked?* she asked.

I nodded. "I've got it." I turned to find Ryuu about three inches away from my face. I yelped and stumbled back a step, but he caught me firmly by both shoulders. I regained control of my breathing and stared into his eyes, waiting, daring him to make a move. Ryuu stared back at me with an intense, frustrated look, obviously wanting to say something. I arched an eyebrow and he finally shook his head, releasing me and then retreating.

Aala sighed at the angsty ninja, annoyed. She'd been standing nearby. She shrugged her shoulders at me in a *what do you do* gesture, and then joined Ryuu as they made their way towards Xuanwu and Qinglong who were waiting beneath the massive glowing tree.

I turned to Pride, who looked entirely too amused at Ryuu's strange behavior. He opened his mouth—

"Okay," I said, cutting him off before he could suggest something horribly inappropriate. Then I summarized the plan the three of us had formulated over the last thirty minutes with Sanguina. "Pride, first. Then me, and then Michael. Remember to anchor your Gateway to my katana, and then layer it on top of the pile, weaving them all together as best as you can," I told Michael, since he was going last. Pride had the easiest job of going first.

"You do remember that we came up with the plan together, and that you've already reminded us five times since we wrapped up our huddle, right?" Pride asked, dryly.

Instead of answering him, I closed my eyes and gathered my will, drawing deep on my bond with Sanguina as I called up the Eternal Metal.

It was time to go to the Neverwas.

I opened my eyes to see my katana rippling like water. I took a deep breath and then yelled at the top of my lungs as I slammed it down into the soil, burying it to the hilt.

I felt Sanguina lash out, solidifying her tether to the long hilt of the katana like a chrome lasso.

"Now!" I shouted at Pride.

The air seemed to darken and the breeze stopped entirely as a ball of wicked black thorns drifted out from his palms. His arms shook and he gritted his teeth as he maneuvered his writhing tangle of thorns a few feet away, using his outstretched hands to shape and control it. He shot me a look and I gave him a firm nod. He roared, the sound ripping through the air like it had come from the throat of an actual lion, and then flung his arms wide. The knot of thorns screamed in protest as it was stretched apart to create an oval window in mid-air. One particularly thick vine lashed out and wrapped around the hilt of the katana so that the shifting ring of thorns looked like a kite in the wind.

Except in the center of that window was a world of embers and sparks rather than Xuanwu's tranquil field. I drew deep on my memory of the land of embers and sparks from my brief visit across the crystal bridge to Castle Dracula with Samael. Seeing it clearly in my mind, but not focusing directly on that exact location, I created a ball of roiling, molten Silver. Then I hurled it at Pride's Gateway, coating the living black thorns in liquid chrome. My power made the air hum as the liquid metal raced down Pride's thorned anchor, strengthening the bond to my katana. My knees wobbled at the surprisingly massive expenditure of power—and the lack of practice I had at using Sanguina's magic in any significant manner.

We both turned to Michael and nodded. He flung his hands forward and blasted the Gateway with glowing white fire. The Gateway of Silver thorns erupted in flame as if it had been doused in gasoline, and I had to leap back a step as the flame raced down the anchor to the katana.

I walked up to the Gateway, admiring our work. Pride and Michael joined me, shaking their heads with awed looks on their faces. "I've never seen anything like it," Pride murmured. "Who knew we could work together so well, eh, brother?" He asked out the side of his mouth, elbowing Michael lightly.

Michael was smiling and nodding, staring through the portal in awe. "It's three stacked Gateways, but woven together to create one," he breathed. He met my eyes. "I don't think magic like this has been done...*ever*," he admitted. Then, "Except for that one time, of course," he said, smiling guiltily as he recalled God creating the universe. Pride nodded somberly—for once, not having a quip ready at hand.

I smiled smugly. "Well, for our next trick, we get to jump through a ring of fire like circus animals, so don't give us too much credit." They nodded grimly, looking more like brothers than at any other moment. I checked the two figurines in my pocket one last time, paranoid that I might have lost them in the last two minutes. I hadn't. "Let's go save the White Tiger and the Vermillion Bird."

"Just say *red*," Pride muttered. "Vermillion sounds like a made-up word."

Michael nodded his agreement.

"People from Kansas City do not say *Red Bird*. On principle, because we were raised Royals. Let those poor souls from St. Louis keep their cardinal," I argued. It was glaringly obvious that they had no idea what I was talking about, which made it even funnier. Must not have baseball in the afterlife.

I leapt through the ring of fire and into the Neverwas. No way in Heaven or Hell was I going to let them go first. History always remembered the first person, rarely the others.

Sidenote—ninety-nine-percent of the time, the first person died.

50

My boots hit the ground and seemed to stick like I'd landed in thick clay—although the surface was bone dry and sent up a cloud of seemingly weightless ash. I quickly lifted the Templar scarf into place over my ears to cover my mouth and nose so I wouldn't breathe any Purgatory particles into my lungs. Call me paranoid.

Embers and sparks danced through the air like swarms of insects, reminding me of the apocalyptic pink cherry blossoms on the other side of the Gateway. I tried lifting my boots, realizing that they hadn't been stuck to the surface, they just felt twice as heavy as normal. In fact, my whole body felt heavy and sluggish, as if it was being pulled down to the ground. The laws of gravity were very different from home, making each step a strain. My shoulders and lower back ached at the pressure.

Which was weird, because the ash seemed to exist in zero gravity. I felt a shiver roll down my spine as my mind entertained any number of horrible theories.

Michael and Pride landed beside me and I watched the effects of the new gravity hit them hard, making their faces noticeably sag as if they'd each aged twenty years. Good lord. I was glad the scarf covered my face or all three of us would have looked like melting candles.

Their wings ripped out of their backs, and I cringed to see that they, too, seemed to sag towards the ground. They clomped around, trying to get familiar with the new environment, and I risked a glance back through the Gateway to see Sanguina snarling at me. Well, at the Gateway, but it sure didn't look that way. I remembered her strange mantra, and grew uneasy.

Summon them! she snapped, sounding strained. And another shiver rolled down my spine to see her suddenly shift two inches to the right without crossing the space between. It looked like one of those video chat calls when the other person has a bad internet connection and they keep freezing and resuming in slightly different positions.

A glitch in the Matrix.

We could not afford a bad internet connection or a glitch. No time to waste.

I turned back to my partners in crime.

A dome of dark light—Hellish protection—slowly expanded around Pride, seeming to press away the gusts of sparks ripping across the desolate, jagged world of raw black and ivory stone.

Michael had a similar dome around him, but his was a pale gray color, representing his Heavenly protection. I let out a sigh of relief, scratching out one of my hidden concerns—that Michael might have actually fallen and lost his Heavenly pension benefits. That would have ruined our whole plan. The two domes intersected without a nuclear explosion, reminding me of a Venn diagram.

I made sure to stay within that overlapping space as the two had fore-warned me. I was mortal, after all, and I would be first to succumb to the effects of the Neverwas without their domes of protection—Heaven and Hell keeping me safe in Purgatory. Who would have guessed it.

I quickly checked our surroundings, balking at the colossal pillars of pale powder and dusty mountains in the near distance. Other than the swirling swarms of sparks—resembling schools of tropical fish moving in concert—in the stormy black sky, we were utterly alone, as if this was some alien planet.

"The Night Currents," Michael commented with a shudder, eyeing the swarms of dancing embers.

The pair instantly tucked in their wings, looking nervous about the Night Currents. "You'd have to be one crazy son of a bitch to try flying in *that*," Pride murmured. I was pretty sure I'd heard Nate tell me that his unicorn, Grimm, had braved those currents once. Hunting rainbows or something. I chose not to mention it. Grimm was certifiable, so it didn't invalidate their fear.

Michael cleared his throat, pointedly. "As fun as this is..."

I blushed beneath my scarf and nodded. I pulled out the two wooden figurines of the White Tiger and the Vermillion Bird that Lilith had given me. Both were carved of a rich, red wood and felt strangely warm to the touch. I swiftly reached down to a throwing knife tucked into my boot and almost dropped the seemingly twenty-pound dagger. I managed to prick the tip of my finger and slip it back into the sheath before a hush fell over the Neverwas.

I looked up in alarm to see Michael and Pride staring down at the ground beneath my hand. A single drop of blood had hit the ash, and already seemed to be boiling. "Shit," I breathed. Because I suddenly heard a stampede of screams in the distance. I looked up sharply to see a cloud about a mile-wide racing down the distant mountain, seemingly headed right for us. My stomach roiled, unable to look away from the rolling, tangled mass of what I imagined was thousands of rubbery, boneless spirits racing our way as fast as they possibly could. In this place, I had no idea how far away they actually were, because distances seemed to slip and slide in my peripheral vision. Maybe a mile? Too fucking close.

"Callie..." Pride growled nervously.

I rubbed my bloody finger over each figurine, ignoring my shaking fingers.

"ZOE! BAI! WE'VE COME TO BRING YOU HOME!"

The figurines abruptly flared with intense heat, smoldering at the edges. I refused to let them go, fearing what would happen if any more of my blood hit the ground. I tried to ignore the distant screams, which was made easier by the fact that I was panting desperately into my scarf, staring at the figurines in frantic desperation. How long had we been here? Two minutes? Longer than Lilith's visit, so that was good.

Directly before me, two translucent spirits fizzled into existence and I almost stumbled back in alarm.

A huge, fully-grown tiger and a phoenix of about the same size as the cat slowly lifted their heads to stare at me. Although basically transparent, their faces were gaunt and hollow and confused. They were staring at the figurines with puzzled, exhausted expressions, as if trying to recall why they looked familiar.

"Oh, my God. It worked," I whispered, feeling my eyes growing misty. I tugged down my scarf and smiled at the phoenix and tiger. "Xuanwu and

Qinglong sent us," I said, pointing at the Gateway. "We're here to rescue you!"

The phoenix let out a weak cry that sounded like a dying peacock, and then shook her head languidly. Her long, translucent tail of feathers stretched out behind her like a limp rag.

"Let's save the Q and A for after we save them," Pride growled. "Come on, Zoe," he said, scooping up the phoenix and lobbing her through the Gateway.

Except she bounced off the surface like it was solid glass. My heart dropped into my stomach. Zoe landed awkwardly on the ground, stumbling. Then she let out another wailing cry, shaking her head more forcefully. Bai, the tiger, let out an agonizing growl, and then shook her body as if to banish excess water from her fur.

"Well, that fucking sucked," Pride said, staring at the Gateway.

"They're moving fast," Michael warned, keeping an eye on the oncoming horde of starving souls.

The tiger plodded over to me drunkenly, and I had to focus intently so as not to lose sight of her almost invisible form. She nudged my hand with her nose as if wanting me to pet her, and my heart broke. "Oh, Bai. What has this place done to you?" I whispered, feeling how frail and hollow she was.

She nudged me again and my bloody finger smeared over her forehead in a crimson streak. Light suddenly flickered through her body like fire following a trail of gasoline, and I gasped. She straightened marginally, puffing out her chest as if taking her first deep breath after a long run. Then the light faded and she sagged again, letting out a sad whine that I felt in my chest.

The phoenix wailed again, tripping towards me, and she sounded downright condescending.

My blood was powerful, able to make people stronger. I'd Blood Bonded Qinglong to me. My blood was also powerful enough to break bonds. But Zoe and Bai were bloodless souls. Yet...Xylo had been a bloodless skeleton, and I had bonded him. I decided to stop thinking about it too hard, because the oncoming wave of vengeful spirits was only growing closer.

I drew my knife and cut deep across both palms. Then I grabbed both of the divines, hurriedly smearing my blood over their bodies as I drew deep on my power. They flared with light and the horde of souls screamed louder as the two Divines roared and wailed, growing less translucent and filling in with color. My head began to swim as I panted, not entirely sure what I was doing. But I felt their minds coming alive, and I tried to pass on my intentions through our bond. The Blood Bond snapped into place and I let out a choking cough, feeling as if my stomach was a black hole of nothingness—as if I would never again feel full.

I. Was. *Starving.*

"What was *that?*" Michael shouted, sounding shaken.

I sagged, wanting nothing more than to fall to the ground. "A Blood Bond," I said, fighting through the yawning void in my center. "It makes them stronger by binding them with my blood," I mumbled, tiredly.

The tiger nudged my cheek, encouragingly, and I sobbed to see that she was now actually a glowing white tiger. Her claws gleamed like freshly polished steel, and her teeth were a perfect match as she curled her lip in an anxious snarl towards the oncoming wave.

The phoenix burned with astonishing red and white feathers, and I saw faint flickers of flame on her long, vibrant tail. She swiftly abandoned us and began frantically pecking at the glass-like surface of the Gateway. My joy crashed and burned, realizing my Blood Bond hadn't been enough. I scrambled over and reached my own hand through to Xuanwu's field without issue.

"Damn it!" I cursed. "My Blood Bond isn't strong enough to get them through!"

The screaming army grew steadily nearer, drawn to the amount of fresh blood in the air. The tiger snarled angrily as she swiped her claws against the invisible barrier of the Gateway to the sound of nails on a chalkboard. I stared at our escape, trying to force my mind to think of a solution as Sanguina continued to spastically snarl and flicker on the other side—the connection between us spotty, despite her anchor. I glanced back to see the horde of souls had covered half the distance. I hoped they were as sluggish as Bai and Zoe had been, giving us a few more precious seconds to come up with our escape. I called up the Spear of Destiny and stared down at it, trying to think of anything I could do to buy us some time. What had my mother expected me to do? Could I send a blast of light at the souls?

"Fighting and hiding are both off the table. What if *we* tried this Blood Bond?" Pride asked, anxiously. "It obviously did *something* helpful since they're no longer transparent," he said, pointing at Zoe and Bai.

Michael shook his head. "Our blood is too potent. And who knows what mixing our two pantheons together would do? It might very well be poisonous to them. May as well stab them in the heart with your weapon."

Which left us with...

My Spear. But how?

I sent up a silent prayer, not knowing what else to do.

Help me, Mom. Please just let me save these girls and bring them home. They've suffered enough.

51

I stared down at my Spear with a frown, Michael's words scratching something deep in my mind. *It is not a weapon.* Ryuu and Aala had been adamant about that. I slowly looked up at the archangel and archdemon. I could visibly see that their domes of protection were weakening and growing smaller, their very aura was being beaten back by the oppressive weight of anti-death that was the Neverwas.

Sanguina snarled at us through the Gateway, her fur visibly steaming and her molten eye sockets blazing with light. I could feel her anxiety and strain to keep the Gateway stable for us—able to see us but reading my mind well enough to know that something was terribly wrong. For whatever reason, she could no longer communicate with me through my mind—our connection was too unstable.

The tiger stalked over to me, growing more lethargic as I watched the power of my Blood Bond begin to fade away. She sat down beside me, nudging me with a sad yowl. The phoenix hopped over, her flaming feathers already growing weaker as she pressed up against my other side, shooting her sister a sad look and voicing an agonizing cry. The fire didn't burn me, but I probably wouldn't have cared if it had.

"The Spear is not a weapon," I whispered, fighting back the heartache caused by their fear and sorrow. At their dashed hopes.

Sanguina managed to somehow send me a whispered message—a repeat of her earlier mantra—and the Gateway rippled as a result, shrinking smaller at her momentary lapse in focus. The Gateway solidified as she focused back on it. I pondered her mantra, gripping my Spear tightly, ignoring Michael and Pride nervously bickering back and forth.

I visualized the metal card from the box in my mother's laboratory—particularly, the strange image I'd found inside it. The Spear of Destiny forming a bridge. Whatever the picture had portrayed, there was no question that it had represented massive power. And the Spear was made for healing, not harming. I slowly lifted my gaze to the two brothers, cocking my head at a crazy, half-baked thought.

Was it enough power to save the two Divines? Was their blood worth the risk?

"I need you both to cut your hands and grab the Spear of Destiny with me," I said, hurriedly. "Maybe it will be enough to bolster my Blood Bond with them. This way we don't have to worry about your blood poisoning theirs." Maybe my Spear would cleanse their potent blood before passing it onto the Divines—like a blood transfusion. I risked a glance past them, cringing at the writhing mass of tortured souls. Like an inbound wave, they stretched to left and right, impossible to evade or withstand. "If you don't, we're all going to die in a few minutes. Less."

"We can escape and come back with a better plan!" Michael shouted, pointing at the open Gateway.

And...he was right.

I shook my head adamantly. "I won't do it. We just rang the dinner bell and painted them with living blood. No *way* am I leaving them behind to be feasted upon after we gave them a taste of hope. *Look* at them!" I said, feeling Zoe and Bai press closer against me, sandwiching me as they wilted in fear of the oncoming wave of anti-death. "They're brimming with life compared to anything else here. The souls will devour them like a school of piranhas. We just turned them into cocaine!" I shouted, feeling my own stomach threatening to pull me down into the ground from my impossible hunger.

Pride gripped Michael's shoulder firmly. "She's right, Brother," he said in a stern tone.

Michael set his jaw and nodded. "I know," he whispered. And the look he gave his brother touched my heart. It was a look of respect. A look of gratitude. And it was a whisper of unspoken sorrow at all the time they had lost with each other. "Thank you for saying what shouldn't have needed to be said," Michael told his brother, dipping his chin, respectfully.

I narrowed my eyes. "Hey. I am right here, and I said it first, you hairy idiot."

Michael shot me a guilty smirk that quickly split into a wide grin. Then the two of them laughed, slapping each other on the backs as they knelt down beside me.

And that's when I noticed that my pockets were buzzing. I frowned, reaching inside to pull out the rings from my mother's box. Both were glowing.

Michael and Pride both froze. Pride leaned close. "Where did you get those?" he breathed. "I thought they had been destroyed."

Michael looked shaken to his core as he reached out and touched one. It flashed brighter and suddenly zipped out of my palm and onto his finger. His name flared on the metal and he let out a sigh of relief.

Pride did the same, and the other ring suddenly appeared on his own ring finger. A name flashed there, starting with an L—obviously not *Pride*—but he lifted his hand to inspect it before I could read it. "You never cease to amaze me, White Rose," he whispered to me with a loving, compassionate look.

I nodded, numbly, knowing we didn't have time for monologues as I handed Pride my dagger.

Pride shot a dubious scowl at the Spear, and then checked the distance of our impending doom. "I'm not going to die a coward," he boasted angrily. "What would everyone say about me? It would ruin my reputation." I could tell that his heart wasn't in the last part, but I saw no need to point it out as he sliced his palm and held the dagger out to Michael with an encouraging nod.

Michael assessed him. "I'm going to regret saying this, but I am proud to call you brother, Lucifer," he said, and then he sliced his palm and grasped his brother's bloody hand with his own.

I blinked, my jaw falling open. "The fuck *what*? You're *Lucifer*?" I shrieked. *That* had been the name on his ring—not *Pride*. I'd seen the L, but not the rest of the damning name. They didn't seem to hear me. I felt a panic attack brewing, so I shook my head, firmly, filing it away for later—if we survived.

Pride—Lucifer—sucked in a breath, surprised and...honored by his brother's praise. "Thank you, Michael," he whispered, lowering his eyes. "You're not too bad yourself, you know."

Michael rolled his eyes and released his grip with Lucifer to grab one end of the Spear. "If an angel can fall, does it not make sense that one could also rise?" he mused, philosophically.

Lucifer nodded with a thoughtful look in his eyes, and then gripped the other end of the Spear. Then he wrapped his other arm around the tiger protectively. "Come here, Bai. Let me help you. I'm not as noble as my brother, but I'll die before I let them take you, girl." He smiled at her so brightly that my heart skipped a beat. She purred like a diesel engine as she rubbed her metal whiskers against his cheek, making him laugh.

A tear of joy fell from Michael's cheek as he cast his brother an adoring smile. Then he mirrored the gesture by wrapping his arm around the phoenix. "Come here, child. Like my brother said, we'll stick with you to the end."

I focused on the Spear, checking the souls in my peripheral vision. They must have been as lethargic and heavy as Bai and Zoe had been, or they would have already been on top of us. I licked my lips, nervously. "You understand this might not work, and that it could kill you," I said. "Kill us all." I eyed their rings curiously, trying to figure out why my mother had kept them locked away—where she had managed to steal a fucking archangel and archdemon's class ring.

Lucifer shrugged. "But think of the story they will tell about me."

Michael chuckled. "None of us will survive long enough to share the story if this fails."

Lucifer nodded with a faint smile. "I felt like I needed to say it," he murmured. In unison, the two abruptly turned to stare at something well *above,* and beyond, the tide of souls. Their rings flared brighter—white hot, but they didn't seem to notice.

"Do you feel that, too?" Michael murmured.

Lucifer nodded. "Yes. It's...strange. Familiar but not."

"Is it dangerous?" I asked, trying to see whatever it was that had caught their attention as I fought down my own soul-deep hunger. Their rings had done something. But what? And why didn't they seem to notice?

"No," Pride, Lucifer, whatever, said absently, turning back to me with a frown. "It's nothing, I'm sure."

Michael cleared his throat. "We're damned if we do, and damned if we don't. Save us, Callie Penrose."

"Hold onto your haloes," I said, focusing on the Spear. "This is going to get bumpy," I muttered. "And in case we don't make it, I love you two for seeing this through with me."

And...I meant it. Aala had told me there was a power in healing. Aphrodite was the goddess of love, and she had devoted her entire life to healing her husband's pain. My Spear was designed to heal, not harm. Maybe...

The Spear of Destiny was designed to forgive two brothers.

Maybe I was here to bring them back together. And...that felt *right*. I had no idea what that had to do with the Daemons, but if love was such a powerful magic...

Maybe it was enough to get us the hell out of here.

"I love me, too," Pride said, dreamily.

Michael sighed wistfully. "I love you, too, Callie Penrose, even though I want to strangle you half the time," he admitted with a playful grin. "And I guess I love you too, Lucy," he added. Then he pulled the flaming phoenix in and kissed her on the top of the head.

Lucifer burst out laughing. "I haven't heard that in *ages*! I thought you'd *forgotten*! Hell, I love you, guys, too," he said, hugging Bai. The tiger replied with a lick from her tongue that spanned from Pride's cheek to his hair. "My hair!" he cried, horrified.

Before he ruined the moment, I opened myself up to the Spear of Destiny.

Almost instantly, it burst into pure light with a piercing scream, and I felt the Spear connecting me with the two brothers. And the image of the metal card abruptly popped into my mind, like an overlay of the scene before me. Michael on one side, Lucifer on the left—both mountains of power in their respective homes, Heaven and Hell.

And their *rings*! They glowed like haloes! The golden rings hovered over their heads—and over the superimposed mountain peaks. With only one or the other joining me today, one of those mountains wouldn't have existed— we wouldn't have survived this long—reminding me of the X I had seen above each mountain. It had been a warning—don't focus on one over the other. Can't have a bridge without two opposite ends.

But both together...

And here, right now, a Spear of light bridged the gap that had kept them apart for so long—bridged the two mountain peaks.

With a gleaming sword in the center. A sword just like Excalibur...

Me. I was the sword in the picture, helping bridge the gap between Heaven and Hell.

And, as we combined, I felt an overwhelming ocean of love from each of them, crashing into me at the same time. But that love didn't just hit me.

It hit Zoe and Bai, too, making them glow like bioluminescent fish, restoring their bodies.

Bai let out a thunderous roar and a distant pillar of rock, hundreds of feet tall, exploded in on itself.

Zoe screamed loud enough for her cry to echo a million miles, and a section of ground abruptly gave way, obliterating a third of the oncoming army of soul-eaters.

A deep bell tolled in the distance, and it had to be the size of a skyscraper, because it made my teeth rattle. Power raged through us, and it was all I could do to hold onto the Spear as I felt the souls less than fifty feet away, seconds away from devouring us. The bell tolled again—louder and deeper and closer—and a shockwave exploded out from our huddle, bowling over the entire tide of starving souls.

Except for one that came out of nowhere, racing towards us from the distant sky like a meteor.

And it was a *big* giant of a soul, made of pure light. Michael and Lucifer's rings blazed like the sun, as if calling it home at long last.

Before I could even acknowledge the fact that we'd survived certain death, that comet of a soul came directly at *me* and slammed into the Spear —somehow fitting into the small space between my two clenched fists. Their rings burned the air and I feared the three would destroy my Spear. My heart dropped into my stomach as a third bell tolled, and I realized that I somehow hadn't been vaporized by the blast of light.

Michael and Lucifer were gasping and sobbing with laughter and sheer joy.

"Something is happening!" I croaked, not finding anything remotely funny about our situation as I held onto the vibrating Spear for dear life.

Zoe and Bai pressed close to me, making terrified sounds as the Neverwas grew too bright for even my supernaturally-protected eyes to see anything. I slammed my eyes shut, fearing the Spear was going to blind us before it saved us. Or destroy us. I couldn't let go.

I tried. My hands felt fused to the haft and I felt Sanguina screaming my name.

Then the Neverwas exploded and I was flying backwards into nothingness.

52

I opened my eyes with a groan and stared up at the starry, purple sky, marveling at the streak of apocalyptic pink flower petals drifting through the air in a constant stream. I sucked in a breath of relief. We were back in the training fields where we'd opened the Gateway, but how had I escaped the Neverwas? I felt drained and hollow, utterly spent from whatever I had done with the Spear. But I no longer felt that gnawing, soul-deep hunger, at least.

I felt a warm presence to my left and turned to see Bai, the white tiger, sleeping soundly next to me. Finally, in full color, I stared in awe, transfixed by her black stripes and the faint metallic sheen to her fur. Long, silver claws curled out from her massive paws as she absently scraped the ground in her sleep.

Zoe was dozing on her feet, but crouched down between her sister's throat and massive paws. Although the heat from her fiery red and white feathers made me squint, her sister's striped fur didn't burn. I reached out tentatively, and gasped as my fingers entered the flames to touch cool feathers beneath.

This didn't make any sense. Had Michael and Lucifer carried us back? I stared up at where the Gateway had been, but it was gone. My katana was still buried in the earth in the center of a ring of black char and silver droplets. I sat up groggily, glancing left and right. Michael and Lucifer were gone. How long had I been asleep? Had they gone to the tree to get help from the others?

I turned to check and croaked out a cry of alarm to see a stranger sitting a few feet away between me and the tree. He was naked apart from a thick silver necklace that held two long feathers against his tanned chest—one black and one white. He was staring at his hands in fascination, twisting them back and forth, mesmerized. He wore a golden ring on each ring finger, and I felt my breath catch. He'd stolen Michael and Lucifer's rings! He didn't even seem to notice me. His long blonde hair shifted in the gentle breeze.

I sat up hurriedly, realizing that I still held the Spear in my hand and that it wasn't damaged.

"Stay right where you are, stranger," I rasped, weakly, pointing the Spear at him.

He looked up at me without a flicker of fear, grinning like a madman. "It's *us*—" he cut off, his smile slipping. "No. It's *me*," he corrected, tasting the word with a bemused yet euphoric look on his face. He saw my confused expression and his smile fell back into place as he lifted his arms in introduction. "Lucifer and Michael," he explained, "and...our Grace, I think. Or our soul." He eyed my Spear pensively. "I feel like you and that oversized needle sewed us all together. Hastily."

I stared at him, alarmed. He did look like a mix of the two brothers, leaning more towards Lucifer's roguish good looks. "I...don't understand," I murmured, staring at the rings on his fingers. How was this possible? I'd barely accepted the fact that I'd been hanging out with freaking *Lucifer* in a Miata, and now I'd done *this*. He held them up, and I caught the two names etched into the metal. I flicked my gaze over his shoulder towards the tree where my other allies had been hiding. Why weren't they rushing over?

"Neither do we—*I*," he corrected himself again. "I feel so strange but so good at the same time. I feel more like Lucifer than Michael," he murmured thoughtfully. He grinned at the sleeping Daemons. "You did it, Callie. You saved Zoe and Bai," he whispered. He glanced down at the Spear again. "But how? And why did you do this to us?" he asked, indicating himself.

A single word from Wrath's prophecy whispered in my mind. *Anghellian.*

Was that referring to...a hybrid angel and demon? An angel and a hellian? I stared at his necklace—the white and black feather hanging side-by-side. *What have I done?* I thought to myself, beginning to panic.

I shook my head, still holding the Spear nervously. What if this was someone else entirely? Where were my friends? Xuanwu? Qinglong? Ryuu and Aala? Where was Sanguina? They should have come running the moment I returned. What if...this was not Michael or Lucifer at all? What if this man had killed everyone else already? "What do you remember?" I asked, carefully, gauging his reaction and trying to blink away my grogginess.

"There was an explosion of power," he whispered. "Nothing like I've *ever* felt before. You brought us together, and that combination of power threw us at the Gateway! I bet every angel and demon in the *world* felt it—"

Twin cracking sounds made me jump, feeling as if lightning bolts had struck within inches of me.

The stranger flinched to find two men looming before him, their faces hard. I only knew one of them.

"Wretched Daemons," Wrath cursed. "I'll roast that turtle alive and eat his heart," he snarled. "How was he able to ward us out for so long?" He wore a crisp suit and he held a small bouquet of white roses in one hand. He slowly turned to look at me, and I watched as his face slowly morphed from hard to downright furious. As if the flowers were a reflection of his mood, they began to wilt and droop, blackening within seconds. Then he dropped the dead bouquet at his feet. The black feathers hanging from his chain stirred faintly in the ever-present breeze.

The other man was eerily tall and muscular with long, straight, white hair, resembling the guy from *The Witcher*. His irises flickered with golden light and his face seemed carved from granite. He was obviously friends with Wrath, but he didn't give off any sort of obedient lackey vibe. Likewise, Wrath didn't appear beholden to him, either, making me think they were equals. I frowned, noticing he wore a similar necklace to Wrath, except the two feathers were perfectly white. "It does not matter. Where are Michael and Lucifer? I felt their power exploding at a level of magnificence that only our Father could have achieved," he snarled, hungrily. "It shook the Pillars of Heaven, and I *know* it rocked the Foundations of Hell," he said, glaring at Wrath. "I thought you had this under control."

Alarm bells began ringing in my ears, recognizing the man's necklace as feathers from an archangel, not an archdemon. And he'd just quoted Wrath's dark prophecy. The prophecy that Wrath had presumed to mean his impending marriage to me.

Looked like the bride had cold feet and an idling getaway car.

The prophecy had meant something entirely different—making an

Anghellian between Lucifer, Michael, and their grace. Even though I didn't understand the details, it was obvious.

Wrath had been wrong.

"You guys wear matching jewelry?" I asked, trying to hide my anxiety. "How...cute."

The archangel turned to look at me and my heart skipped a beat as terror filled me. I'd never felt such an instinctive reaction from a mere look. Zoe and Bai had come awake, likely from the thunderous cracking sounds of the new arrivals. They let out frightened whimpers, pressing into me like terrified babes. I lifted the Spear in a shaking fist, already knowing that I was utterly spent and had no power to defend myself.

Not that it would have made a difference anyway.

Wrath's friend pursed his lips and lifted his hand to point at me with a bone-chilling smile. "My jewelry is much better than gaudy rubies," he growled. "You foolish, vapid human," he snarled disgustedly. "To have to suffer through your wonton attempt at seducing me. You—a vile, daughter of Eve! Cloaked in sin, tried to seduce me, God's chosen!" he growled.

Goosebumps raced up my arms and I almost dropped the Spear of Destiny. Rubies...

My eyes widened and I stared at him, only feeling *more* confused. As I looked closer at his face, I saw similarities to the valet who had brought me my towels—the one I had flaunted my robe and jewelry for in hopes of drawing out Envy.

But Envy hadn't been the only mole in my castle. Wrath had been playing both sides against the middle, and I suddenly understood how Michael and Lucifer had been so swiftly set up and pinned for crimes they did not commit.

I had asked the valet if he preferred my sapphires to rubies. It hadn't been Envy, though. It had been this man. This archangel I'd shamed and embarrassed. The only archangel I could think of was Michael's boss.

I gasped, taking a stab in the dark. "Gabriel."

Michael's boss and Envy had both been in my castle, watching me, working with Wrath.

Gabriel nodded. "To the goddaughter of the world's first whore, Lilith... good riddance—"

He snarled, suddenly jerking his hand back as blood spurted in the air. Wrath shouted out in alarm, crouching warily as his eyes darted back and forth, looking for the unseen assailant. Gabriel did the same, and the two smoothly shifted into a back-to-back position, slowly spinning in a circle.

"The Angel Killer!" Gabriel roared.

"Halo Breaker!" Wrath bellowed with a vicious snarl.

I jumped as a smoke pellet exploded to my right, and then three more in rapid succession all around me. Wrath gasped, letting out a string of curses as he clutched his side, and Gabriel staggered, grabbing at his thigh. Blood flowed freely, and I found myself grinning toothily. Ryuu!

"Dance for me, darling," Ryuu taunted, seeming to hop from one direction to the next, inhumanly fast. "Because no one steps on my rose garden, and no one *dares* pluck my rare lotus blossom from her mountain boulder. She. Is. Mine."

My heart dropped into my stomach, recalling his story about Buddha. He...

Ryuu had been talking about *me*.

Gabriel and Wrath roared in outrage, hurling blasts of black and white fire at every source of sound, but they weren't louder than Ryuu's bitter, mocking laughter. Twice more, Gabriel and Wrath stumbled as Ryuu's dark blade bit deep, drawing more blood from the archdemon and archangel.

Ryuu laughed again and Wrath raised his arm to throw something at him. A coil of translucent rope wrapped around his wrist, yanking it back so that he punched Gabriel in the head, bathing him in black fire. The archangel roared, swatting out the fire with one hand while hurling his own white fire at the source of the attacker with the rope—which obviously hadn't been Ryuu.

I heard a grunt, and Aala materialized, clutching at her abdomen with bloody fingers. Gabriel flicked a hand and she flew a dozen feet, crashing into the ground near the white tree. Ryuu snarled as Wrath finally found him —probably distracted by Aala's injury—and a dark, metaphysical fist punched the ninja so hard that he flew across the field and slammed into the glowing tree, causing a downpour of apocalyptic pink petals. He didn't get back up.

I pointed the Spear at the two brothers, willing anything I had left into it, but nothing happened.

Gabriel and Wrath dismissed me and both focused on the Anghellian, who had climbed to his feet at some point and was glaring back at them with his fists clenched at his sides. For the first time, I noticed that the wind had ceased. Entirely. A hush fell over the field, and the Anghellian's eyes flickered with silver light, reminding me of Sanguina. The feathers on his necklace smoldered around the edges, but they didn't actually burn up—as if they were made of hot coals.

A distant part of me began to wonder how they had found us. How they had broken into Xuanwu's protected sanctuary, but then I remembered what the Anghellian had said. About how every angel and demon had to have felt the surge of power I'd unleashed with the Spear. The surge of power strong enough to Frankenstein an archangel, an archdemon, and the supposed grace from purgatory. But...it was just too fucking crazy. How could two angels be the same person? Or be fused together like this? Wasn't that pure blasphemy?

More words from Wrath's prophecy came to mind, and I realized, with a faint grin, that it hadn't meant what Wrath thought, at all. *Her love will rock the pillars of Heaven and rattle the foundations of Hell, burning away all that once was in a purifying bridge of Anghellian fire.*

The power from the Spear of Destiny had been stained with our love as we all volunteered to give up our lives rather than abandon Zoe and Bai. And that power had rocked and rattled Heaven and Hell, bringing Wrath and Gabriel here, now. I really, really hoped my new pal knew how to call up some Anghellian fire, because I was all out of magic tricks. I hugged Zoe and Bai close, knowing they were too weakened to protect themselves, and I wasn't about to abandon them when I'd only saved them halfway.

Wrath and Gabriel stared at the Anghellian, no longer looking as brave. And I didn't blame them.

Not. One. Bit.

Because two terrifying, ephemeral apparitions abruptly loomed behind him like security guards. One was white, and one was black, and they were easily ten-feet-tall with muscles growing out of their muscles in a display that would have put the Incredible Hulk to shame. Their shoulders were bigger than my damned head. They wore hooded scarves, reminding me of Xylo's crimson cowl, so I couldn't see their faces. Just two sets of glowing blue eyes.

Although I had never seen them before, I was pretty sure I was staring at Michael and Lucifer's arch-level forms. And despite being significantly smaller than Samael's giant demon form...

These two were much, much scarier. My lips were trembling and I was too frightened to even blink. I hugged my new stuffed animals and prayed for the monsters to go away. Not the Anghellian. He was my friend...wasn't he?

Gabriel and Wrath lifted their hands and each let loose a purplish super-nova of power from their fists—enough to incinerate a building in two seconds flat.

The Anghellian didn't even flinch, but his two apparitions abruptly bent over him and caught the attacks in their palms, absorbing the power as if blocking laser pointers. Gabriel and Wrath released their beams and took an instinctive step backwards, their faces gaunt and incredulous.

"What have you done?" Gabriel whispered. "You are human. I can *feel* it!"

Wrath shot me a quick look, seeming to ask the same question with his big, terrified eyeballs.

The naked Anghellian smiled wryly. "I evolved, brothers." Which sounded about as blasphemous as something Lucifer would have said. Then he flung his hands out and an unseen blast of power hit Gabriel and Wrath in their chests, causing a burst of embers and sparks on contact, and the archdemon and archangel flew back, slamming into the earth like lawn darts.

*

53

Their chests smoked as they scrambled to their feet, swatting out the charred marks on their chests. They shot each other a quick look and promptly disappeared with two thunderous cracking sounds that echoed across the field.

I saw Ryuu sprinting towards me with an anxious look on his face.

He was coming to protect his lotus blossom. And I was okay with that.

I dropped the Spear with a sigh of relief and it winked out of existence, returning back inside me where it belonged. At least, I hoped it still belonged there and I hadn't inadvertently created a new type of monster. An all-powerful human with god-level powers and two spiritual bodyguards—

The naked Anghellian wobbled unsteadily and the apparitions winked out behind him. "I...don't feel so good," he mumbled as Ryuu finally reached us.

And then the Anghellian vomited on the white tiger, causing her to let out a feral snarl of anger. Zoe, being a clever old bird, squawked, hopped back a safe distance, and then spread her wings and burst into a pillar of flame that made me jump.

"Oh, god. I'm turning inside out!" the Anghellian shrieked, hyperventilating, not even seeming to notice the ten-foot-tall bonfire a few feet away. "I'm dying!"

Ryuu grimaced distastefully. "You're fine. You just threw up—"

The man doubled over, throwing up on his own bare feet. "Ah! My insides are on my outsides. I'm liquifying!" he cried, wiping his forearm across his mouth and dry-heaving. Bai yowled angrily, realizing that she couldn't get close enough to murder her target without getting tagged again, and began to pace back and forth, snarling in frustration.

"Calm down, man. You're *fine*," Ryuu said, side-stepping clear of the blast radius. He pointed toward the nearby pond. "Go jump in the pond. It will...stop you from liquifying," he said, hiding his smirk. The Anghellian lurched upright and awkwardly sprinted towards the pond, screaming in terror the whole way. Bai thought about chasing him, but decided against it. Zoe's flame winked out and she lifted her head away from her vomit-coated sister with a haughty cry.

Ryuu stared at the pair with an awed look, and then turned back to me, shaking his head incredulously. His happiness shifted to concern as he knelt down beside me, checking me for wounds. I stared at the bloody wound in his own side, alarmed by how deep it looked. Was that bone?

"I'm fine, Ryuu," I snapped, swatting his hand away. He obviously didn't want to talk about his flowery taunts against Gabriel and Wrath. Perhaps he was embarrassed about it.

Idiot.

He nodded with a breath of relief and clasped my hands between both of his, staring me in the eyes. "Let's all go for a swim," he said, smiling crookedly. "Sanguina and my sister are already down there." And then he was tugging me to my feet before I had time to answer. As if he hadn't just mentioned...

"Your *sister?*" I sputtered.

Ryuu frowned. "Yes. Aala. My sister—"

Xuanwu and Qinglong suddenly appeared at my side, making me jump in alarm, worried that Gabriel or Wrath had returned to kill or abduct me. Xuanwu laughed delightedly and scooped up the pissed off white tiger with one massive claw and pulled her close to his shell. He abruptly hissed, angling his head about as far away from her as he could. "Who vomited on my sister?" he demanded protectively.

I pointed at the fleeing, screaming Anghellian. "The new guy."

Qinglong reared up on his hind legs so he could use his front claws to scoop up the phoenix. He closed his eyes and let out a shuddering breath as he hugged her tightly, seemingly unbothered by her flames. "You're alive," he whispered. Then he shot me a desperate, overwrought smile. "You saved them, White Rose," he breathed, choking up.

I nodded, lowering my eyes. I couldn't bear to look at the raw emotion on his face. And I was too exhausted to do more than stand and blink at the same time. Which was where Ryuu volunteered his services. Without warning, he scooped me up in both arms to carry me horizontally across his chest. I reared back to punch him, but hesitated upon remembering his wounded ribs.

"Put me down! You're the wounded one!" I argued.

"And I'll die from blood loss waiting for you to hobble down the hill by yourself," he muttered, entirely too amused. Putting proof to his words, he began walking towards the pond, ignoring my weak protests. Xuanwu and Qinglong flanked us, staring adoringly down at their sisters in their arms, who had apparently both fallen asleep after their brief, yet eventful, time awake. They probably needed days of sleep and had only awoken thanks to Wrath and Gabriel's sudden arrival.

I gave them a quick rundown of what had happened beyond the Gateway, and how I'd accidentally made the Anghellian by combining Michael and...Pride. I kept his other name to myself, thank you very much. Once I was finished talking, I looked ahead, studying the Anghellian wading out into the pool beside Ryuu's sister—who looked perfectly fine after her dip in the healing pool. "I'm glad she's okay," I told Ryuu.

I felt his arms tighten involuntarily. "I'm thankful that *you're* okay," he murmured. "I've never been that scared," he whispered, as if the words had been pulled out of him. "When I saw the explosion and then saw you just lying there..." He stiffened and I pressed my cheek into his chest affectionately. "I don't quite remember making that first slash at Gabriel," he admitted with a frown. "I was suddenly just there, ready to kill both of them. I'm lucky my sister chased after me."

I thought about pestering him on the sister thing, but there was entirely too much sibling drama going on at the moment. I stared at the Anghellian, wondering what I was supposed to do with him.

"Xuanwu?" I asked. The turtle loomed over me, using his long neck to his advantage. "Is he human?"

The Black Tortoise considered the question, glancing ahead. "I believe so."

"You must not have seen his shadows," I muttered. "Hulking archangel and archdemon apparitions."

He grunted. "Oh, we saw. The power on the field today," he said, sounding troubled, "was guaranteed death, even for Divines. It took everything we had to keep the wards up before all of Heaven and Hell descended upon my sanctuary."

I arched an incredulous eyebrow.

"We were too weak to stop Wrath and Gabriel, though," Qinglong added.

"Any sane person wouldn't have dared enter the fray," Xuanwu said. Ryuu kept his eyes forward, pretending we were talking about the weather.

Ryuu and I had a lot to talk about after I recovered. *The minute I recover, not later*, I promised myself, cringing at the last word. "How are your sisters?" I asked Xuanwu.

He glanced down and smiled. "Asleep." Qinglong echoed his agreement, sounding amused. "But they are healthy, Callie. You saved them, and for that, I am eternally grateful."

Again, Qinglong echoed his sentiment.

"Good," I said with a tired smile. "Because I fear we managed to piss off both sides. Heaven and Hell won't stand for this. Whatever *this* is," I said, gesturing at the Anghellian. He was laughing with Aala, which I took for a good sign. I saw Sanguina dozing on a patch of grass, but I could see her wet fur and knew that she would be fine after her rest. If not for her holding open the Gateway, I wasn't sure any of us would have survived.

"We've been here for two days, waiting," Ryuu said meaningfully, noticing my glance at Sanguina. "I've never seen that much power held for so long." Xuanwu and Qinglong murmured their agreement, sounding beyond impressed. "She's exhausted, but fine."

"Two days," I breathed. "What happened while I was gone? Because I'm almost confident that Gabriel himself was spying on me from within the Keep. And judging by his appearance here with Wrath, I'm wondering if we weren't all lied to. Wrath and Gabriel were working together the entire time. It had nothing to do with Envy, and it also explains why Michael and...Pride were targeted. Why they were set up," I said, hoping no one noticed my hesitation on his name. Lucifer.

Ryuu cast a glance back at Xuanwu, processing the information about Gabriel. Finally, he nodded. "That makes more sense," he admitted. "Apparently, the rebels at Castle Dracula surrendered. They walked right up to the Keep and asked to turn themselves in to the Bone Heir."

I sucked in a breath. "You're kidding. Xylo?"

Ryuu smirked, nodding. "They seemed very confused on what they've been up to the last few weeks, but they found enough evidence to realize they'd been doing something...ill-advised. They all mentioned the name Envy, however, speaking like they'd been brain-washed." I frowned, suspiciously. "Xylo believed them," he added.

I pursed my lips thoughtfully. "Which means Envy and Gabriel were *both* at Castle Dracula," I murmured, troubled. "Envy must have fled, abandoning his cause. I wonder if that was at Wrath or Gabriel's command, or if it was just self-preservation."

He shrugged, shifting my weight in the process. "Either way, they will come back twice as hard."

The Anghellian settled his gaze on me as we finally reached the edge of the pond. "And we will be waiting for them," I told Ryuu out of the side of my mouth. He smirked, setting me back on my feet but remaining close to catch me if my wobbling legs gave out. "What do we call you, now?" I asked the Anghellian.

He thought about it. "Lucifer and Michael," he mused, scratching at his cheek. Ryuu stiffened, bouncing me up and down in the process, but Xuanwu and Qinglong didn't bat an eye. "How about Luchael?" the Anghellian asked, frowning thoughtfully at the made-up name. It sounded like he'd said *Lucky-el.*

"How about Lucky?" I asked. "Kind of fits since luck got us out of the Neverwas in one piece."

Luck and love.

"Lucky," he repeated, nodding. "I like it. I feel more like Lucifer than Michael. Maybe because my demon side knew how to exercise more free will..." A ghost of a frown drifted across his face and he clutched his stomach nervously. "I think I'm still adjusting to this. My stomach hurts," he said, glancing down to poke his chiseled stomach with his finger. He frowned, poking it harder. "But it hurts on the *inside*. How curious," he murmured, poking it even harder and faster, practically stabbing it.

Ryuu shot me a mischievous grin. "I think you're talking about *hunger*," he suggested. "Humans need to eat food. I'm taking it that this wasn't a concern as an angel? Or a demon?" he added.

Lucky shook his head. "I've eaten before, but only to see what all the fuss was about. Everything tasted the same, though," he said, frowning. "Except for Frappuccinos," he clarified, licking his lips dreamily.

"I think your taste buds might be different now. You ever had bacon?" Ryuu asked, smiling.

"No."

"Do you want to?"

"Absolutely. What's it taste like?" he asked, excited about the new adventure of discovering tasteful foods.

Ryuu chuckled. "You'll see. Your life will never be the same. I'll cook some up for you when we get back. It's the least I could do for you risking your life to save them," he said, pointing at the sleeping Divines. "And for defending Callie," he added, bowing his chin in a show of respect and appreciation.

Xuanwu and Qinglong silently waded out into the pond, speaking soothing words to their sisters so as not to startle them when they felt the water. Judging by the typical reaction of cats to water, Xuanwu was in for a rough time. Good thing he had a shell.

I squawked as a blast of water hit me in the face, soaking me. Lucky burst out laughing, splashing me again. "Thanks for saving me, too, Callie! You saved my grace from Purgatory!"

Rather than dive into the theology of angelic and demonic souls, I dove into the pond, vowing to dunk the Anghellian into the pond to establish dominance.

And the rest of the night was spent on what truly mattered.

Teaching Lucky how to be human. Magic and war, and Heaven and Hell could wait. There were some things in life worth taking a step back from the craziness for.

Like bacon.

And Frappuccinos.

DON'T FORGET! VIP's get early access to all sorts of Temple-Verse
goodies, including signed copies, private giveaways, and advance notice of
future projects. AND A FREE NOVELLA! Click the image or join here:
www.shaynesilvers.com/l/219800

*Callie returns in 2020... Subscribe to my NEWSLETTER to receive an
email when it's live!*

Turn the page to read a sample of **OBSIDIAN SON** - *The Nate Temple Series
Book 1 - or* **BUY ONLINE**. *Nate Temple is a billionaire wizard from St. Louis. He
rides a bloodthirsty unicorn and drinks with the Four Horsemen. He even cow-tipped
the Minotaur. Once...*

(Note: Nate's books 1-6 happen prior to UNCHAINED, but they crossover from then
on, the two series taking place in the same universe but also able to standalone if you
prefer)

Full chronology of all books in the TempleVerse shown on the 'BOOKS BY SHAYNE
SILVERS' page.

TRY: OBSIDIAN SON (NATE TEMPLE #1)

There was no room for emotion in a hate crime. I had to be cold. Heartless. This was just another victim. Nothing more. No face, no name.

Frosted blades of grass crunched under my feet, sounding to my ears like the symbolic glass that one would shatter under a napkin at a Jewish wedding. The noise would have threatened to give away my stealthy advance as I stalked through the moonlit field, but I was no novice and had planned accordingly. Being a wizard, I was able to muffle all sensory evidence with a fine cloud of magic—no sounds, and no smells. Nifty. But if I made the spell much stronger, the anomaly would be too obvious to my prey.

I knew the consequences for my dark deed tonight. If caught, jail time or possibly even a gruesome, painful death. But if I succeeded, the look of fear and surprise in my victim's eyes before his world collapsed around him, it was well worth the risk. I simply couldn't help myself; I had to take him down.

I knew the cops had been keeping tabs on my car, but I was confident that they hadn't followed me. I hadn't seen a tail on my way here but seeing as how they frowned on this kind of thing, I had taken a circuitous route just in case. I was safe. I hoped.

Then my phone chirped at me as I received a text.

I practically jumped out of my skin, hissing instinctively. "Motherf—" I cut off abruptly, remembering the whole stealth aspect of my mission. I was off to a stellar start. I had forgotten to silence the damned phone. *Stupid, stupid, stupid!*

My heart felt like it was on the verge of exploding inside my chest with such thunderous violence that I briefly envisioned a mystifying Rorschach blood-blot that would have made coroners and psychologists drool.

My body remained tense as I swept my gaze over the field, fearing that I had been made. Precious seconds ticked by without any change in my surroundings, and my breathing finally began to slow as my pulse returned to normal. Hopefully, my magic had muted the phone and my resulting outburst. I glanced down at the phone to scan the text and then typed back a quick and angry response before I switched the cursed device to vibrate.

Now, where were we?

I continued on, the lining of my coat constricting my breathing. Or maybe it was because I was leaning forward in anticipation. *Breathe*, I chided myself. *He doesn't know you're here.* All this risk for a book. It had better be worth it.

I'm taller than most, and not abnormally handsome, but I knew how to play the genetic cards I had been dealt. I had shaggy, dirty blonde hair—leaning more towards brown with each passing year—and my frame was thick with well-earned muscle, yet I was still lean. I had once been told that my eyes were like twin emeralds pitted against the golden-brown tufts of my hair—a face like a jewelry box. Of course, that was two bottles of wine into a date, so I could have been a little foggy on her quote. Still, I liked to imagine that was how everyone saw me.

But tonight, all that was masked by magic.

I grinned broadly as the outline of the hairy hulk finally came into view. He was blessedly alone—no nearby sentries to give me away. That was always a risk when performing this ancient rite-of-passage. I tried to keep the grin on my face from dissolving into a maniacal cackle.

My skin danced with energy, both natural and unnatural, as I manipulated the threads of magic floating all around me. My victim stood just ahead, oblivious to the world of hurt that I was about to unleash. Even with his millennia of experience, he didn't stand a chance. I had done this so many times that the routine of it was my only enemy. I lost count of how many times I had been told not to do it again; those who knew declared it *cruel, evil, and sadistic*. But what fun wasn't? Regardless, that wasn't enough to stop me from doing it again. And again. And again.

It was an addiction.

The pungent smell of manure filled the air, latching onto my nostril hairs. I took another step, trying to calm my racing pulse. A glint of gold reflected in the silver moonlight, but my victim remained motionless, hopefully unaware or all was lost. I wouldn't make it out alive if he knew I was here. Timing was everything.

I carefully took the last two steps, a lifetime between each, watching the legendary monster's ears, anxious and terrified that I would catch even so much as a twitch in my direction. Seeing nothing, a fierce grin split my unshaven cheeks. My spell had worked! I raised my palms an inch away from their target, firmly planted my feet, and squared my shoulders. I took one silent, calming breath, and then heaved forward with every ounce of physical strength I could muster. As well as a teensy-weensy boost of magic. Enough to goose him good.

"*MOOO!!!*" The sound tore through the cool October night like an unstoppable freight train. *Thud-splat*! The beast collapsed sideways onto the frosted grass; straight into a steaming patty of cow shit, cow dung, or, if you really wanted to church it up, a Meadow Muffin. But to me, shit is, and always will be, shit.

Cow tipping. It doesn't get any better than that in Missouri.

Especially when you're tipping the *Minotaur*. Capital M. I'd tipped plenty of ordinary cows before, but never the legendary variety.

Razor-blade hooves tore at the frozen earth as the beast struggled to stand, his grunts of rage vibrating the air. I raised my arms triumphantly. "Boo-yah! Temple 1, Minotaur 0!" I crowed. Then I very bravely prepared to protect myself. Some people just couldn't take a joke. *Cruel, evil,* and *sadistic* cow tipping may be, but by hell, it was a *rush.* The legendary beast turned his gaze on me after gaining his feet, eyes ablaze as his body...*shifted* from his bull disguise into his notorious, well-known bipedal form. He unfolded to his full height on two tree trunk-thick legs, his hooves having magically transformed into heavily booted feet. The thick, gold ring dangling from his snotty snout quivered as the Minotaur panted, and his dense, corded muscles contracted over his now human-like chest. As I stared up into those brown eyes, I actually felt sorry...for, well, myself.

"I have killed greater men than you for lesser offense," he growled.

His voice sounded like an angry James Earl Jones—like Mufasa talking to Scar.

"You have shit on your shoulder, Asterion." I ignited a roiling ball of fire in my palm in order to see his eyes more clearly. By no means was it a defensive gesture on my part. It was just dark. Under the weight of his glare, I somehow managed to keep my face composed, even though my fraudulent, self-denial had curled up into the fetal position and started whimpering. I hoped using a form of his ancient name would give me brownie points. Or maybe just not-worthy-of-killing points.

The beast grunted, eyes tightening, and I sensed the barest hesitation. "Nate Temple...your name would look splendid on my already long list of slain idiots." Asterion took a threatening step forward, and I thrust out my palm in warning, my roiling flame blue now.

"You lost fair and square, Asterion. Yield or perish." The beast's shoulders sagged slightly. Then he finally nodded to himself in resignation, appraising me with the scrutiny of a worthy adversary. "Your time comes, Temple, but I will grant you this. You've got a pair of stones on you to rival Hercules."

I reflexively glanced in the direction of the myth's own crown jewels before jerking my gaze away. Some things you simply couldn't un-see. "Well, I won't be needing a wheelbarrow any time soon, but overcompensating today keeps future lower-back pain away."

The Minotaur blinked once, and then he bellowed out a deep, contagious, snorting laughter. Realizing I wasn't about to become a murder statistic, I couldn't help but join in. It felt good. It had been a while since I had allowed myself to experience genuine laughter.

In the harsh moonlight, his bulk was even more intimidating as he towered head and shoulders above me. This was the beast that had fed upon human sacrifices for countless years while imprisoned in Daedalus' Labyrinth in Greece. And all that protein had not gone to waste, forming a heavily woven musculature over the beast's body that made even Mr. Olympia look puny.

From the neck up, he was now entirely bull, but the rest of his body more closely resembled a thickly furred man. But, as shown moments ago, he could adapt his form to his environment, never appearing fully human, but able to make his entire form appear as a bull when necessary. For instance, how he had looked just before I tipped him. Maybe he had been scouting the field for heifers before I had so efficiently killed the mood.

His bull face was also covered in thick, coarse hair—he even sported a long, wavy beard of sorts, and his eyes were the deepest brown I had ever seen. Cow-shit brown. His snout jutted out, emphasizing the golden ring dangling from his glistening nostrils, and both glinted in the luminous glow of the moon. The metal was at least an inch thick and etched with runes of a language long forgotten. Wide, aged ivory horns sprouted from each temple, long enough to skewer a wizard with little effort. He was nude except for a massive beaded necklace and a pair of worn leather boots that were big enough to stomp a size twenty-five imprint in my face if he felt so inclined.

I hoped our blossoming friendship wouldn't end that way. I really did.

Because friends didn't let friends wear boots naked...

Get your copy of OBSIDIAN SON online today!
http://www.shaynesilvers.com/l/38474

Turn the page to read a sample of **WHISKEY GINGER** *- Phantom Queen Diaries Book 1, or* **BUY ONLINE***. Quinn MacKenna is a black magic arms dealer in Boston. She likes to fight monsters almost as much as she likes to drink.*

TRY: WHISKEY GINGER (PHANTOM QUEEN DIARIES BOOK 1)

The pasty guitarist hunched forward, thrust a rolled-up wad of paper deep into one nostril, and snorted a line of blood crystals— frozen hemoglobin that I'd smuggled over in a refrigerated canister—with the uncanny grace of a drug addict. He sat back, fangs gleaming, and pawed at his nose. "That's some bodacious shit. Hey, bros," he said, glancing at his fellow band members, "come hit this shit before it melts."

He fetched one of the backstage passes hanging nearby, pried the plastic badge from its lanyard, and used it to split up the crystals, murmuring something in an accent that reminded me of California. Not *the* California, but you know, Cali-foh-nia—the land of beaches, babes, and bros. I retrieved a toothpick from my pocket and punched it through its thin wrapper. "So," I asked no one in particular, "now that ye have the product, who's payin'?"

Another band member stepped out of the shadows to my left, and I don't mean that figuratively, either—the fucker literally stepped out of the shadows. I scowled at him, but hid my surprise, nonchalantly rolling the toothpick from one side of my mouth to the other.

The rest of the band gathered around the dressing room table, following the guitarist's lead by preparing their own snorting utensils—tattered magazine covers, mostly. Typically, you'd do this sort of thing with a dollar-bill, maybe even a Benjamin if you were flush. But fangers like this lot couldn't touch cash directly—in God We Trust and all that. Of course, I didn't really understand why sucking blood the old-fashioned way had suddenly gone out of style. More of a rush, maybe?

"It lasts longer," the vampire next to me explained, catching my mildly curious expression. "It's especially good for shows and stuff. Makes us look, like, less—"

"Creepy?" I offered, my Irish brogue lilting just enough to make it a question.

"Pale," he finished, frowning.

I shrugged. "Listen, I've got places to be," I said, holding out my hand.

"I'm sure you do," he replied, smiling. "Tell you what, why don't you, like, hang around for a bit? Once that wears off," he dipped his head toward the bloody powder smeared across the table's surface, "we may need a pick-me-up." He rested his hand on my arm and our gazes locked.

I blinked, realized what he was trying to pull, and rolled my eyes. His widened in surprise, then shock as I yanked out my toothpick and shoved it through his hand.

"Motherfuck—"

"I want what we agreed on," I declared. "Now. No tricks."

The rest of the band saw what happened and rose faster than I could blink. They circled me, their grins feral...they might have even seemed intimidating if it weren't for the fact that they each had a case of the sniffles —I had to work extra hard not to think about what it felt like to have someone else's blood dripping down my nasal cavity.

I held up a hand.

"Can I ask ye gentlemen a question before we get started?" I asked. "Do ye even *have* what I asked for?"

Two of the band members exchanged looks and shrugged. The guitarist, however, glanced back towards the dressing room, where a brown paper bag sat next to a case full of makeup. He caught me looking and bared his teeth, his fangs stretching until it looked like it would be uncomfortable for him to close his mouth without piercing his own lip.

"Follow-up question," I said, eyeing the vampire I'd stabbed as he gingerly withdrew the toothpick from his hand and flung it across the room with a snarl. "Do ye do each other's make-up? Since, ye know, ye can't use mirrors?"

I was genuinely curious.

The guitarist grunted. "Mike, we have to go on soon."

"Wait a minute. Mike?" I turned to the snarling vampire with a frown. "What happened to *The Vampire Prospero*?" I glanced at the numerous fliers in the dressing room, most of which depicted the band members wading through blood, with Mike in the lead, each one titled *The Vampire Prospero* in *Rocky Horror Picture Show* font. Come to think of it...Mike did look a little like Tim Curry in all that leather and lace.

I was about to comment on the resemblance when Mike spoke up, "Alright, change of plans, bros. We're gonna drain this bitch before the show. We'll look totally—"

"Creepy?" I offered, again.

"Kill her."

Get the full book ONLINE! http://www.shaynesilvers.com/l/206897

MAKE A DIFFERENCE

Reviews are the most powerful tools in my arsenal when it comes to getting attention for my books. Much as I'd like to, I don't have the financial muscle of a New York publisher.

But I do have something much more powerful and effective than that, and it's something that those publishers would kill to get their hands on.

A committed and loyal bunch of readers.

Honest reviews of my books help bring them to the attention of other readers.

If you've enjoyed this book, I would be very grateful if you could spend just five minutes leaving a review on my book's Amazon page.

Thank you very much in advance.

ACKNOWLEDGMENTS

Team Temple and the Den of Freaks on Facebook have become family to me. I couldn't do it without die-hard readers like them.

I would also like to thank you, the reader. I hope you enjoyed reading *ANGHELLIC* as much as I enjoyed writing it. Be sure to check out the two crossover series in the Temple Verse: The **Nate Temple Series** and the **Phantom Queen Diaries**.

And last, but definitely not least, I thank my wife, Lexy. Without your support, none of this would have been possible.

ABOUT SHAYNE SILVERS

Shayne is a man of mystery and power, whose power is exceeded only by his mystery...

He currently writes the Amazon Bestselling **Nate Temple** Series, which features a foul-mouthed wizard from St. Louis. He rides a bloodthirsty unicorn, drinks with Achilles, and is pals with the Four Horsemen.

He also writes the Amazon Bestselling **Feathers and Fire** Series—a second series in the TempleVerse. The story follows a rookie spell-slinger named Callie Penrose who works for the Vatican in Kansas City. Her problem? Hell seems to know more about her past than she does.

He coauthors **The Phantom Queen Diaries**—a third series set in The TempleVerse—with Cameron O'Connell. The story follows Quinn MacKenna, a mouthy black magic arms dealer in Boston. All she wants? A round-trip ticket to the Fae realm...and maybe a drink on the house.

He also writes the **Shade of Devil Series**, which tells the story of Sorin Ambrogio—the world's FIRST vampire. He was put into a magical slumber by a Native American Medicine Man when the Americas were first discovered by Europeans. Sorin wakes up after five-hundred years to learn that his protege, Dracula, stole his reputation and that no one has ever even heard of Sorin Ambrogio. The streets of New York City will run with blood as Sorin reclaims his legend.

Shayne holds two high-ranking black belts, and can be found writing in a coffee shop, cackling madly into his computer screen while pounding shots of espresso. He's hard at work on the newest books in the TempleVerse— You can find updates on new releases or chronological reading order on the next page, his website, or any of his social media accounts. **Follow him online for all sorts of groovy goodies, giveaways, and new release updates:**

Get Down with Shayne Online
www.shaynesilvers.com
info@shaynesilvers.com

facebook.com/shaynesilversfanpage

amazon.com/author/shaynesilvers

bookbub.com/profile/shayne-silvers

instagram.com/shaynesilversofficial

twitter.com/shaynesilvers

goodreads.com/ShayneSilvers

BOOKS BY SHAYNE SILVERS

CHRONOLOGY: *All stories in the TempleVerse are shown in chronological order on the following page*

NATE TEMPLE SERIES

(Main series in the TempleVerse)

by Shayne Silvers

FAIRY TALE - FREE prequel novella #0 for my subscribers

OBSIDIAN SON

BLOOD DEBTS

GRIMM

SILVER TONGUE

BEAST MASTER

BEERLYMPIAN (Novella #5.5 in the 'LAST CALL' anthology)

TINY GODS

DADDY DUTY (Novella #6.5)

WILD SIDE

WAR HAMMER

NINE SOULS

HORSEMAN

LEGEND

KNIGHTMARE

ASCENSION

CARNAGE

FEATHERS AND FIRE SERIES

(Also set in the TempleVerse)

by Shayne Silvers

UNCHAINED

RAGE

WHISPERS

ANGEL'S ROAR

MOTHERLUCKER (Novella #4.5 in the 'LAST CALL' anthology)

SINNER

BLACK SHEEP

GODLESS

ANGHELLIC

PHANTOM QUEEN DIARIES

(Also set in the TempleVerse)

by Cameron O'Connell & Shayne Silvers

COLLINS (Prequel novella #0 in the 'LAST CALL' anthology)

WHISKEY GINGER

COSMOPOLITAN

OLD FASHIONED

MOTHERLUCKER (Novella #3.5 in the 'LAST CALL' anthology)

DARK AND STORMY

MOSCOW MULE

WITCHES BREW

SALTY DOG

SEA BREEZE

HURRICANE

BRIMSTONE KISS

CHRONOLOGICAL ORDER: TEMPLE VERSE

FAIRY TALE (TEMPLE PREQUEL)

OBSIDIAN SON (TEMPLE 1)

BLOOD DEBTS (TEMPLE 2)

GRIMM (TEMPLE 3)

CARNAGE (TEMPLE 14)

ANGHELLIC (FEATHERS...8)

SHADE OF DEVIL SERIES

(Not part of the Temple Verse)

by Shayne Silvers

DEVIL'S DREAM

DEVIL'S CRY

DEVIL'S BLOOD

NOTHING TO SEE HERE.

Thanks for reaching the last page of the book, you over-achiever. Sniff the spine. You've earned it. Or sniff your Kindle.

Now this has gotten weird.

Alright. I'm leaving.

Made in the USA
Coppell, TX
05 April 2022

76002965R00189